Waltz with a Stranger

PAMELA SHERWOOD

sourcebooks
casablanca

Published by Sourcebooks Casablanca, an imprint of Sourcebooks, Inc.
P.O. Box 4410, Naperville, Illinois 60567-4410
(630) 961-3900
Fax: (630) 961-2168
www.sourcebooks.com

Printed and bound in Canada.
WC 10 9 8 7 6 5 4 3 2 1

To Winston Graham and Edith Wharton, for inspiration,
To my mother, for understanding,
And to my sister, because Christina Rossetti was right.

To be fond of dancing was a certain step towards falling in love.

—Jane Austen, *Pride and Prejudice*

One

London, May 1890

IF SOCIAL SUCCESS WAS MEASURED BY THE NUMBER OF guests the hostess could cram into a limited amount of space, then Lady Talbot's ball honoring her daughter's betrothal to Viscount Maitland's heir was an unqualified triumph. James Trelawney wished he could be properly appreciative of such an achievement, instead of counting the minutes until he could make his escape. Another half hour or so before the break for supper—perhaps he could slip away then.

"I see you made it after all," a familiar voice remarked at his shoulder.

"Thomas." Despite the crowd hemming them in, James managed to turn his head to smile at his closest friend. "Well, Jess is my cousin, and my aunt can be very persuasive."

"So she can. Pity the army doesn't recruit women. Lady Talbot would make a formidable general. Here." Thomas Sheridan held out a brimming champagne flute. "This should help."

"Do I look that uncomfortable?" James took a sip of the excellent wine.

"Like the proverbial fish out of water. Wishing yourself back in Cornwall?"

"When am I not?" James sipped his champagne again, thinking longingly of the open spaces and crisp, salty air of his home county. "I only come up to London when I must. Frankly, I don't know how you stand it, Thomas. You're an artist, for God's sake!"

His friend's eyes glinted. "There's beauty and grace to be found even here, James. Or perhaps I should say *especially* here."

He meant women, of course—being something of a connoisseur. Amused, James surveyed the ladies gracing the ballroom. Most were attractive, he supposed, but there were lovely women to be found in Cornwall too. He was just about to point that out to Thomas when the musicians struck up a waltz. The couples assembled on the floor began to move, the ladies' jewels glittering beneath the radiance of the gas-lit chandelier, their pastel skirts belling out behind them with each whirling turn. He glimpsed his cousin Jessica, all in white, floating rapturously in the arms of her betrothed.

A flash of vivid blue among the preponderance of white and pink caught his eye. Idly, his gaze followed the motion of that swirling gown, traveled upward to the wearer's face...

He ceased to breathe, as if a fist had driven the air from his lungs. Beauty. Grace. *Oh, yes.*

Eyes as blue as her gown, the color of sunlit summer skies; a creamy complexion blushed with rose; smiling lips of a deeper rose hue; and a glory of spun-gold hair, bright as any coronet.

"Thomas." His voice sounded husky, even far away. "Thomas, who's that—in blue?"

His friend followed the line of his gaze, stilled abruptly. "Ah. *La Belle Américaine*."

An odd note in that cool, cultured voice, like the faintest crack in a bell. James glanced at his friend but saw only Thomas's habitual expression of ironic detachment.

"Miss Amelia Newbold," Sheridan continued. "Amy, to her closest friends. The latest heiress to cross the Atlantic and lay siege to our damp, foggy island."

"An heiress. From America?" That might explain her vivacity; English misses tended to carry themselves more demurely, with downcast eyes and half-smiles reminiscent of *La Giaconda*. Miss Newbold looked as though she was on the verge of laughter—enchantingly so.

"New York, to be precise. The father's in shipping, I understand. Miss Newbold arrived in London with her mother and sister about two months ago and proceeded to cut a swathe through our susceptible young—and not so young—aristocrats. I've heard she'll accept nothing less than a peer. They don't lack for ambition, these Americans! And as you see," Thomas nodded toward the waltzing couples, "she already has Kelmswood in her toils."

James glanced at Miss Newbold's partner, noticing him for the first time: a tall, athletically built young man whose dark good looks seemed the perfect foil for the American girl's golden beauty. The thought gave him no pleasure whatsoever. "An earl, isn't he? I suppose they're as good as betrothed, then."

"I wouldn't bet on that." Thomas's mouth crooked. "Glyndon's entered the lists as well."

James's brows rose. "Good God, really?" Viscount Glyndon, Thomas's cousin, was heir to the Duke of Harford. "How do their graces feel about that?"

"My uncle and aunt are maintaining a well-bred silence

on the subject. However, I doubt their plans for my cousin's future include an American bride."

Having met the duke and duchess, James was inclined to agree with his friend. Not that it mattered—could matter—to him; the likes of Amelia Newbold were out of his humble star. He made himself look away from her and her handsome, eligible partner. "I think I'll go and get some air. If you'll excuse me?"

Thomas relieved him of his now-empty flute. "Of course, old fellow."

James threaded his way through the crowd toward the French windows, standing open to the warm spring night. Just as he was about to step onto the terrace, a raucous male laugh assailed his ears. A raucous, all-too-familiar male laugh.

Damn, and damn again. Gritting his teeth, James ventured a glance onto the terrace and saw several men leaning against the balustrade in a haze of cigar smoke. In their midst he spotted a familiar blond head, a heavy profile: his cousin Gerald, Viscount Alston.

He ought to have expected this; Aunt Judith was the family peacemaker. If she'd invited one of her nephews to attend Jessica's betrothal ball, she would certainly invite the other, despite knowing that he and Gerald met as seldom as possible. They both preferred it that way.

Memories stirred, a dark tide with a deadly undertow. James forced them away, turned from the doors. The conservatory—he'd go there instead. Even if other guests had sought refuge in the same place, they could hardly be less congenial company than Gerald and his cronies.

But at first glance, the conservatory appeared to be deserted. Moonlight poured in through the glass-paneled walls, bathing the plants and stone benches in an otherworldly glow. Loosening his collar, James inhaled the warm, jasmine-scented air and felt himself relax for the first time that evening.

Hands clasped behind him, he strolled along the nearest

walkway. Feathery ferns, sinuous vines, potted palms...
he could not identify more than a few of the more exotic
species, but it scarcely mattered. Here, at last, were peace and
tranquility. Then he rounded a corner, came to a halt at the
sight of the figure standing in the middle of the conservatory,
the moonlight frosting her golden hair and casting a silvery
sheen upon the skirts of her blue ball gown. Her eyes were
closed, her slim form swaying gently in time to the waltz
music drifting in from the ballroom.

James wondered if he'd lost his mind. Hadn't he just seen
her mere moments ago, dancing in the arms of an earl? Then,
looking more closely, he saw that the shade of her gown was
closer to turquoise than azure, her hair dressed a touch less
elaborately—subtle differences but telling nonetheless. What
had Thomas said? "She and her mother and her sister..."

He must have made some sound, some movement,
because the girl suddenly froze like a deer scenting a hunter,
apprehension radiating from every inch of her.

James spoke quickly, seeking to reassure her. "Pardon me,
Miss Newbold. It is Miss Newbold, is it not?"

❧

Aurelia fought down a rush of panic and an irrational urge to
flee—for all the good it would do her. The stranger's voice
was deep and pleasant, with a faint burr she could not place.
She wondered if he was as attractive as he sounded; the
thought made her even more reluctant to turn around.

But it would be rude not to acknowledge his presence.
Keeping her face averted, she nodded. "I am Aurelia Newbold."

"Miss Aurelia," he amended. "My name's Trelawney.
Again, I ask your pardon. I could not help but stare—no one
told me that you and your sister were identical twins."

Aurelia swallowed, knowing she could no longer delay
the inevitable. Best to get it over with, as quickly as possible.
"We are twins, sir. But—no longer identical."

She turned around, letting him see the whole of her face now—thinner and paler than Amy's, despite their maid's skilled application of cosmetics. But no amount of paint or powder could disguise the scar that ran along the left side of her hairline before curving sharply across her cheekbone like a reversed letter *J*. She forced herself to meet Mr. Trelawney's eyes, even as her stomach knotted in dread over what she would see.

And there it was—that flash of pity in his eyes; dark eyes, in a strongly handsome face that recalled portraits of dashing adventurers and soldiers of fortune. At least they held no distaste or revulsion: a small mercy. Or perhaps he was simply better at hiding them.

"A riding accident," she said tersely, anticipating the question he was trying not to ask. "Three years ago. It's left me with a limp as well."

"I am sorry." His voice was kind. "That must be difficult to bear. Do you need to sit down? I could escort you back to the ballroom, find you a chair."

Aurelia shook her head. "That won't be necessary, sir. I just—came to admire the conservatory." And to escape all the stares, whether curious or pitying. She'd have preferred to stay behind in their suite at Claridge's tonight, but Amy had refused to attend this ball without her. Beautiful Amy, who looked the way *she* had used to look.

"I see." And as his dark eyes continued to study her, Aurelia had the uncomfortable feeling that Mr. Trelawney did indeed see.

"They fade, you know," he said, almost abruptly. "Scars. When I was a boy, I knew a man who'd served in the Crimea and had a saber cut down one side of his face. Many saw it as a badge of honor. In later years, some even thought it made him look distinguished."

"Scars on a man may be distinguished, Mr. Trelawney," Aurelia said, more sharply than she intended. "On a woman, they're merely ugly. And there was nothing—honorable or heroic about the way I acquired mine." *Merely stupid.*

His brows drew together. "Surely you need not be defined by your scars, Miss Newbold."

She felt her lips twist in a brittle smile. "It's hard not to be, when they're the first things about me that people notice."

"But you are under no obligation to accept their valuation of you. And would *you* judge another solely on the basis of injury or illness?"

He spoke mildly, but she heard the faint rebuke in his voice, nonetheless. Flushing, she looked away, ashamed of her outburst. She'd thought herself resigned, if not reconciled, to her disfigurement; what was it about this man that unsettled her so? "I would hope not, especially now. Pardon me, sir, I let my—disappointment get the best of me. A graceless thing to do, and I'm sorry for it. If you'll excuse me, I'll return to the ballroom." Still not looking at him, she turned toward the conservatory doors.

"Wait." The urgency in his voice stopped her in her tracks. "Miss Newbold, may I have this dance?"

Aurelia whipped her head around, astonished. "Dance? Pray do not mock me, sir."

Dark eyes gazed steadily into hers. "I have never been more serious in my life. You have a fine sense of rhythm—I noticed that when I first saw you. Are you fond of the waltz?"

"Well, yes," she admitted, after a moment; there'd been a time when she loved nothing better than to whirl about the floor in her partner's arms. "That is, I was before. But my limp—"

"A limp is surely no worse than two left feet—and the latter affliction has not prevented quite a number of people from dancing tonight."

A breath of unwilling laughter escaped her. Mr. Trelawney's eyes seemed to warm at the sound. He held out his hand. "I do not ask this out of mockery—or pity," he added with a perception that surprised her. "Will you not indulge me? We need not return to the ballroom. We can have our dance here, unseen, among the flowers. Unless you find it too physically taxing?"

He'd just handed her the perfect excuse. All she had to do was plead fatigue or discomfort, and Mr. Trelawney, gentleman that he was, would surely let her retire and not importune her further. Instead, she stepped forward—and placed her hand in his.

He smiled at her and her knees wanted to buckle; she made herself stand fast and look him in the eye. She could feel the warmth of his hand through the evening gloves they both wore, and smell his cologne, an appealing blend of citrus and clove. Then he drew her to him, his hand resting lightly on the small of her back, and led her into their dance.

Her first steps were halting, hesitant, and she felt her face flaming anew, but Mr. Trelawney took her clumsiness in stride, adjusting his movements to hers. A few more bars and Aurelia found herself dancing more easily, as if some purely physical memory had taken over, leaving her mind free to concentrate on the beauty of the moonlit conservatory and the light pressure of Mr. Trelawney's arms enfolding her as gently as if she were made of porcelain.

Together, they waltzed along the paved walkways, around benches and garden beds, beneath the light of the moon and stars. With each circling turn, Aurelia felt her spirits rise, a sensation that had become as alien to her as a man's touch. Mr. Trelawney danced with an easy assurance that seemed in keeping with his forthright manner and confident air. No other man she'd waltzed with had ever made her feel this safe—not Papa, not Andrew…not even Charlie.

That last realization was so startling that she almost stumbled; Mr. Trelawney steadied her at once, concern in his eyes. Aurelia summoned a smile that surprised her as much as it did her partner, and they waltzed on, whirling back toward the center of the conservatory and the pool of moonlight on the tiled floor.

The music ended, the last chords quavering into silence, and Mr. Trelawney swirled them both to a stop. Aurelia stifled a pang of regret at how quickly the time had passed.

"Thank you," she said, and meant it. She was slightly breathless, and her bad leg twinged after the unaccustomed exercise; it would be worse in the morning, but she felt not even a particle of regret.

He gave her that knee-weakening smile again. "The pleasure was mine, Miss Newbold."

The sound of a throat being discreetly cleared drew their attention to the doorway, where a liveried footman now stood. "Mr. Trelawney?"

His brows rose inquiringly. "Yes?"

"Lady Talbot wishes to speak with you, sir. In the supper room."

"Ah. Tell her I'll be along straightaway."

"Very good, sir." The footman withdrew at once.

Mr. Trelawney turned back to Aurelia. "Pardon me, Miss Newbold, but I must wait upon my aunt. May I escort you back to the ballroom now?"

She shook her head. "No, thank you. I'd like to remain in the conservatory a while longer." Solitude would give her the chance to recover her poise—and invisibility.

"As you wish." But he lingered a moment longer. "Thank you for the waltz. Perhaps we might attempt it again sometime?"

Aurelia swallowed, deliberately not allowing herself to dwell on that possibility. "Perhaps we might, at that. Good evening, Mr. Trelawney."

He raised her hand briefly to his lips. "And to you, Miss Newbold."

He bowed and strode from the conservatory. Much to Aurelia's vexation, her traitorous gaze followed him, long after he had disappeared into the crowded ballroom.

Two

A little more than kin, and less than kind.

—William Shakespeare, *Hamlet*

JAMES MADE HIS WAY ALONG THE PERIMETER OF THE dance floor. The ball was still in full swing; only the music had changed—to a lively polka this time. And there was Amelia Newbold, partnered no doubt by some scion of the nobility and romping like thistledown through the set.

Looking at her immediately brought her sister to mind. Again James seemed to feel Aurelia's hand resting uncertainly on his shoulder, the arch of her slender—too slender—back against his palm as they stepped into their secret waltz. She'd smelled of lavender. The discovery had startled him; he'd have expected a wealthy young woman—an heiress, no less—to choose a more exotic perfume, like orchid or frangipani. Not simple English lavender. But he'd loved the scent since childhood—hanging in a fragrant haze over his mother's garden or wafting from the stillroom where she concocted her creams and lotions. Even now, he associated the smell of lavender with a more innocent time, a time when he'd been unreservedly happy.

Happy...James frowned, his thoughts taking a different

turn. Aurelia Newbold was not happy, for which he could hardly blame her. It had startled him at first to see such beauty marred. And yet, even with scars she was no Gorgon—her eyes were as blue, her hair as lustrous as her more fortunate sister's. And when she forgot her insecurities and smiled...

James shook his head. He'd no business thinking of Aurelia Newbold's smile, any more than he had thinking of her twin's. What had he to offer but admiration, or, in Aurelia's case, a momentary act of kindness? Perhaps, in time, she might overcome her dread of being stared at and venture out into Society; there were kind people as well as cruel ones even in London.

He had reached the supper room at last. Lady Talbot, a still-comely matron in her fifties, turned at his entrance and held out her hands to him. "Dear James!"

"Aunt Judith." He took her hands and kissed her cheek, scented with roses and vanilla.

She smiled at him. "I am so glad you came. I know you're not overfond of London. You will be attending the wedding, won't you?"

"Of course. Next month, isn't it?"

Lady Talbot nodded. "At midsummer—my Jessica's to be a June bride. And at St. George's, Hanover Square, of course. The Maitlands won't hear of anyplace else."

James did his best to look impressed, though he couldn't tell one Society church from another. "Was there something more you wished to discuss with me?"

"As it happens, yes. I wondered whether you might extend your stay in town—just for a few days. The Hastings are arriving from Surrey, and I know Felicia, in particular, would be delighted to see you again," she added. "She's been sadly pulled with influenza this past winter, and I'm sure she'd benefit from a change of scene and perhaps some congenial company?"

Reading between the lines all too plainly, James stifled

a sigh. Felicia Hastings, Lady Talbot's goddaughter, was a pretty, sweet-natured girl, but he'd never felt the least degree of romantic interest in her. "Well, I wish her a speedy recovery. Unfortunately, I've urgent business I must attend to in Cornwall. In fact, I was planning to leave tomorrow."

"Then, by all means, don't let us keep you," a familiar voice drawled from the doorway. "Cornwall's gain is sure to be ours as well."

"Gerald!" Lady Talbot's voice was sharp with disapproval.

James stilled, schooling his face into impassivity before turning to regard his cousin. "Good evening, Alston. Let me assure you, the feeling is entirely mutual."

The viscount shouldered himself away from the doorway. He'd put on weight, James observed dispassionately. While most Trelawneys were dark and slender, even wiry, Gerald favored his mother's side of the family: fair and big-boned. For a time, his size had given him the advantage in boyhood altercations, until James had learned other ways of fighting back.

Alston gulped his champagne in the manner of one who'd have preferred whiskey. "I must say, I'm surprised to see *you* here. I thought you'd be at home, tumbling a chambermaid."

"I leave such exploits to you, cousin," James replied pleasantly. "But then you haven't had much success in that endeavor lately, have you?"

Alston scowled, doubtless remembering one "chambermaid" James had forcibly prevented him from tumbling. But before he could respond, their aunt stepped between them.

"That's enough, both of you!" Lady Talbot fixed her nephews with a steely glare. "This is Jessica's evening—and I won't have it spoiled by a vulgar brawl. I realize that you'll never like each other, but I expect you to be civil while you're under the same roof!"

Out of respect for his aunt, James refrained from pointing out that, where he and Gerald were concerned, it was far easier to be civil under different roofs. Instead, he summoned a conciliatory smile and bowed over Lady Talbot's hand. "I beg your pardon, ma'am. As it happens, I've an early start tomorrow, so I'll take my leave now."

"But James—"

He shook his head and turned away, pointedly ignoring Gerald. "Good night, Aunt Judith—and my love to Jess. I'll see myself out."

❧

"Wasn't it a splendid evening, Relia?" Amy asked as the maid brushed out her hair for the night. "Lord Kelmswood and Lord Glyndon both asked for *two* of my waltzes!"

"Splendid," Aurelia echoed. Already dressed for bed, she drew the covers up over her knees and settled back against the pillows. Her mind was far away, however, remembering a deserted conservatory and a dark-eyed man guiding her around the flowerbeds. Where had he gone? She'd looked but hadn't seen him for the rest of the evening.

Amy lowered her voice to a conspiratorial whisper. "I think Lord Glyndon wanted to claim a third waltz, but I understand that would've been tantamount to a proposal here!"

Aurelia frowned, eyeing her twin more closely. "Do you like him, Amy?"

"Oh, well enough. He's good-looking and considered quite the catch. Lord Kelmswood's handsomer, but he's only an earl. Still, an earl trumps a viscount, even if he is heir to a dukedom. Aunt Caroline says the Duke of Harford may live a good twenty or thirty years yet."

Aurelia bit her lip. As the wife of Baron Renbourne, their aunt—godmother, really—was well-acquainted with the intricacies of British society; who better to shepherd two American girls through their first London Season? But it troubled her to hear Amy parroting Lady Renbourne's remarks with a jaded air more suited to a dowager of sixty than a girl of nineteen.

Amy dismissed Mariette and headed, yawning, for her own bed. "Such a night!" she declared, snuggling down into the bedclothes. She glanced at her twin. "Did *you* have a good time too, Relia? I know you didn't want to come at first—"

"Oh, yes," Aurelia hastened to reassure her. "Better than I expected." And strangely enough, that was the truth. While she hated being stared at, no one had been overtly unkind to her. And there had been Mr. Trelawney.

"Oh, good. I did so want you to enjoy yourself." Amy paused, then continued a bit diffidently, "Aunt Caroline says that the English have much better manners than Americans, at least in public. They aren't as likely to pry into one's business or ask…awkward questions."

Such as, how did you get that awful scar? Aurelia thought. She had to admit that Aunt Caroline and Amy were both correct on that score. While she'd seen curiosity and even speculation in the eyes of several people, no one had been intrusive enough to ask. But she herself had told Mr. Trelawney outright…

Her sister's voice cut into her musings. "You'd tell me, wouldn't you, if someone said something to upset you? Promise you'll tell me?"

Aurelia smiled into her twin's anxious eyes. "As long as you do the same, dearest. You and I, *contra mundum*." She quoted the Latin motto from one of their brother's old schoolbooks.

"*Contra mundum*," Amy agreed, smiling back. Abruptly, her smile became a yawn. "Goodness, I'm sleepy! I can barely keep my eyes open." She turned down the lamp beside the bed, and the room sank into shadow. "Good night, Relia dear."

"Good night," Aurelia echoed. She lay down, listening to her sister's breathing. Within minutes, Amy had drifted into an enviably sound sleep.

Not so Aurelia herself. While she could not see the mantel clock from where she lay, she envisioned the minute hand circumnavigating its broad glass face as she stared into the darkness. Sighing, she shifted position and felt her bad leg throb at the movement; it would be worse tomorrow, she knew, because of the unaccustomed exertion tonight.

If she got up and fumbled her way to the washstand, she'd find a small bottle of laudanum there. A modest dose would grant her a night of unbroken slumber, even if she paid for it with lethargy and a loss of appetite in the morning. Not that she had much appetite at any time. She was thinner than she'd been three years ago—her face as well as her figure, which made her scar look disproportionately larger.

She folded back the bedclothes but found herself reluctant to rise—and not because of the pain. In her memory, she heard the lilting strains of waltz music, felt the warmth of a strong, masculine hand at her waist, smelled the sharp fragrance of citrus and clove.

Your scars need not define you.

Easy for someone without scars to say, but he'd spoken with such conviction that she found herself wanting to believe him. And wanting with a sudden, desperate hunger to be free of the prison she'd made of her life. Free of the pain and desolation of these last three years.

After her accident, her parents must have consulted every physician in New York on how to hasten her recovery. Some had prescribed sedatives and tonics to ease the pain of her broken thigh and the gash on her face. Others had suggested European spas and clinics where she might build up strength in her weak leg. Little could be done about her face, unfortunately—save to wait and hope that the scarring might prove to be less severe than feared. Or that it might fade in time.

As far as Aurelia was concerned, the damage was done. One moment of recklessness, and she was lamed, disfigured, and abandoned by the boy she'd loved and dreamed of marrying. What future could she hope for, maimed as she was? Sometimes she felt she'd have saved everyone a great deal of trouble by breaking her neck instead of her leg that day.

"Don't even think that!" Amy had blazed when Aurelia had confided as much to her during the long dreary days of convalescence. "Not for a single second!"

And then she'd burst into tears, shocking them both because Amy hardly ever cried. Aurelia had never expressed that sentiment again, and in time, she even ceased to feel it. Not often, anyway. To give up on life would be to hurt Amy beyond measure—their parents and brother too, but Amy most of all.

She glanced over at her sister's sleeping form. *My twin, my face, my heart.* They no longer had the same face, but they would always have the same heart. Which made the decision she was about to make that much harder. She only hoped Amy would understand.

The waltz in her head tinkled on, insistent as a music box tune. But now she seemed to hear a hidden promise in every chord: health, happiness, a whole new beginning—if she had the courage to reach for it. A whole new Aurelia, who could walk a city block without tiring, meet strangers' eyes without flinching...and dance the night away with a handsome young man.

Unbidden, Mr. Trelawney's face rose in her mind: the bold planes, the brilliant dark eyes. They might never meet again, and yet, waltzing in his arms tonight...

For the first time in three years, she had felt beautiful.

From Amelia Louise Newbold to Aurelia Leigh Newbold. 21 June 1890.

...I hope you and Mother had a safe crossing and are now comfortably settled at Bad Ems. What an inauspicious name for a spa! I do understand why you had to go, and

I hope Doctor Strauss lives up to all of Aunt Caroline's recommendations, but oh, I miss you terribly! Please get well and strong as soon as possible, because London just isn't the same without you. In fact, it's downright insipid, earls and viscounts notwithstanding. Please write soon—love to Mother.

Love always,
Amy

༺ঙ

From Judith, Lady Talbot to Jessica Maitland, on the death of Joshua Trelawney, 5th Earl of Trevenan. 3 July 1890.

…At the last, your uncle went peacefully—a marked contrast to the choler with which he had lived most of his life. Pray do not worry about cutting short your wedding trip to attend the funeral. My presence and your papa's will suffice for our side of the family. Gerald and James are both to be pallbearers. I only hope I can keep them from each other's throats until the service is concluded. At least Helena was absent. According to Durward, any sort of carriage or railway travel nauseates her in her present condition. I shudder to think how much greater the tension would be if she attended…

༺ঙ

From Lucretia, Lady Featherstonehaugh to Augusta Beauchamp-Burton, on the death of Gerald Trelawney, 6th Earl of Trevenan. 8 January 1891.

…Quite the scandal! Found dead at the bottom of a cliff, barely six months after he inherited! It's enough to make one believe in family curses, isn't it? Rumor has it that he was intoxicated. It can't possibly have been suicide. I suppose the cousin will succeed now, the one whose mother

was a miner's daughter. A stroke of luck, indeed, though I confess I can't help wondering where he was when his cousin had his unfortunate accident…

❧

From Victoria, Duchess of Harford to Charlotte, Countess Savernake. 21 March 1891.

…I perfectly understand your concerns, my dear, but you know how rebellious the young can be! If it will set your mind at ease, Harford and I have already determined to have a long talk with Glyndon. While it is only to be expected that a young man will sow his wild oats, he cannot continue to sit in the pocket of this American arriviste, however pretty her face or sizable her fortune. Really, the effrontery of these girls knows no bounds, and far too many of them have married into our ranks as it is! In twenty years or so, the English aristocracy will be unrecognizable. We at least need make no concessions as yet to bloodlines or breeding where the future duchess is concerned. Rest assured that our son will do his duty—by Harford and your daughter. And no later than this summer, if I have anything to say about it…

❧

From Aurelia Leigh Newbold to Amelia Louise Newbold. 10 April 1891.

…Just one more month and I'll be joining you in London! Do you know, dearest, I've actually found myself homesick for the place? And looking forward to all the diversions I was too weary or self-conscious to enjoy last spring: the theater, the opera, even the shops! All my gowns have had to be let out. Doctor Strauss is delighted by my increased energy and appetite! Mother is delighted too, as it gives

her the perfect excuse to stop in Paris to order new gowns. I must admit I'm not protesting too much; it will be lovely to have a new wardrobe to go with the new me. But the most important thing is that we'll be together again, at last! I know you came to spend Christmas here, but that's not at all the same thing.

Write soon, and love always,
Relia

Three

Doänt thou marry for munny, but goä wheer munny is!

—Alfred, Lord Tennyson,
"Northern Farmer: New Style"

London, April 1891

"I DON'T THINK I'VE EVER IN MY LIFE SEEN ANYONE LESS pleased at becoming an earl," Thomas observed, topping off James's glass with his best port. Barlow, his trusted manservant, had cleared away the dinner dishes and brought in the dessert course of cheeses, grapes, and nuts.

James grimaced as he reached for the glass; three days in London and he was already being driven to drink, he thought only half-humorously. Even here, in Thomas's comfortably masculine rooms in Half Moon Street, he felt confined and hedged-about. "How many new-made earls inherit a mountain of debts along with their title?"

"Entirely too many these days." Thomas refilled his own glass, then leaned back in his chair. "How bad is it, exactly?"

"Bad enough. Allingham and Daviot—the family's solicitors—estimate the amount to be in excess of fifty thousand pounds." James smiled without humor. "Uncle Joshua may have been a miser, but Gerald more than made up for it. He ran through his mother's legacy years ago, but I still can't believe he managed to spend so much in a mere six months as Trevenan!"

"A sad truth about fortunes—they take decades to build and no time at all to spend. And your cousin was always one for cutting a dash. He aspired to the Prince of Wales's circle, and they get wilder by the year."

James scowled into his glass, reflecting without pleasure on the excesses of the Marlborough House set. "Wilder and more extravagant, I understand. I'll give Uncle Joshua his due—he did what he could for Pentreath and its tenants. Gerald never contributed as much as a farthing." He took a swallow of port. "Aunt Judith would be shocked to hear me say this, but the estate, at least, is better off without him. Not that he ever spent much time there to begin with. I still don't know what he was doing there the night he died."

"I was surprised to hear that as well," Thomas remarked. "Knowing his proclivities, I'd have expected him to spend Christmas at one of his friends' estates. Somewhere in the Shires, perhaps, where there'd be hunting." He swirled the port in his glass, regarded his friend with searching green eyes. "This hasn't caused trouble for you, has it? With the inquest?"

James shook his head. "None. It helps that I was visiting my mother's relations at the time. My cousin, Sir Harry Tresilian, was hosting a party in honor of the New Year. Even Helena—Gerald's sister—could make nothing of that. The coroner brought back a ruling of death by misadventure. Apparently, Gerald had been drinking before he fell off that cliff. He might have lost his footing in the dark." He cracked open an almond. "Well, however he met his Maker, he's left me one hell of a mess to clean up."

Thomas idly rolled a grape between his long fingers. "Will you sell off some land?"

"No." The vehemence of his response surprised them

both, but the certainty was there, James discovered, as solid and enduring as the Cornish cliffs. "I never expected to inherit," he continued slowly. "And God knows I never *wanted* the earldom. But now that it's mine, I'm not parting with a single acre, save as a last resort. Pentreath deserves better of me than that."

He might have few pleasant memories of Uncle Joshua and none whatsoever of Gerald, but Pentreath had been home to the Trelawneys for centuries. Even for him, coming there as a desolate orphan of twelve. Once again, he saw the estate in his mind's eye: gracious and silver-grey, its mullioned windows facing out upon the surging sea. Pentreath—one of the few things his uncle had loved with all his flinty heart.

But Gerald, like his fashionable mother, had disliked Cornwall, spending most of his time in London or the Shires once he was of age. Certainly he'd never troubled himself about maintaining the estate that was his birthright or looking after those who lived and worked there.

Well, that would have to change. "I suppose," James began dubiously, "I could borrow the money to make the most pressing repairs to Pentreath and the tenants' cottages. And arrange to pay it back out of my profits from the mines. It would take time, of course, but—"

"There's a quicker solution," Thomas interposed. "Marry an heiress."

"Marry?" James stared at his friend as if he'd grown another head.

"Why not? That's what many men in your situation do, if they can manage it. And you've arrived just in time for the Season, so there should be plenty of candidates to choose from."

James pulled a face. "I hadn't thought to turn fortune-hunter."

"Think of it more as a trade: your title and estate in exchange for your bride's dowry." Thomas's mouth crooked in its familiar ironic smile. "According to Mother, there are a number of eligible young ladies who'd be delighted to make your acquaintance."

"None of whom would have given me the time of day when I was plain Mr. Trelawney," James pointed out. "If Gerald were alive, they'd be setting their caps at him just as eagerly."

"Perhaps not quite as eagerly," Thomas corrected him. "Your cousin may have been a peer for a good deal longer, but he was also a prize boor. You, on the other hand, have no such prejudice to overcome." He added, more sympathetically, "It needn't be as cold-blooded as you think. Some of the ladies Mother mentioned are good-natured as well as rich—and pretty, especially the Americans. Not that *you* heed such things, but it's practically the fashion these days for an English lord to take an American bride—and the wealthier the better."

James paused, his glass halfway to his lips, as a memory rose in his mind: a radiant, golden-haired girl laughing as she waltzed. It was succeeded almost at once by that of another girl, alike and yet so different from the first. Joy and sadness, sun and shadow…

"—and there's a Miss Leiter from Chicago," Thomas's voice broke into his thoughts, "who's been much admired this year, ever since the Prince danced the quadrille with her at Grosvenor House. She's got at least one sister, too."

"Talking of sisters," James began, keeping his tone casual, "what about the Newbold twins? Have they returned to America?" Just his luck if they had.

"One of them has gone abroad for her health, I hear. But Miss Amelia is still among us—and unmarried."

"Unmarried?" James felt his heart give a slight lurch at the news. "But what about Glyndon—or that other fellow, Kelmswood?"

Thomas shrugged. "Kelmswood tired of the chase last summer. No staying power. Glyndon still fancies her, but as I've said before, his parents have other plans for him."

"You don't think he'll defy them and go his own way?"

"Not on this. There's too much at stake. He might bluster and fume at first, but in the end, he'll dance to their piping." Thomas paused, his eyes oddly hooded in the lamplight. "So, you have a liking for Miss Newbold?"

James fidgeted with his glass. "That might be putting it too strongly. We haven't even been introduced yet. I spoke to her sister once."

Spoke to her, danced with her…He remembered the painful flush on her cheek, her low, vehement words: *Scars on a man may be distinguished. On a woman, they're merely ugly.*

And now she'd gone abroad—to recover her health, as Thomas had said. He hoped she found it, along with some peace of mind. Aurelia, fragile and brittle as a blown-glass butterfly.

"But you do find her attractive, don't you?" Thomas pressed on.

"Who wouldn't?"

"Indeed." Thomas steepled his fingers. "My mother's holding a garden party this weekend," he announced, almost abruptly. "At Richmond. Miss Newbold will be there, along with several other heiresses. That should be as good a place as any to start looking."

ود

Havenhurst—Lady Julia Sheridan's Richmond estate—was a haze of purple bloom. Sprays of lilac and dangling clusters of wisteria filled the air with their intoxicating perfume.

Amy Newbold blended in perfectly; indeed, she had taken great pains to do so. A little complacently, she smoothed the lavender kid gloves that matched her lavender muslin afternoon dress. Not every lady showed to advantage in lavender, but the color became her admirably well, as did the straw hat trimmed with white and violet flowers. She'd spent a good ten minutes before the mirror getting it positioned at just the right jaunty angle. The perfect ensemble in which to stroll through the gardens—and receive a proposal of marriage.

She glanced about the garden, seeking Glyndon's broad shoulders and golden-bronze hair. As Lady Julia's nephew, he was certain to attend this affair; he'd said as much to her two nights ago at the Eveshams' ball. And surely, if he were familiar with Havenhurst's grounds, he must know of some secluded place where they might go to settle things between them. As a matter of fact, he'd made a point of mentioning the Wilderness Garden…

A few feet away, Aunt Caroline was conversing with Viscountess Ashby and her daughter Harriet, who were both noticeably more cordial this Season, now that Lord Kelmswood was no longer paying court to "that encroaching American girl." Privately, Amy wished Miss Ashby joy of the earl. Handsome though he was, he'd proven quite dreadfully fickle. She felt a renewed surge of fondness for Glyndon; at least *his* affections hadn't changed with the seasons!

Talking of seasons, would a June wedding be too soon? If not, they could have it in London, at St. George's, Hanover Square, that church so popular with English aristocrats. Or a September wedding in New York, after everyone was back from Newport. Maybe at St. Thomas's: fashionable, Anglican, and large enough for a choir of more than fifty strong.

Yes, the more Amy thought about it, the better she liked the idea. A grand New York wedding—and one in the eye for those stodgy Knickerbocker families who had never been able to decide whether to welcome her and Aurelia because of their father's name or snub them because of their mother's money. Too often it had turned out to be the latter.

Aurelia…Amy's heart lifted at the thought of her twin. Just one month and they'd be together again. It had been wonderful to see her at Christmas, looking and acting so much more like her old self. Amy would ensure that every door in London was open to her and she had her pick of suitors. A peer would be ideal, though Aurelia had never cared about titles. But someone splendid, nonetheless, who could make her forget all about that stupid Charlie Vandermere!

Of course, she conceded, that might have to wait until after her own nuptials. But once that was accomplished, surely no one would dare to snub the sister-in-law of a future duke. Pity Glyndon's younger brother was only a schoolboy, but he might have a cousin who'd be suitable. What a coup it would be if Aurelia could marry into the family too!

She looked for her ardent suitor again, but failed to find him. Well, perhaps he was running late. Glancing over her shoulder, she saw Aunt Caroline still in conversation with Lady Ashby, and a pretty redhead whom she didn't recognize was now speaking to Miss Ashby. Having already met the people her godmother had most wanted her to meet, Amy saw no reason not to take advantage of her momentary freedom and explore the grounds—the Wilderness Garden, for example. Aunt Caroline, an indulgent chaperon, would not mind as long as she didn't stay away too long or wander too far afield. And if she happened to come back *engaged*, Amy thought with a secret smile, her peccadilloes would be forgiven in an instant.

Catching up her skirts, she hurried across the grass. Paths unrolled in all directions before her, some leading to formal gardens where spring flowers bloomed in exquisitely regimented order, others to plots where nature had been permitted freer rein. The Wilderness Garden probably lay down one of the latter. Her guess confirmed by a passing footman, she set off down the indicated path and soon found herself in what appeared to be the very heart of spring.

No sign of Glyndon yet, but rhododendrons and azaleas—in every shade of white, pink, and red imaginable—bloomed in splendid profusion on every side of her. Some bushes were short, reaching barely to her knee, while others towered over her head. For a moment, Amy imagined her arms full of azaleas as she drifted down the aisle toward Glyndon, then she reluctantly abandoned the fantasy. If she meant to marry in September, azaleas would be long gone by then. But roses would still be available, and orchids—even more magnificent.

She wandered through the flowering wilderness, her mind still full of wedding plans. Gown by Worth, of course, satin trimmed with seed pearls...no, pearls were for tears and she didn't want those on her wedding day. But Brussels lace, a train, and a veil of the finest tulle.

What should Aurelia wear as maid of honor? Ice blue to set off her eyes, or perhaps a delicate peach to flatter her complexion. It might be Amy's day, but she wanted her twin to shine as well. She had no patience with brides who dressed their attendants unbecomingly so they might look better by comparison. Such a petty thing to do!

"—a paltry thing to do!" A male voice spoke up suddenly from the other side of a towering wall of rhododendrons.

Amy stopped, jolted from her reverie. That voice—she knew she'd heard it before.

"Leave off, Thomas!" snapped a second voice that sent a shudder of recognition down Amy's spine. *Glyndon*..."It's none of your affair!"

"On the contrary, it's very much my affair since you're on my mother's property," Thomas retorted. "You were thinking of meeting Miss Newbold here, weren't you?"

"And if I were?" Spoken with sulky schoolboy bravado. "I'm still a free man, cousin."

"Not for long. Your engagement to Lady Louisa's due to be announced any day now."

Amy froze. Blood, breath, and heartbeat slowed to the speed of a melting glacier.

"You have no matrimonial intentions toward Miss Newbold," Thomas continued inexorably. "And it's no kindness to let her think you do."

Amy closed her eyes, willing Glyndon to assure him otherwise. Seconds dragged on like hours, like days, and then—

"All right," the viscount said heavily. "I'll stay away from her."

There was a pause, then Thomas said, "You don't intend to tell her about the engagement?" His tone was oddly devoid of expression.

"What's the point? She'll find out soon enough, when the notice appears in the *Gazette*." Glyndon gave a short laugh. "Miss Newbold's sharp enough to figure things out from there."

"You show touching concern for the lady's well-being."

"Don't pretend you care, Thomas," his cousin scoffed. "You've said yourself these American girls are all pirates. I'll wager she has another string to her bow, even as we speak."

Amy clenched her fists, her fingernails digging into her palms even through her gloves. Mortification and rage flooded hotly through her, dissolving the ice in the pit of her stomach.

Glyndon was continuing, "I suppose Mater and Pater are right. Harford Park would best be served by a proper English duchess, not an American upstart."

Amy had heard enough. Head high, she spun on her heel and stalked from the garden. She reached the path again within moments, following it back the way she had come. Her face was flushed—she could tell by the rising heat in her cheeks—and her heart thumped against her ribs with healthy fury. Fury at herself as well as at Glyndon, a small part of her was perceptive enough to recognize. How stupid she'd been, how complacent and naïve to have believed his protestations for even a moment! She'd have married him in good faith, done her best to be a loyal wife and a worthy duchess. And all the time he'd just been amusing himself, flirting with the "American upstart" before taking a proper English bride. How dare he? How dare they? Well, they could both go to the devil, Glyndon and that supercilious cousin of his!

Buoyed by her anger—infinitely preferable to tears—she rounded the last corner and saw Aunt Caroline standing almost exactly where she'd left her. Amy paused to collect herself further, then assumed a polite smile and ventured forth. Her face had cooled slightly; she hoped that meant her flush had subsided into something less hectic and more becoming.

"Amy, my dear," Lady Renbourne greeted her with a fond smile. "I was hoping you'd return from your rambles soon. There's someone I should like you to meet," she added, indicating the tall, dark-haired man standing beside her. "Amy, this is the Earl of Trevenan. Lord Trevenan, my goddaughter, Miss Amy Newbold."

An earl. Summoning up all the charm and grace in her arsenal, Amy extended her hand to the newcomer and flashed her most dazzling smile. "How do you do, Lord Trevenan? I'm delighted to make your acquaintance."

Four

Two lovely berries moulded on one stem;
So with two seeming bodies, but one heart...

—William Shakespeare,
A Midsummer Night's Dream

Bad Ems, May 1891

THE TRUNKS WERE PACKED AND THE PORTER SUMMONED
to carry them downstairs. All that remained was to wait for
the carriage that would take them to the station.

Aurelia took one last look in the glass as she pinned her
hat into place with hands that trembled only slightly. The face
that gazed back at her was a far cry from the one she'd seen
on arriving here eleven months ago: fuller and rosier. But it
was the expression that made all the difference; her eyes were
no longer shadowed but bright with anticipation, and, despite
her apprehension, her mouth wanted to turn up in a smile.

She could not see her leg in the glass, as it was decently
covered by her traveling dress. But she knew how much
it had improved as well. Oh, her limp did become more
pronounced when she was fatigued, but most of the time it
was scarcely noticeable. And as for her scar...

A discreet knock on the door broke into her thoughts.

"Mother?" Aurelia called. Laura Newbold had been finishing her own toilette when her daughter had looked in on her five minutes ago.

"*Mais non, m'amie*—it is I." The mellifluous, slightly amused female voice that replied had been known to bring countless audiences to their feet.

Smiling, Aurelia opened the door. "Claudine," she greeted her friend with equal warmth. "I hoped I would see you before we left."

Claudine Beaumont, the sometime toast of Paris, brushed her cheek against Aurelia's in a fleeting caress. "*Vraiment,* I have come to wish you and your mother *le bon voyage.* You will give my love to Paris, when you see her?"

"I will, though I'll miss you terribly. I feel you helped me just as much as Dr. Strauss."

Claudine gave a slight shake of her head. "*Eh bien*, I could not have done so, were you not so apt a pupil, *ma petite.*" Slipping one elegant finger beneath Aurelia's chin, she gently tilted her face up to the light and, after a long considering moment, smiled. "*Bon.* I see the queen and not the little mouse. Even the so-cold English will notice the difference."

"Do you think so?" Aurelia asked, unable to keep the eagerness from her voice. "I should so like to make a…better impression than I did last year."

"*Mais oui.*" Claudine's dark eyes regarded her shrewdly. "Is there someone in England you particularly wish to impress?"

Aurelia felt herself coloring. "Well, 'impress' might not be the word, exactly," she temporized. "But someone I might like to see again, now that…things are different."

Mr. Trelawney—the name was never very far away. Other young men had come to Bad Ems this past year; some had even been quite attentive, especially after she and Claudine had become friends and taken to wandering about the town together. But Aurelia had to admit—if only to herself—that, compared to *him*, they all seemed rather bland and characterless.

What harm could there be in making discreet inquiries after Mr. Trelawney when she returned to London? He was Lady Talbot's nephew—that much she did recall. And what could be more natural than to ask after an acquaintance when she had been away so long? And if some thought her forward and gauche for doing so—well, so be it. She was American, after all.

Claudine's voice, laced with amused affection, recalled her to the present. "I shall wish you *bon courage* then. And hope that you meet again this someone who has put the stars in your eyes." She took Aurelia's hands and kissed her lightly on both cheeks. "*Au revoir, ma chere.*"

Aurelia embraced her friend in turn. "What of you? Are you staying on here?"

Claudine shook her head. "*Non.* I shall be leaving for Nice at the end of the week. A dear friend has invited to me to stay. Should you like to have my direction?"

"Very much." Aurelia wondered if Claudine's "dear friend" was a man or a woman, but decided it would be impertinent to ask. "I can give you mine too, if you like. According to my sister, we're renting a house in London for the Season."

They quickly exchanged information before bidding each other a last fond farewell. Moments after Claudine's departure, the porter rapped on the door. The carriage had arrived.

Following her mother and the porter downstairs, Aurelia felt her heart pounding in mingled excitement and trepidation. Paris and London—those two dazzling, terrifying cities—still lay ahead, but at this moment, she felt equal to whatever they held in store for her.

⤜✥⤐

London, two weeks later

Descending from the train in her mother's wake, Aurelia caught her breath when she saw the familiar figure waiting on the platform. Looking at Amy might no longer be like looking into a mirror, but she could still pick out her twin in a crowd.

Before she could wave or call out, Amy's head turned in her direction—and a welcoming smile blazed across her face. "Mother! Relia!"

Hands outstretched, she came toward them, and Aurelia found herself moving forward as well. They met in a fierce embrace, half-laughing, half-crying. Breathing in her twin's favorite rose-and-jasmine scent, Aurelia felt that she was home at last.

"That will do, my dears," Laura reproved, but her blue eyes were smiling as she regarded her newly reunited daughters. "Amy, you haven't misplaced Caro, have you?"

"No, Mama." Releasing Aurelia, Amy greeted her mother more decorously. "Indeed, I believe she was right behind me."

"Beside you, now," Lady Renbourne corrected her crisply, but she, too, wore an indulgent expression. "Laura, Aurelia." She kissed her cousin and her goddaughter in turn, then stood back to survey them from head to toe. "You're both looking very well. No trouble during the crossing?"

"None at all, Aunt Caroline," Aurelia reassured her. "We were both fine throughout."

"You look it. And the spa seems to have agreed with you, to say nothing of Paris!"

"Monsieur Worth was very obliging," Mrs. Newbold informed her cousin. "He's designed a whole season's wardrobe for Aurelia, and at such short notice!"

"Excellent," Lady Renbourne said briskly. "Although I am certain you'll both want to visit the London shops too. Now, let's find a porter for all your luggage. The carriage is waiting."

Amy linked her arm through Aurelia's. "Wait till you see the house! It's in Grosvenor Square, right in the heart of Mayfair and terribly grand. And I have so much to tell you…"

⌘

No. 17 Grosvenor Square was indeed "terribly grand," both outside and in. Bemused, Aurelia let her twin, still talking nineteen to the dozen, lead her to a chamber decorated in soft blues and lavenders, with an Aubusson carpet and a four-poster bed worthy of Marie Antoinette.

"I'm just across the hall," Amy told her as they sat down on a blue brocaded chaise longue. "In the room with the rose-covered wallpaper. We can trade if you like."

"No, this room is lovely," Aurelia assured her. Suzanne, her new maid, was already unpacking her trunks and hanging the gorgeous Worth gowns in the wardrobe.

"You look wonderful, by the way," Amy remarked. "Even better than at Christmas." She tilted her head to one side, studying her sister intently. "Your hair, for one thing…"

"Do you like it?" Aurelia fingered the short, feathery fringe that softened the expanse of her forehead and—better yet—rendered the scar at her hairline far less visible. "I thought it might help make my face look—not quite as thin."

"Oh, it's very becoming," Amy assured her at once. "Your face does look fuller and healthier. I like the curls too, at the side," she added, gently touching a wispy tendril.

"So do I." The side curls drew the eye downward, away from her scarred cheek. "My friend Claudine calls them 'à la Grecque' because they remind her of Classical sculpture."

"Who on earth is Claudine?"

"Her full name is Claudine-Gabrielle Beaumont. She's a French actress," Aurelia explained. "She arrived in Bad Ems for a rest cure, about a week after you and Father left."

Amy's eyes widened. "Mama let you associate with a French *actress*?"

"Not at first. I liked her right away, but Mother didn't know what to make of her. But then when she was bedridden with the grippe, Claudine came to visit. She brought flowers and hothouse fruit and was so kind that Mother couldn't help softening her stance. So while she was resting, Claudine and I would go for walks in the gardens or about town. After Mother recovered, she would join us now and then." Aurelia smiled at the memory. "Once, the three of us had a picnic near the ruins of a Roman castle."

"That sounds wonderful," Amy said wistfully. "Is your friend very beautiful?"

"Not exactly. She said herself her nose was too long, her mouth too wide, and her cheekbones too high. But she could make you *think* she was the most beautiful woman in the room, by sheer charm alone."

And charm had been the most important quality Claudine tried to instill in her. Exercise and Dr. Strauss's treatments had strengthened her weak leg, but Claudine's tutelage had helped restore much of the confidence she'd lost after her accident and Charlie's defection.

"She took you under her wing, didn't she?" Amy observed shrewdly.

"I suppose she did. And she gave me tons of advice on how to get on when I was back in Society. How to dress, how to move, how to carry myself…'You must stand tall, *hein*?'" Aurelia quoted in a fair imitation of her friend's accent. "'And walk like a queen, not creep about like the little mouse.'"

Amy laughed appreciatively. "Oh, I do like the sound of her! What else did she suggest? I wouldn't mind picking up some French sophistication myself."

"Oh, she recommended certain creams and lotions to make the skin supple. And cosmetics." With difficulty, Aurelia refrained from touching her scar. Claudine had surprised her by rejecting any sort of heavy maquillage for a light dusting of powder and occasionally rouge. "Her maid Françoise cut my hair, by the way. But Claudine said that the secret to being beautiful and poised is to believe you are— and not let anyone convince you otherwise. Not even your own reflection." She paused, feeling self-conscious again, and smiled at her twin. "But enough about me! What's been happening with *you*? You sounded so mysterious in your last letter."

Amy flushed. "I'm sorry. I didn't mean to. It's just—well, things weren't quite settled when I wrote, and even now, nothing's been officially announced. But Father and Aunt Caroline approve," she rushed on. "And I'm sure Mother will too, once she knows—"

"Approve of what?" Aurelia demanded, catching her sister's hands in hers. "For heaven's sake, Amy, spit it out!"

Amy took a deep breath. "I'm engaged—to be married."

"Married?" Aurelia echoed, astonished. "Good heavens!" She sifted through her memories of Amy's many admirers. "Is it Lord Glyndon?"

Amy's mouth twisted as if she'd bitten into something sour. "No. Lord Glyndon is unofficially engaged to Lady Louisa Savernake. *I* am marrying the Earl of Trevenan."

"Trevenan." The name meant nothing to Aurelia. "Was he courting you last year?"

Amy shook her head. "He came into his title very unexpectedly—just this past January, in fact. But he says he saw me once when he was in London and never forgot me." A dimple quivered at the corner of her mouth. "You can imagine how flattering that was to hear!"

"What's he like?" Aurelia asked, relieved by her twin's returning good humor.

"Tall, dark, and handsome—like someone out of a gypsy fortune-teller's predictions. And he has a London townhouse and an estate in Cornwall, though the latter needs repairs. He apologized for that, but I told him my dowry should take care of any problems." Amy shrugged lightly. "I was glad he didn't pretend not to need money. We should deal well together, I think."

Aurelia fretted her lip at this dispassionate assessment. "Are you in love with him?"

Amy flicked her an amused glance. "*You* were always the romantic one, Relia. I do like and respect Lord Trevenan, but we've only been acquainted for a month."

Aurelia stared at her. "Only a month—and you're marrying him?"

"It'll be at least three months before the wedding— plenty of time to get to know each other better. And he's invited us all down to spend part of the summer at his estate. I wonder if Cornwall's anything like Newport—" She broke off with a little laugh. "Goodness, Relia, your face! You'd think I'd just told you I was engaged to Bluebeard or Henry the Eighth!"

"I can't help worrying," Aurelia pointed out with dignity. "Any more than you could if I were to tell you I was marrying someone I'd known for just a month."

Amy sighed. "Well, you needn't. Lord Trevenan is quite the upstanding citizen." She began to tick off his virtues on her fingers. "Well-educated, clean-living, hard-working—"

"I thought English aristocrats prided themselves on never having to lift a finger."

"I told you, he hasn't been an earl very long. Before that, he had to earn his bread. His mother's family owns a tin mine. He inherited her shares and helps run the business. That's one reason Father approves of him. Trevenan's not afraid of dirtying his hands.

"In fact, he's been in Cornwall for the last week taking care of things there," Amy went on. "But he's supposed to be back by this evening. We're seeing *The Gondoliers* at the Savoy. You will come, won't you? I want very much for you to meet—and like each other."

Aurelia knew she could make but one answer; laying her doubts aside, she squeezed her twin's hand. "Of course, dearest. Now, why don't you help me pick out a gown for tonight?"

⌾⌾⌾

From the private box the Newbolds had hired for the Season, Aurelia glanced around the theater. Seats were filling rapidly, even though *The Gondoliers* had played here for more than a year. Nonetheless, according to Aunt Caroline, the Savoy remained an excellent place at which to be seen, if one were a lady in Society.

Amused, Aurelia plied her fan and admired the luxury of the Savoy's trappings: the décor—all white, gold, and red, the gold satin stage curtain, and the steady luminescence of the theater's electrical lamps. More than a thousand of them, Amy had said. She spared a moment to hope her scar wasn't too visible in this light, then she made herself put the thought aside. She was meeting Amy's intended tonight; that was the important thing.

All the same, she'd dressed with care in a Worth creation of violet satin with glittering silver trim; her earrings—dangling twists of silver wire and tiny amethysts—had been chosen to complement the gown. Like her new coiffure, the earrings drew the eye down and away from her cheek; another trick Claudine had taught her. Despite her resolve, she'd felt a flutter of apprehension in her midriff before they left the house, but the sight of her reflection and the delighted approval of her mother, godmother, and twin had reassured her. She did look well; more importantly, she *felt* well—and quite determined to enjoy the evening.

A knock on the door of their box brought Amy to her feet, her peach silk gown rustling around her. "That must be Trevenan," she said, going to answer it.

"Oh, good. You're here," Aurelia heard her say as she

opened the door. "Do come in, my lord, and meet the rest of my family." She stood aside, smiling, to admit her fiancé. "Mother, Aurelia—may I introduce the Earl of Trevenan?"

Aurelia caught her breath as a tall man in evening dress stepped into the light.

Dark hair, dark eyes in a strongly handsome face, and the scent of citrus and cloves...

The only thing missing was the sound of waltz music.

Five

I do desire we may be better strangers.

—William Shakespeare, *As You Like It*

AURELIA FROZE IN HER CHAIR, UNABLE TO DO MORE than stare as Amy's betrothed came forward to take her hand and raise it to his lips before turning to greet the other ladies.

Mr. Trelawney. The newly made Earl of Trevenan. The first man to make her feel alive in four years was engaged to her sister—to Amy, whom she loved with every beat of her heart. She didn't even have the consolation of hating her rival.

A voice inside of her howled at the injustice of it: *Not fair, not fair—I met him first!* Another voice, quieter and more insidious, murmured, *Of course he would choose the whole twin. The one who was perfect and unscarred.*

Aurelia swallowed, feeling her hard-won confidence crumble into dust. For a moment, she wanted nothing more than to rise and flee from the box. Then, like a dash of cold water in the face, rational thought came flooding back.

No one was to blame for this situation. Amy and—Lord Trevenan had not become engaged to hurt her. How could they have done so, when neither of them knew what she'd felt that night at the Talbots' ball? She had never spoken a word to Amy about that secret waltz, and, despite her nebulous hopes, she could not be certain of seeing Mr. Trelawney—as she'd known him—again. Nor did she have any reason to believe that their private dance in the conservatory had meant anything to him beyond a stray charitable impulse. He'd been kind to her—that was all. An act of chivalry, if not the pity she'd dreaded.

"And this is my sister, Aurelia." Amy's voice penetrated the fog in her head.

And now the earl was turning to *her*, having already greeted Mother and Aunt Caroline. She swallowed again, feeling the panic rise in her throat.

Dear heaven, what would Claudine do in a situation like this?

Mercifully, some of her friend's words flashed into her mind. "When in public, you must not let anything appear to vex or distress you," Claudine had counseled. "You must cultivate *le sangfroid*—the cold blood. The English, they are famous for it."

"I'm not English," Aurelia had pointed out.

"But you will be living among them, *n'est-ce pas*? So, in England, do as the English do."

"Cold blood." Aurelia had rather doubted her ability to master that quality. But she had to admit that it had its uses just now—and so did nearly twenty-one years of lessons in deportment. Drawing upon her reserves of both, she summoned a smile and extended her hand.

"Lord Trevenan," she began, relieved to hear how calm her voice sounded. "I am pleased to make your acquaintance at last."

He took her hand, his clasp light and warm through the silk of her glove. Would he allude to their previous encounter, or had he forgotten it entirely? And if, by chance, he *did* remember, would he find it easier—as she did—to pretend they were meeting for the first time?

"The pleasure is mine, Miss Aurelia." His voice was the same—deep, pleasant, with that faint but attractive burr; the Cornish accent, perhaps. "Your sister has told me much of you."

She risked a glance at him. Was that recognition she saw in his eyes, or merely a reflection of her own desire? She could not be certain, but she felt again that stirring of attraction, followed by a pang of longing. Suppressing both, she said lightly, "All good, I trust?"

"Relia!" Amy protested, laughing. "As if I'd say anything else!"

His eyes warmed, just as they had that night. "Entirely good. I can but hope that she was even half as complimentary when speaking to you of me."

"You need have no fears on that score, Lord Trevenan. My sister speaks of you in only the most glowing terms." Which wasn't wholly inaccurate, Aurelia thought; Amy's admission that she liked and respected her betrothed must count as high praise, coming from her.

"I'm relieved to hear it." He smiled at Amy, and Aurelia had to stifle another rebellious twinge at the sight.

"The house lights are dimming," Aunt Caroline announced from behind them. "I do believe the performance is about to start."

"I've saved you a place, Trevenan." Amy indicated the vacant seat on her left.

Thanking her, he moved to occupy it. Achingly aware of his every movement, Aurelia turned her attention toward the stage, hoping fervently that whatever happened there would be enough to distract her from Lord Trevenan's presence in their box.

❧

"I love the Savoy operas, don't you?" Amy murmured to James as the overture began.

He murmured polite agreement, even though he'd only seen *The Mikado* and *The Pirates of Penzance*. Airy trifles, but he'd enjoyed both productions well enough. And since Amy was so fond of them, he would see that she had the chance to attend on the occasions when they were in London. And they would come to town from time to time, he acknowledged with an inner sigh. A successful marriage involved some compromises, after all.

He glanced at his fiancée's exquisite profile, scarcely able to credit that she'd accepted his suit: a provincial earl who had held his title less than six months and still felt far more comfortable poring over account books and galloping along the Cornish shore than frequenting London balls and receptions. Even with Kelmswood and Glyndon out of the running, she might have set her sights higher than James. And yet, for all her ambition, Amy was not without heart, as her obvious love for her family showed. James thought she liked him well enough, and he'd found it easy to care for so sweet and charming a girl. And desirable—surely no man with a drop of blood in his veins could deny her appeal. A deeper affection could easily develop between them, and in time, there might be children, a family of their own.

Family. His gaze strayed to Aurelia, sitting on her sister's right. He'd scarcely recognized her; despite what Thomas and Amy had both told him of her sojourn abroad, he had not expected so dramatic a change. The girl he remembered as a wounded bird had met his eyes squarely, with a bright, confident smile—and no sign of the brittle delicacy that had informed her every word and gesture in their previous encounter.

And no visible sign of recognition either, when they were introduced just now. Granted, there was no reason why she should remember, he supposed. A year had gone by, and so much had changed for both of them. Perhaps she'd left the memory of that night behind, along with her past unhappiness, to emerge from her chrysalis newly and joyously transformed.

And her transformation was indeed remarkable to behold. The new clothes helped. She'd been well-dressed last year too, but the gown she wore tonight fit her better, or perhaps it was merely that she had put on some weight and no longer seemed painfully thin.

She wore her hair differently too; the waving fringe across her brow and the wispy curls at her temples partly concealed her scar, though he could still detect its tracery upon her cheek, softened by the electrical light. But the skin of her throat and shoulders gleamed with the same pearly translucence as Amy's, promised the same warmth and satiny smoothness…

Good God! Startled by the turn his thoughts had taken, James forced them back to the woman sitting beside him: Amy, his lovely fiancée. He wondered uneasily if other men courting twin sisters experienced this sort of momentary confusion.

The overture ended, and Amy leaned forward, her lips parting slightly in anticipation. Catching the drift of her scent, James let it anchor him to her side and the present moment, as the gold curtains opened on a scene in Venice.

Rather to her surprise, Aurelia discovered it was possible to close off a part of her mind and focus on the spectacle before her: the colorful bands of gondoliers and contadine, the lavishly painted sets and backdrops, and the soaring voices of the principal singers.

As the curtain descended at the interval, Amy turned to her with sparkling eyes. "Isn't this wonderful, Relia? I think I like it as much as *The Mikado*, and far more than *The Yeomen of the Guard*!"

Aurelia nodded agreement. "*The Yeomen of the Guard* was too sad for me. I hated how Jack Point ended up heartbroken and alone—" She broke off, flushing, at the vehemence that had crept into her tone.

Fortunately, no one else seemed to have noticed. Shaking out her skirts, Amy rose from her chair. "Goodness, I'm stiff! Trevenan, might we take a turn about the foyer?"

"Of course, my dear. Ladies," he addressed the other inhabitants of the box, "may I escort you there, or would you prefer to remain here during the interval?"

"You'll come, won't you, Relia?" Amy entreated.

The last thing Aurelia wanted was to play gooseberry between her twin and Lord Trevenan, but how could she possibly explain that to Amy?

"Why don't we all go?" Aunt Caroline suggested, and that settled that.

Gentlemen in evening dress and ladies in silks and jewels crowded the foyer, talking animatedly amongst themselves. Staying close to her mother's side, Aurelia caught snatches of conversation as they passed, some pertaining to tonight's performance, others to subjects completely unrelated; the London Season was in full swing, after all. Various people nodded in passing or stopped to exchange brief pleasantries. To Aurelia's surprise, several welcomed her back to London with every indication of sincerity, as well as complimenting her on her improved appearance. She smiled and thanked them, bemused that anyone remembered her when she'd done her best to avoid Society whenever possible last year.

"Amy, dear." Aunt Caroline's voice, low-pitched but holding a note of urgency, broke into Aurelia's musings. Startled, she glanced at her twin and saw her stiffen visibly.

Two more people were strolling toward them in a manner too deliberate to be accidental: Viscount Glyndon and a young lady, gowned in the height of fashion. Could this be Lady Louisa Savernake? She certainly carried herself like a person of consequence. Indeed, there was an air of the triumphal procession about them both, though the lady looked noticeably more pleased than her companion. "Smug" might be a better word, Aurelia thought.

Pausing before them, Lady Louisa gushed a greeting. "Why, Lady Renbourne, Miss Newbold. I'm simply delighted to see you here tonight. This must be the rest of your family?"

"Good evening, Lady Louisa, Lord Glyndon." Amy's voice and smile were equally bright. "Indeed, it is." She undertook the introductions without further ado. Lady Louisa's pale blue gaze passed over Mrs. Newbold and Aurelia with only cursory interest, though Lord Glyndon clasped Trevenan's hand and punctiliously bowed over each lady's.

He seemed to linger a moment longer over Amy's, and Aurelia wondered if he was ruing his bargain. Lady Louisa was fair-haired and fine-boned in the typical English fashion, but to Aurelia's admittedly biased eye, she hadn't so much as a spark of Amy's charm or vitality.

"I simply adore the works of Messrs. Gilbert and Sullivan," Lady Louisa declared. She gave Lord Glyndon's arm an unmistakably proprietary squeeze. "And seeing this one has convinced me: we simply must go to Venice on our wedding trip!"

"A delightful notion," Amy replied with just the right amount of polite interest. "Allow me to congratulate you on your engagement. Have you set a date yet?"

Lady Louisa simpered; there was no other word for it, Aurelia decided. "June is the best month, of course, but we're considering July and August too. And at St. George's, Hanover Square, naturally." She tightened her grip on Lord Glyndon's arm; Aurelia thought she saw a flicker of annoyance in the viscount's eyes. "But what of you, Miss Newbold? Have you made any plans for *your* big day?"

"Oh, Lord Trevenan and I are still discussing the details," Amy said airily.

"Of which there are many," the earl interposed with equal

smoothness. "But my intended can rely upon my indulgence in whatever she decides, from the church to our wedding trip."

Well said, Aurelia thought as Amy smiled up at Lord Trevenan; her mother and Aunt Caroline regarded him with approval as well.

Lady Louisa seemed slightly flummoxed by their solidarity, perhaps because it provided such a contrast to Lord Glyndon's sullen silence. "How charming," she began, then broke off to exclaim, "Oh, look—there are the Elliots! I simply must go and give them my regards."

"Yes, you *simply* must," Amy agreed dulcetly. Aurelia hid a smile behind her fan.

Impervious to irony, Lady Louisa excused herself and departed, towing her fiancé in her wake like a tugboat pulling a recalcitrant barge. Aurelia darted a glance at her twin, who was still sporting a bright, fixed smile. Not for the first time, she wondered just what had passed between Amy and Lord Glyndon. If the viscount had led her sister on, when he'd no honorable intentions…A gust of protective love swept through her as she remembered the coolness that had greeted them on their debuts in New York society. Insulated by her love for Charlie, Aurelia had not cared as much, but Amy had felt the slights and snubs almost as keenly as their mother. How intolerable for her to encounter the same treatment in England!

"My dear, are you well?" Lord Trevenan asked. Aurelia's throat tightened at the warmth and solicitude in his voice; how he must adore her sister.

Amy turned to him in evident relief. "Perfectly well, my lord. Shall we return to our seats? The interval must be nearly over by now."

"Of course." He proffered his arm and she took it, smiling more brilliantly than ever.

They made such a striking pair, Aurelia thought wistfully as she followed them back into the theater: Lord Trevenan so darkly handsome, her twin so radiantly fair. And she herself had cause to know that he was as kind as he was handsome, easily worth a dozen of Lord Glyndon. And wasn't that what she wanted for Amy: a good man, an estimable man, who would value and cherish her? And his title, albeit the least of his attractions as far as Aurelia was concerned, would certainly provide all the social cachet her sister could desire.

Mastering the ache in her heart, she steeled herself with a new resolve.

She would not ruin this for Amy, no matter what it cost her.

Six

…She never told her love
But let concealment like a worm i' th' bud
Feed on her damask cheek…

—William Shakespeare, *Twelfth Night*

"A GENTLEMAN TO SEE YOU, LORD TREVENAN," THE butler announced. "A Captain Mercer."

James looked up from his correspondence. "Did he state his business, Roberts?"

"Not entirely, but he says it's a matter of some urgency, pertaining to his late lordship."

Gerald? Frowning, James put aside the letter he'd been reading. All was well at Pentreath, according to his estate manager. Mercer…the name was unfamiliar. Still, what harm could it do to hear his business? "Thank you, Roberts. Show him in here, if you would."

"Very good, my lord." The butler withdrew.

Of all the things to which James had yet to become accustomed since inheriting the title, being addressed as "my lord" counted chief among them. So did acting as master of this huge Belgravia townhouse he had entered no more than three times in his life. Perhaps one day he'd adapt to both conditions; his household had already adjusted with surprising ease. "Captain Philip Mercer, my lord," Roberts announced from the library doorway.

The newcomer—a tall, brown-haired man perhaps in his thirties—advanced into the library. "Good morning, Lord Trevenan. I hope I am not disturbing you?"

"Not at all," James said with more politeness than truth. He gestured to an armchair opposite his desk. "Pray, be seated."

"Thank you." Mercer came forward and sat down.

Navy? James wondered as he studied his visitor more closely. *Or perhaps the merchant service?* Mercer had the sun-browned complexion and slightly rolling gait of someone who spent a lot of time at sea, but his accent sounded refined enough to James's ears. For a sailor, he was quite the polished article, not at all like the hearty, sporting types with whom Gerald had usually kept company. "You wished to speak to me? On a matter of some importance?"

"Indeed, my lord." Mercer leaned forward, his eyes—a striking pale grey—intent on James's face. "At the risk of distressing you, I must inform you that this matter concerns your late cousin. He and I had become business associates in the months before his death."

James raised his brows. "Gerald—in business?" To his knowledge, Gerald had displayed neither interest nor acumen in any business enterprise, much to the disgust of his father. Still, his cousin had always needed money to support his way of life in town.

"Last spring, Lord Alston—as he then was—acquired a number of shares in my company, Mercer Shipping," the captain continued. "By autumn, he had taken a more active interest in certain…practical aspects of the business."

"I see." James could imagine Gerald, at his most arrogantly bullish, thrusting himself into the middle of things and trying to take over without any real understanding. Most people *would* find that galling, as Mercer clearly had, to judge from his tone and expression.

"Quite." Mercer paused, brows drawing together. He appeared to be weighing his words carefully. "Alston…well, to make a long story short, part of a shipment from last December—just before Christmas—has gone missing, and I have been unable to determine its whereabouts. I have searched several warehouses, but to no avail. As your cousin oversaw the unloading of this shipment, I wondered if he might have redirected it to some other location, and if, as his cousin, you might have been privy to this information."

James shook his head. "I am afraid I know nothing of this, Captain Mercer. Gerald and I were not close. Indeed, I was unaware until now that he had invested in your company."

"Ah." Mercer shifted in his chair. "That is another matter I hoped to discuss with you. As your cousin's successor, you inherited the bulk of his estate, did you not?"

"I did," James replied guardedly. "Except where noted in his will." Although, if truth be told, Gerald's will was a sketchy document at best. Like countless young men, he'd never considered the possibility that he might die prematurely and without heirs of his own body.

"Including his shares in Mercer Shipping?"

"I would assume so." James kept his tone neutral. "Only our family solicitors know the whole of Gerald's assets."

"I see." Mercer cleared his throat. "Well, I would very much like to buy back your cousin's shares, and I'm prepared to negotiate a fair price for them. Starting at—" He paused and then named an amount that made James blink.

Control must be the crux of the matter, he realized, after the first shock had worn off. Having endured Gerald's interference in his business, Mercer clearly did not wish to tolerate anyone else's; James could scarcely blame the man for that. But he was in no position to grant Mercer's request. "I fear I cannot make a decision of this nature without first consulting my solicitors. Given the extent of Gerald's debts, they may advise against such a course at present."

Something inimical flickered in Mercer's eyes; for a moment, James thought he was about to protest, then, abruptly, he capitulated. "Very well. I understand your concerns, my lord. But if you should decide to part with those shares, would you be so good as to contact me?" He took out a silver card case and handed James one of the cards. "This is my direction in London."

"Thank you. I will bear your offer in mind," James assured him, setting the card down on his desk. Somewhat to his relief, he heard the mantel clock chime the hour. Eleven o'clock—he was expected at the Newbolds' this morning. He rose to his feet, a signal for his visitor to do likewise. "If you'll excuse me, Captain, I have an appointment I must keep. Good day to you."

Perceptive enough not to overstay his welcome, Mercer tendered his own farewells and departed. James waited five minutes, then asked for the carriage to be brought around.

❧

As the carriage headed toward Grosvenor Square, James mulled over his conversation with Mercer. Missing shipments, goods vanishing without a trace...the whole thing disturbed him more than he cared to admit. For all their mutual animosity, he did not like to think Gerald might have been a thief as well as a bully and a lout.

And yet...he could not dismiss the possibility that his cousin might have done something underhanded, especially if he'd needed the money badly enough. Mercer had not been exactly forthcoming about the nature of the goods his ships transported, but if they were sufficiently rare and costly, might Gerald have sold them secretly and pocketed the profits for himself? Or planned to do so, before he met his death on the cliffs?

Unease prickled at the back of his neck, but he could not have said whether he was more troubled by Gerald's possible theft or the all-too-real glimmer of hostility he had sensed beneath Mercer's polished veneer. The man was determined to regain those shares, and left to his own devices, James might have obliged him. But something seemed…off, somehow.

He'd talk to his solicitors at the earliest opportunity, he decided. And if they thought he should sell the shares back to Mercer—well, he would do so. Mr. Newbold had already advanced him a considerable portion of Amy's dowry to make repairs to the estate where she would one day be mistress, but James was reluctant to spend any of it on settling Gerald's personal debts.

Arriving at 17 Grosvenor Square, he was shown into the sitting room, furnished in Heppelwhite and decorated in soft blue. The family would be informed of his arrival, he was told. Idly studying the rather uninspired landscape painting over the mantel, he heard rippling notes of piano music coming from the room just down the passage. He listened as the notes ran up and down the scale, then shaped themselves into a somewhat familiar air.

Chopin, he thought, after listening for a few more moments—a composition he'd heard a few times before when his cousin Jessica was practicing. But this player, while no virtuoso, was far more proficient than poor Jess. Intrigued, he left the sitting room to investigate the sound.

What he found in the music room made him smile. He hadn't known Amy even played the piano, much less this well. From the doorway, he glimpsed her straight back and the proud set of her head and shoulders, though wisps of spun-gold hair had escaped from her chignon to tease the tender nape of her neck. Seemingly unaware of this distraction, she played on, her fingers skimming over the keys with exhilarating speed and unerring accuracy.

Well, perhaps not entirely unerring, he amended, as she struck a wrong note.

"Drat," she muttered, just audibly enough for him to hear. And then, more vehemently, "*Merde*," just before she resumed playing with the same fierce concentration.

James stared at her, astonished. His own French was little more than passable, but some words one did not forget. Then his mouth quirked; truly, his fiancée had unknown depths. And far from shocking him, her lapse made her seem more endearingly human, less a golden goddess than a flesh-and-blood woman with the same imperfections and insecurities as other mortals.

But the occasional error notwithstanding, her dedication to her music amazed him. He would never have guessed she could play with such intensity, such single-minded passion. Never before had she revealed this side of herself to him. Never before—

He froze, struck by a sudden realization. And took a closer look at the pianist.

Not Amy. Aurelia.

Why hadn't he remembered she was musical? The image of her swaying in time to the waltz flashed into his mind with blinding clarity. Such unconscious grace, despite her professed infirmity, and now, such unexpected skill, displayed just as artlessly.

Loath to interrupt, he remained in the doorway, watching and listening. She'd come a long way from the girl she'd been a year ago, and yet she drew him as strongly now as she had then. Not from pity this time, but admiration—and something more he did not care to name.

❧

Someone was watching her. Aurelia could feel the weight of that unseen gaze upon her, but she continued to play, working her way through the alternating slow and fast movements of the piece to the last chords, which ended as softly as a sigh.

Lord Trevenan's voice spoke from behind her. "Well done, Miss Aurelia."

Aurelia wondered why she was not more surprised to discover it was he. But then, she reflected wryly, last night had taken the cake as far as surprises went. "Thank you, Lord Trevenan." To her relief, her voice sounded steady and calm. "Have you been listening long?"

"Long enough." He came further into the room. "I was not aware that you played."

"I hadn't, not for a while," Aurelia confessed. After the accident, she had shunned anything that might call attention to herself, including music. "But I discovered that I regretted giving it up. There was a piano at our hotel in Bad Ems, so I asked if I might practice on it. I hope to regain some degree of proficiency soon."

"From what I heard, I would say you already have." He paused beside the piano.

Aurelia made herself look at him and smile, grateful that her face did not show the ravages of a sleepless night. "That is kind of you to say, my lord."

"Not at all. As a Cornishman, I can be very exacting about music," he explained. "I've heard my cousin perform this piece, but not so well. Chopin, isn't it?"

"Yes. Waltz in C sharp minor." She felt the betraying color rising in her cheeks; it *would* have to be a waltz she was playing!

Lord Trevenan glanced aside, and Aurelia had the sudden impression that he felt just as self-conscious and awkward as she. Then he looked back, his gaze locking on hers with an intensity that made her pulse quicken. "Talking of waltzes…perhaps you might favor me with another some evening."

Aurelia stilled, hands clenching in her lap. He'd done it now, dismantled last night's mutual pretense in a mere handful of words. "You remember, then."

He hesitated, then nodded. "Yes. But I wasn't sure if you did."

Oh, God. When every moment of that waltz seemed permanently etched upon her memory—and her body. The warmth of his hands, the scent of his skin…

The flood of longing that had nearly overwhelmed her at their last encounter threatened to rise again; she forced it back with grim determination. "I remember," she told Amy's fiancé. "But last night did not seem an appropriate time to mention that—we'd met before." She attempted a light shrug. "Life has changed so much since then, for both of us."

"So it has," he conceded.

Aurelia took a steadying breath. "So, perhaps it's best if we go on as if we only met for the first time last night, because in a way, we truly have."

Something stirred in the depths of his eyes; she could not tell whether it was relief or regret. Then, "No doubt you're right," he said, almost too quickly.

Aurelia stifled a sigh, refusing to be hurt by his ready compliance. What good would it do to dwell upon the past? "That settles that, then. May I wish you every happiness with Amy?"

"Thank you." He paused, then continued, almost diffidently, "I've come to know your sister better over this past month. She is lovely and charming, and—I believe we would suit."

There were few things less pleasant, Aurelia discovered with a sinking heart, than hearing the man of one's dreams praise another woman, even if that woman was one's beloved sister. But Amy's happiness meant more to her than those secret yearnings—and so did her own recovery. Her twin's impending marriage to Lord Trevenan could not take away what she had accomplished: the long journey back to health and strength. She would not falter now.

Lifting her chin, she mustered her brightest smile. "How

could anyone *not* love Amy? I should be happy," she managed not to stumble over that word, "to welcome into the family any man who cherishes her as she deserves."

He smiled back. "I would be no less honored to call you sister, Miss Aurelia."

And she must learn to call him *brother*, Aurelia told herself firmly. "Since we are to be related, I think you can leave off the 'Miss,' Lord Trevenan."

"Very well, if you're likewise willing to dispense with formality and call me James."

James Trelawney. *A good, masculine name*, she thought, *straightforward and unaffected*. "What does my sister call you?"

"Trevenan. She's asked me to call her Amy, but unfortunately, I haven't been able to persuade her to use *my* name yet." His eyes held a glint of rueful amusement. "She told me that her first pony was called 'James.'"

Aurelia was startled into a laugh. "So he was! And my pony was called Jack. I'm afraid they were horrid little beasts, contrary as donkeys and thoroughly spoiled." She sobered abruptly. "Forgive me, my lord, but I don't feel I can use your Christian name if my sister does not."

He nodded. "Understood. Would you consider dropping the 'Lord' and just making it 'Trevenan'? Perhaps I'll get used to it faster if you and your sister both call me that."

"I believe I can manage that," she assured him.

"Relia! Trevenan!" Amy's voice hailed them from the doorway. "I thought I heard your voices. My goodness, how serious you both look!" she added, regarding them with a quizzical eye. "Have I missed something?"

"We were merely discussing possible excursions," Trevenan replied, as Aurelia busied herself with putting away her music. "I know how eager you've been to see the exhibition at the Royal Academy. Would you and your sister—and your mother, for that matter—like to go today? One of my closest friends has a painting on display this year."

"That sounds wonderful!" Amy turned to her sister. "You're coming, aren't you, Relia? I know you enjoy looking at art as much as I do!"

The queen and not the little mouse, Aurelia reminded herself. Disappointed hopes or not, she was not creeping back into the shadows; her days of hiding were over. She smiled at her twin as she rose from the piano. "Of course I'm coming. Let's go find Mother."

Seven

Painters and poets alike have always had license to dare anything!

—Ovid, *Ars Poetica*

WHILE FLATTERED BY THE EARL'S INVITATION, LAURA chose to stay behind and rest, so it was a party of three that arrived at Burlington House and made their way inside to the gallery.

Walking at her sister's side, Aurelia gazed about her in awe at the sheer number and diversity of the paintings covering the walls. Nearly as impressive was the fashionable crowd that wandered at a stately snail's pace through the exhibition: ladies in lace-trimmed afternoon gowns and feather-and-flower bedecked hats and gentlemen scarcely less fine in morning dress and silk toppers—and all of them prepared to voice decided opinions on whatever they saw, whether on the walls or the other people in attendance.

"How vulgar," a dowager pronounced, peering through her lorgnette at one painting. A few feet away, a gentleman with a loud, rather pompous voice dismissed another effort as "too conventional, even insipid," while his female companion—dowdy and unobtrusive as a peahen—murmured timid agreement. Nearby, two girls close to Aurelia's age ignored the paintings but murmured less than flattering remarks about the frocks worn by some of the other ladies there.

Aurelia glanced down self-consciously at her spring-green afternoon dress, then caught sight of Amy doing the same to her own rose-pink ensemble. Their eyes met and they looked away at once, struggling not to laugh. As Trevenan led them through the throng, they encountered some acquaintances of his or Amy's and stopped to exchange brief pleasantries. Aurelia accustomed herself to being introduced anew to Society, though she was again agreeably surprised by the cordiality with which she was received.

The press of people made reading the placards difficult, but Aurelia endeavored to do so anyway. Few of the names were recognizable, though she was charmed to see two new paintings by Waterhouse: a dramatic rendering of Ulysses and the Sirens and a quieter portrait of an auburn-haired girl in classical dress, daydreaming before an altar decked with flowers. Aurelia admired both but preferred the more contemplative mood of the latter.

"*Flora*," she read from the accompanying placard.

"So serene," Amy said on a sigh. "And the model is lovely. I wonder who she is. It must be fascinating to pose for an artist."

"Maybe, but think of having to sit still all that time," Aurelia pointed out. "Or stand—or hold some other uncomfortable position for hours."

"Or pose in a full bathtub, like the model for Millais's *Ophelia*," Trevenan added. "I understand he was so intent on his work that he never noticed when the water became too cold for her and she took a severe chill. She sent him the doctor's bill later."

"I hope he paid it. It seems the very least he could have done, under the circumstances!" Aurelia declared roundly.

Amy nodded agreement. "I hope not all artists are as oblivious as Mr. Millais. Still, his model should have said something. *I* certainly wouldn't have just lain there freezing to death!"

"It does take the idea of suffering for one's art to an extreme," Trevenan agreed. He offered his arm to Amy. "Shall we continue?"

By now they had traveled more than halfway around the room and the crowd was beginning to thin, slightly but appreciably. Perhaps visitors were recalling luncheon or other engagements, Aurelia speculated; she wouldn't mind some refreshment herself, once they were finished here. But for now, it was simply a relief to have a clearer view of the remaining works.

Further along the wall, they paused before another painting that, like Waterhouse's, appeared to have a mythological theme. A young woman clad in flowing white robes sat at her loom, but her hands were idle, her rapt gaze fixed upon what looked like a huge mirror hanging before her. Reflected there were the shadowy forms of a man and a woman walking entwined beneath a softly glowing full moon.

"Why, it's the Lady of Shalott!" Amy exclaimed after several moments' perusal.

And indeed it was, Aurelia discovered upon reading the placard. "*But in her web she still delights / To weave the mirror's magic sights*," she quoted softly. "*For often through the silent nights, / A funeral with plumes and lights and music / Went to Camelot...*"

Trevenan took up the recital, his deep voice sending a shiver down her spine. "*Or when the moon was overhead, / Came two young lovers lately wed, / 'I am half-sick of shadows,' said / The Lady of Shalott.*"

"Who's the artist?" Amy asked eagerly.

"Thomas Sheridan," Aurelia reported, consulting the placard again.

Amy stiffened—just enough for a twin to notice. "I see." Her tone cooled. "Was this the friend you mentioned, Trevenan?"

"Indeed," he replied, smiling. "This is Thomas's first showing at the Royal Academy. Do you like the painting, my dear?"

She shrugged. "It's quite pretty, but perhaps a bit—derivative? There have been so many treatments of the subject, after all."

Aurelia glanced at her in surprise. It was so unlike Amy, with her keen interest in paintings and portraits, to damn fine work with faint praise. But her twin's face was an impenetrable mask, showing not so much as a trace of her previous enthusiasm.

"True enough," her fiancé agreed, sounding more amused than offended. He turned to Aurelia. "Do you agree with your sister, Miss Aurelia?"

"Oh…" Wishing she wasn't quite so conscious of Trevenan's dark gaze, Aurelia turned back to the painting. "Well, I have seen other versions of *The Lady of Shalott*. But I do think each artist can bring something new to a familiar subject and make it his own." She paused, peering more closely at Sheridan's work. "I like the artist's use of light and dark here, but I think it's the lady's expression that makes the painting truly memorable. How sad, how wistful she looks watching the lovers. Even her hands have fallen still. You can tell she's seeing all the things she can never have. And the title—'Half-Sick of Shadows'—is inspired," she added.

"Thank you," a new voice remarked behind her. "I was rather pleased with it myself."

Startled, Aurelia turned to see that a lanky man with brown hair and clear green eyes had joined them.

"Thomas!" Trevenan clasped the newcomer's hand. "What brings you here today?"

"Well, I've received a few offers for the Lady—good ones, as it turns out—but I wanted to see if I could bear to part with her." Sheridan's smile was quick and rueful. "No one tells you what a double-edged sword it can be—producing a painting good enough to sell."

Trevenan smiled, clapping his friend on the shoulder. "Well, it's a fine piece of work—whatever you decide to do." He turned to Amy. "You know my fiancée, Miss Newbold."

"Good day, Miss Newbold." Sheridan bowed over Amy's hand; she gave a cool nod in response, showing none of her usual warmth and friendliness. Watching, Aurelia wondered uneasily just what the story was there.

"And this is her sister, Miss Aurelia," Trevenan resumed.

Sheridan turned, and Aurelia found herself the focus of those startlingly green eyes. "Enchanted, Miss Aurelia." The painter bowed over her hand as well and smiled more warmly this time; the effect was little short of dazzling. "I hear you've been abroad and have just recently returned to London."

"Very recently," Aurelia confessed. "I arrived only yesterday. Before, I was at Bad Ems."

He regarded her keenly. "Your sojourn there appears to have done you a world of good."

"Thank you, it did." Somewhat to her surprise, Aurelia felt neither threatened nor offended by his scrutiny. But there was no malice in Sheridan's assessing gaze, though it seemed to encompass her every feature, scar and all.

"Pardon me, Miss Aurelia," he began, "but if I may take the liberty?"

He meant to touch her, she realized. Too astonished even to consider refusing, she nodded bemused consent. Much in the way Claudine had done, Sheridan slipped a finger beneath her chin and tipped her face up to the light; his touch was gentle, even respectful, despite his own acknowledgment of taking liberties.

"Very clever," he said, after a moment. "One might even say artistic—the effect of the hair *and* the earrings." He brushed a finger against one of the teardrop pearls dangling from her ears before releasing her chin.

"Thank you," Aurelia said, a little uncertainly. "A friend of mine—a Frenchwoman—gave me some advice on both."

"Ah, that explains it. Frenchwomen have a matchless sense of style."

"They do, indeed. When I visit Paris, I can't help feeling like a frump by comparison, no matter how well I dress," Aurelia confessed.

"If it's any consolation, you don't look like one," he assured her. "In fact, I would say you embody the best of both worlds: the sophistication of the Old and the freshness of the New."

Aurelia felt herself coloring, not just at the compliment but at the open admiration she saw in those penetrating green eyes. *Charm to spare*, she thought, *and a way of making you feel as if you were the only person in the room*. She wondered why Amy disliked him so.

"Thomas, would you kindly refrain from flirting with my future sister-in-law—at least, not quite so blatantly?" Trevenan's amused tone seemed laced with a faint irritation.

"Slander, James!" Sheridan protested. He gave Aurelia another winning smile. "I assure you, Miss Aurelia, I intend nothing so idle and frivolous as mere flirtation. To be completely frank, I should like to paint you."

"Paint me?" Aurelia echoed, astonished. "Good heavens, why?"

"Why not?" he retorted. "As it happens, I am always looking for new faces to paint. And not just pretty ones, though yours is certainly that," he added hastily. "Interesting ones—the kind that capture and hold the eye, that compel one to look more closely."

"You think *I* have such a face?" Aurelia tried not to sound as incredulous as she felt.

"Without a doubt. Your eyes and mouth are very expressive, and that's what I look for in a model. I've seen Society beauties with perfect features but no animation whatsoever," he went on. "Like wax dolls. And then I've seen ordinary, even plain, women whose faces were so mobile, so alive with every thought and emotion, that I could not look away."

"Oh, my," Aurelia said faintly. "I don't know what to say, Mr. Sheridan."

"Say that you'll consider it?" he persisted. "And perhaps allow me the chance to persuade you over tea?"

"I believe *I'm* supposed to say that," Trevenan interposed with some acerbity. "Ladies, I was just about to ask if you would care for tea, once we were finished here."

"Tea sounds delightful, my lord," Amy replied at once, giving him a brilliant smile. "And *I* am quite ready to take some refreshment now. What about you, Relia?"

"Yes, yes, of course," Aurelia said hurriedly. "Why don't we all go?" she added, not wishing to snub Mr. Sheridan.

"Indeed." Trevenan turned to his friend. "What place do you recommend, Thomas?"

"Well, Fortnum and Mason serves excellent pastries," Sheridan replied. "And it has the advantage of being just across the street…"

❧

"I'll have the chocolate gateau, please," Amy announced, pointing at the luscious-looking slice on the cake trolley. A smiling waitress served her promptly, then turned to Aurelia.

"Um…" She fretted her lower lip as she gazed at the pastries, each one more tempting than the last. "The mille-feuille for me, please," she said at last and just managed not to sigh with delight as the layered confection, bursting with rich pastry cream, was set before her.

"That looks wonderful," Amy said, eying it appreciatively. "I'll trade tastes with you?"

"Of course." Aurelia carefully cut off a morsel of her pastry for her sister and accepted a bite of Amy's gateau in exchange. "Delicious," she declared after swallowing the mouthful.

Amy's response to the mille-feuille was similarly enthusiastic. Trevenan and Mr. Sheridan smiled like indulgent uncles at their pleasure. Between the four of them, they'd consumed an astonishing amount of food, Aurelia reflected: a variety of filled sandwiches, still-warm scones with jam and cream, and now savories and cakes.

She ate another bite of mille-feuille, savoring the feather-light layers of pastry, and gazed out the window at the bustling thoroughfare that was Piccadilly in mid-afternoon.

"More tea, Miss Aurelia?" Mr. Sheridan inquired from his place beside her.

"Yes, thank you." She let him refill her cup from the silver tea service.

"Have you given my proposal any further thought?" he asked.

She took a sip of the hot, fragrant tea. "About your painting me, you mean?"

"Indeed." His eyes glinted. "I'm prepared to bribe you with mille-feuilles, if necessary."

Aurelia surprised herself by laughing. "Too many of these, and I won't be able to fit into my gowns—or your canvas!"

"Then I'll simply take a leaf out of Rubens' book when you pose for me," he retorted. "Believe it or not, his ideal of womanhood is still much admired, especially by men."

Aurelia shook her head, smiling. "You have an answer for everything, Mr. Sheridan."

"He does, indeed," Trevenan said dryly. "I should warn you, Miss Aurelia, Thomas is notoriously single-minded in pursuit of his goals. You might as well say yes now, because he's not about to take no for an answer."

"The curse of having friends who know you too well," Sheridan lamented. "But James is quite right. I intend to be obnoxiously persistent about this."

"Well, obnoxious at any rate," Amy murmured from behind her napkin, just loudly enough for Aurelia to hear.

Aurelia kicked her twin's ankle under the table, though Sheridan gave no sign of having heard. How odd that he wanted to paint her and not Amy, whose features were practically identical and unscarred to boot—not to mention that Amy would probably enjoy sitting for an artist. "Just what exactly did you have in mind, Mr. Sheridan?" she asked, hoping fervently that his ideas did not involve nudity. "A portrait?"

He shook his head emphatically. "Oh, no. While I do paint portraits on commission, I prefer classical or literary subjects when left to my own devices."

"Like your Lady of Shalott?"

"Exactly. Although," he paused, studying her face anew, "I do not think I would choose an Arthurian setting for you. Shakespearean, perhaps—you would make a charming Perdita from *The Winter's Tale*. Or Miranda from *The Tempest*. Are you familiar with either?"

"With both, actually. Believe it or not, Mr. Sheridan, we read Shakespeare's plays in America too," she assured him dryly.

He flashed her a rueful smile. "My apologies, Miss Aurelia. Believe me, I was not casting aspersions on your country so much as decrying the general state of education for young ladies. My own sisters seldom read anything but fashion magazines or Marie Corelli's dreadful books."

"Well, you may rest assured that our governess—Miss Witherspoon—was far too strict to allow that," Aurelia replied, trading an amused glance with her twin. "We read not only Shakespeare, but Milton, Wordsworth, and Tennyson too."

"Impressive. Your Miss Witherspoon seems to have taken her duties seriously."

"She did. In fact, I believe she hoped one of us might even go on to college, Vassar or Smith." And if not for the accident, Aurelia thought she might well have done so. "So, did you have any particular scenes in mind—from the plays, I mean?"

"I was thinking Perdita as a shepherdess, before she discovered she was a lost princess. Or Miranda, pleading with her father to allay the storm. Or even Viola, disguising herself to serve Orsino," Sheridan added, struck by a fresh inspiration. "You would make a fetching Cesario, if you don't consider it improper to pose in breeches—"

"Amy Newbold, is that you?" a young female voice interrupted, cutting off not only Sheridan's remarks but several other conversations. "And Aurelia? I can't believe my eyes!"

Aurelia's eyes met her sister's, the same shock of recognition going through them both in an instant. Then, as one, they slid their gazes toward the voice, the owner of which proved to be a petite brunette, no older than seventeen, with a beaming smile and guileless brown eyes.

Sally Vandermere, Charlie's younger sister, was approaching their table; her mother, Alberta Vandermere, followed at a more dignified pace.

"Look, Mama!" Sally exclaimed, quite unnecessarily. "It's the Newbold twins!"

Amy recovered first, inclining her head with a regality worthy of Queen Victoria. "Why, hello, Sally," she greeted the girl cordially. "What a surprise to see you here in England. Mrs. Vandermere," she added, as the older lady neared.

Mrs. Vandermere, a taller, statelier version of her daughter, nodded in return. "Amelia, Aurelia. You're both looking well."

Her smile did not quite reach her eyes, Aurelia thought, feeling strangely numb. Fortunately, nothing seemed to be required of her at the moment; Amy, with her usual aplomb, was making all the introductions. While clearly impressed to be meeting an earl and an artist, Sally was not too intimidated to chatter away with her usual bright artlessness.

"We just came over three days ago," she announced. "We saw the Tower of London yesterday, and today we've been visiting all the shops. But I told Mama we must have a real English tea in a tearoom." She cast a longing glance at the remains of the gateau on Amy's plate. "Everything looks scrumptious, and I'm simply famished!"

"Sarah, dear," Mrs. Vandermere broke in, using her daughter's full Christian name, "we should find a table and stop intruding on the Newbolds. If you'll excuse us," she added with another nod at the twins.

Aurelia forced herself to respond. "Of course, Mrs. Vandermere, Sally." The words came out easily enough. "Enjoy your tea. The scones are particularly good here."

"Thank you," Mrs. Vandermere returned. "Do give my regards to your mother."

"We'll be sure to do so," Amy promised.

"And we'll be sure to tell Charlie we saw *you*, when we get back to Claridge's," Sally added. "If he's not still out gallivanting around London."

Aurelia froze, feeling a return of her earlier paralysis. As if from a great distance away, she heard Amy ask, "Your brother's in London too?"

"Yes, and so is Papa," Sally said blithely. "Wouldn't it be jolly if we all ran into each other again? We could have such fun together. Well, I must be going now. Good-bye." With a little wave, she hurried after her mother.

"Relia," Amy murmured once the Vandermeres were gone. "Are you all right?"

They were all looking at her now with varying degrees of concern—not unmixed with curiosity in the case of the men. Aurelia reached for her cup, feeling a certain detached gratitude when her hand did not shake, and took a bracing sip of tea. "Quite all right, Amy dear."

Her voice did not shake either. But her thoughts had sped miles away, years away, to a gazebo covered in summer roses. In her mind's eye, she moved among the roses, drinking in their heady perfume and reveling in the sound of a young man's voice as it whispered in her ear.

"Miss Aurelia, you are the sweetest girl…"

Eight

In secret we met—
In silence I grieve,
That thy heart could forget,
That thy spirit deceive.

—Lord Byron, "When We Two Parted"

THEY PARTED COMPANY AFTER TEA, THOMAS HEADING for his studio, James and the Newbolds returning to Grosvenor Square. Aurelia said little on the brief drive, James noted, but Amy watched her all the time with a concern that seemed almost maternal.

Once they were back at the house, Aurelia excused herself at once, pleading fatigue.

"Is it your leg, dearest?" Amy asked solicitously.

Aurelia shook her head. "Not at all. But there was a great deal to take in at the exhibition, wasn't there? So much to see. I think I'd like to go up and rest for a while before dinner."

She did look weary, James observed. Worse, he saw a shadow in her eyes that reminded him of the broken girl she had once been, and the sight pained him more than he dared to admit.

To judge from her expression, Amy saw it too. "Of course," she said. "Do you need me to help you with anything?"

"Good gracious, no!" Aurelia exclaimed. "I can ring for Suzanne, if necessary. Besides, you and Trevenan should have some time alone together as an engaged couple. I'll see you at dinner," she added, cutting off her twin's further offers of assistance and heading for the stairs.

Amy stared after her twin, worrying her lip even after Aurelia disappeared from view.

"Let her go, my dear," James said quietly. He touched his fiancée's arm and nodded toward the sitting room. They could speak privately there.

Reluctantly, she followed him into the sitting room, and he closed the door behind them.

"Now, what exactly is the problem, Amy?" he asked.

"There are *four* problems," she said darkly. "And their names begin with a V."

"You mean the Vandermeres?"

"Who else?" Amy paced the floor, her skirts swirling agitatedly about her ankles. "Oh, bother that stupid Charlie!" she exploded at last. "I should have known he'd ruin everything!"

Charlie? James frowned, thinking back to that meeting in the tearoom. "Miss Vandermere's brother?"

She gave a tight-lipped nod. "I could tolerate the others if I had to, but not *him*."

"Is he, perhaps, a former suitor of yours?" That would explain the acrimony in her voice.

"No, thank heavens!" Amy exclaimed. She seemed about to say more, but paused instead, her face troubled. "It's hard to explain. For one thing, it's not wholly my story to tell."

"My dear, I'd already guessed that there's some sort of connection between your family and the Vandermeres," James assured her. "Is it a close one?"

"Not exactly. At least, not anymore." She bit her lip. "The Vandermeres are a Knickerbocker family, much better placed in New York society than we are—although, to their credit, they were always cordial enough to us. My father often had dealings with Mr. Vandermere, who's a banker, and Andrew—our brother—and Charlie were schoolmates and then went off to Harvard together. We've been summer neighbors at Newport for years.

"The summer Relia and I turned sixteen, our parents had a special party for us. With dancing, even though we weren't officially out yet. But the Vandermeres were invited. Andrew and Charlie had just finished their freshman year..." Her voice trailed off, and she glanced at the floor, her expression suddenly set and stony.

"Aurelia," James realized. "Charlie Vandermere was courting your sister."

Amy nodded. "Relia and Charlie—well, they became sweethearts. Not that there was anything official. They were both too young for that. But...I suppose you could say they had an understanding." She hesitated, then resumed doggedly, "Relia didn't think she should say very much about it to our parents, not until she and Charlie were older and in a position to become formally engaged. But she confided in me, of course. She was in love with him, simply head over heels. And she thought—we both thought—it was the same for him. Except it wasn't."

James suspected he knew what was coming; what surprised him was the surge of anger he felt at the thought of it.

Amy's next words confirmed his suspicions. "He abandoned her, right after the accident, when she needed him most. He broke her heart, and I'll *always* despise him for that."

Her lovely face was implacable, the delicate features set like marble; James did not blame her one bit. Charlie Vandermere sounded like a proper ass.

"Why did he have to come to England? Why couldn't he have stayed in New York?" She brooded over this unwelcome development a moment longer, then turned to

James, urgency in her blue eyes. "Trevenan, do you have any dashing friends who'd be willing to—to pay attention to Relia at balls and dinner parties? Just in case she runs into Charlie here in town, which is all too likely, under the circumstances." Her lips thinned. "It will do him good to see she hasn't been pining away for him all these years."

"I'll do what I can, my dear," James promised, amused and touched. Amy's fierce loyalty to her sister was, beyond a doubt, one of her finest traits. "But I doubt your sister will need much assistance in attracting potential suitors," he added, smiling. "She's already made a conquest in Thomas."

"Oh." Amy's tone conveyed a distinct lack of enthusiasm. "Yes. Mr. Sheridan. Do you really think that associating with him will help Relia, socially?"

"He's a duke's grandson and a noted artist." Not for the first time, James wondered at the hostility his fiancée appeared to harbor toward his closest friend. But now was clearly not the right moment to ask her about that. "And he doubtless knows several gentlemen who would be delighted to make your sister's acquaintance. Indeed, I suspect Thomas knows at least half the aristocracy and is related by either blood or marriage to the other half."

"I suppose that could be helpful," Amy conceded, though she still sounded dubious. "I just can't bear to think of Relia being hurt again."

"I know." James took his intended's hand and gave it a brief squeeze. He found himself equally unwilling to see Aurelia's newfound peace of mind threatened.

"She's come so far. I don't want to see her dragged down, least of all by stupid Charlie."

"I'll do my best to ensure that doesn't happen," he promised.

"Thank you, my lord." She squeezed his hand in turn. "You are so good—to both of us."

"It's no hardship, I assure you." A fugitive corner of his mind offered up the thought that it was all too easy to care what became of Aurelia. Ignoring it as best he could, he suggested, "Now, why don't we take advantage of the opportunity your sister has so generously provided and take a turn about the garden—or what passes for a garden in Grosvenor Square?"

She gave him the smile that had first enchanted him in his aunt's crowded ballroom. "Yes, why don't we?" she agreed, taking his proffered arm.

∝

The heart of the rose was a deep, pure pink, shading outward to paler petals nearly white in hue. The color of a maiden's blush, she'd been told. Wide-eyed, she gazed into the face of the young man who had given her the flower. That suddenly dear face, with its frank blue eyes and ready smile, topped with a thatch of fine, tow-colored hair.

"The sweetest girl," Charlie whispered again, brushing his fingers against her cheek…

The tap on the door recalled her to the present; she knew who it was even before her sister called tentatively, "Relia, are you all right? May I come in?"

Aurelia stifled a sigh. "Yes," she replied, in answer to both questions.

The door opened, and Amy slipped inside. "I'm sorry. I know you'd probably prefer to be alone, but I had to make sure you weren't—" she broke off, flushing guiltily.

"That I wasn't curled up in a corner, crying my eyes out over Charlie Vandermere?"

"*Stupid* Charlie Vandermere," Amy corrected automatically. Aurelia felt her lips quirk in reluctant amusement. "But I'm glad you're all right, because he's not worth a single tear."

"I know." Aurelia made room on the chaise longue, and they sat side by side.

"Why did they have to come over here and spoil everything?" Amy lamented.

No need to ask who "they" were. "Mrs. Vandermere

probably wants Sally to acquire some polish abroad before she makes her debut." She took a breath. "Well, forewarned is forearmed. At least we know the whole family's in London."

"Do you think they'll call on us?"

"I don't know. Mrs. Vandermere didn't seem too happy to see us." Charlie's mother, Aurelia remembered, was a distant connection of the Astors, and while she had never been less than civil to the Newbolds, that civility had never quite warmed into active friendship.

"Too bad for her," Amy retorted. "We were here first." Her eyes sparked. "In fact, as the future Lady Trevenan, I might have a little influence in certain quarters—"

"Oh, don't!" Aurelia interposed at once. "I know it's a temptation, but Sally's the one who'd suffer, and none of *this* is her fault."

"No," Amy conceded, after a moment. "You're right. It *wouldn't* be fair." She sighed. "Drat! What do we do now?"

"I don't think we should do anything at all," Aurelia said after a moment.

"But what if you should run into *him*?" Amy persisted.

Aurelia's insides quavered like a blancmange at the very thought; she forced back the slight queasiness and attempted an insouciant shrug. "Then I'll have to face it out, I suppose. But I doubt he's any more eager to meet than we are."

"Probably not, considering the way he behaved." Amy fretted her lip. "Relia, are you sure this won't overset you? I know how much you cared for him."

Aurelia stared at her hands for a long moment before replying. "When you came in, I was thinking about him," she confessed. "And how it once was between us. How sweet, how dear…but so much has changed since then." She blinked stinging eyes and made herself look up. "I'm not still in love with him. How could I be, when I remember how it ended?"

Amy pulled a face. "Stranger things have happened.

And some girls just can't help caring for fellows who treat them badly."

"Well, I hope I've more pride than that." Unconsciously, Aurelia straightened her back and shoulders. "And more sense than to pine over someone so shallow, cowardly, and weak!"

"That's the harshest thing I've ever heard you say about Charlie," Amy marveled.

Aurelia gave her a wintry smile. "It's time, don't you think, that I was angry at him?"

"Past time," Amy agreed. "Does it feel good?"

"It feels—freeing." Especially after all those years of holding her anger and hurt inside, trying to be patient and accepting of her lot. Well, rebelling against her lot had proved far more satisfying—and produced far better results. "I'm nearly twenty-one," she said aloud. "It's high time to put Charlie Vandermere away, along with other childish things."

"Twenty-one," Amy echoed, eyes widening. "Good heavens, I almost forgot!"

Aurelia raised incredulous brows. "You forgot we're coming of age in two weeks?"

"No, not that. But Father, Trevenan, and I were discussing this just before Father returned to New York. Would you mind, dearest, if Trevenan and I announced our engagement at our birthday ball?"

She'd known it was coming, but the news still evoked a pang of regret for that lost dream she'd cherished this past year. "Not at all," she said gamely. "What better time could there be?"

"That's what we thought too. Trevenan wants everything settled so we can leave for Cornwall as quickly as possible. And I must say," she added, "knowing the Vandermeres are in London makes the prospect sound that much more appealing."

"It does indeed," Aurelia said fervently, getting to her feet. Her forgotten reticule slid from her lap, spilling several objects onto the carpet. "Bother!" She stooped to retrieve them and smiled involuntarily when she saw Mr. Sheridan's card. Although she had not yet agreed to sit for him, he'd insisted on giving her the address of his studio in Half Moon Street. Flattering to know one man in London was interested in her, even if it was only in the artistic sense.

Amy read the card over her shoulder and frowned. "Are you really going to sit for that—peacock?"

"I haven't decided yet," Aurelia replied absently, then frowned in turn at her sister's remark. "Why do you dislike Mr. Sheridan, Amy? I found him charming."

Amy hesitated, then shrugged. "Perhaps *I* find him a bit too charming to be sincere."

"So you think he wasn't serious about wanting to paint me?" Aurelia couldn't quite prevent an anxious note from creeping into her voice.

"Oh, no—that's not what I meant at all!" Amy exclaimed at once. "I'm sure he was serious about that. It's just—" she broke off, biting her lip again. "We don't get along. I never feel comfortable when we meet, even with Trevenan there to break the ice."

"Well, he's Lord Trevenan's friend. Oughtn't you try, at least, to get along with him?"

"I don't think Mr. Sheridan approves of me," Amy confessed. "Or wants me to marry Trevenan. And it doesn't help that he's Lord Glyndon's cousin and obviously thought I wasn't good enough for *him*, either."

"Well, snubbing him or trying to put his back up at every opportunity isn't going to help change his mind about you," Aurelia pointed out. "What is it Mother's always saying about catching more flies with honey than vinegar?"

"What about arsenic?" Amy suggested, then sighed at Aurelia's reproving stare. "Oh, all right. I suppose I could try a little harder, for Trevenan's sake—and yours."

Aurelia put an arm around her twin. "It shouldn't take

much effort, dearest. You have more charm in your little finger than the likes of Lady Louisa has in her entire body. I'm sure if you set your mind to it, you could have Mr. Sheridan eating out of the palm of your hand."

Amy's mouth twitched in a reluctant smile. "Now there's a picture I'd like to see!"

"A subject fit for Waterhouse himself," Aurelia agreed.

Laughing, they turned their discussion to their upcoming birthday celebration.

Nine

Pluck from the memory a rooted sorrow…

—William Shakespeare, *Macbeth*

AURELIA WOKE WITH A START. FOR A MOMENT, SHE lay clutching the bedclothes to her, feeling her heart knocking against her ribs. Then, gradually, she became aware of her surroundings.

She was safe in Grosvenor Square, the grey light of dawn just appearing in her room.

The dream had felt so real, so immediate. The summer sun beating down upon her, the galloping stride of the horse beneath her, and the fence looming up before them. Obedient to her lightest command, Bramble had gathered himself for the familiar jump, soaring high into the air like Pegasus…

And plummeting to earth like Phaeton, hooves thrashing wildly as he screamed in agony. Aurelia had lain where she'd fallen, too winded to speak or even cry out, though one side of her face felt on fire and her left leg was oddly numb. She had fainted when she tried to move.

The days that followed had passed in a haze of pain and laudanum. They'd had to shoot poor Bramble; she remembered crying over that, tears trickling sluggishly down her face and wetting the pad of bandages on her cheek. More than a week had passed before she was allowed any visitors who weren't part of the family. And then Charlie had come...

Aurelia sat up, shaking her head to dispel the memories that had descended like a cloud. She knew now why she'd dreamed of the accident.

Charlie in London. For a moment, she let the feelings engendered by the knowledge wash over her: sorrow, apprehension, and finally, the welcome burn of anger that had set her free of him. Then, laying them all aside, she tossed back the bedclothes and swung her feet to the floor. Time to get on with the day.

Her left leg twinged as she made her way over to the washstand. Sobered, she tested her weight on it and felt insensibly relieved when it held firm. Dr. Strauss had told her there was no reason her leg should not continue to improve as long as she remained active and performed the exercises he had recommended. She would make a point of doing so this morning.

She splashed cold water over her face, banishing the last sticky traces of sleep. Then, as she dried herself, she caught sight of her reflection in the glass. Beneath the strands of wet hair at her brow, she glimpsed the beginning of her scar. Like one studying a map, she traced its course along her hairline and down to her cheek. While it no longer stood out so sharply, it was futile to deny its presence. Or how much her life and she herself had changed as a result of her injuries.

But not where it truly mattered. She must remember that, carry the realization with her like a talisman, or her time abroad meant nothing.

All the same, Claudine's advice had never been put to the test like this. Charlie in London, with his entire family...Despite her words to Amy, she had no idea what she'd say if they happened to meet. After all this time, was she the queen or the little mouse?

"Squeak," Aurelia muttered, glowering at her reflection.

But that would never do; indeed, she would despise herself if she took to creeping into corners again, just to avoid a man best forgotten. *Aurelia Leigh Newbold, where is your pride?* Facing the glass again, she said in her best French, "*Vive la reine.*"

Long live the queen. Foolish as the ritual might seem, she felt oddly heartened by it. Turning away from the glass, she went in search of the tunic and loose trousers she wore to perform her exercises.

✤

"Good morning, Lord Trevenan," James's solicitor, a fair, middle-aged Scot, greeted him with just a hint of surprise. "What can I do for you today?"

"Good morning, Mr. Daviot." James rose from his chair in the anteroom. "I realize this is short notice, but I have questions regarding my cousin's estate that I hoped we might discuss."

"Of course. Miss Carlisle," the solicitor addressed his secretary, a competent-looking young woman of perhaps twenty-five, "I'll be needing the late earl's papers at once."

Abandoning her typewriter, Miss Carlisle retrieved them with her usual efficiency. File now in hand, Daviot beckoned James into the office and closed the door behind them.

James took the seat opposite the solicitor's desk. "I received a visit yesterday from a Captain Philip Mercer," he began. "About some shares Gerald had acquired in his company, Mercer Shipping."

"Ah." Daviot nodded as he sat down at his desk. "Yes, I do remember the name. One of your cousin's last investments, I believe."

"What can you tell me about the company?"

Daviot consulted the file. "Well, to begin with, Mercer Shipping is rather a recent venture, started within the last five years or so. But it's turned quite a profit since its inception."

"What do they deal in?" James inquired.

"Most of their goods appear to come from the Far East—namely, India and China. Antiquities, tea, silks, porcelain..."

All things that would fetch a fine price on the market, James thought, his unease growing. "Had Gerald acquired a controlling interest in the company before his death?"

Daviot glanced over the papers again. "Not quite that," he reported. "But more than a third of the business. Enough to exercise some influence, I should think."

James shifted in his chair. "Undue influence?"

"I could not say, my lord." The solicitor frowned slightly. "If you don't mind my asking, Lord Trevenan, what precisely was the nature of Captain Mercer's visit?"

James hesitated, remembering Mercer's report of the missing shipment, but he was reluctant to mention Gerald's possible involvement at this point. "The captain expressed a strong desire to buy back my cousin's shares. In fact, he made quite a generous starting offer."

He named the captain's price and had the satisfaction of seeing Daviot's brows rise.

"That is indeed generous," the solicitor remarked. "However, given the extent of your cousin's debts, I would advise against parting with those shares, or with your shares in *any* company counted among your present assets, until your marriage to Miss Newbold is finalized and the full settlement is made."

That bad, was it? Well, James had expected to hear as much. If Mercer Shipping was as successful an enterprise as Daviot suggested, the wisest thing to do would be to retain his shares and wait until their value rose before selling off. A sensible decision—and yet something still niggled at him. "Would you happen to know how my cousin became involved in Mercer Shipping in the first place?" he asked. "To my knowledge, Gerald never demonstrated much aptitude or interest in business. Was it on the advice of our banker?"

"Not exactly. That is, your cousin did act on the advice of a banker in purchasing his later shares in Mercer Shipping, but not the one most associated with the Trelawney family. A friend of his supplied him with the name, I think."

James frowned. "His *later* shares?"

"He actually acquired them over a period of several months, my lord, and through somewhat…unorthodox means." Daviot's tone took on the faintest note of censure. "In fact, I believe he won the first shares in a card game…"

Sobered and more perturbed than he cared to admit, James departed Lincoln's Inn Fields. A card game—so Gerald's involvement in Mercer Shipping had been questionable from the start. And according to Mr. Daviot, his cousin had then bought up the shares of another investor barely a month later. That was perhaps less questionable, but why this company and why such haste? And who, if not the family banker, had advised him to do so?

Definitely the matter required more looking into, he thought. But not today, not at present. He had gifts to purchase—chief among them, he recalled with an odd little shock, an engagement ring. Hailing a hansom, he set off for Piccadilly.

Even at this hour, when the fashionable were barely beginning to stir, the thoroughfare was crowded with shoppers. Alighting in front of Hatchards, one of the few establishments in which he felt wholly comfortable, James gazed in trepidation at the scene before him, which seemed to embody everything he enjoyed least about London: noise, bustle, and so many people one could scarcely turn around without colliding with someone.

The bookshop seemed a good enough place to start, he decided. And by virtue of its trade, it stood a fair chance of being quieter than most of the other establishments; there was something soothing, even lulling, about the smells of leather and parchment.

He had taken no more than three strides toward his destination when a young woman stepped out of the shop: a slender, moderately tall young woman, with golden hair and the faint tracery of a scar on one otherwise flawless cheek.

Aurelia.

James stopped in his tracks, watching her. She wore a walking dress in a deep, rich shade between navy and cobalt blue, and a black straw hat trimmed with ostrich plumes that made her hair gleam more brightly by contrast. Her dangling earrings were twists of gold, hung with bits of some blue stone—lapis lazuli, perhaps.

It was not, he thought with an inward smile, the sort of outfit a woman trying to escape notice wore. Indeed, more than a few passersby cast an admiring glance in her direction, though Aurelia paid them no heed, intent as she was on the book in her hand. She looked like a child sorely tempted by a sweet but determined not to succumb until her meat and greens were eaten.

James stepped directly into her path. "Miss Aurelia."

She glanced up from her book, her blue eyes widening. "Lord Trevenan! Good morning. I'm surprised to see you out and about so early."

"I might say the same," he countered. "What brings you here at this hour of the day?"

"I have some shopping to do."

"Alone? Shouldn't you have brought your maid with you?"

"Poor Suzanne's got a cold. The English climate doesn't seem to agree with her. So I thought it would be a kindness to leave her at home. I'm not going anywhere out of the ordinary," she added, a touch defensively. "It's silly having someone follow you around on perfectly mundane errands just because you happen to be female."

James sighed. "It may be silly, but it's for your own

safety," he pointed out. "I'm surprised Amy didn't insist on accompanying you."

"Amy had business of her own to attend to this morning," Aurelia replied. "Besides, the sort of shopping I had in mind is best done without her. I need to buy her a birthday present."

"Good Lord!" he exclaimed, startled by his own forgetfulness. "Of course. And I need to do the same." He paused, realizing that—in the absence of the twins' father and brother—he'd become, in some fashion, the man of the family. In which case, offering Aurelia his escort was the only right thing to do. "Perhaps we might go shopping together," he suggested. "I could use some advice on what your sister might like as a gift."

He could tell from the faint glint in her eyes that she'd seen through his motives, but, to his relief, she raised no objection. "All right. Did you have anything already in mind for her?"

"Well, I'd thought to start at Hatchards. Would *that* be for Amy, by any chance?" He indicated the book she still held, angling his head to read the title. "*Tristram of Lyonesse*?"

Aurelia flushed. "That would be for me, actually. I'm fond of poetry. Amy prefers novels, but I didn't see anything that might appeal to her, at least not today." She tucked the book into her reticule. "You could go in and look around yourself, if you like."

He shook his head. "I trust your judgment here. Let's move on, shall we?"

She glanced at him quizzically. "Where should we go next?"

"I was rather hoping you might have some suggestions," he confessed, feeling like a schoolboy caught not knowing his lessons. "I don't do a great deal of shopping in London. In fact, I tend to avoid it whenever possible. So I'm afraid I have only the most general idea of where to look for things."

"I see." To her credit, Aurelia did not laugh, although her lips quivered suspiciously for a moment. "Well, my father and brother don't care much for shopping either, so you're in good company," she said diplomatically. "I suppose we could try the Burlington Arcade; they have lots of shops to choose from. We should be able to find something for her there."

"An excellent idea," James said, feeling considerable relief—not least because he actually knew where the Burlington Arcade was. He offered his arm, and, after a moment's hesitation, Aurelia laid a gloved hand on the crook of his elbow. To his surprise—and disquiet, he seemed to feel that light pressure all the way down to the bone.

Ignoring the sensation as best he could, James started up the street. As they walked, he shortened his stride to match Aurelia's. But her limp was barely observable now; he suspected only someone aware of her past injuries would notice the slight halt in her step. She had indeed come a long way in the past year.

"So, what were you thinking of getting Amy?" he asked.

"I haven't decided yet. But a twenty-first birthday present ought to be special." She paused, considering. "Maybe a piece of jewelry—a locket or a brooch?"

"Then we'll start by finding a jeweler's. I need to look at engagement rings, in any case."

Aurelia's brows arched. "You haven't purchased the ring yet?"

"Not just yet, no," he admitted. "I haven't got round to asking which stone your sister prefers or what size ring she wears. Would you happen to know the answer to either?"

"Well, as to the first, Amy admires many kinds of gems." She paused again, flushing slightly. "And as to the second, she and I wear the same size gloves—and shoes, for that matter. So, if you need the ring fitted properly, I should be able to help with that."

James hesitated; it felt strange and not quite fair to ask this of her, though he could not have said why if his life depended on it.

Aurelia looked up at him, and he had the uncomfortable sense that she knew exactly what he'd been thinking. "It's all right," she said, quite gently. "You know I'd do anything for Amy."

&

Even last year, when she could hardly bear to go out in Society at all, Aurelia had rather admired the Burlington Arcade. Its orderly, well-tended calm presented such a welcome contrast to the rest of Piccadilly, like an island in the middle of a turbulent sea. One could browse at one's leisure without feeling pressured or rushed along by other shoppers. The harried look on Trevenan's face disappeared once they were safely inside, she observed with some amusement.

Wickes and Taylor, the first jeweler they found, appeared to be doing a brisk business even this early in the day, which augured well for their search. Entering the shop just ahead of Trevenan, Aurelia spied a clerk showing a magnificent diamond necklace to a prosperous-looking gentleman of middle age. At the other end of the jewelry counter, a dark-haired man and a red-haired woman were studying a tray of sapphire rings and carrying on an animated discussion of their merits. The woman's lilting voice would have been pretty if it weren't so imperious, Aurelia noted absently, feeling a little sorry for the man, who seemed the patient sort.

A third clerk now came forward to greet them. "Good morning, sir—and madam," he added, nodding to Aurelia. "How may I assist you today?"

"I am…Trevenan." He sounded as if he were still getting used to calling himself that, Aurelia thought. "And I would like to see some of your engagement rings."

"Certainly. We have a fine selection of them, with a variety of gems and settings." He turned a beaming smile on Aurelia. "Does the young lady have a particular preference?"

"Oh, I'm not—"

"Miss Newbold isn't—"

They spoke at the same time, then broke off, equally embarrassed. The clerk glanced from one to the other in obvious confusion. "This lady is not your fiancée, my lord?"

"Lord Trevenan is marrying my sister," Aurelia explained.

"But Miss Newbold wears the same glove size as my betrothed," Trevenan added. "So, with her assistance, we can ensure a proper fit for the ring."

The clerk recovered at once, but then he'd probably heard stranger explanations. "Of course, my lord," he said smoothly. "What would you and Miss Newbold like to see first?"

Aurelia glanced toward the jewelry counter. The red-haired woman had made her selection at last. She was smiling triumphantly down at her no longer bare ring finger, while her suitor appeared to be settling accounts with the clerk.

"Why don't we start with sapphires?" she suggested. "Since there are some out already."

Once the other couple had exited the shop, the clerk brought over the tray of rings.

"These certainly are beautiful stones," Aurelia said, gazing down at them. Sapphires had always been her favorite gem, reminding her of mountain lakes and summer skies at evening.

Trevenan studied them in his turn. "Indeed. Some of them are the color of the sea in Cornwall on a fine day." He picked out a ring with a square-cut stone surrounded by an intricate frame of gold filigree. "Do you think Amy would like this one?"

Aurelia pursed her lips doubtfully. "It's very impressive, but perhaps a bit too heavy to suit my sister. Maybe something more delicate?"

"You have a point." He returned the ring to the tray. "Gold or silver for the setting?"

The clerk gave a discreet cough. "If you'll pardon me, my lord, I must point out that our engagement rings are set in either white gold, yellow gold, or platinum. And platinum has become increasingly popular in the last few years," he added.

Trevenan glanced at Aurelia. "Which would your sister prefer?"

"That would depend on the stone," she replied. "Rubies always look best set in yellow gold, but emeralds and sapphires can look well in either. Personally, I prefer yellow gold, simply because it seems warmer—and a better contrast to the stone."

"I believe I agree with you." Trevenan turned back to the tray, then, after several seconds' perusal, he picked up another ring. "What about this one?"

"Much better," Aurelia approved. Ravishing, in fact. The round-cut stone was a clear cornflower-blue, smaller than the first sapphire but of remarkable clarity; a circle of tiny, rose-cut diamonds surrounded it like the petals of a flower.

Trevenan held out the ring to her. "Would you mind trying it on?"

After a moment's hesitation, Aurelia tugged off her glove and slipped the ring onto her finger. The slender gold circlet, cold at first, grew warm against her skin; the diamonds twinkled with rainbow sparks and the sapphire shone like the heart of a sunlit sea.

"Excellent taste, my lord," the clerk declared.

"It *is* very beautiful," Aurelia said, watching the light kindle in the stone's blue depths.

"It is."

Some note in Trevenan's voice made her look up. He was watching her with the most unfathomable expression in his dark eyes. She felt her cheeks grow warm and her pulse flutter in response. Annoyed at herself, she dropped her own gaze and tugged off the ring. "Amy might like this one. But perhaps you should look at a few more, just to be sure."

"Perhaps I should," the earl said after a moment. He turned to the clerk. "Would you be so good as to show us some of your diamond engagement rings?"

"Of course, my lord," the clerk agreed. "Very fashionable

they are—diamond rings. Especially nowadays, owing to the mines in South Africa."

White diamonds, colored diamonds, in simple and elaborate settings, alone or in combination with other gemstones…Wickes and Taylor boasted an assortment that Garrard and Company, jewelers to the royal family, would not have disdained. When consulted, Aurelia gave her opinion of the rings Lord Trevenan singled out for closer inspection; when asked, she presented her hand for the proper sizing. She was careful not to reveal her own preferences too plainly. This was to be Amy's ring, chosen by Amy's man, and she'd do well to remember that.

Trevenan finally selected a half-hoop ring: a trio of diamonds set in a carved band of yellow gold. Though the stones weren't particularly large, they were of fine quality, flashing white fire with every movement of the hand. It was splendid without crossing the line into vulgar, and Aurelia thought it would suit her sister admirably.

Afterwards, she asked to see some brooches, choosing one in the shape of a ribbon bow, fashioned of yellow gold and set with tiny winking brilliants. It would provide a glittering accent to anything Amy wore, from shirtwaists to ball gowns. The price made a sizable dent in the money she'd brought with her, but surely a coming of age was ample excuse for extravagance.

Their business concluded, they left the jeweler and engaged in some desultory window-shopping among the Arcade's other establishments. Trevenan found Amy's birthday present in a small shop specializing in articles of women's finery: a silk fan painted with a design of flowers and butterflies in delicate pastel shades, perfect for whatever Amy chose to wear for the ball.

"Thank God that's settled," he remarked as they left the shop.

"Yes, and you even managed to survive it," Aurelia said lightly. As had she, come to that.

"Just barely, I'll have you know," he retorted, then gave her a reluctant smile. "Thank you for your assistance—and for remembering the Arcade. I suspect I'd have found this experience much more trying elsewhere. Now, have you any more shopping left to do?"

Aurelia shook her head. "Nothing that can't wait. What about you?"

"That depends. What would you like for your birthday?"

Taken by surprise, she protested, "Lord Trevenan, it's not necessary to—"

"Yes, it is," he contradicted her gently but inexorably. "You're coming of age too. It's only right that you should receive a gift."

Aurelia flushed; he did have a point, and she was making far too much out of the matter. Quickly, she sifted through her memory for unexceptionable gifts. "All right. I should like some new sheet music. I hadn't realized how limited our selection was until I took up the piano again."

"More Chopin?" he asked, smiling.

"I was thinking of some popular tunes. Maybe some of the songs from *The Gondoliers*?"

"I'll bear that in mind," Trevenan replied. He consulted his watch. "It's well past noon. Would you care for some refreshment? We can go back to Fortnum and Mason, if you like."

Aurelia hesitated, remembering yesterday's unfortunate encounter. "Refreshment would be welcome, thank you. But perhaps someplace else this time."

"Of course. Shall we try Gunter's instead? Unless you think it's too cold for ices."

"Unless we're in the middle of a snowstorm, I can always eat an ice!" she assured him.

He laughed outright. "A woman after my own heart! Then let's go and find a hackney."

❧

Situated in Berkeley Square, Gunter's Tea Shop displayed a sign marked with a pineapple—an emblem of hospitality, Trevenan informed a fascinated Aurelia. Entering, they found a table in a quiet corner of the tearoom—not yet filled with patrons—and seated themselves. A smiling waiter hurried up at once to greet them and offer suggestions on what to order. Bemused by his attentiveness, Aurelia agreed to try the Neapolitan, one of Gunter's specialties.

"Good heavens!" she exclaimed when the confection was set before her: three luscious-looking layers of pink, green, and white ice cream, topped with red rosettes made from currant water ice. "I've heard the saying 'too pretty to eat,' but I've never believed it, until now."

Trevenan grinned at her over his own dish of strawberry ice. "Well, I think you'd better try to eat it, because it won't be nearly as pretty when it melts."

"True." Aurelia picked up her spoon. The first taste, a mingling of strawberry, vanilla, and pistachio, astonished her. "Oh, my. We have ice creams in America too, but not like this!"

"Gunter's ices are something special," Trevenan agreed. "I still remember my first one. I must have been all of seven years old at the time, visiting London with my parents."

He'd been orphaned young, Aurelia remembered; a sailing accident in Italy, Amy had told her. "Did they often come to the city—your parents?"

"Only on business or for a brief holiday. They were Cornish to the bone, and happiest at home. As I am," he added. "In fact, I never feel quite myself when I'm anywhere else."

"You must be counting the days until you can return," Aurelia remarked.

"I am, indeed. I only hope your sister takes to Cornwall—and the rest of you, of course."

"Oh, Amy enjoys the seaside very much," Aurelia assured him. "She loves going to Newport in the summer. Is Cornwall very like Newport?"

The door swung open, cutting off his reply and admitting a burst of laughter and chatter.

"Well, girls, let's have ourselves a real English tea!" a boisterous female voice declared.

The words and the speaker's familiar, flattened vowels rang in Aurelia's ears, seemed to stop the blood in her veins. Not again. Fate could not be so unkind. Steeling herself, she glanced casually toward the door—and almost sagged with relief. American girls, without a doubt—chaperoned by an older grey-haired lady—but not a Vandermere among them.

Silently thanking providence, she turned back to Trevenan. "You were saying, my lord?"

His expression told her he was not deceived; his words confirmed it. "Are you all right?"

Aurelia tried to smile. "Of course. Why wouldn't I be?" She popped another spoonful of her Neapolitan into her mouth to avoid answering; fortunately, the chattering group of Americans had moved to a table on the other side of the room.

Trevenan sighed. "There's no need to pretend, my dear. I know what's troubling you—your sister's already informed me."

Aurelia swallowed, feeling a sudden chill in the pit of her stomach that had nothing to do with the ice cream. "Amy told you—about Charlie and me?"

"Yes. I hope you will not be too upset with her. I asked her just what the relationship was between your family and the Vandermeres." He paused, then resumed gently, "I'm so sorry you were hurt by someone you cared for so deeply."

Aurelia exhaled slowly. The memory his words evoked was painful, but it was the dull pain of an old wound, not the raw agony of a new one. "I did care for him," she admitted. "Very much. There was a time I thought I'd never get past the caring—or what came after."

Trevenan's face darkened. "The way he abandoned you, you mean?"

"It's a little more complicated than that." She fiddled with her spoon. "It's not that I'm absolving Charlie from all blame. I blame him for plenty, believe me! But what happened was partly my responsibility. If he abandoned me…well, I made it easy for him to do so."

He frowned. "No honorable man would abandon the woman he loved if she was injured!"

"Perhaps not. But would an honorable woman—facing disability and disfigurement—insist that he stay?" Aurelia countered. She took a breath to quell her agitation before going on, the words spilling from her in a barely controlled torrent.

"When Charlie came to visit afterwards, he could barely look at me. I could tell what my accident was doing to him, how frightened he was at the thought of being tied to a cripple for life. And I knew what his family expected of him. He was supposed to make an advantageous marriage to a woman who'd be the perfect Society hostess, beautiful and charming at all times. I couldn't promise any of that anymore, so I offered to set him free. And he accepted." She paused, smiling wryly. "My own fault, I suppose, that I was in any way surprised. He praised me for my selflessness and told me I'd always be as dear to him as a sister. He even said his family would be willing to assist mine with my care, should the need arise—"

"God, what an unmitigated ass!" Trevenan interrupted in tones of deep disgust. "Did anyone in your family happen to overhear this self-serving rubbish?"

His blunt speech was oddly comforting. "No. But the doctor came in, fortunately, and told Charlie to leave because he was clearly distressing the patient. Mind you, he didn't know the half of it, but I couldn't bear to tell anyone in my family what had happened."

"Except Amy."

"Except Amy, and even then, not right away. Of course, she's referred to him as 'Stupid Charlie' ever since."

"She's being entirely too generous." Trevenan paused, his

face still thunderous. "Well, if it's any consolation, I am sure he'd be kicking himself if he could see you now!"

Aurelia felt herself color. "Thank you. That's quite a compliment."

"It's no less than the truth. You've turned your life around since then. You should be proud of that." He looked at her and smiled, the last signs of anger vanishing. "Very proud."

Her heart lifted at his words. He was right; no one could take away or mar the triumph of her recovery—least of all the Vandermeres. "I'll try to remember that from now on."

"Well, you'll have Amy—and myself—to remind you, lest you forget." Leaning back in his chair, he added briskly, "Now, let's finish our ices before they turn into soup!"

Smiling, Aurelia picked up her spoon again.

Ten

A queen in opal or in ruby dress,
A nameless girl in freshest summer greens,
A saint, an angel—every canvas means
The same one meaning, neither more nor less.

—Christina Rossetti, "In an Artist's Studio"

AMY FROWNED DOWN AT THE CARD IN HER HAND, then looked back up at the house before her. No mistake in the address, although she'd envisioned something quite different from this rather handsome terraced townhouse.

Of course, Mr. Sheridan was grandson to a duke, she reminded herself. Not some penniless bohemian toiling in a squalid garret in Soho or Chelsea. He mightn't be exceptionally wealthy, but he could certainly afford to lease a house like this and have his studio on the same premises.

No one knew she was here, which was just as well, as she suspected Aurelia at the very least might have tried to talk her out of it. Originally, she'd planned on taking her maid, but Mariette had shown signs of the same cold that had felled her sister's maid Suzanne. Instead, Amy had donned a hat with a thick veil that concealed her features before venturing out.

Screwing her courage to the sticking place, she marched

up the walk and rapped smartly on the door. A middle-aged woman in a severe black dress answered her knock.

"May I help you, ma'am?" she inquired in a pleasant, well-modulated voice.

"Good morning. I am Miss Newbold, and I've come to see Mr. Sheridan...in a professional capacity," Amy added at once.

"Mr. Sheridan has stepped out for the moment, miss, but he's expected back shortly."

"Perhaps I might wait for him in his studio?" Amy suggested with her most winning smile. "It is a matter of some importance, I assure you."

The housekeeper—as Amy assumed she must be—pursed her lips but finally nodded. "Very well, miss. If you'll follow me?"

Amy obeyed, relieved not to have encountered greater resistance. But then, she reasoned, Mr. Sheridan must receive many visits, whether from potential patrons, collectors, or models.

"In here, miss." The housekeeper showed Amy into a large salon on the ground floor. "I'll tell Mr. Sheridan of your arrival as soon as he comes in," she added, and withdrew.

Left alone, Amy gazed around the studio with interest. Canvases of varying sizes, in different stages of completion, hung from the walls or sat propped upon easels, and the room itself smelled not unpleasantly of turpentine and linseed oil. Too curious to sit down, she folded back her veil and wandered about the studio, examining the paintings one by one.

A few landscapes—certainly not on par with Turner or Constable, but Amy had to admit that they were gracefully rendered, with what appeared to be special attention to the qualities of light and shadow. An autumn scene, rich with images of ripening fruit and turning leaves, seemed bathed in a mellow radiance that evoked a sense of shorter days and cooler temperatures. In another painting, a lighthouse shone blindingly white against the brilliant blue of a summer sky and the shimmering green of a turbulent sea.

Mr. Sheridan was indeed talented, Amy conceded grudgingly but fairly. At sixteen, she'd have given her eyeteeth to paint even half as well; acknowledging her own lack of artistic ability had been a bitter pill to swallow, though she'd come to terms with it, for the most part. Nonetheless, she would have enjoyed finding a serious flaw in at least one of Mr. Sheridan's paintings. But even his portraits were well-executed, far superior to the stiff family likeness her parents had commissioned five years ago, which now hung in the library of their Fifth Avenue home. Reading the placards, she discovered that several members of Sheridan's family had posed for him, though not—to her relief—Lord Glyndon. One portrait in particular drew her eye—that of a brown-haired girl in a green dress sitting on a fallen tree trunk. A book lay open on her lap, but she gazed straight out from the canvas with merry brown eyes and the barest hint of a welcoming smile. She looked like someone who had just caught sight of a dear friend and was about to spring up to greet her—or him, Amy amended. Despite her best efforts, she found herself oddly charmed by the sitter's open, guileless expression.

"The Honorable Elizabeth Martin, Aged 17," the placard read.

"Honorable"—Amy knew that meant the child of a baron at least. A young girl of good birth, painted with obvious affection—perhaps a cousin, or some other connection? Trevenan had mentioned that Mr. Sheridan was related by blood or marriage to several aristocratic families.

Voices reached her from the passage—the housekeeper's, and a deeper, masculine one. Unconsciously, Amy straightened her spine, readying herself for a confrontation from which she was determined to emerge victorious.

The studio door opened, and the man she was coming

to think of as her nemesis stepped over the threshold. "Miss Aurelia," he began. "May I just say I'm delighted that you've—"

He broke off as Amy turned around, affording him a full view of her unveiled face. The momentary change on his own was startling to behold, eyes widening, lips parting in unfeigned astonishment. Then, just as swiftly, it was replaced by an expression of mild inquiry.

"Miss Newbold. This is most unexpected." Sheridan's tone was level, almost uninflected.

"I know." Amy tried to match his nonchalance. "You were expecting my sister."

"Indeed, I was, but how may I assist you?" he asked, coming further into the room.

Amy eyed him warily as he approached. For all her distrust of him, she had to admit he was an attractive man: every inch the aristocrat, in fact, with his lean build and fine-boned elegance. His brown hair was slightly overlong, in her opinion, but it suited his narrow, angular face and set off those vivid green eyes. Uncanny eyes that saw things they'd no business seeing, she thought, wishing she could find a flaw in his person as well as in his paintings.

Remembering her errand, she made herself smile brightly at him. "If I recall correctly, Mr. Sheridan, you mentioned yesterday that you paint portraits on commission. I wish to employ your services in that capacity."

To her annoyance, the smile famous for captivating ballrooms of susceptible men appeared to have no discernible effect on Sheridan, who merely raised his brows. "I am flattered, Miss Newbold, but are you certain I would be the right person for whatever you have in mind?"

Amy flushed; his tone seemed to imply that he expected her to commission a likeness of her dog or something just as foolish. "Indeed, I am," she retorted with another smile, one that felt more like a grimace—or a snarl. "I wish to give

Lord Trevenan a portrait of myself as a wedding present. Whom should I ask but his closest friend, whose work he already admires?"

His eyes widened fractionally; she'd surprised him again, Amy saw with satisfaction, but he made another quick recovery. "I see. So this portrait is actually intended for James."

"After seeing further examples of your work, I believe you to be eminently suited to the task. I found this one, for example, to be utterly charming," she added, gesturing toward the portrait of Elizabeth Martin.

To her astonishment, Sheridan tensed at her words, something unreadable flickering behind his eyes. "Thank you," he said at last, his face and voice equally colorless.

"Such a sweet expression," Amy went on, eyeing him curiously. "And such speaking eyes. Is she a relation of yours, by any chance?"

He shook his head. "Just a friend—a family friend." Glancing away from the wall, he asked abruptly, "What had you in mind for this wedding portrait?"

"You're willing to accept my commission?" Amy tried not to sound too triumphant.

"I am willing to consider it," he returned.

She chose her next words with care. "If you think the amount insufficient, I am prepared to—negotiate terms. As this is to be a gift for my future husband, I wish to spare no expense. Moreover," she added, struck by a sudden inspiration, "if you were to agree to paint me, my sister might be more amenable to letting you paint *her*."

That caught his attention. "Indeed? Has Miss Aurelia said as much to you?"

"Relia has no idea that I'm even here today. But I know my sister, Mr. Sheridan. She's more likely to agree to a venture that includes both of us. As am I, for that matter."

Something that might have been humor warmed those cool green eyes. "I suppose that's only to be expected, given the nature of your bond. Two of my own sisters—while not twins—are quite close in age and similarly inseparable."

"Relia and I have no difficulty separating from each other," Amy corrected him sharply. "I came here on my own, after all. We simply—prefer to do certain things together."

He inclined his head, his expression closed and formal again. "I stand corrected, Miss Newbold. And I should be glad of whatever influence you might bring to bear upon your sister."

Seeing her opening, Amy pressed, "So, you *are* taking the commission, Mr. Sheridan?"

He stared at her for a moment, then said dryly, "It appears I have agreed to, at that. But then, as you say, it's a gift for James. And my friendship with him happens to mean a great deal to me, Miss Newbold—perhaps even as much as your bond with your sister means to you."

Amy just managed not to register her surprise. Perhaps her dislike had blinded her, but she'd always thought Trevenan cared more about Sheridan than the latter cared about him.

"Have you any particular ideas of how you wish to be painted?" Sheridan continued. "A gown you wish to wear, or a place you would like to use as a setting?"

"I—hadn't quite decided yet." Indeed, she'd thought no further than achieving her immediate objective. "Not my wedding dress," she said hastily. "That won't be ready for months. I'll look through my wardrobe for something suitable." She hesitated a moment, then ventured on. "Do all your patrons know beforehand how they wish to appear in their portraits?"

"No, not all. Some have very clear ideas about what they want from the start, while others are perhaps more willing to give me free rein. More often than not, we compromise. They present their idea to me and I…refine it." A ghost of a smile softened the severe line of his mouth. "One lady envisioned herself as Cleopatra reclining on a hideous Egyptian-style divan."

Amy felt her lips quiver treacherously at the image, but she had come to charm Mr. Sheridan, not the other way around. "Well, I assure you, *I* have nothing so grandiose in mind."

"Perhaps not, but I understand your family is both affluent and influential. Do you not wish your portrait to reflect such things about you?"

"My family's wealth notwithstanding, I have no wish to make a vulgar spectacle of myself, Mr. Sheridan," she said, with all the dignity she could muster. "My aim is to present my intended with a portrait he will enjoy looking at. Did you perhaps have a theme in mind?"

"Let me think." He regarded her with thoughtful green eyes; Amy forced herself to remain composed beneath their scrutiny. "Vitality," he mused aloud. "Candor. Classic beauty…classic." He lapsed into silence for several moments. "Come to think of it, that might be just the way to go, " he said at last. "With the Classics. Atalanta, perhaps, or Artemis."

Amy flushed, stung. Hunting references: Mr. Sheridan probably envisioned her roaming through the forests of England, seeking to fell aristocrats with her bow and arrows. "Classics?" she inquired with dangerous sweetness. "As in nymphs and shepherdesses? But how conventional, Mr. Sheridan! Why not something more—daring?"

His brows arched. "Daring, Miss Newbold?"

"Why, yes. Daring, adventurous…even swashbuckling." She gave him another of her brilliant smiles. "Do you know, I quite fancy myself as a buccaneer. Pistol at my hip, cutlass in my hand, my hapless victim bound and squirming at my feet…surely there could be no more appropriate depiction of an American heiress in London. Would you not agree, Mr. Sheridan?"

He stilled, his face growing shuttered and wary. "That seems—rather a harsh assessment of yourself, Miss Newbold."

Amy raised her brows. "Does it, indeed? But I understand that you hold just such a view of my kind. Indeed, I have it on no less an authority than your own words."

His own brows lanced together. "When have you ever heard me say such a thing?"

"Barely a month ago, at your mother's garden party." She noted with wintry satisfaction the realization dawning on his face.

He was staring at her, clearly appalled. "You were there. In the Wilderness Garden."

Amy nodded. "As you have no doubt guessed, I came there hoping to meet Lord Glyndon. I heard—or more accurately, *overheard*—the two of you discussing me. He quoted you as saying that all American girls were pirates." She mustered a brittle laugh. "I suppose it's true that eavesdroppers hear no good of themselves."

Sheridan was silent for a moment. "That was discourteous of me," he said at last. "I ask your pardon, Miss Newbold."

"For saying such a thing, or simply being careless enough to be overheard?"

He met her gaze without a flinch. "Neither is the act of a gentleman. I hope you will accept my apologies, and perhaps we might continue our acquaintance on more—amicable terms now." He paused, then said almost abruptly, "For what it's worth, Glyndon has been pursued as a matrimonial prospect ever since he reached his majority. You would not be the first heiress—or even the first American—to hope for an offer from him. Although," he added, "you might be the first to have tempted him to make one."

Amy regarded him narrowly. "Is that meant as a sop to my pride, Mr. Sheridan?"

"I wasn't aware your pride required one." His tone was dryer than ever.

"Touché," she acknowledged, feeling a reluctant stirring of amusement. Tempting though it was to refuse this irritating man's olive branch, she could not let her animosity blind her to her larger goal. "Well, then. For Trevenan's sake, I am willing to try to set our past differences aside. It would be awkward for him to have his future wife and his friend continually at odds."

"It would. And James deserves better from us both." Sheridan paused again, then continued more formally, "I have two commissions that I must complete first. But I could let you know when I can accommodate you with regard to sittings. Is that acceptable, Miss Newbold?"

"Perfectly acceptable, Mr. Sheridan," Amy assured him. "And in the meantime, I can devote some further thought as to how I wish to appear in my portrait."

"An excellent idea. Although, if you'll forgive the liberty..." again that faint smile warmed his eyes, "I think pirate dress would scarcely do you justice."

Feeling unaccountably flustered, Amy bade him a dignified farewell and took her leave, drawing her veil over her face as she left the house.

Eleven

Unbidden guests
Are often welcomest when they are gone.

—William Shakespeare,
King Henry VI, Part One

"Mr. Augustus will see you, Lord Trevenan."
The butler sounded almost astonished to be making such
an announcement.

James felt rather surprised himself. He'd called twice before,
only to be told that the man he sought—the second son of
Baron Shenstone and one of Gerald's former cronies—was
not at home. Today, however, the butler showed him into
a spacious breakfast parlor, where the Honorable Augustus
Burton was filling his plate from a laden sideboard.

Nearly noon, and Burton was just sitting down to
breakfast; James had never understood how Londoners could
sleep the whole morning away. Glancing at his host's pallid
complexion and bleary eyes, however, he suspected Burton
had likely spent the previous night carousing with his friends
and not got in until quite late. Gerald had been the same,
when he was alive.

Somewhat curtly, Burton invited his guest to partake of

the various dishes on the sideboard. Although James had already breakfasted, he took a slice of toast, poured himself a cup of coffee from the silver urn on the table, and sat down opposite his host.

"So, what brings you to my door, Trevenan?" Burton inquired, looking up from his plate.

"I wished to speak with you on a business matter," James replied. "I understand from my solicitor that my late cousin acquired some shares from you—in Mercer Shipping?"

Burton's face darkened. "What of them?" he asked brusquely, forking up his kedgeree.

Undeterred by his host's lack of graciousness, James continued mildly, "I was hoping you could tell me more about the company itself."

Burton shrugged. "Don't know what you expect to hear from *me*, Trevenan. I had those shares for just a few months—legacy from a distant cousin on my mother's side. Never got the chance to find out more before I lost 'em."

Or simply couldn't be bothered. James suspected that Burton, like Gerald, was generally disinclined to concern himself with the nature of his assets, beyond the fact of whether they made money or not. But he kept that opinion firmly to himself.

Burton stared gloomily down into his cup. "Hadn't intended to, but I'd already bet everything else that night—didn't want to throw in my hand. I was sure my luck would turn if I stayed in. So I put 'em on the table, and Alston won the whole pot on his next trick!" He lapsed into brooding silence.

James waited for him to continue. Fortunately, Burton's sense of grievance was still strong nearly a year after that fateful card game.

"Didn't know those damn shares would return such a profit, or I'd never have parted with them to begin with. Alston wouldn't sell either when I approached him about buying them back," Burton added resentfully. "Even *after* I was back in funds. He decided to purchase more of the bloody things instead. Didn't even have the decency to let me know who the other shareholders were so I could have a chance at them myself."

"How did Gerald find out who the other shareholders were?"

"Paid *my* solicitor a large retainer to look into it, if you can believe the bloody cheek," Burton said, scowling. "He's the one who handled the transfer of shares from me to Alston. Ought to sack him for his disloyalty, but he's been in charge of my family's finances for years."

"Might I trouble you for his name?"

"Dunning. Alfred Dunning. He's got his offices in Lincoln's Inn." Burton paused, peering at James suspiciously. "Might I ask what your particular interest is in this affair, Trevenan?"

James hesitated, but he saw no reason to bring up Mercer and his offer to buy back the shares, not when he had his doubts about the man. "As Gerald's heir, I wish to learn as much as possible about his investments and holdings," he replied. "My solicitor informed me that Mercer Shipping was quite a recent acquisition and his own knowledge of the company is incomplete."

Burton's pouchy eyes brightened. "I don't suppose you'd consider parting with your shares, if I offered you a good price?"

"I'm afraid I'm in no position to entertain an offer at this point, Mr. Burton," James said as pleasantly as he could. He pushed his chair back from the table. "I must be going now. Thank you for your time—and good day."

As he took his leave, it occurred to him that he hadn't heard a word of regret or sorrow from Burton regarding Gerald's death. His cousin's cronies did not appear to greatly mourn his loss. A sobering reflection, given how much time he'd spent with them. But then, James did not know how deeply Gerald himself would have grieved, had one of his companions perished last New Year's Eve. All the same, it seemed a sad thing to leave the world at barely thirty years of age and have no one care one way or the other.

Taking a hansom to Lincoln's Inn, he discovered from Mr. Dunning's secretary that the solicitor had left London to attend to a client in Manchester. Undaunted, James secured an appointment for the day Dunning was expected back; his new title accomplished that at least.

One more stop after that, to the office of an inquiry agent Thomas had recommended for his competence and discretion. Once that business was concluded, James headed home, just in time to dine and dress for the ball to which he was escorting Amy, her mother, and sister.

Stepping into his carriage, he reflected bemusedly that he was coming to lead a double life, investigating shady business dealings by day, attending the most exclusive Society functions by night. What a relief it would be when this business was settled and he could return to Cornwall with his future bride and her family. Comforted by the prospect, he leaned back in his seat and resigned himself to yet another glittering evening.

"More rouge, mademoiselle—or a soupçon more powder?"

"No, thank you, Suzanne. That will be all, I think." Aurelia studied herself in the glass. The curled fringe at her brow and the ringlets at her temples worked their usual magic in drawing the eye away from her scar, the line of which had been softened, though not concealed, by powder. "Never let anyone think you have something to hide, something of which you are ashamed," Claudine had told her when first teaching her how to apply cosmetics. "That will make everyone believe you are something to be unmasked, stripped bare."

Sound advice, Aurelia thought now. She mightn't be proud of her scars, but she'd learned to live with them. It was up to her to convince through her own demeanor that they were the very least part of her appearance. All the same, she was glad that the rest of her toilette passed muster. She wore green tonight, a bright, clear shade, along with earrings and a necklace in the shape of enameled leaves, green and gold. The color became her, gave her added confidence that she knew she needed tonight. Her first ball, her first major public appearance since her return, held by Lady Warrender—a fashionable young matron who'd become friendly with Amy.

"You look wonderful, Relia," Amy declared, coming up behind her.

Aurelia smiled at her twin, bright as a sunbeam in a jonquil-yellow gown. "So do you." Picking up her fan, a delicate creation of painted silk mounted on ivory sticks, she rose from her chair. "Enough primping. Time we were on our way."

Suzanne placed the velvet evening cloak over her mistress's shoulders, and the sisters went downstairs, where their mother and Lord Trevenan awaited them. The carriage conveyed them to a splendid mansion on Park Lane, large enough to have its own grounds and gardens, as well as a ballroom spacious enough to accommodate the cream of Society. Lady Warrender and her husband—an attractive, fair-haired man of perhaps thirty-five—stood at the head of the stairs, greeting their guests with what appeared to be genuine pleasure.

After welcoming Lord Trevenan and Mrs. Newbold, Lady Warrender turned to Amy. "Delighted you could attend, Miss Newbold. And this must be your sister?" The baroness's brown eyes were warm and friendly. "The resemblance is truly remarkable."

Aurelia did not doubt their hostess had seen her scar. But her breeding, along with the kind heart Amy had sworn she possessed, would have precluded any mention of it.

"My twin, Aurelia," Amy confirmed. "She's just returned from abroad."

"So glad to make your acquaintance, Miss Aurelia," Lady Warrender said, smiling at both sisters. "Is this your first ball of the Season?"

"Indeed it is, Lady Warrender," Aurelia replied. "Though I hope it may not be the last."

"So may we all, my dear. I hope that you enjoy every moment of it," she added, before turning to greet the guests who had come up behind them.

Lord Trevenan offered Amy his arm and led the way down the grand staircase into the lavishly bedecked ballroom. As always, they looked wonderful together, their contrasting good looks emphasized by his dark evening clothes and her golden gown. Accompanied by her mother, Aurelia followed in their wake, buoyed by the memory of her reflection in the glass. If no longer her sister's equal in looks, she felt she was no disgrace to her present company.

As was only to be expected, Amy and her betrothed attracted most of the attention, though Aurelia was conscious of a few glances cast in her direction—more curious than hostile, fortunately. But she kept a smile upon her lips, letting her gaze rove about the ballroom, hung with pale peach-colored silk and decorated with massive arrangements of roses at the height of their bloom. Lady Warrender clearly had exquisite taste.

More guests arrived, and the musicians struck up a quadrille, the opening dance of the evening. Scarcely had the first notes sounded when Lady Warrender appeared, accompanied by a tall, broad-shouldered young man with fair hair and an open, attractive face whom she introduced to Aurelia as William Sutcliffe, Viscount Sutcliffe's heir.

Mr. Sutcliffe bowed. "Might I have the pleasure of this dance, Miss Newbold?"

His face and manner were both so pleasant that Aurelia did not hesitate to accept. Conscious of her mother and sister's delight, she let him lead her onto the dance floor. Her left leg did not so much as twinge when she walked, though she supposed the slight halt in her step might be noticeable to someone consciously looking for it. Still, a quadrille was far more sedate than a polka or a galop. And after three years of being a wallflower, she felt a thrill of excitement at once again taking part in the very first dance at the ball.

Smiling at her partner, she took her place opposite him in the set. A new era in her life was about to begin, and she meant to enjoy every moment of it.

❧

"Enjoying yourself, my dear?" James asked, drawing his betrothed into their first waltz.

Amy's blue eyes sparkled. "Oh, yes! Everything's going splendidly. Have you noticed that Relia has danced almost every dance so far?"

"Indeed I have," he assured her. "She's having quite the triumph this evening." With difficulty, he managed not to glance in the direction of a certain green gown swirling in and out of the throng; its wearer was well on her way to becoming the belle of the ball tonight.

"It's just what she deserves," Amy declared stoutly. "Do you know, I don't think she's looked back once since that quadrille with Mr. Sutcliffe. One of your friends, my lord?"

James shook his head. "I'm afraid I can't claim the credit for that association. Sutcliffe is one of Thomas's friends, a viscount's heir and a very good fellow, I've been told."

"Oh!" Amy's brow furrowed slightly. "Did Mr. Sheridan *tell* him to ask my sister to dance? As a favor, perhaps?"

"He might have made the initial suggestion, but he wouldn't have required Sutcliffe to claim more than one dance. As you see he has already done." James nodded toward the couple.

"A quadrille *and* a waltz," Amy mused aloud. "That might prove fruitful ground, mightn't it, Trevenan?"

"It might." James quickly suppressed the odd pang he felt

at the thought. Aurelia was a lovely young woman coming into her own, he reminded himself, or rather, coming *back* into her own. No wonder London society was so eager to make her acquaintance, the young men especially. As Amy had said, she deserved every moment of this triumph.

Amy—his betrothed, who deserved *his* full attention.

Fortunately, she did not appear to notice any neglect on his part. In fact, her attention had strayed to another corner of the room. "Talking of Mr. Sheridan, I did not realize that he and Lady Warrender were on such close terms."

Following the line of her gaze, James observed that Thomas had arrived and was engaged in conversation with their hostess, who was smiling warmly up at him.

A faint, speculative frown creased Amy's brow. "Is she perhaps a patroness of his?"

Surprised at her curiosity, James said, "She might be, but I doubt that's the reason. They've known each other since they were children—their families are neighbors in Devon."

Amy's eyes widened. "Really? I didn't know."

"I told you Thomas has a vast number of connections," James reminded her. "I don't know the Martins well personally, but—"

"Martins?" Amy interrupted him. "Would Lady Warrender's Christian name happen to be Elizabeth, by any chance?"

Elizabeth? James just managed to contain his surprise. How had his fiancée found out about *her*? Surely not from Thomas. "Lady Warrender's Christian name is Eleanor. Elizabeth was her older sister, I believe."

"Was?" Amy echoed, clearly startled.

James hesitated a moment before replying. "She died some years ago."

"Oh!" An expression that seemed equally composed of shock, regret, and remorse flashed across Amy's lovely face. "How very sad."

"Yes." James debated whether to say more, then decided any further details were Thomas's to relate, not his.

Once the waltz had quavered to a close, he bowed to his intended and led her from the floor. Her partner for the Lancers Quadrille would be waiting—and so would his, he realized with an odd little shock. He was engaged to dance it with Aurelia.

⁓

"Thank you, Mr. Sutcliffe," Aurelia said somewhat breathlessly, fanning herself as they left the floor. "That was a delightful waltz."

He smiled down at her. "The pleasure was mine, Miss Newbold. Might I have the honor of partnering you for the supper dance?"

Aurelia consulted her dance card. "I'm afraid that I have already promised it to another," she said with genuine regret.

"Then, the first dance after supper?"

That, fortunately, was unclaimed, and Aurelia penciled in Mr. Sutcliffe's name beside it. He bowed to her one last time, then approached another young lady, one of several seated in this particular corner. She rose with alacrity, and they strolled toward the middle of the dance floor, a number of envious gazes following them.

Not at all surprising that they should, Aurelia thought. Mr. Sutcliffe was both eligible and attractive: fair-haired, blue-eyed, broad-shouldered…as her first love had been. But where Charlie had been a youth, scarcely more than a boy in some ways, Mr. Sutcliffe was unquestionably a man. She realized with a not unwelcome shock that for the first time in memory, she had thought of Charlie without pain.

Plenty of fish in the sea, her mother and her sister had assured her during those years she had mourned Charlie's defection. Now, she found she might just be ready to believe that truism; dancing almost every dance did wonders for one's confidence. She hoped that she was not so naïve as to think that all the gentlemen attending this ball had been struck by the light of her *beaux yeux*. Indeed, she suspected that Amy and perhaps even Trevenan had had a hand in the number of partners who had presented themselves to her before each dance. But more than one young man, like Mr. Sutcliffe, had asked for a second dance after the conclusion of the first, which Aurelia dared to think might actually have something to do with *her*.

Better still, she had yet to glimpse on anyone's face the revulsion she had once dreaded to find. She had seen surprise from her partners, even a touch of pity, when they beheld her scar, but no disgust. None had averted his gaze or angled his head so as to avoid looking at it, or her. Most remarkable of all, the pity had faded once she had demonstrated her own determination to enjoy the evening. Faded and given way to respect, a triumph far sweeter than the most extravagant of compliments.

She glanced down at her card and felt a sudden frisson when she saw the name beside the next dance. But of course Trevenan had committed himself to one dance with her; they were to be brother and sister, after all. And if one secret part of her still experienced a wistful ache at knowing they could not be more to one another, she had that part well under control.

And here they came, Trevenan and her sister. The twins exchanged fond glances—as ever, not needing words to convey how they felt at this moment. But as Amy and Trevenan neared, a feminine murmur grew behind Aurelia, sharpening into disastrous clarity at the exact moment the musicians paused to tune their instruments and a lull descended upon the room.

"—those twins! Beauty and the Beast…"

"Oh, hush!"

From that horrified whisper and the awkward silence that followed, Aurelia knew exactly of whom they had been speaking. Impossible *not* to know. Amy's eyes widened, then blazed, and her cheeks flew two scarlet flags. She, too, had heard.

Aurelia's heart seemed to stutter to a stop, the cold of utter shock stealing through her veins. The first unkindness. The first breath of malice since her return...

And the moment she discovered what she was made of. Whether she was indeed the queen—or merely the little mouse.

She lifted her chin and gave the approaching couple her most dazzling smile. "Ah, there you are, dearest," she greeted her twin, pitching her voice just loudly enough to be heard in that whispering corner. "Did you enjoy the waltz?"

Amy rallied at once. "Indeed, I did. Thank you, my lord," she added to her fiancé.

Trevenan raised Amy's hand to his lips. "The pleasure is mine—to be partnered with *two* such lovely women. Are you ready for our dance, Miss Aurelia? I've been looking forward to it."

"As have I, Lord Trevenan. And as this is to be rather a lengthy dance," she took care to emphasize the word *lengthy*, "perhaps you might tell me more about Cornwall during the set?"

"Delighted to oblige." He proffered his arm and Aurelia took it, stepping out onto the floor without a backward glance at the now-glowering wallflowers. And to think she'd felt rather sorry for them before—clearly a waste of sympathy!

"Brava, Miss Aurelia," Trevenan said softly as he led her to their place in a newly formed set. Amy's partner, a Mr. Ashby, was doing likewise on another part of the floor.

Aurelia attempted Claudine's Gallic shrug, hoping she looked even half as nonchalant. "I'm done with hiding in corners. Or cowering in fear of an unkind word."

"They're envious, you know."

"Because I've managed to find some partners, despite my limp and scar?"

"Because you've made those things irrelevant. Don't undervalue yourself—or the pleasure you've given to your partners tonight."

Startled, she glanced up at him and saw that he was in earnest, his dark eyes intense as he returned her gaze. She felt herself flush and hoped that the heat of the ballroom could account for her change in color. Before she could sink deeper into confusion, the music came to her aid.

Five figures in a Lancers Quadrille. Years ago, as a schoolgirl just learning to dance, that knowledge had filled her with dismay. Now, however, she was relieved to have so many steps on which to focus. She remembered to smile as she danced, and after the successful completion of the second figure, the smile felt more genuine and less forced. She caught Trevenan's eye then, and felt her heart give an odd little jump when he smiled back and half-closed his eye in a wink. *Concentrate*, she reminded herself sternly as the third figure began.

Trevenan acquitted himself well in the quadrille, and during the moments they came together, he even managed to impart a few details about Cornwall—mainly regarding the north coast: its towering cliffs and many echoing caves, the latter carved out by the relentless wash of the sea, so beautiful and turbulent. It did sound magnificent, Aurelia thought, if not much like Newport, and she looked forward to the day when she and Amy would see it for themselves.

The dance now concluded, Trevenan escorted her from the floor, leading her to a different corner of the room this time. She was just about to thank him for his consideration when another unwelcome voice assailed her ears.

"Aurelia! How lovely to see you! I *told* you the Newbolds were still in London, Charlie."

Aurelia stilled, waiting for the sudden humming in her ears to subside. Under her hand, the muscles of Trevenan's arm went hard as iron as the earl also registered the identity of the person addressing her. Surely some cosmic irony must be at work that she should have to face *this* trial tonight as well. But at least she was not facing it alone.

Affixing a bright, inconsequential smile to her face, she turned around—and there they were. Sally attired in a frilly, girlish white gown, and her brother standing stiffly beside her.

He looked older, Aurelia thought, broader in the chest and shoulders, his face more defined and less boyishly soft. But then, it had been three years—nearly four, now.

She regarded them with a serenity she was far from feeling. "Mr. Vandermere. Miss Vandermere. Good evening to you both." To her relief, her voice sounded almost normal.

Charlie's throat worked as he swallowed; he looked nervous, and she could not be sorry for it. "Miss Aurelia. Good evening. And to you, sir?" He glanced uncertainly at Trevenan.

"This is the Earl of Trevenan, Amy's betrothed," Aurelia replied. "My lord, you have already met Miss Vandermere. This is her brother, Charles Vandermere."

"Of course." Trevenan inclined his head with a haughty air not at all like his usual demeanor. "Sir. Miss Vandermere." His tone thawed only fractionally when he addressed Sally, who appeared too awed by his position to be offended by his coolness. "You must excuse us. I am taking Miss Aurelia for some refreshment. Good evening."

Amused in spite of herself, Aurelia let herself be swept off on his arm.

"Well played, my lord," she murmured, once she was certain they were out of earshot. "I've never seen such airs and graces. You sounded positively imperial."

"I've never seen such unruffled calm," he countered. "My dear, are you sure his presence here has not distressed you?"

Aurelia sighed. "I own, I wasn't best pleased to encounter him tonight. But with the Vandermeres in London, I suppose it was only a matter of time before we ran into each other.

I'm just—relieved that I was able to carry off the meeting with some degree of assurance."

"You have carried off *everything* tonight with the assurance of a princess."

Incredibly, she felt her lips quirk in a smile. "Or a queen?"

"A very empress," he told her, smiling back.

"Thank you." Aurelia took a deep breath. "Now I can concentrate on this evening, and the rest of our stay in London, without worrying about whether I'll meet him again or not. Though perhaps we should find and warn Amy that he's here. Otherwise she might commit a breach of etiquette and call him 'Stupid Charlie' to his face!"

"From what I've learned of your sister, she might consider that almost worth the social opprobrium," Trevenan remarked.

Aurelia rolled her eyes. "Well, *I* don't!" she declared, and glanced about for her twin.

❦

At the conclusion of the quadrille, Mr. Ashby led Amy toward a corner occupied mainly by older ladies whose dancing days appeared to be behind them. She felt at once relieved and regretful. A part of her would have enjoyed putting the fear of God into those spiteful cats who'd mocked her twin. But for the sake of propriety, she supposed she was better where she was.

Mr. Ashby bowed and withdrew to claim his partner for the next dance—a galop, Amy noted, on consulting her card. She had no partner listed, but after the intricacies of the Lancers, she was glad enough to sit out this set and catch her breath. Fanning herself, she glanced about the ballroom, then stiffened when she caught sight of Mr. Sheridan, less than twenty feet away, in deep conversation with a stunningly beautiful woman gowned in peacock-blue.

And not just any woman, Amy discovered on further inspection, but Sybilla Crowley—the dashing widow of an elderly but wealthy baronet. She'd emerged from mourning late last summer, opulent as a full-blown rose, with her lush figure, auburn hair, and vivid blue-green eyes. Lady Crowley had also received numerous mentions in *The London Lady* and *Town Talk*, two widely read Society magazines. The most exclusive establishments vied for her patronage, and her photograph was to be found, with that of other professional beauties, in almost every print shop in London. Not since Lillie Langtry had a woman enjoyed such a meteoric rise to prominence, and Amy had been heartily sick of her by the time the Season ended. Lady Crowley had gone to winter on the Riviera, and in her absence, other fashionable wives and widows had succeeded her in the limelight, though she now seemed intent on reclaiming her place there.

And from the admiring look on Mr. Sheridan's face, she was succeeding. Even as Amy watched, Lady Crowley tossed her head back to laugh, then tapped him on the shoulder with her fan, a gesture at once playful and intimate, as if she were accustomed to taking such liberties.

Amy caught her breath as the artist gave Lady Crowley a lazy smile, then took her hand and raised it to his lips. She smiled back with almost feline satisfaction and leaned in a little closer, until their bodies were mere inches apart. Sheridan then tucked Lady Crowley's hand into the crook of his arm, and they strolled away together—not toward the dance floor, but toward the French windows that opened onto the terrace. Moments later, they disappeared from sight.

Face suddenly aflame, Amy looked away. So Mr. Sheridan and Lady Crowley knew each other. But she would eat her best hat if their association was as innocent as the childhood friendship he supposedly shared with Lady Warrender. She racked her brain furiously, trying to recall if gossip had ever linked these two, in the past or the present, and for how long. How had they met? Had Mr. Sheridan painted Lady Crowley's portrait, perhaps, or had she sought him out for some other purpose? He had so many aristocratic connections, after all.

Not that it mattered, Amy told herself. She was aware of the rumors surrounding Mr. Sheridan; for all she knew, he could have had affairs with half the women in attendance tonight. What possible difference could it make to her? But the knowledge brought a sharp, unpleasant stab of... disappointment? Really, after all his remarks about preferring the unusual to the obvious in regards to beauty, she'd have expected him to have better taste! And to think she'd been feeling almost kindly toward him, after hearing about Elizabeth Martin's untimely death. That had to have affected him, given the closeness of their families.

Amy shook her head, trying to recapture that more charitable mood. She'd resolved to get on with Sheridan better for James's sake, and for the sake of the portrait. And, after all, it was his own business with whom he chose to flirt. Turning her attention back to the dancers, she saw her sister and Trevenan approaching, moving a little more quickly than was usual in a ballroom.

Something was definitely off, Amy sensed at once. Concerned, she went to meet them, skirting the perimeter of the dance floor. "Relia, is everything all right?" she asked in a low voice when they were face to face.

"Fine." Aurelia hesitated and exchanged a quick glance with Trevenan. "But we thought you should know—Sally Vandermere is here tonight, with Charlie. There's no need to worry, dearest," she added hastily at Amy's involuntary hiss of fury. "I've already seen and spoken to them—and I can assure you, the sky did not fall."

"Your sister kept her composure admirably," Trevenan said with obvious approval. "I venture to say, it was Mr. Vandermere who appeared uncomfortable."

"Well, that's something, I suppose." Amy tightened her hold on her fan and her fraying temper, and mustered a tight smile that felt more like a grimace. "The Vandermeres—here, tonight. Why, this evening just gets better by the minute!"

"It hasn't been all bad," Aurelia reminded her. "In fact, I'd say most of it has been very pleasant. Besides, it will be over soon."

Their eyes met in perfect understanding. A lady did not make a scene or lose her temper in public, their mother had instructed them years ago. In private, however, she might vent or rage as much as she needed. Not even Laura Newbold expected complete restraint under the most trying circumstances—and tonight had provided plenty of those!

Amy expelled a pent-up breath. "Yes, it will be over soon," she conceded, and turned to accept Trevenan's arm for the next dance.

Twelve

And when we meet at any time again,
Be it not seen in either of our brows
That we one jot of former love retain.

—Michael Drayton, "Sonnet LXI"

CORA FITZGERALD, MAJOR FREDERICK RAWLINGS—
two more names that Alfred Dunning had been reluctant to
divulge. But divulge them he had, ultimately, once James
had made it clear that he wasn't leaving the solicitor's office
until he knew from whom Gerald had obtained his remaining
shares in Mercer Shipping.

There was little mystery about either the major or the
widowed Mrs. Fitzgerald, as it turned out: both had needed
ready money and had parted willingly with their shares once
informed of Gerald's generous offer. *Too generous*, James had
thought on hearing the amount his cousin had paid. Gerald
must have wanted those shares very badly to offer such a
sum, especially given his spendthrift life in London and his
aspirations to the Prince's set. But why?

He was still pondering the question when he returned
to Belgravia to find the post had arrived and his correspondence awaited him in the library. Sorting through the

usual selection of bills—most of those for the repairs on Pentreath—James paused when he recognized the return address of the inquiry agent he'd hired to look into the business history of Mercer Shipping.

Breaking the seal on the envelope, he extracted the contents, which included a detailed list of the various holdings of Mercer Shipping. For a relatively young company, it nonetheless had cast a wide net, leasing warehouses in numerous ports of significance, including London, Bristol, Liverpool…and Falmouth.

James told himself he should not have been surprised. As a Cornishman, he knew exactly how important Falmouth was as a shipping center, and the railways, built within the last thirty years, had only increased the town's importance. Goods newly unloaded from ships could be dispatched from ports to inland towns with astonishing speed…unless those goods mysteriously disappeared without a trace.

James dropped the letter onto his desk. Feeling strangely cold, he paced to the window, stared out at the square without seeing it. He had not asked Mercer from which warehouse that missing shipment had vanished; he suspected he already knew now, and the knowledge only increased the unease he felt about Gerald's venture into the shipping business. And raised even more questions that could not readily be answered.

Perhaps those answers lay in Cornwall, where his cousin had died. And where he himself was soon to travel with his future bride and her family. He only hoped he would be able to keep those two matters separated. Not for the world would he endanger her or those she held dear—who had become dear to *him* as well.

Putting those troubling thoughts aside for the moment, he turned resolutely from the window. This evening he was expected at 17 Grosvenor Square, to dine with his in-laws-to-be. Mr. Newbold and his son Andrew had arrived from New York just three days before.

❧

Dinner, served on the hour, was typically excellent—the Newbolds had engaged a French chef for the Season—and the service irreproachable. The atmosphere, however, was less formal than at most English dinner tables and the conversation ranged freely over a wide variety of topics, most of them related to New York. While James had little to contribute to the discussion personally, he enjoyed watching the way his future in-laws interacted. They were clearly an affectionate family who took sincere pleasure in each other's company. James got on well with Adam Newbold, his prospective father-in-law, and Andrew Newbold seemed an estimable enough young man with a frank, open face and the same fair coloring as his sisters.

Amy had told James that her parents were distant cousins and a fond rather than a passionate pair. But—she added hastily—they had formed a successful partnership in which her father managed the family business while her mother presided over the family home. James did not doubt it: Mr. and Mrs. Newbold shared an easy, comfortable rapport. If they did not complete each other's thoughts and sentences as some long-married couples were wont to do, they seemed to hold similar views on most subjects, and their pride in their children was unmistakable.

James wondered to what extent her parents' union had shaped Amy's practical views on marriage. He glanced at Aurelia, who looked exceptionally well tonight, her face bright with animation and her fair complexion warmed by a shell-pink gown. Did she hold the same views as her twin, or had she come to adopt them after her painful disillusionment? By her own admission, she had loved that ass Vandermere dearly…

"Do you ride, Trevenan?" Mr. Newbold's voice roused him from his musings.

"I do, sir," James replied. "Though seldom in London.

I come to town so infrequently that it makes little sense to board my horses here. But I keep a good stable at Pentreath. You and your family are welcome to make use of any horses during your stay."

"Excellent," Mr. Newbold said, smiling. "I used to ride every morning when I was a boy in the country. Nowadays, I fit it in when I can, which isn't often."

Andrew looked up from his plate. "Talking of horses, Father, I met Charlie Vandermere riding in Hyde Park today. I mentioned that we were celebrating the twins' birthdays in style."

"Oh, Andrew, you didn't!" Amy exclaimed reproachfully.

James glanced involuntarily at Aurelia and saw that she was gazing fixedly at her plate. He could not decipher her expression, but even by gaslight, she looked pale and tense.

"Why not?" Andrew cast a perplexed glance around the table. "It's not a secret, is it?"

After a pause, Mrs. Newbold said, "The Vandermeres aren't on the guest list, Andrew."

"They're not?" Andrew stared at her. "But Charlie's one of my closest friends, and the Vandermeres have been our summer neighbors for years. Why wouldn't they be invited?"

Again the silence threatened. Beside him, James sensed Amy mustering up the nerve to speak, but her father's next words stopped her short.

"My dear, you might do well to reconsider and send them an invitation as soon as possible," Mr. Newbold addressed his wife. "I still have to do business with Vandermere in New York. It could get very awkward if he thinks we're slighting his wife and daughter in any way."

Mrs. Newbold flushed, perhaps remembering the times Mrs. Vandermere had slighted *her* family. "Very well. I will think further on the matter," she said with obvious reluctance.

If Mr. Newbold noticed the stiffness in her tone, he chose to ignore it. "Thank you, my dear." He turned to James again. "Do you sail as well, Trevenan? From what I've heard, Cornwall sounds like a capital place for yachting."

❧

Leaving the gentlemen to their port, the Newbold women made their way to their drawing room. Once the doors closed behind them, Amy erupted into furious speech.

"Oh, Mama, how can Papa and Andrew ask such a thing of us?"

"Hush, Amy," Mrs. Newbold remonstrated, though her own expression was no happier. "I am sure your father has his reasons." She glanced at Aurelia. "All the same, if having to invite the Vandermeres should cause you distress, dearest, I can explain to him and Andrew—"

"No, Mama!" Aurelia broke in. "Please, I should prefer not to make more of this than there is. Nor do I wish to cause trouble for Papa or even for Andrew. He and Charlie have been friends for many years, for much longer than Charlie and I were sweethearts."

"Hah," Amy said darkly. "I wonder just how long that friendship would survive if Andrew knew how Charlie had treated you."

Aurelia fixed her twin with a stern stare. "Pray do not even consider putting that to the test! It wouldn't be fair, especially since my association with Charlie is at an end." She took a deep breath, willing herself to calm. "Of course, I don't desire a second meeting with him. But if we send an invitation, we at least control the circumstances of that meeting."

Her mother gave her a searching look. "Are you sure about this, my dear?"

"I think so." Aurelia did her best to smile reassuringly. "Send the invitation, Mother. Perhaps they will be already engaged for that evening, or simply decline to attend."

"Either one would suit *me*," Amy grumbled. "But our ball is shaping up to become one of the Season's grandest events, especially since Aunt Caroline's letting us hold it at Renbourne House. Sally will almost certainly want to attend, and she'll probably talk the rest of them into obliging her. Drat them all! Are we never to be free of them?"

"That's enough, Amelia!" Mrs. Newbold scolded. "Your sister's arguments make excellent sense. Besides, we will have quite enough on our hands that evening, since we'll be announcing your engagement as well. I daresay we needn't concern ourselves with the Vandermeres any more than with our other guests." She paused, listening for a moment. "The gentlemen are about to join us, so let us find more agreeable topics to discuss."

❧

Entering the drawing room on Mr. Newbold's heels, James found his gaze going at once to the twins, who were sitting side by side on the sofa. Only a faint shadow seemed to hover about them now. Amy, he observed, looked slightly less mutinous than she had on leaving the dining room. Not that he blamed her; it was damnable that her own father wanted to invite to their ball the family who'd caused her sister such distress.

He glanced at Aurelia, who seemed to have regained her color and her composure, smiling warmly at her father and brother as they approached. Not for the first time, he admired her mettle. She might be considered the quieter and less daring of the twins, but she lacked neither courage nor spirit. She'd faced down her former sweetheart once before; James did not doubt she could do it again, should circumstances require it.

Mr. Newbold sat down beside his wife, but it was to his daughter that he spoke next. "Aurelia, my dear girl, would you favor us with some music?"

"Certainly, Papa. Is there anything in particular you wish me to play?"

He smiled fondly at her. "I find myself homesick for some of my old favorites, if you happen to have the music handy."

Aurelia laughed, and the hovering shadows retreated to the far corners of the room. "After all this time, Papa, I think I can manage those without the sheet music." She rose to her feet. "Which would you like to hear first?"

"Why not the one you were named for?" he suggested.

She pulled a slight face, half-comical, half-serious. "Are you sure you don't want something a bit livelier to start?"

Mr. Newbold shook his head. "Call me a sentimental old fool, my dear, but I found myself thinking of this one often while you and your mother were away. Humor me."

Capitulating with good grace, she went over to the piano.

"Your sister was named for a song?" James murmured to Amy.

"In a way. I was named Amelia for my maternal grandmother, and Mama wanted another name starting with 'A' for my sister. So Father suggested his favorite song. You'll understand when you hear it."

"Will you join me, dearest?" Aurelia called from the piano bench.

At James's nod, Amy went to stand beside the instrument. Aurelia played a rippling chord, and their voices—clear, sweet sopranos—rose together in effortless song:

"As the blackbird in the spring,
'Neath the willow tree,
Sat and piped, I heard him sing,
Singing Aura Lea.
Aura Lea, Aura Lea,
Maid of golden hair;
Sunshine came along with thee,
And swallows in the air."

Not too difficult to see how her parents had derived "Aurelia" from that, James mused. But the name—"golden"—suited her, and so did the words of this song, sentimental though they were. Not that James minded. His own mother had loved and often sung the sentimental folk songs she had grown up hearing in Cornwall.

The twins sang on, bringing the brightness of spring into the room with every note. Mr. and Mrs. Newbold, their earlier friction forgotten, listened with obvious pleasure to their daughters' performance while Andrew looked on tolerantly. And James, watching the two slender, shining figures at the piano, thought he had never seen or heard anything lovelier.

"Music hath charms to soothe the savage breast." So Miss Witherspoon had told the twins in the schoolroom, and while Aurelia would not describe her breast as "savage," she had to admit it felt distinctly unquiet. But after playing and singing her way through several of her family's favorite songs, she felt calmer—mistress of herself again. Not wanting Lord Trevenan to feel excluded, Aurelia went on to some Gilbert and Sullivan tunes, including a few from *The Pirates of Penzance*. Fortunately, most of her family knew those as well and sang along heartily, gathering at the piano as they'd sometimes done in the evenings at home in New York.

The room was still ringing with the last strains of "With Catlike Tread Upon Our Prey We Steal" when the servants brought in the coffee and tea service. Amy laughingly declared herself parched and in need of refreshment after her musical efforts. The group around the piano began to disperse, though Lord Trevenan lingered as Aurelia began to put her music away.

"Well played, Miss Aurelia," he said, his voice pitched for her ears alone.

"Thank you." She managed a smile. "I'm happy to have regained some of my old skill."

"I was not referring to your performance at the piano,

delightful though it was." He studied her with those penetrating dark eyes. "The Vandermeres are to be invited, are they not?"

"They are," she admitted. "And with my consent. But even if they attend, they will be but a few among many guests. I refuse to let their presence spoil the evening for me or Amy."

"Oh, bravely done," he said softly. "But then I expected no less from you."

As always, his approval sent a rush of warmth through her. "Oh, Amy's the brave one," she demurred, keeping her tone light. "But I am not so poor-spirited as to let the Vandermeres overset me on what is supposed to be a happy occasion."

"Trevenan, Relia!" Amy called brightly to them. "Do you not mean to join us?"

"In a moment, dearest," Aurelia replied. She motioned to the earl to join the party now gathered on the other side of the room, where Mrs. Newbold presided over the coffee service. He hesitated for a bare moment, then gave her a slight bow and complied.

Aurelia stowed her sheet music in the bookcase, resolutely not looking as Trevenan made his way toward Amy. The pang of yearning that shot through her at the thought of their betrothal, so soon to be formalized, shocked her with its intensity. Furious at her own weakness, she forced back that yearning, along with the jealousy that could so easily poison her best intentions. What good could come of caring more for James Trelawney than a sister should? And what of *her* sister? The very idea of hurting Amy...

Who could have imagined, Aurelia wondered bleakly, that she'd someday have to face a sterner test than meeting Charlie Vandermere again? But this was a test she was determined to pass with flying colors. Summoning her most brilliant smile, she went to join her family.

Thirteen

When you do dance, I wish you
A wave o' th' sea, that you might ever do
Nothing but that; move still, still so,
And own no other function.

— William Shakespeare, *The Winter's Tale*

Long-expected one and twenty...

WHICH, AURELIA HAD TO ADMIT, DID NOT FEEL MUCH different from twenty all by itself. But tonight supposedly marked a new chapter in her life—and Amy's—in more ways than one.

She took a deep breath and met the knowing gaze of her image in the cheval glass. All her secrets, all her worries seemed reflected back at her. She only hoped they were not as visible to the rest of the world.

At least she had the consolation of knowing she looked her best tonight in a new ball gown made just for the occasion. *Ciel*-blue silk-satin beneath a draped overskirt of silver net, the close-fitting bodice trimmed with crystal beads that shimmered with each breath, each change of light. Monsieur Worth had outdone himself. While she had worn many of his creations with pride this Season, this one seemed by far the loveliest.

Suzanne had done her best to bring the rest of her mistress up to snuff, applying cosmetics with a light but expert hand, brushing her hair until it gleamed like a river of molten gold, then coiling and pinning it up most elegantly with pearl-studded combs. Aurelia's ringlets—freshly curled—still dangled to her shoulders, providing the same indispensable camouflage as the teardrop pearls in her ears.

Amy's face appeared behind her in the glass. "You look absolutely angelic in blue."

Aurelia smiled at her twin. "Thank you, dearest. You look utterly exquisite yourself."

As one, they studied their paired reflections. The only thing they had in common were the pearl necklaces clasped about their throats—birthday gifts from their father. Not since their days in the schoolroom had they dressed alike. Their mother had insisted upon it, declaring that her daughters were individuals, not copies of one another. Bewildered at first, the twins had come to appreciate this wisdom more and more over the years.

Even without Aurelia's distinguishing scar, there could be no question as to who was who tonight. Amy's gown—another Worth creation—was as white as the wedding gown she would soon commission, trimmed with the palest pink silk gauze, like the most delicate and maidenly of blushes. Silk rosebuds of the exact same shade were woven into her coiffure; her gloves and slippers matched as well, and she carried the painted silk fan that was Lord Trevenan's birthday gift to her. Even to Aurelia's partial eyes, her twin glowed as though lit from within. Excitement, merely—or something more? Something to do with Trevenan, who would be announced as her future husband tonight? What if Amy was in love at last?

Aurelia dropped her gaze, trying to conceal a flash of pain

even as she reminded herself fiercely that Amy deserved to love and be loved by someone as wonderful as Trevenan.

"I've brought our flowers up!" Amy announced, happily oblivious to her twin's inner turmoil. "Roses, of course—white for you, pink for me."

She turned away and picked up the two boxes that held their posies. Except for the color, these were identical: delicate arrangements of rosebuds, just large enough to grace their corsages.

After some judicious consideration, Suzanne pinned Aurelia's posy to the left shoulder of her bodice. Amy immediately secured hers to her right shoulder, and after a last glance in the glass to make sure all was in order, the twins linked arms and left the room together, descending the long, curving staircase to the drawing room where they would soon be receiving their guests.

Aurelia felt her composure waver momentarily at the prospect—because three of the Vandermeres would be attending, including Charlie. She pressed her lips together, refusing to think about it further. According to her mother and Aunt Caroline, Renbourne House would be bursting at the seams tonight. If Aurelia were lucky, she mightn't even have to converse with the Vandermeres, except in the most superficial terms.

And she wasn't the only one who might have to see some not entirely welcome faces tonight. The Harfords—whom Lady Renbourne had deemed too important to slight—had sent back an acceptance as well. No doubt they would breathe a sigh of relief to see Amy engaged to Trevenan and thus no longer a threat to their heir's engagement to Lady Louisa Savernake. Amy, however, wasn't shaking in her shoes at the thought of meeting *her* former suitor, Aurelia reminded herself. High time she took a page from her twin's book and conducted herself more bravely and with greater aplomb. Why else, after all, had she gone away in the first place?

Amy turned her head and smiled at her. "Ready, Relia dear?"

Aurelia returned the smile. "As I'll ever be."

Heads high, side by side, they swept into the drawing room. The delighted smiles of their family upon their entrance assured them that they looked their very best. Cheered, Aurelia made her way to her mother's side, as did Amy, to welcome their first guests.

His betrothed's coming-of-age ball and the occasion of their official engagement—James only wished those circumstances could have made him more comfortable this evening. Unfortunately, he found the crowds as oppressive and the noise as deafening as ever. According to Thomas, nearly everyone who was anyone had come here tonight. The twins must surely be the reason. American or not, new money or not, Amy had won over much of Society with her beauty and vivacity. Aurelia too had attracted a coterie of admirers since her return to London.

They were both in their best looks tonight: Amy warm and glowing in pink, Aurelia cool and ethereal in blue. They flitted through the ballroom like brightly hued butterflies, in a near-perpetual blur of color and motion, and the captivated gazes of young men, the envious glances of young women seemed to follow wherever they alighted next.

He'd danced the first quadrille with Amy when the ball officially began, then yielded her to a succession of other partners for most of the next hour. Even now, she was romping through a polka with a young man who appeared to possess more enthusiasm than skill. But she had promised the next dance on the programme—a waltz—to him.

For his part, James had done what was required of him— from partnering other ladies to accepting the good wishes of the fashionable strangers surrounding him. Although the betrothal announcement would not be formally made until just before the supper break, word seemed to have got out that he and Amy were soon to marry. James thought he detected a certain wistfulness from several of the young men offering their congratulations. Odd to think that a year ago he had been among them, watching the exquisite Miss Newbold waltzing with a peer of the realm and believing her far beyond his reach. One year—and so many changes...

The strains of the polka faded away. James glanced back toward the dancers to see Amy's partner escorting her from the floor and back toward the corner where the chaperons sat. From his contrite expression and agitated gestures, he seemed to be trying to apologize to her, an interpretation borne out by Amy's response. She was smiling, but there was a hint of strain about her eyes and mouth that suggested irritation or impatience barely held in check. Frowning, James hurried toward her, even as her now red-faced partner withdrew.

"Is everything well, my dear?" James asked on reaching his intended's side.

"Quite well. Only—" Amy lifted her skirts just enough to reveal the lace dangling from a satin flounce. "Mr. Elliot stepped on my hem during the polka. I need to have it repaired before I damage it further or trip myself up." She gave him an apologetic little smile. "I am so sorry, Trevenan, but I'll have to sit out our waltz."

"No need to apologize. We're engaged for at least one more dance this evening."

"Why don't you ask one of the other ladies to—Relia!" Amy hailed her sister, approaching on Thomas's arm, with relief. "There you are!"

Aurelia's brows rose. "Yes, love. Is everything all right?"

Amy explained about her torn hem. "So I'm off to the retiring room," she concluded. "But that leaves Trevenan without a partner. Are you engaged for the next set?"

Aurelia colored slightly as she consulted her dance card. "Er, no, actually—"

"Perfect!" Amy declared, turning with a bright smile to James. "Why don't you dance with Relia, my lord? That way neither of you is obliged to sit out."

"A most elegant solution, my dear," James said after a moment. He met Aurelia's wide, startled eyes. "May I have this dance, Miss Aurelia?"

✺

May I have this dance?

Memories rose like an unstoppable tide at his words, the ones he had spoken to her a year ago in a moonlit conservatory. The words that had started her on the journey back to health and to this new self she'd created in hopes of seeing him once more. Not in her wildest dreams could she have imagined hearing them again and on such an occasion: his engagement to her sister.

Aurelia forced her thoughts back to the present. A dance was just a dance, when all was said and done, she reminded herself. This waltz held no greater significance than the Lancers Quadrille she and Trevenan had danced at Lady Warrender's last week. They were to be family now, and what could be more mundane than dancing with one's future brother-in-law?

"Certainly you may," she replied, smiling, and set her hand upon his proffered arm.

They took up their place in the set and assumed the proper position, observing the requisite distance between their bodies. All the same, Aurelia found herself excruciatingly aware of him—the warmth of his hands through his gloves, the achingly familiar scent of his cologne. They'd both come so far since that secret waltz, but at this precise moment she felt once again like that shy cripple, touched and dazzled by the kindness of a handsome stranger. Her Mr. Trelawney. If only it had been possible to forget.

A year ago only the moon had witnessed their dance.

Tonight all of Society would be watching as she took to the floor with Amy's fiancé. And she must take care that Society saw nothing untoward in her demeanor. Esteem, respect, even—heaven help her—sisterly affection, but not yearning, not desire…and not love.

The music started—Strauss, of course. She lifted a smiling face to Lord Trevenan's and took her first step in the dance.

∾

Full circle. The thought popped into James's mind as the waltz began and refused to leave it even as he and Aurelia circled the floor with the other couples. Impossible not to remember that night, though so much had changed.

The same woman, but the face turned up to his was no longer shadowed and wan but glowing with health and vitality. The self-loathing he'd glimpsed in her then was likewise a thing of the past; the poise and assurance she had developed in the last year made her scar and limp of no account. Indeed, he would not even have noticed the latter had he not already known of it, for she moved with the liquid grace of flowing water.

And yet—James found himself more unsettled by what *hadn't* changed. Like her scent, still the elusive fragrance of lavender. And the feeling of her in his arms as they glided and twirled across the polished floor—that too was the same. And she wore blue, as she had that night, though she filled out this gown rather better. No need to ask if she remembered their first waltz. He knew it was etched as indelibly in her memory as it was in his.

They had not spoken then, in the conservatory. The music, the moonlight, and the solitude had combined to weave a spell that made speech undesired—and somehow unnecessary. Very different from his waltzes with Amy, who seemed to expect, even require, conversation when they danced. Not that there was any fault in that, but this complete absorption in the dance and in his partner was something he'd not experienced with any woman but Aurelia. Absorption—and the sense, both now and then, that he was holding the world in his arms.

Unnerved, he moved to break the spell. "You look lovely this evening."

"Thank you." Her bright, social mask relaxed into something warmer and more intimate. If her smile was perhaps a degree less vivacious than her sister's, it was—sweeter somehow, as if she'd learned not to take compliments for granted. Indeed, he suspected she had. "Fine feathers, of course. It's hard not to look well in a Worth gown."

"The gown is the least part of it, I assure you." *And could I sound any more banal?* James wondered rather savagely as he maneuvered Aurelia into a turn.

She followed effortlessly, appearing not to mind his descent into platitudes. "Then perhaps it is the occasion."

He seized thankfully upon the rope she'd thrown him. "Very likely. My best wishes on your coming of age."

"Oh!" Her eyes widened, impossibly blue in the light of the chandelier. "Well, thank you again, my lord. I was— actually thinking of your engagement to Amy."

Startled, James regarded her more closely, but her gaze did not waver. "Of course," he said, feeling as though he'd spoken just a fraction too late. "Our engagement."

"You must be anticipating it eagerly," Aurelia went on. "I know my sister is." Again, her lips curved up in that achingly sweet smile. "I wish you both every happiness, Lord Trevenan, from the bottom of my heart."

He did not doubt the truth of her heart, even for a moment. It was his own heart that seemed to be rebelling, suddenly crying out against the fate he'd been so willing to embrace mere weeks ago. That wondered, wildly and far too late, how it could be right to pledge himself to one woman when it was another who stirred such feelings in him—tenderness, longing, and passion, beyond what he had known before.

And yet—he could not betray Amy. Not that bright, laughing girl who had accepted his proposal in good faith and for whom he had genuinely come to care. Even to think of jilting her was monstrous…and Aurelia would hate him for it, even if she knew the true cause. Worse, she would hate herself if she *did* know, and he could not allow that to happen.

Either way, she would be lost to him. And he had given his word: his betrothal to Amy must stand.

So he did his best to return Aurelia's smile and steer her through the dance that had brought them together and must now dictate the end of whatever else they might have shared.

And as mad and dangerous as it was—sheer folly, no doubt—he found himself wishing that this waltz would never end.

The repair was accomplished quickly, though the seamstress exclaimed in dismay at the tears in the fragile lace and suggested that Amy replace it as soon as she had the chance.

Just outside the ballroom, she paused, listening intently. The strains of Strauss told her that the waltz was still in full swing. No doubt Trevenan and Relia were among the couples swirling about the floor. It did Amy's heart good to think of her sister waltzing the night away, as she had before the accident. And how pleasant that she and Trevenan should get along so well. Though Amy would not have owned it for the world, she had been somewhat worried that her twin and her betrothed would not be at ease in each other's company. Instead, they appeared to be on quite friendly terms; they'd even gone shopping together for her birthday present.

"Miss Amelia." A familiar but thoroughly disliked voice spoke up from behind her.

Amy felt her spine stiffen and the smile congeal upon her face. Drat this man. Wasn't it enough that they'd had to invite him and his wretched family tonight? After what he'd done, he should at least have the decency not to approach her or, worse, Aurelia.

She turned around, not bothering to hide her displeasure. "Mr. Vandermere."

Her sister's betrayer looked slightly older, but he'd kept his fair good looks, Amy conceded grudgingly. Pity he hadn't grown fat or started losing his hair prematurely. He looked ill at ease, however; she took some comfort from that.

"I wanted," he began, then paused to clear his throat. "That is, I would like to wish you happy on your birthday."

"Thank you. I hope your family is enjoying the ball?" she inquired, hoping nothing of the sort. The Vandermeres were more likely to leave early if they *weren't* enjoying themselves.

"Indeed. Sally claims she hasn't had to sit out one dance yet. Speaking of which," he paused again, "I was wondering if you might honor me with a dance?"

Amy's eyes widened. What could have prompted such a request from Stupid Charlie? Surely he must know she felt only antipathy for him after the way he'd broken Relia's heart. Unless, of course, he was hoping to ingratiate himself to Aurelia through her...

Well, he might as well save himself the trouble. Recollecting her wits, she stared him down coolly. "I fear all my dances are claimed, Mr. Vandermere. *For the rest of the night.*"

Even Stupid Charlie could not misconstrue that hint. He flushed slightly and sketched a stiff bow. "Another time, perhaps. I wish you a pleasant evening."

He withdrew, making his way into the ballroom, where the crowd soon swallowed him up. Coldly satisfied, Amy watched him go. Let him carry tales to his father if he were so inclined, though she doubted he would feel comfortable mentioning this snub to anyone.

"I can't believe you just did that!" another familiar voice exclaimed indignantly.

Dismayed, Amy turned around again, this time to see her brother glowering at her. "It's not what you think, Andrew."

"It's not?" he challenged, folding his arms. "You mean, I *didn't* just see you snub my best friend? Tell me what I did see, then!"

"You are making a scene!" she hissed at him. A few people standing near the ballroom doorway were glancing in their direction, looking understandably curious. Just what she needed—to be caught arguing publicly with her brother at her own birthday ball.

Andrew glanced distractedly at them, then grasped her by the elbow and pulled her into an alcove to continue their discussion in more private surroundings.

"What the devil is wrong with you?" he demanded, his voice lower but no less furious. "Snubbing Charlie like that! Where are your manners, Amelia?"

"My manners are just fine, thank you!" she flashed back, losing her own temper now. "Where is your judgment? Don't you even *care* about what your *best friend* did to Relia?"

"Relia?" her brother said blankly. "What has she to do with this?"

"Charlie jilted her," Amy told him, and felt a stab of angry satisfaction when she saw his eyes widen. "She *loved* him—and he abandoned her when she was injured. I guess he didn't want a sweetheart with a limp and a scar. Not the scion of the almighty Vandermeres!"

Andrew paled. "No. I can't believe—no one has ever said—"

"He broke our sister's heart!" Amy snapped. "And it's high time you knew about it. Go ask Mama if you don't believe me!"

Andrew opened his mouth as if he would protest further, then shut it just as quickly and hurried from the alcove without challenging her again. Amy's sense of righteous anger lasted all of two minutes after he had gone, to be speedily replaced by dismay and remorse.

Dear heaven, what had she just done? And would Relia forgive her? She knew she was right to be angry on her twin's behalf, but Charlie's betrayal was Aurelia's secret to tell, and she'd just blurted it out to their brother, Charlie's best friend.

Stifling a groan, Amy pressed her hands against her hot cheeks. Her wretched tongue! Mama and Aunt Caroline would have been mortified by her outburst, no matter how justified it was. She needed…solitude, a few minutes to calm herself and regain her composure.

And then she would go and apologize abjectly—using sackcloth and ashes, if necessary—to Relia for her appalling lack of discretion.

She had just told, if not the biggest lie in her life, something less than the full truth. And the sky had not fallen. Nor had her heart cracked in two, though it still ached treacherously for what might have been.

Much to Aurelia's relief, Trevenan did not speak again. They finished their waltz in silence, and he led her off the floor, escorting her back to the chaperons' corner.

Again she mustered a smile. "Thank you, Lord Trevenan. It was a pleasure to waltz with you. But then it always is."

He regarded her with somber dark eyes. "The pleasure was mine, Miss Aurelia."

It always is. The words hung unspoken on the air between them, and she hastened to fill the silence with words of her own.

"I am sure Amy will be returning to the ballroom soon," she said brightly. "And no doubt longing to make up for the dance she missed."

"No doubt," Trevenan agreed, picking up his cue at once. Another brief exchange of pleasantries, and he had moved off through the crowd in search of her sister.

Aurelia turned away, fanning herself. This next dance, a schottische, was another she'd left unclaimed, to give herself time to catch her breath. But she'd never guessed she would need that respite so desperately as she did now.

As unobtrusively as possible, she sidled toward the French doors, standing open in the sultry night, and stepped out onto the terrace. The spring air, cool and mild, caressed her face deliciously. Closing her eyes, Aurelia drank in the scents of jasmine and honeysuckle. Five minutes of this, and she could endure whatever else happened this evening.

The moment when Amy and Trevenan's betrothal was announced.

Unbidden, her thoughts returned to their last waltz, the sensation of his arms around her, leading her effortlessly through every turn and twirl…how was it that—on the night he was to become her sister's affianced husband—he should feel more hers than ever?

Madness. She had to stop thinking—feeling—this way, for all their sakes. Perhaps if they never danced together again, it might help. A sharp pang went through her at the realization that the next occasion on which they might be expected to do so would be Amy's wedding. She felt an even sharper one at the thought of everything else that would follow.

Amy's life would be here, in England, with James. Almost certainly she would invite Aurelia to stay with her, but that could not happen yet. Amy must never discover how keenly her twin coveted her husband. And until Aurelia could meet the Earl and Countess of Trevenan without experiencing even a moment's envy or regret, keeping an ocean between herself and them was surely the right—the *only*—thing to do.

No one ever told you how much doing the right thing hurt.

It mightn't be so bad, Aurelia told herself firmly. She and Amy had managed to weather their separation while she was at Bad Ems, after all. Their parents and brother would be in New York. She could move in Society again; after London, she suspected nothing in New York could intimidate her. She could even go to college, as she had once considered before the accident. And perhaps, in time, in either Europe or America, there might be a man whom she could care for, with whom she could have a future and a family.

Her life needn't end with Amy's marriage. Indeed, she could turn it into a new beginning. The future was what one made of it, after all, and she meant to make the best of it.

She took another breath of the fragrant night air, opened her eyes, and turned around to reenter the ballroom.

Charlie Vandermere stood on the terrace, blocking her way.

Fourteen

Ill-met by moonlight…

—William Shakespeare,
A Midsummer Night's Dream

AURELIA STOPPED, AGHAST, THEN NEARLY LAUGHED
aloud. Of course. It needed only that.

"Mr. Vandermere," she said with what she hoped was
cool composure. "Good evening. I was on my way back to
the ballroom. Pray excuse me."

Picking up her skirts, she started to move past him, when
he sidestepped, again placing himself directly in her path.

"Miss Aurelia, I—I need to speak with you." His words
came out jerkily, in disjointed bursts. "If you would grant me
but one moment of your time—"

"I do not believe we have anything to say to one another,
sir," Aurelia replied steadily. "I came out here for a moment's
privacy, and now I wish to return to our guests. I would
appreciate it if you would respect my wish and step aside."

His face was resolute. "Not until I have spoken my piece!"

Aurelia cast a frantic glance over his shoulder toward the
ballroom. No one seemed to be looking in their direction
just yet—a small mercy—but how long could they expect

to remain undisturbed? "Pray lower your voice," she urged, lowering her own. "I will not tolerate a scene, not tonight of all nights!"

"Hear me out, and I will be as circumspect as you could wish." His voice was lower but no less urgent—or determined.

Aurelia looked longingly toward the sanctuary of the brightly lit salon behind them, so close and yet so far, and made herself take a fortifying breath. "Very well. You may have your moment, but I fail to see what you hope to gain by it."

His gaze intensified, that brilliant blue gaze she had once adored. "Can you not?" he asked, and the melting tenderness in his voice sent a betraying tremor through her. "Since seeing you again, I must confess, you have been constantly in my thoughts."

Aurelia raised her brows. "Indeed?" She infused the word with a wealth of cool skepticism. "I fear I cannot return the compliment, sir. You have *not* been constantly in mine."

"No, nor could I expect to be, after—what passed between us." Charlie paused, moistening his lips, as nervous as she had ever seen him. *All the better*, a part of her observed with a satisfaction bordering on the vindictive. "What I did… four years ago," he resumed haltingly, "was unforgivable. As callous as it was callow—"

Aurelia shrugged and looked away. "True enough, but it is over and done with. What purpose is there in dwelling upon the past?"

"Because I have not known a day's peace or happiness since parting from you." Charlie's voice was hoarse, his blue eyes now burning with an emotion Aurelia feared to name. "Because I now understand the worth of what I threw away so carelessly! I *always* did, in my heart of hearts," he amended before she could voice her incredulity. "But like a coward and a cad, I told myself ending things was best for both of us."

"And now you believe otherwise?" Deliberately, Aurelia

brushed the fringe back from her brow, exposing her hairline. "Those things that led to our parting have not changed, Mr. Vandermere. I am still crippled, still scarred—"

"And still beautiful," he broke in. "As beautiful as you've ever been. Even more so to *my* eyes than any other woman in the world."

The conviction in his voice took her breath away, even as she berated herself for a fool ten times over. But his eyes—he was gazing at her directly, as he had not done that dreadful day four years ago. And what she saw reflected there made her pulse quicken, her heart stutter...what flesh-and-blood woman could remain unmoved by such ardor?

Helpless as a bird mesmerized by a snake, she stood stock still as he drew closer, his gaze still intent on hers. "Can you ever forgive me? Give me a chance to make things right?"

Shock rippled through her at his words. "M-make things right?" she echoed. "But how..." Her voice trailed off uncertainly.

Charlie swallowed. "Like this, my dearest girl." He leaned in, his hands cupping her face as they had that long ago evening in her parents' gazebo, and covered her mouth with his.

Years fled away before the touch of his lips, the warmth of his palms against her cheeks. Too startled to resist, Aurelia succumbed to his embrace. At that moment she was sixteen again, lost in rose-tinted dreams of true love with the boy next door.

Then, even through the haze clouding her brain, she heard a step behind them on the terrace—and a low, furious voice.

"Get away from my sister, Vandermere," Andrew said tautly.

Awareness came rushing back at his words. With a gasp, Aurelia pulled free, even as Charlie dropped his hands to his sides. Good heavens, *what* had she been doing? Mortified, she turned to her brother, only to find that he was glaring not at her, but at Charlie, and with an intensity that sent a shiver of apprehension along her spine.

Wait—another realization struck. *Vandermere?* Since when had Andrew addressed Charlie by his surname? Biting her lip, she glanced from one to the other. Something was going on, something important—beyond this small indiscretion—but she could not begin to guess what.

After what seemed an eternity, Andrew spoke. "My God, it's true. You and Aurelia—" He broke off, shaking his head in disgust. "Why, you cowardly cur!"

Aurelia's eyes widened. *He knew?*

Charlie flushed, but made no attempt to defend himself.

His expression stony, Andrew offered his arm to Aurelia. "Let me take you back to the ballroom, sister."

His tone brooked no argument, even if Aurelia had been inclined to give one. Instead, she meekly took his arm and let him lead her away. Neither of them looked back.

No sign of Amy, so far, James observed as he scanned the ballroom for a golden head and a pink gown. Perhaps the repairs to her hem had taken longer than expected. In such a crush, hers was surely not the only gown to have suffered damages.

Or perhaps she had opted for a breath of air on the terrace before returning. No harm in going to check, and he could do with a brief respite himself from all this noise and bustle. Something to clear his head, remind him of where his honor lay—and with whom.

Somberly, he began to thread his way through the crowd, when a sudden motion by the French doors caught his eye: Andrew Newbold, his face white and set, had just reentered the ballroom, with Aurelia on his arm. At the sight of *her* face, equally pale and strained, James had to check an impulse to go to her. But she was with her brother, one of the men with whom she could be considered indisputably safe, who would surely look after her.

All the same, his gaze followed them as they skirted the

perimeter of the ballroom, heading not for the chaperons' corner but toward a more distant destination. They paused at last before a doorway—one leading to a smaller salon just off the ballroom, if James recalled correctly—and then passed through it, disappearing from sight.

What the devil—? Frowning, James glanced back toward the French doors—and stiffened when he recognized the man just slipping through them as Charlie Vandermere.

James hissed a breath between his teeth. What had that bastard done to upset Aurelia? Hands fisting, he took an involuntary step forward…

Dear God, what was he doing? He stopped short, fury and frustration curdling in the pit of his stomach. And horribly unsure which he resented more: Vandermere's presumption—or his own impotence.

He could not champion Aurelia as fully as he wished and as she deserved. Not with her father and brother present. Not when he was promised to her own sister: Amy, his future bride and the woman of whom he should be thinking most tonight.

Taking a deep breath, James forced his fists to unclose. The dislike that seemed to bubble up from his very soul was directed wholly at himself right now. What sort of man pledged his faith to one woman, but continually yearned for another, as he was doing? And on what basis could he possibly justify it? Familial loyalty could only account for so much.

Broodingly, he watched Vandermere until the young man was swallowed up by the crowd in the ballroom. Perhaps Andrew Newbold would take it upon himself to avenge the slight to his sister. Meanwhile, James's own duty and his faith lay with Amy, wherever she might be.

He turned his back on the French doors and renewed his search for her. A sense of having betrayed someone still gnawed at him, but he could not have said at that moment whether it was his intended, Aurelia, or himself.

"Not one word," Andrew had muttered in Aurelia's ear just before they'd reentered the house. And so they had silently made their way to the blue salon, closing the door behind them.

Now, however, her brother exploded into speech. "Hang it, Relia, why didn't you tell me Charlie was courting you?" he burst out, running an agitated hand through his hair. "Or that he jilted you after the accident?"

Aurelia moistened her lips. "How do you know?" she ventured, avoiding his question.

"Amy told me."

Shock, followed by betrayal, lanced through her. "She had no business doing so!"

Andrew sighed. "Don't be too mad at her. She wouldn't have said anything if I hadn't started in on her about being nicer to Charlie." He shook his head at his own folly. "Gad, it's a wonder she didn't throw something at me!"

"I am sure the thought crossed her mind," Aurelia said dryly.

"I didn't want to believe what she told me, so I came out to confront him." Andrew gave a short laugh. "No need for that. His guilt was written all over his face. Why didn't you tell me?" he repeated. "Then or now? I could have done something about it!"

Aurelia raised skeptical brows. "You mean, challenge him? Duels are illegal—here and in New York."

Andrew's face darkened. "Well, I'd have knocked him down, for a start."

"Just like a man," she scoffed. "Thinking fists solve everything!"

He glowered. "Tell me that *wouldn't* have made you feel better—just a little!"

Aurelia opened her mouth, thought for a moment, then closed it with a sigh. "Perhaps at first," she conceded. "But it wouldn't have changed anything in the end. What happened between Charlie and myself was private, and I meant it to stay that way. Amy knew, of course, and Mother figured it out once Charlie stopped visiting. But I didn't want to make trouble for Papa—he said himself that he still has business dealings with Mr. Vandermere. And Charlie is your closest friend."

"*Was* my closest friend," Andrew corrected her. "But you'll always be my sister."

"Then, as your sister, I'm asking you to let this go—for all our sakes!" Aurelia insisted. "I am *not* some pathetic weakling, pining over a man who jilted her four years ago, and I refuse to be treated as one. I'm well, I'm strong, and I'm certainly not wearing the willow for Charlie Vandermere these days!"

"Then why were you kissing him tonight?" Andrew demanded.

"I wasn't kissing him; he was kissing *me!*"

"Pretty hard to tell the difference from where I was standing," he retorted. "Are you sure you don't still care for him? Because if you don't, letting him kiss you like that is downright stupid. If you'd been caught by anyone but me, you'd probably be engaged to him right now—whether you wanted to be or not!"

Aurelia flushed guiltily, unable to deny the truth of his words. It was mortifying to realize that possibility hadn't even crossed her mind out there on the terrace—and after all those lectures from Mother and Aunt Caroline about young ladies needing to observe the proprieties and maintain a spotless reputation. She could have been compromised so easily tonight, and it would have been her fault as much as Charlie's.

"Do you still care for him, Relia?" Andrew persisted, his voice gentler now.

Aurelia dropped her gaze to her gloved hands, lying clenched in her lap. How she wished she could say that she'd felt nothing at all during that moonlit kiss! But that would have been a lie—and for Amy's sake, she'd already resolved to live with one such lie for the rest of her life.

"I don't know how I feel about him," she admitted in a low voice. "He said he wants a chance to make things right, whatever that means. I don't know how to feel about that either."

Her brother stared at her in disbelief, then his mouth twisted in what was almost a smile. "Then I guess we're in the same boat, because neither do I. Are you going to tell anyone?"

"You mean Mother or Amy? I haven't decided yet." Aurelia pressed her fingers to her throbbing temples. "Everything might look different in the morning, for everyone. But I know I *don't* wish to speak of this any further just now. This is Amy's big night, and I'm not going to spoil it for her." She rose, summoning up all the assurance she had gained in her year abroad. "Would you take me back to the ballroom, please? Papa will be making the announcement as soon as the break for supper comes."

At first, she feared Andrew would continue to argue, but after several moments of visible internal struggle, he capitulated.

"As you wish," he said with a wry smile, and held out his arm.

The conservatory at Renbourne House was a haven of silence and serenity, as well as being mercifully unoccupied for the moment. Amy breathed in the fragrance of countless exotic plants and willed her pulse to stop racing. No question that she'd made a mess of things over Charlie and Andrew. Relia would doubtless be upset with her, and with reason, but surely she would understand what had prompted her sister's outburst. Understand and forgive.

Amy felt her lips tremble. She could not bear even to think of Relia not forgiving her—and over a faithless cad like Charlie Vandermere, to boot! Not for the first time, she vowed that she would *never* let a man hurt her, as Charlie had hurt her twin. Even the coldest, most distant marriage of convenience had to be preferable to that!

Footsteps sounded somewhere behind her. Another person—surely a man, by the heaviness of his tread—had entered the conservatory. Amy turned at once, but could see nothing among the numerous plants and shrubs.

"Andrew?" she called tentatively. "Trevenan?"

A familiar figure stepped out from behind a potted palm. "No, sweeting, it is I."

Amy recoiled. "Lord Glyndon!"

He smirked at her as if they'd both done something exceptionally clever. "I didn't know how we'd manage it until I saw you slip away from the ballroom. You gave me quite a chase."

Amy drew herself up to her full height. "I left to have my gown mended, and for no other reason. I certainly did not intend for anyone to follow me. You are not here at *my* invitation, Lord Glyndon. Shouldn't you return to the ballroom? Your parents and betrothed must be missing you."

To her dismay, he showed no sign of heeding her words. "Oh, come now, darling, there's no need to pretend any longer!"

"Pretend?" Amy echoed, incredulous. Could he really be so conceited as to believe she had arranged this encounter? She watched uneasily as he continued to approach, walking with the exaggerated care of someone slightly the worse for drink. Enlightenment dawned: the viscount was intoxicated.

"You are not fit company in your present condition," she said coldly. "If you will not withdraw, then *I* shall. Good evening."

Drawing up her skirts, she started to move past him, when he reached out and caught her by the arm. The strength of his grip startled her, and for the first time, she felt a stirring of fear in her stomach. "Let me go!" she demanded, trying to pull herself free.

Lord Glyndon licked his lips, and for the first time, Amy noticed how full they were—not sensual, but oddly petulant, like a pouting baby's. His eyes burned with a strange, hot gleam as he scanned her from head to toe. "God, I don't know how I've stood it all these weeks—watching you with *him*."

"Lord Trevenan is my betrothed." It was at once a reminder and a subtle threat.

"Once we're both safely married, we needn't keep apart for long," Glyndon went on, as though she had not spoken. "Lady Louisa will be a complaisant wife, I have no doubt, as long as I make her a future duchess."

Amy stared at him, scarcely able to credit what she was hearing or what he was suggesting. She gave a brittle laugh. "Why, how delightful. You'd make her your duchess and me your—your paramour. Forgive me if I don't fall prostrate with gratitude at your feet."

He chuckled, and the sound made her nape prickle unpleasantly. "You American girls have such spirit! I've always admired that about you—among other things."

Amy lifted her chin. "You shame us both by such a proposal. Lord Trevenan has offered me his name and his honor. I wouldn't betray him for the world—and certainly not for the likes of *you*! Now let me go before I scream the house down!"

Some of her anger finally seemed to penetrate the viscount's sodden brain. "You can't intend to remain faithful to that provincial yokel—"

"You're not fit to black Trevenan's boots!" she flashed. "He's worth a hundred of you!"

"The devil he is! Tell me you haven't thought of this." Glyndon's voice was thick, congested. "Tell me you haven't wanted this, every bit as much as I." He pulled her to him, his mouth coming down hard and hot on hers, his arms closing around her in a stifling embrace.

Amy struggled frantically, but Lord Glyndon held her

fast, her arms pinioned to her sides. The combined reek of whiskey and perspiration made her head reel, and her lips felt bruised and swollen beneath the insistent pressure of his. The world was going grey around her when a new voice, sharp and imperative, sliced through the haze like a whetted knife.

"Get away from her, you drunken bastard!"

A mighty wrench, and then she was stumbling backwards, dazed but free of that hateful embrace, able to breathe again. Through still-blurred vision, she saw two dark shapes struggling; the leaner one appeared to have the more thickset one in a headlock. There were sounds of a scuffle that seemed to be moving farther and farther away. Putting out an unseeing hand, she felt the slim trunk of a young tree and gratefully steadied herself against it.

"Miss Newbold—" Another figure was looming over her now, but the voice was gentle, even solicitous. Still dazed, Amy blinked hard to clear her vision—and looked up into a familiar pair of green eyes.

"Glyndon is gone." Thomas Sheridan's tone was one of grim satisfaction. "He will not trouble you again—my word on it."

"M-Mr. Sheridan." Amy swallowed a treacherous lump in her throat, stifled a wild urge to burst into tears.

His eyes widened with what appeared to be genuine concern. "Here—you may feel better if you sit down." He took her gently by the elbow, led her unresisting to one of the stone benches. "Do you need me to fetch anyone?" he asked. "Your mother, perhaps—or your sister?"

Amy shook her head, beyond speech at the moment. Sheridan's face darkened further. "I cannot apologize enough for my cousin. His behavior was disgraceful, and I shall ensure that he does not approach you again—tonight or at any other time."

Amy found her voice again, shaky though it was. "I can't— I can't believe I *ever* esteemed him, future duke or not!"

To her eternal gratitude, Mr. Sheridan did not say, "I told you so." Instead, he passed her his handkerchief without a word. The urge to weep had receded, but she vigorously wiped her mouth to rid herself of even the feeling of Glyndon's unwanted kiss.

Sheridan continued to eye her solicitously. "Might I at least fetch you a glass of water?"

Amy shook her head. "I will be all right presently. I just need—a few moments to compose myself." She pressed the handkerchief to her lips again, suppressing a shudder. "Thank you, Mr. Sheridan, for coming to my rescue. And for your kindness now."

He inclined his head. "I am glad to have been of service, Miss Newbold, though tremendously sorry that it was necessary and that a member of my own family should have offered you such an insult."

She cast him an apprehensive glance. "How much did you witness, exactly?"

"I heard you tell him to let you go, and then I saw him embrace you, clearly against your wishes." Sheridan frowned. "You mean, he gave you further offense?"

"In a manner of speaking." Amy forced herself to speak calmly despite her lingering sense of outrage and insult. "He told me that—once we were married to our respective spouses—we needn't keep apart. By which I inferred that he wishes me to become his mistress."

Sheridan stilled, his fine features hardening, his eyes turning to emerald ice. "Forget that," he said curtly. "And forget him."

"With pleasure," she said fervently.

"Amy?" A new voice spoke from the doorway, and she turned her head to see her betrothed standing on the threshold.

"James," Amy said weakly. For a moment, she felt dangerously close to tears again.

"My dear?" He came further into the conservatory, his dark eyes scanning her anxiously. "Are you all right?"

Amy rose from the bench and surprised them both by flinging herself into his arms. Trevenan rallied almost at once, however, his arms closing around her—and oh, how blessedly different his embrace felt from the one Lord Glyndon had forced upon her! Gentle, but reassuring—the touch of a trusted friend and protector. Not trusting herself to speak yet, she rested her head against his shoulder, warm and solid beneath his evening coat, and breathed in the comforting scents of citrus and cloves. Safe.

"Amy?" He looked down at her, then glanced at Sheridan. "Thomas, what happened?"

"Glyndon." The single word dripped with censure. "He forgot himself and imposed his unwanted attentions upon Miss Newbold."

Trevenan stiffened. "Go on," he said to his friend in a voice every bit as hard and cold.

Sheridan complied, as tersely as possible; by the end of the recital, Trevenan looked as angry as Amy had ever seen him.

"By God, I will not stand for this!" His dark eyes held a dangerous light that might have alarmed Amy if it had been directed at her. "My dear," he studied her with renewed concern, "shall I take you to your mother?"

Amy shook her head. "I'm all right, my lord." With difficulty, she summoned a smile. "And I refuse to let this evening be spoiled by a drunken cad."

"That drunken cad will answer for what he's done," he told her. "And when I find him—"

"No, James," Sheridan interposed. "Glyndon is my cousin. Let *me* handle this!"

"It was my intended whom he assaulted!"

"And my family whom he embarrassed by his shameful conduct. My Uncle Harford will be informed of this, and I assure you, he will mete out as severe a punishment as you could wish. Short of flaying alive, perhaps," Sheridan added with a wry quirk of his lips. "Glyndon is still his heir, after all."

"*I* would be content simply never to set eyes on him again," Amy declared. "Let Mr. Sheridan deal with this, James. I don't wish you to soil your hands or even your horsewhip on Lord Glyndon. He is not worth the use of either."

Trevenan sighed. "I beg to differ, with regard to the horsewhip, at least, but I will abide by your wishes." He met Sheridan's eyes. "Thank you, Thomas."

Sheridan nodded. "I'll see to it at once. If you'll pardon me, Miss Newbold?" He sketched an abrupt bow and strode from the conservatory.

Trevenan turned to Amy. "My dear, are you recovered now, or do you need more time to collect yourself?"

She shook her head. "I think I've seen quite enough of this room for tonight. Let us rejoin our guests. Papa will be announcing our betrothal soon." She smiled at him, feeling a rush of gratitude for all that he was—and was not. "And if you'll forgive me for sounding like a brazen American hussy, I am looking forward to it very much."

"As am I." He offered her his arm. "And I give you fair warning, Amy—I intend to remain at your side for the rest of the evening."

Touched, she laid her hand upon the crook of his elbow. "You are gallant, my lord."

"Not at all." A peculiar expression flickered across his handsome face; if Amy hadn't known better, she might have described it as self-reproach. But what had Trevenan to reproach himself for? "I am merely resolved to take better care of you, in future."

Puzzled but agreeable, Amy let him lead her back into the ballroom.

From Victoria, Duchess of Harford, to Charlotte, Countess Savernake. 3 June 1891.

...So, as of two nights ago, Miss Amelia Newbold was officially betrothed to the Earl of Trevenan! Harford is most relieved, as am I, by this turn of events. I will concede that Miss Newbold is quite the beauty, and I suspect she will do well enough as a countess to a provincial earl, however ill-suited she might be as the next Duchess. I have heard that the Newbolds are departing within the week for Lord Trevenan's estate in Cornwall, where they will remain for at least a month. No Society there, of course, but the scenery is said to be breathtaking.

Of the matter that most concerns us, you will be glad to hear that Glyndon appears to have undergone a change of heart with regard to Miss Newbold. I suspect we may continue to plan Louisa's wedding for this coming autumn. For the time being, however, Harford means to dispatch Glyndon to Scotland, to oversee some matter at our northernmost property. Doubtless he will be bored, as most persons of consequence are remaining in London until August, but I daresay the solitude will afford him abundant opportunities for reflection. And time to recover from the rather nasty black eye he apparently acquired from a collision with a door...

Fifteen

Many a heart is aching,
If you could read them all;
Many the hopes that have vanished
After the ball.

> —Charles K. Harris, "After the Ball"

"HAVE YOU ANYTHING FURTHER TO REPORT, MR. Norris?" James asked the inquiry agent seated across the desk from him.

John Norris, a nondescript man who looked to be in his mid-thirties, shook his head. "I'm afraid not, my lord. Captain Mercer left London yesterday to attend to his interests in Bristol. Beyond that, I've learned nothing further regarding Mercer Shipping or your late cousin's involvement in it."

"Well, I appreciate your efforts on what you've learned so far, Norris," James replied. "And if you should discover anything more, send the information on to me in Cornwall. I leave for my estate tomorrow morning."

"I will continue to look into the matter here," the agent promised, rising to take his leave. "By the by, I saw the notice of your engagement in the papers. May I wish you happy, my lord?"

James thanked him, thinking how odd it felt to *be* engaged, then saw his visitor to the door. Returning to the library, he drifted to the window and stood there awhile, lost in thought.

So Mercer had left town, at least for the present. Only time would tell if he made contact again, in pursuit of those shares he appeared to want so intensely. Norris's investigation of Mercer Shipping likewise seemed to have reached a dead end.

Perhaps, James mused, the agent had found nothing more because—there was nothing more to be found? One could not overlook the possibility that the simplest explanation was the most accurate one—that Gerald had found a profitable venture and sought to maximize its advantages to himself by buying up as many shares as possible. And that Mercer had resented Gerald's intrusion in his business, especially after his unwanted "partner" added theft to his list of offenses. An unsavory scenario, without a doubt—and one that cast an unflattering light on his cousin—but not particularly sinister.

And yet…while he might hope there *was* nothing more to it than that, he couldn't help the uneasy feeling that they'd scratched only the surface of the problem. The rest of it lurked underfoot like a hidden mine shaft—and just as dangerous.

Cornwall. He needed to get back there, clear his head; he *thought* better in Cornwall. And he had responsibilities too long neglected there: the estate, the mine…though at least Harry could be counted on to have taken care of things at Wheal Felicity, as he had ever since James had inherited. He also needed to devote more attention to the Newbolds, and make sure that they enjoyed their stay at Pentreath. It was to be Amy's new home, after all.

Well, whatever ugly business Gerald had got up to in his last months, it would not touch his fiancée or her family, James vowed to himself. He'd as good as promised them a carefree holiday in his beloved home county, and that was just what he meant to give them, Gerald and Captain Mercer be damned.

"More flowers!" Amy caroled, swooping down upon the latest floral offering ensconced on the mantel. "Roses this time—Gloire de Dijon!" She indulged in a rapturous sniff of the luxuriant blooms and glanced at the accompanying note. "And from Mr. Sutcliffe, no less. Relia, dearest, you have made a conquest!"

"Oh, I don't know that I'd go that far," Aurelia demurred. "Mr. Sutcliffe is probably just being chivalrous."

Amy rolled her eyes. "Of course he is. And so are Lord Richard Vaughn, George Atherton, and Bertram Ashby, who sent you flowers as well. It's almost a shame that we're leaving London tomorrow. I am sure you could secure a proposal in no time if we were to stay."

Aurelia shook her head, refusing even to think of that. Flattering as it was to receive flowers and compliments from such eligible gentlemen, she felt confused enough about her present feelings without bringing another suitor into the mix. Personally, she was relieved that they would be departing so soon for Cornwall and Lord Trevenan's estate. "I'm in no hurry, dearest. Let us see you safely married first!"

"That's some months away as yet," Amy objected, seating herself on the sofa across from Aurelia's chair. "I should think we could at least make a push to find someone suitable for you before then." Her face brightened. "How wonderful if you were married or at least engaged within the year! You could stay with Trevenan and me until your own wedding."

Aurelia dropped her gaze to the floor. She had not discussed her plan to remain in New York after Amy's wedding. How could she, knowing how it would distress her twin? Nor had she mentioned that moonlit encounter with Charlie at their birthday ball, or Charlie's attempts to call on her these last two days; fortunately, she had been out of the house at both times. So many secrets she was keeping now—and from the one person to whom she had once told everything.

And Amy had had her share of distressing experiences that evening. All the Newbolds had been shocked to hear that Lord Glyndon had made such improper advances toward her, and grateful that Trevenan and Mr. Sheridan had been on hand to save her. Amy had been so shaken by the encounter that Aurelia hadn't had the heart to be angry with her for telling Andrew about Charlie, especially after her twin had apologized profusely for her breach of confidence.

She looked up at a sound from the doorway and saw a footman entering the sitting room bearing the morning post on a silver tray. Letters for both of them today, along with the latest issues of the Society magazines Amy read so avidly. Receiving her own mail, Aurelia broke into a smile when she saw the direction and French postage stamp on the topmost letter. Whatever the delights of Nice or Paris, Claudine had not forgotten her young American friend.

She glanced up to share the news with Amy, only to find that she'd fallen silent. Too silent—and *The London Lady* and *Town Talk* both lay forgotten on the sofa beside her. "Dearest, what is it?"

For answer, Amy held out the letter she had been reading. "It's from Lord Glyndon."

"Lord Glyndon?" Aurelia echoed, dumbfounded. "What on earth—?"

"It's—I think it's his idea of an apology."

Astonished, Aurelia took the letter and ran her gaze over it. Only a few lines, but the meaning—however stiffly worded—seemed clear enough, as did the phrases "deeply regret" and "sincere apologies for the offense." The page also bore Glyndon's full signature, and the envelope Amy had passed her along with the letter carried the Harford seal.

"Well," she said at last, "it appears genuine enough. At least he is *attempting* to make proper amends."

Amy's lips curved in a faint, wintry smile. "Oh, I very much doubt Lord Glyndon came up with the idea of writing this himself."

"Then who?"

"I suspect Mr. Sheridan had a hand in this."

"You think *he* wrote the letter and signed his cousin's name?"

"No." Amy's expression thawed fractionally. "But I suspect he pressured Glyndon into doing so. He did say—that night—that he would see to the matter."

Aurelia handed back the letter. "Well, if he is responsible for Glyndon owning up to his behavior, I can only applaud him."

"Yes." Amy surprised her by agreeing. "I should call on him, I suppose—and thank him again for his intervention." She stood up. "I have to speak to him anyway, about my portrait."

"Do you need me to accompany you?" Aurelia asked, reluctantly laying her letters aside.

Amy shook her head. "No, thank you, dearest. If I require a chaperon, I can always take Mariette." She glanced at her morning dress. "I'll just go up and change."

Looking somewhat distracted, she left the sitting room. Aurelia gazed after her in bemusement. Matters did seem to have improved between her sister and Mr. Sheridan, she mused, which must be a relief to Trevenan.

Her glance fell on Lord Glyndon's discarded missive, and the thought occurred to her that the viscount's letter had served at least one more useful purpose: Amy had become far too preoccupied to continue the subject of finding her a husband. She picked up her letters again, sifted through them—and froze when she saw the handwriting on the last one. Handwriting she had not set eyes on in more than three years.

Charlie—making one more attempt to reach her.

❧

As before, Mr. Sheridan was out but expected to return shortly, so, at Amy's request, his housekeeper again showed her into the studio to wait for him.

She was not, however, destined to wait alone, for the studio was already occupied. A fashionably dressed young woman with brown hair stood before the nearest wall, admiring Sheridan's handiwork.

"Lady Warrender!" Amy exclaimed in startled recognition.

"Miss Newbold." The baroness sounded surprised but not at all perturbed by Amy's presence here. "Have you come to offer Thomas a commission?"

Thomas. Belatedly, Amy recalled what Trevenan had told her of the friendship that had existed between Sheridan's family and Lady Warrender's. "Indeed. Mr. Sheridan has agreed to paint my portrait as a wedding gift for my fiancé."

"An excellent notion. You could not have chosen a more gifted artist, or one whose work is more likely to please Lord Trevenan. Have you decided upon a gown and a setting?"

"Not just yet. Those are among the details I hope to discuss with him today."

"Well, Thomas will certainly do you justice. He has the most extraordinary way of capturing the very heart and soul of his subjects." Lady Warrender's gaze went to Elizabeth Martin's portrait, and her smile turned soft, even wistful. "The very heart and soul."

Amy glanced at the portrait as well, remembering how she had admired it on her first visit. She could now see the resemblance between the girl in the painting and the woman gazing at it so fondly, though the girl's expression was merrier. "And this was your sister?" she asked, though she already knew the answer.

"Yes, my sister Elizabeth. She died when she was only seventeen. We were just two years apart, and very close."

"I am so sorry," Amy said with complete sincerity. How could she not sympathize with one who had lost a beloved sister? Those first days after Relia's accident, when they had all feared for her life, were permanently etched on her memory. Even thinking about them chilled her to the very marrow.

Lady Warrender regarded her for a moment. "Yes, you, of all people, would understand," she said more warmly, then sighed. "She was the elder, in life. Now I am almost a decade her senior. It has been … difficult to accept, at times." She looked back at the portrait. "Thomas finished this six months after her death. The original is at my parents' estate, in Devonshire."

"The original?" Amy echoed. "You mean, this is a copy?"

"As close a one as he could manage. I hope it comforted him as much as ours did us."

"He held your sister in high regard, then?"

"They were to be married, my dear." Lady Warrender paused. "And it was a love match."

"Really?" Amy glanced at the portrait again. This laughing, fresh-faced girl and the sophisticated, blasé artist, who'd had a number of discreet liaisons with equally sophisticated, blasé Society women, if rumor were to be believed? And yet he could not have always been so.

"Our families have been neighbors for years, in Devonshire," Lady Warrender explained. "My brothers, my sisters, and I were playmates of the Sheridans." She paused, lips curving at the memory. "We were this great pack of children running wild over the Devon moors, squabbling over our tea, and planning endless excursions here and there.

"But even then there was something special between Thomas and Elizabeth. He was her staunchest defender when she was a little girl, while she was his most loyal ally when he chose to study art. They had a deep trust in each other that was—quite beautiful to see." Lady Warrender's brown eyes misted slightly. "And so, in due course, they became engaged and planned to wed after Thomas was finished at university. But during his first year at Oxford, she took a severe chill and died within a few days. It was…a very great shock to us all. She had always been so lively and robust." She paused again, fished a handkerchief from her reticule, and dabbed at her eyes. "Oh, dear. Please forgive me…"

"No need, Lady Warrender," Amy broke in hurriedly, half-wishing she'd never asked the question that led to this painfully sensitive subject. "I understand completely."

The baroness gave her a sweetly tremulous smile before tucking the handkerchief away. "So," she resumed, "Thomas has always been dear to our family, for his own sake and for hers. I rejoice in his success, as Elizabeth would have done, and I like to think that she watches over him, even now. Although," she added, "I cannot think she would approve of *everything* he has done in the last ten years. Or of the company he has sometimes kept." The faint censure in her tone made her meaning unmistakable, and Amy's own thoughts went irresistibly to Lady Crowley. "On reflection, I really do think it would be best if Thomas were to marry."

Amy found the thought of Mr. Sheridan married even more disconcerting than the thought of him engaged. But Lady Warrender knew him far better than she. "A suitable wife would surely be a benefit to his career," she ventured.

"Oh, indeed. But that is not why I propose it." Lady Warrender studied the portrait once more. "Thomas's own gifts and his dedication will ensure his success as an artist. But for Thomas the man…I should like to see him in love, truly in love, again. And loved in return."

"You would not mind that, even though he was betrothed to your sister?"

"Oh, I admit, I once would have found it difficult to see Thomas with someone in what should have been Elizabeth's place," Lady Warrender confessed. "But to expect him to remain a bachelor forever, when he might find happiness elsewhere, would be selfish and unreasonable. Elizabeth loved him dearly; they were the best of friends, as well as true sweethearts, but she had the most generous of hearts. I think she would want him to be happy again, after—"

She broke off at the sound of footsteps in the passage. The door opened a moment later, and the man they'd been discussing stepped into the room. To Amy's surprise, Sheridan's face lit with a genuine smile of welcome at the sight of Lady Warrender.

"Eleanor, this *is* a surprise! And Miss Newbold," he added, nodding in Amy's direction. "To what do I owe the honor of being visited by two lovely women this afternoon?"

"Silver-tongued as ever," Lady Warrender declared, with a fond shake of her head. She came forward, hands outstretched to clasp Sheridan's own, and they exchanged a light, brief kiss.

"You know how I love to visit and see all your latest works," the baroness continued. "But today I have a particular purpose in mind. My son will be a year old in September, and Warrender wishes to have a portrait painted of the three of us. I know how much in demand you've become these days, so I wanted to give you plenty of notice."

"Much obliged, my dear," Sheridan said, with mock-gravity. "Is it to be Wyldean Hall?"

"Where else? I shall be at some pains to convince Warrender to relax and appear more natural. He does take his role as head of the family so seriously."

"Between us, we might be able to persuade him to unbend a trifle. To say nothing of young Piers."

They continued in this vein, bantering lightly back and forth as Sheridan arranged the time and place of the Warrenders' first sitting. Amy remained silent, studying her former nemesis with new eyes. The cool, detached artist who had roused her distrust and—at times—her dislike was gone; in his place stood a far more engaging stranger. But then, he could not always have been as jaded or cynical as she'd first thought him. He and James were close friends, and just now she had seen the unguarded affection on his face when he greeted Lady Warrender. She could imagine *that* man as Elizabeth Martin's lover—warm, ardent, alight with youthful hopes and dreams. Had her loss frozen that warmth into insensibility? She found herself hoping it was not so, then wondered with some irritation why it should matter to her.

"But I must be going now," Lady Warrender said at last. "And Miss Newbold, who has been waiting so patiently there, no doubt has business to discuss with you as well." She gave Sheridan a brief parting kiss. "Take care, dear Thomas."

He lowered his head to return the salute. "And you, my dear Eleanor."

After Lady Warrender had taken her leave, he glanced quizzically at Amy. "You are here about the wedding portrait, I surmise?"

"Among other things." She hesitated, then pressed on firmly, "First of all, I owe you my thanks for the other night. For coming to my aid against your own cousin."

Sheridan actually smiled at her. "You need not reproach yourself on that account, Miss Newbold. Glyndon and I are not especially close."

"Perhaps not, but I should not like to cause trouble between you and the Harfords."

"On the contrary, I believe I stand in fairly good odor with them at present." A corner of his mouth quirked up. "My encounter with Glyndon has apparently given him more enthusiasm for his marriage to Lady Louisa."

"I wish her joy of him then," Amy said feelingly. It still rankled, that she'd been so taken in by Glyndon's polish—and his title, she admitted—that she hadn't seen far sooner what a lout he was. A lout and a milksop, too spineless to stand up to his parents but not above fondling another man's fiancée in private. Her skin crawled at the memory; James would never grope her so. He had been so gentle, so understanding with her in the conservatory. As had Mr. Sheridan.

"I rather doubt Lady Louisa *expects* joy from Glyndon, but it's a laudable sentiment all the same," Sheridan said dryly.

Amy suppressed a reluctant smile, and continued, "In addition, I have received a letter of apology from Lord Glyndon this very morning. I assume I have you to thank for that as well?"

"Ah." Sheridan paused. "Only in part. Let's just say that my Uncle Harford and I convinced Glyndon that an apology should be forthcoming. I am relieved to hear that, graceless as his behavior has been, my cousin has performed his duty in that regard."

"And I assume my duty is to accept that apology?" Amy sighed. "Well, I can do that much, I suppose. I only hope he does not feel obliged to call on me as well."

"You may rest easy on that score, Miss Newbold. There will be no meeting between you and Glyndon, for he has left London as of this very morning."

Amy felt an almost palpable sense of relief at the news. "He's been sent to Coventry?" she inquired, recalling that unusual English phrase that meant severe punishment.

"Northernmost Scotland, actually, but the result is essentially the same. My uncle has sent him to tend to an estate matter there."

She frowned. "Is that truly an appropriate punishment?"

"To one who enjoys Society as much as Glyndon, it is severe indeed," Sheridan replied. "But at least his face should have time to recover."

"His face?" she echoed, startled.

"He's—acquired a few bruises since last you saw him."

Sheridan's tone was neutral, but Amy's gaze went at once to his right hand, now resting casually upon the mantelpiece. Did his knuckles look—just a trifle swollen? Before she could muster the nerve to ask, he changed his position—and the subject.

"But enough of Glyndon. What was it you wished to discuss, regarding the portrait?"

Amy did her best to rally. "Well, I had wondered if we

might manage one sitting this week," she began, "but I'm to leave for Cornwall tomorrow."

"Would you prefer to wait until your return to London?"

"Would that give you enough time? We are to be at Pentreath for at least a month, and then I expect I will be returning to New York soon after that to prepare for the wedding." Amy paused, fretting her lower lip. "I am not sure how best to manage this…"

"There might be a way around the problem," Sheridan interposed. "If you are amenable to it, that is." He paused, his expression unreadable. "James has invited me to Cornwall as well. He points out that I have long wanted to paint the sea there. I have not yet given him a response."

"But you are his friend. Why would you not go? And why would you think me not amenable to it? Indeed," she added, struck by a sudden inspiration, "your coming to Cornwall might be the perfect solution. You know James barely tolerates London. Cornwall is his true home. What could be better than having my portrait painted *there*, in one of his favorite places?"

"The garden at Pentreath, perhaps." Sheridan's green eyes took on a dreamy cast. "Or even upon a cliff-top, gazing out to sea, like Iseult the Fair. Toward Ireland—no, toward Brittany and Tristram…"

"Whichever you prefer." Personally, Amy had never been much interested in Arthurian legends. Relia found them far more intriguing; the other day, she'd pointed out that mythical Lyonesse was often identified with Cornwall and hoped that they might see Tintagel Castle. Amy was more eager to see Pentreath, the estate of which she would soon be mistress. Carpenters, roofers, and stonemasons were already at work on the parts of the house most in need of repair; it was only good sense to see how the Newbold money was being spent. "So, will you come? You could kill two birds with one stone—paint the sea *and* fulfill your commission."

"Most efficient," he agreed, a faint smile hovering about his lips. "Very well, Miss Newbold. You may consider me persuaded. I'll send my acceptance to James at once."

"Excellent," Amy said briskly. "Shall you be traveling down with us as well?"

"No, I've some business to attend to in London first. But I'll be along a few days later."

For just a moment, Amy wondered if that business included Lady Crowley or someone like her. Then she put that thought firmly aside; it was none of her affair, after all. "Very well—we shall expect you then." She picked up her reticule from the sofa. "Thank you, Mr. Sheridan. I wish you a pleasant afternoon."

"And you, Miss Newbold," he returned, escorting her cordially to the door.

Not until she was well on her way home did Amy pause to reflect that the prospect of Mr. Sheridan's joining them in Cornwall did not strike her as unwelcome or unpleasant.

A change indeed, from the way she had formerly regarded his company.

All that I said to you that night is true. I feel that truth more deeply with each passing day. My past actions are difficult to forgive—indeed, you may find it impossible to do so. But I urge you to recollect how it once was between us. No other woman has taken your place in my heart, which, I assure you, is not the callow, thoughtless organ it was four years ago. I offer it to you now, my dearest Miss Aurelia, in the hopes that you might find it within your own heart to forgive—and to permit me another chance to court you as you deserve...

Safe in the privacy of her own room, Aurelia exhaled shakily and laid the letter aside. Dear heaven, what on earth was she to say to such a missive?

Anger surged up, hot, fierce, and welcome. How dare he put her in this position, after all this time! Perhaps she should simply throw his letter on the fire and have done with it. But that would hardly deter him from sending another. Nor, if she were being wholly honest with herself, could she deny that his plea had stirred something inside of her, other than anger or scorn.

If only she could have felt nothing at all on reading his words. Indifference, not hate, was the true antithesis of love. And she had loved him so much once, with all a young girl's passion and ardor. Her disillusionment in him had been every bit as intense—and shattering. For the first time in her life, she had believed it was possible to die of a broken heart. But she had found the strength to go on, in spite of it. More to the point, she had found *herself* again, a victory of which she was justifiably proud and of which she would not allow Charlie or his family to deprive her.

And yet this letter must be answered, if only for her own peace of mind. But what could she possibly say, with her thoughts and feelings in such a jumble? If she could just talk to someone about all this—but neither her mother nor Amy was a possibility. The same went for her father or Andrew; the latter's face still darkened at even the mention of the Vandermeres.

Aurelia straightened up at a sudden inspiration: Claudine, her friend and sometime confidante. Older, sophisticated, a woman of the world—surely it could do no harm to write to her. And surely Claudine would have some guidance or, at the very least, some comfort to offer.

Crossing to her desk, she sat down and reached for pen and paper.

From Aurelia Leigh Newbold to Claudine Gabrielle Beaumont. 4 June 1891.

…I seem to have found myself in a situation I could never have predicted. The man of whom I spoke in Bad Ems, the one I hoped to meet again, is betrothed to my sister. And another man, whom I believed lost to me long ago, has renewed his suit. I cannot pretend that my feelings for him are as they once were. And yet I cannot deny that I do feel something. As you see, I cannot confide in my sister, nor even my mother. So, my dear friend, I have turned to you for some sorely needed advice…

Sixteen

This is my own, my native land...

—Sir Walter Scott, *Lay of the Last Minstrel*

"MY GOODNESS, I FEEL AS THOUGH WE'VE TRAVELED TO the ends of the earth!" Amy exclaimed, stepping out onto the railway platform in Truro.

"Some might consider Cornwall the next closest thing," Trevenan observed, turning to assist Mrs. Newbold and Aurelia down the last steps. Mr. Newbold and Andrew followed.

Aurelia glanced around the station, relieved that the long journey was over, or nearly so. The air felt soft against her face, and a watery sun glinted off the spires of a great stone building that looked like some sort of church. A *Gothic* church, Aurelia discovered, much to her surprise. She had not expected to find such a lofty edifice here, in a place that so many of their London acquaintances dismissed as a backwater.

Trevenan spoke up from behind her. "That's the Cathedral of the Blessed Virgin Mary."

Aurelia felt herself flushing at the realization that he'd been watching her. "Do you admire the new cathedral, Trevenan?"

"I have a preference for some of our smaller, more intimate churches, but this promises to be a handsome structure."

He smiled. "It's been several centuries, I believe, since a new cathedral was built in England. Perhaps I might offer you a tour at some point during your stay?"

"I'd like that. We all would, wouldn't we, Amy?" she appealed to her twin.

Amy glanced toward the cathedral. "Indeed. Very fine, I am sure," she said, sounding more dutiful than enthusiastic. "My lord, will we need to hire carriages to take us to Pentreath?"

Trevenan shook his head. "The carriages should arrive momentarily, my dear, if they are not here already. I wired my aunt two days ago with the full details of our arrival—" He broke off as a man in livery approached. "Ah, here we are!"

The earl's aunt had sent three carriages, enough to convey him, his guests, and their servants to Pentreath. Aurelia climbed resignedly into the same one as Amy and Trevenan, as her twin appeared to expect. Fortunately, Andrew chose to ride with them as well, so she no longer had to play goose-berry, as she had on the train.

Settling back against the seat, Aurelia found herself smiling in anticipation: adventure, a journey into the unknown. A year ago, she might have shied from the prospect; now, it seemed like a splendid idea, a welcome escape from the social whirl of London. "There is no Society there to speak of," one of Amy's witty friends had warned them, but Aurelia had personally found that idea more attractive than off-putting. Besides, she'd read that Truro boasted a theater, a museum, and some fine shops, all of which should please town-loving Amy.

She glanced at her twin, who seemed uncharacteristically quiet—weary from the long journey perhaps. Aurelia felt a little tired herself, and her left leg had begun to twinge; strangely, it seemed to prefer exercise to inactivity. Well, she might be able to appease it with some rambles in the country, or on the beaches for which Cornwall was so famous. Across from them, the earl appeared more relaxed, now that he was headed back to the place he loved best.

"How far are we from Pentreath, my lord?" Amy asked as the carriage began to move.

"Slightly more than a dozen miles. I'm afraid the train comes no closer as yet, though there's been talk of putting in a track between Truro and Newquay, just north of Trevenan."

"That would speed things up a bit," Andrew approved. "Not that I have anything against carriage rides," he added hastily. "It's just that I've gotten more used to the train."

"No offense taken," Trevenan assured him. "Progress is inevitable, after all."

"Is Newquay the town that's become something of a seaside resort?" Aurelia asked.

"Indeed." Trevenan sounded mildly regretful but resigned. "I understand several hotels have been built or are in the process of being built there. My maternal cousins—the Tresilians—tell me that the fashionable have taken to coming here in droves for sea-bathing and other such diversions. And I can't fault their taste—Newquay is beautiful in the summer."

"More beautiful than Trevenan or Pentreath?" Amy teased.

He smiled. "Oh, I don't know that I'd go that far. I'd say Trevenan has its own charms—and I admit I'm in no great hurry for the outside world to discover them yet."

"Tell us more. Unlike Relia, I haven't packed my trunk full of travel books of the area."

Aurelia blushed at Trevenan's quizzical glance. "I like knowing a bit beforehand about the places I'll be going," she explained. "It's just common sense, and it makes everything seem more real, somehow." She decided not to mention that she'd also packed *Tristram of Lyonesse*, with which she had quite fallen in love but which could not be described as even the least bit realistic. But to her way of thinking, one needed poetry as well as prose on one's travels.

"So it does," Trevenan agreed, and Aurelia thought he sounded approving. "Well, then," he turned back to Amy, "where should you like me to begin?"

"At the beginning, of course," she said with the air of one settling in for a bedtime story.

Trevenan chuckled, a low, warm sound that sent an answering ripple of warmth through Aurelia. Flustered, she darted a guilty glance at Amy, who appeared unaffected, and wondered how she could remain so in her intended's presence. "If I give you the full history of the Trelawneys at Trevenan, you will be asleep long before we reach our destination."

"Perhaps the most basic details, then," Aurelia suggested. "I understand Cornish to be a highly unusual tongue, and rarely spoken these days. What does 'Pentreath' mean?"

"'Top of the beach,' which is fitting, as Pentreath stands upon a rise overlooking the sea. One of my ancestors had a set of stairs carved into the stone, so he and his family could make their way directly down to the beach from the house. We've since improved on his efforts, and we keep that staircase in good repair, for our pleasure and that of our guests."

He warmed to his theme as the carriage wound its way along the country lanes, revealing that he had family in both the village of Trevenan and its nearest neighbor, St. Perran— home of his mother's relations, the Tresilians, whom he often visited. "Though rather less of late since I inherited," he added regretfully. "Between estate matters and my affairs in London, I haven't spent as much time with them as I would like. Nonetheless, my closest cousin and I are partners in the family mine, Wheal Felicity. I expect to see quite a lot of him on my return."

"I should be pleased to make his acquaintance," Amy assured him. "And the rest of the family, of course. Have you informed them of our engagement?"

"Indeed. I have written to Harry and his mother, my Aunt Isobel." He smiled at Amy. "They are all looking forward to meeting you."

Aurelia could hear the warmth in his voice when he

mentioned his mother's family, a contrast to his guarded tone when he spoke of his father's. She wondered if Amy had also noticed and deduced how important the Tresilians were to her betrothed. She did not doubt that her sister would charm them from the very first meeting. And if the Tresilians were as estimable as Trevenan's affection for them suggested, it would be no hardship to befriend them.

Andrew was now asking about the fishing in Cornwall, which Trevenan assured him was excellent. "We've pilchards and mackerel in the sea, and a stream for trout on the estate if you prefer not to venture out on the open water. Indeed," he added, his expression suddenly grave, "I would not advise a newcomer to brave the tides here without an experienced sailor beside him. The seas on the north coast can be very rough, even before the storms set in."

"Storms?" Amy sounded alarmed. "Do you have many of those here, my lord?"

"Some, mainly in the autumn and winter." He glanced at Amy with concern. "Does that frighten you, my dear?"

"Oh, not frighten, exactly," Amy said, not altogether truthfully. "But I confess, I'm not too fond of storms. I once saw a tree at our country home blasted by lightning when I was a girl. I've never forgotten it."

Aurelia remembered that day too. They'd been twelve or so, watching from their bedroom window when the lightning struck. And Amy, usually so bold, had paled on seeing the smoking remains of the horse-chestnut tree under which they'd so often played. She'd been frightened too, yet oddly exhilarated; for the first time, she had understood what Miss Witherspoon had told them about having to respect the raw power Nature had at her command. She had tried to share that understanding with Amy later, but her twin had only shuddered and pulled the bedclothes over her head.

"An alarming sight," Trevenan agreed with sympathy.

"But Pentreath has withstood many generations of storms, though not without some wear and tear," he added ruefully.

Amy relaxed, smiling back. "Oh, I'm sure we can deal with those now, Trevenan. Might I ask how repairs to the estate are going?"

"Well enough. I've had the roof fixed, and the main wing is sound. You and your family will be lodged there. The north wing is being renovated, but the overall structure of the house is in better condition than expected." Trevenan paused. "My late uncle—was not an easy man to live with, but he set great store by Pentreath. He was too proud to let it fall to rack and ruin, though he lacked the resources to maintain it as well toward the end of his life."

"Then it's fortunate indeed that matters have turned out as they have," Amy asserted. "Pentreath can be made as fine as it ever was—and perhaps even better." She paused in her turn, going slightly pink. "Er, if it is not too indelicate to ask, might I inquire about the plumbing?"

"Pentreath does have a water closet," Trevenan replied. "More than one, actually. And I've had central heating installed in the main wing, though not yet in the rest of the house."

"Oh, excellent," Amy declared. "I am especially relieved about the water closets."

"I think we're *all* relieved about those, Amy," Andrew put in dryly; Aurelia hid a smile.

Trevenan chuckled, unoffended. "I am pleased to have allayed your concerns, then. Pentreath does contain most modern conveniences, and my aunt, Lady Talbot, has taken pains that all should be in readiness for your stay. I trust her completely and hope you will as well."

"There can be no higher recommendation," Amy assured him. She glanced out the carriage window. "We're approaching a gateway, my lord. Does that mean we've arrived?"

Trevenan looked through his own window. "Indeed it

does." And Aurelia could hear the anticipation in his voice, the barely contained eagerness.

She understood that eagerness when their carriage passed through the gateway and bowled along the gentle curve leading up to the house. Aurelia caught her breath as Pentreath rose before them, solid and silvery-grey, its mullioned windows glinting in the light of the westering sun. The curving Dutch gables added a touch of whimsy that made her smile.

"Most of Pentreath was built during Tudor times," Trevenan said. "But improvements were made over the years—without altering the character of the house, I am happy to say."

"It's certainly a handsome estate," Amy observed. "In an unusual way. And the view must be splendid from those windows."

"There is hardly any prospect that can fail to please." The pride in the earl's voice was almost palpable. "I hope that you can see yourself as mistress here, Amy."

"Any woman would be proud to call herself mistress of such a place," she replied.

The carriage came to a stop, and they alighted before the short flight of steps leading to the massive front door. Trevenan's aunt awaited them at the foot of those steps. Remembering Lady Talbot's poise and graciousness, Aurelia was surprised to see hints of strain about her eyes and mouth now. Two other people stood beside her: a fair-haired woman and a rather weedy-looking gentleman. To judge from their expressions, neither appeared friendly.

"Good Lord! Helena?" Trevenan sounded at once surprised and aghast by these new arrivals. "And Durward? What brings you to Cornwall?"

"James, I tried to make her see sense," Lady Talbot began, but the remainder of her explanation was lost as the fair-haired woman straightened to her full height, stalked up to Trevenan, and dealt him a ringing slap across the face.

"Murderer!" she shrilled.

Seventeen

Open your ears; for which of you will stop
The vent of hearing when loud Rumour speaks?

—William Shakespeare, *2 Henry IV*

MURDERER. THE ANCIENT STONES OF PENTREATH SEEMED to give back the echo.

Dumbstruck, Aurelia stared at Trevenan, who had gone slightly pale but appeared otherwise composed. His face bore the reddening mark of the fair-haired woman's hand, but he did not so much as raise his own to touch it.

"That's quite a greeting, cousin," he said at last, his tone level, almost uninflected. "Whom am I supposed to have murdered?"

Cousin? Aurelia looked more closely at—Helena, Trevenan had called her—but saw no close resemblance. This must be one of his other relations, from his father's side of the family.

"Don't play the innocent with me, *cousin*!" Helena practically spat the last word at him. "The coroner may have exonerated you in my brother's death, but *I* am not so blind!"

Aurelia felt her sister stiffen beside her, heard Andrew's faint intake of breath. For her part, she remained silent, watching the cousins intently.

Trevenan said as calmly as before, "I have done nothing of which I need be ashamed where Gerald was concerned. I am sorry for your loss, Helena, but I am not responsible for it."

"Indeed not!" Lady Talbot stepped between her niece and nephew. "And the sooner you accept that and stop conducting yourself like a madwoman or a spoiled child the better!"

Helena's face grew mottled. "Simply because you have always taken his part against Gerald's or mine—"

"That will do!" Trevenan's voice rang with an authority Aurelia had never heard him use before. It had the welcome effect of silencing Helena, though she still practically vibrated with fury. "I understand you have a quarrel with me, cousin, but I will not have you enacting an ill-bred scene before my guests. Pelham," he addressed a black-clad butler who had just appeared in the doorway. "Please escort Lord and Lady Durward to the library for the time being."

"Very good, my lord," the butler returned with the imperturbable calm Aurelia had come to associate with English servants. "Lord Durward, Lady Durward—if you will follow me?"

"This isn't over," Helena hissed up at Trevenan, who merely inclined his head. Incensed by his lack of response, she gathered up her skirts with a sharp twitch and stalked up the steps and into the house. Lord Durward, clearly a nonentity, shot Trevenan what might have been an apologetic look and all but skulked after his wife.

Trevenan exchanged a significant glance with his aunt, then turned back to face his guests. "I am sorry you were all subjected to that. Forgive me."

"There's nothing to forgive." To Aurelia's relief, Amy showed no sign of being affected by Lady Durward's venom. "Having unpleasant relations is a cross many of us have to bear."

"Well, rest assured that they shall be dealt with promptly," he replied. "In the meantime, Amy, may I present to you my aunt, Lady Talbot? Aunt Judith, this is my intended, Amelia Newbold, her sister Miss Aurelia, and their brother Mr. Andrew."

"I am delighted to meet you all." Lady Talbot smiled warmly. "And I bid you welcome to Pentreath. Your parents have accompanied you too, Miss Newbold?"

"They have, Lady Talbot," Amy replied. She glanced over her shoulder. "Indeed, I believe that is their carriage just entering the gate."

Aurelia followed her sister's gaze and saw the two remaining carriages now approaching the house. How fortunate that their parents were arriving now and not five minutes earlier, when Lady Durward was throwing about those vile accusations!

Moments later, Lady Talbot was welcoming Mr. and Mrs. Newbold to Pentreath and inviting everyone inside for a cup of tea and some light refreshment while the servants took their luggage up. Trevenan excused himself with a smile and disappeared into the depths of the house.

Aurelia gazed after him, suspecting he'd gone to deal with those awful Durwards. Fervently wishing him every success, she followed Lady Talbot and the rest of their party inside.

Helena, pacing the floor like a caged tigress, rounded on James the moment he entered the library. "How dare you keep me waiting, like some hireling!"

"How dare *you* arrive uninvited and make a scene in front of my guests?" he countered, meeting her fire with ice. "A Billingsgate fishwife would have shown more self-restraint."

The comparison infuriated Helena enough to shock her into silence, though James knew better than to hope it would last. He studied her dispassionately as she flushed and sputtered. Like Gerald, she was tall, fair, and large-boned—not a bad-looking woman, in an Amazonian way. Also like Gerald, she could be domineering, even something of a bully. Despite her rank and dowry, she'd gone three London Seasons without an offer, for which James suspected her disposition was largely to blame. When Lord Durward had broached his suit during her fourth Season, her father had practically demanded she accept his proposal or risk being disinherited.

James glanced at the earl, lurking in a far corner of the room and looking distinctly uncomfortable, and wondered—not for the first time—how such a mild, self-effacing man could have brought himself to marry a termagant like Helena. Money, he suspected, and she had produced an heir within the last year. Little doubt that she ruled the roost at their estate in Wiltshire. It probably came as a rude shock that she could not do so here at Pentreath.

To his regret, Helena found her tongue at last. "I suppose a miner's brat would know all about Billingsgate fishwives!"

"Mine *owner's* brat," James corrected, without rancor. He had long since ceased to respond to gibes about his mother's family. As far as he was concerned, the Tresilians needed no defending—unlike the Trelawneys. He crossed over to his desk and sat down, knowing it would infuriate Helena to see him making himself at ease. "From your earlier outburst, I gather that you have concerns regarding Gerald's death," he resumed coolly. "Now, if you have something of substance to say, cousin, then say it. If you have merely come here to spew abuse and unfounded accusations, then you and Durward may depart this instant."

The earl uttered a self-deprecating cough. "I think, Trevenan, you'll find my wife has cause for concern," he began tentatively, only to be silenced by Helena's basilisk glare.

"They are *not* unfounded!" Turning back to James, she reached into her reticule and drew out an envelope. "This letter arrived at my home in Wiltshire three days ago!" she snapped, flinging it onto the desk before him. "Now read that, and tell me—if you dare—how I am mistaken!"

James picked up the letter, examining the envelope first: no return address, and Helena's name and direction were printed in block capitals—difficult, if not impossible, to trace. He experienced a sudden unease as he extracted the single sheet of stationery. Good quality paper, heavy and smooth. But he kept his face impassive as he unfolded the page and read the contents.

No direct salutation, he noticed at once, and the thick, slanting handwriting was unfamiliar, but it was the tone—slyly insinuating rather than openly accusatory—that set his teeth on edge. Halfway down the page, his own name jumped out at him, and he read more closely.

> *—that while he has not soiled his hands with the blood of his predecessor, he may have attained his present position through means no gentleman would employ. Indeed, it is rumored in the county that, with the aid of his confederates, Sir H—— T———— and R———— P————, he did enlist the services of ruffians to accost the late Lord Trevenan as he walked the cliffs on this past New Year's Eve, resulting in the untimely death of his lordship. Proof of this vile deed has been found and will be offered once certain conditions are met.*

It was signed "A Concerned Friend."

James stared at the letter a moment longer, feeling the slow roil of anger in his stomach. Of all the vile, damnable slurs…

"Well?" Helena demanded sharply. "Do you deny it?"

"Entirely," he replied, dropping the letter back onto the desk. "If that letter represents the sum of your evidence against me, cousin, I can't say much for your powers of discernment. Or your correspondent's reliability, for that matter. I haven't much use for someone who lacks the conviction either to identify these supposed culprits by name or to sign his own."

She flushed an unbecoming scarlet. "Doubtless he feared

reprisals from you and your—confederates!" Snatching up the letter again, she brandished it furiously at him. "But I'll wager *you* know who they are! And I demand that you tell me at once!"

James rose to his feet; his cousin was a tall woman, but he still topped her by several inches, an advantage he was fully prepared to exploit at the moment. "So that you may slander two more innocent men? I think not."

Helena drew an affronted breath, but before she could launch into another heated tirade, the library door opened and Lady Talbot entered the room.

"Our guests are being shown to their chambers now," she reported. "So I've come to see if I could be of any assistance here."

"Thank you," James said.

"Hiding behind our aunt's skirts again?" Helena gibed. "Well, it won't help you this time! *I* know now, and the rest of the world will too, how you schemed against my brother!"

"The rest of the world will know better than to credit *your* baseless slanders, Helena!" Lady Talbot retorted quellingly.

"Not baseless—I have proof of what I say!" Helena thrust the letter under her aunt's nose.

At James's nod, Lady Talbot took the letter and read it through.

"Oh, this is absurd!" she exclaimed, looking up a few minutes later. "Nothing more than gossip, hearsay, and malicious innuendo! You're a fool to put any credence in it, Helena. But then you were ever one to jump to conclusions," she added scathingly.

Helena's nostrils flared. "A fool, am I? Well, we'll see about that." She glared at James. "How would your fine guests like to know how you inherited your title? Your rich American bride and her even richer father?"

James held on to his patience—barely. "As I said before, I have nothing to hide or of which to be ashamed. My future in-laws are already aware of the circumstances under which I inherited—and that I was cleared of any possible involvement in Gerald's death. You would do well," he added, "to consider who might have written to you with such insinuations nearly six months after the fact. And what his motives for doing so might be."

"And what he hopes to gain by it," Lady Talbot added. She glanced down at the letter still in her hand. "'Proof of this vile deed has been found and will be offered once certain conditions are met.' If that doesn't sound like a bid for remuneration, I don't know what does." She regarded her niece with cool disfavor. "For the right price, your correspondent could no doubt produce 'evidence' implicating James in the Whitechapel Murders. Try to show a little sense, Helena. You're past the age for such credulous folly."

For just a moment, James saw Helena's bravado waver, the flicker of doubt in her eyes. Then she rallied. "You think to dismiss me with that? Well, I won't have it! I *will* be answered, and Gerald will have justice!"

"Indeed he will," James broke in smoothly.

Helena stopped short, eyes narrowing. "What do you mean by that?"

"I mean that, while I am not the least bit culpable, I have come to the conclusion that the circumstances of Gerald's death are mysterious enough to warrant further investigation," he replied. "At the very least, I should like to discover the source of the rumors reported in that letter. Two other men, whom I believe as innocent as myself, have been libeled—if only by implication. I owe it to us all to locate and silence their defamer before their reputations and honor are irretrievably damaged."

"Fine words," she scoffed. "Well, *I* won't be silenced, cousin, or sent away!"

"I had not thought to suggest it," James replied evenly. "If you seek answers, you are best off remaining in Cornwall for the present."

Helena gave him a tight-lipped nod. "I shall stay here, of course," she announced, flinging out the words like a challenge.

James inclined his head. "You are a Trelawney born, and an earl's daughter. I would not deny your right to stay here, especially since you have traveled such a distance." He spared a moment to be thankful that the Durwards' infant heir had been left in Wiltshire with his nurse.

His aunt's face showed a brief flicker of dismay, but consummate hostess that she was, she quickly concealed it. "It shall be as you say, James." She turned to her niece. "I shall summon Pelham to see that chambers are prepared for you and Durward. Your old rooms will suffice, I think," she added in a tone that brooked no argument.

If Helena was offended by the not too subtle implication that James's other guests were occupying the best chambers, she had the sense not to show it. Instead, she nodded stiffly, while Durward murmured a pallid acknowledgment of James's hospitality and fell silent again.

A flurry of activity followed, and then the Durwards were conveyed upstairs, Helena throwing a triumphant glance over her shoulder at James as she left. He kept his expression neutral, betraying neither displeasure nor dismay at her continued presence in his home.

"Well," his aunt remarked, when they were alone in the library, "that was—unpleasant."

"Deeply," James agreed.

"I wouldn't have blamed you if you'd sent them both off to an inn. We Cornish may be hospitable, but I'm not sure hospitality should extend to those intent on slandering their host."

"Likely not. But better she be lodged under this roof, where we can keep an eye on her, rather than elsewhere, spreading her poison throughout the county."

"There is that," Lady Talbot acknowledged.

"I'm bearing that old saying in mind: keep your friends

close and your enemies closer." James pulled a face. "I realize there's no affection between Helena and myself, but I had not thought of her as an enemy."

"Unfortunately, that appears to be how she regards *you*." Lady Talbot glanced at the letter, now lying on James's desk. "What do you mean to do with that?"

"Hold on to it, for now. If I destroyed it, I would appear guilty indeed. And, libelous though it is, this letter represents evidence of some grudge against me—and my relations."

"Sir Harry Tresilian, you mean."

"So you recognized the initials."

"I recognized *his*. Unlike Joshua, I saw no reason to shun your mother's family, and Sir Harry has always seemed an estimable young man. But I have no idea whom R. P. might be."

"Nor I. Harry might, however, once he sees this." James locked the letter in the topmost drawer of his desk. "I'll ride over tomorrow and show it to him. Perhaps he can also tell me if this malicious rumor is indeed spreading through the county. But tonight," he smiled wryly at his aunt, "we have the Newbolds to entertain. If such a thing is possible, under the circumstances."

"You may leave that to me," Lady Talbot asserted. "I will not allow Helena to poison your guests against you, or mar what was supposed to be a pleasant interlude for you and your intended bride. My dear niece," she added in a tone that was anything but affectionate, "will keep a civil tongue in her head while she's under this roof, if she knows what's good for her!"

Knowing both women, James felt fairly certain of his aunt's success. "Thank you. I am deeply grateful Talbot was able to spare you this month. Though you may have got more than you bargained for, coming here," he added ruefully.

"Nonsense, I am a Trelawney, a Cornishwoman, and more than equal to any rubbish Helena serves out. We'll find a way to nip that nasty rumor in the bud." She patted his arm. "Gerald's death was a shock and a tragedy—if only because he did not live long enough to improve his character. But I have never once believed you involved with it, even before the coroner's evidence exonerated you completely."

"One wonders why that wasn't enough for Helena," James remarked. Despite himself, he could not prevent a hint of bitterness from creeping into his tone. "From the sound of it, she actively *wants* me to be guilty, though for what reason I cannot imagine."

His aunt sighed. "Oh, who knows what ails her this time? She was always a willful, headstrong child, better at making enemies than friends. But in all fairness, neither her father nor her mother did right by her. Joshua cared only for Pentreath, and Augusta cared only for Gerald. And Gerald himself was quite the egoist, as we both know. Well, put all this from your mind tonight, if you can," she added briskly. "Your guests are here, expecting a fine dinner and a pleasant evening. We shall ensure that they have both."

"Indeed, we shall," James agreed, with a new appreciation for her sangfroid. "So, I had best go up and wash, hadn't I?"

He kissed his aunt's cheek and strode from the room.

Refreshed after a nap and a hot bath, Aurelia dried her hair before the fire and studied her chamber. Such a pretty room, decorated in soft blues, silvery greys, with the faintest touches of green—like the sea on a misty summer morning. The bed's canopy was worked in the same misty blues and greys as the curtains at the window, which afforded a stunning view of the sea in the distance. According to Tamsin, the housemaid who'd conveyed her upstairs, this had been Lady Talbot's room as a girl. Aurelia hoped her family was equally pleased with their chambers.

With characteristic efficiency, Suzanne had put away all of

Aurelia's clothes while her mistress slept. Now she laid out a dinner gown and matching slippers in a soft, misty shade of green; sea green, Aurelia thought with a smile. And pearls for adornment, she decided—the strand she'd received for her birthday—and her teardrop pearl earrings. Suzanne approved her choice and brought out silver-and-pearl combs for her hair as well.

Once Aurelia was dressed for dinner, Suzanne draped a light shawl about her shoulders, observing—a touch critically—that it seemed cooler in Cornwall than in London.

"Indeed it does," Aurelia replied. "But I understand that high summer is approaching, and Cornwall becomes beautifully warm then. Even the sea."

Suzanne still looked dubious. "If you say so, mademoiselle."

Aurelia hid a smile as she smoothed her gloves. "I'll go and see how my sister is faring," she said, and slipped out of her chamber.

Amy's room was located a short distance down the passage; Aurelia knocked lightly on the door. "Amy, are you ready?"

"Not yet, Relia," her twin called back. "But please, come in."

Aurelia obeyed, closing the door behind her. Amy was sitting at the dressing table, while Mariette brushed and coiled her hair into an elegant upsweep.

"You look lovely, dearest," Aurelia said, smiling at her.

Her twin wore ivory tonight—a good shade for her, usually, but she looked slightly pale. Weary from the journey, Aurelia wondered, or—the unwelcome reminder struck her—troubled by the unpleasant business that had marred their arrival? How had Lord Trevenan dealt with Lady Durward and her dreadful accusations? Aurelia could only hope he'd sent her packing.

"Amy, are you feeling quite well?" she asked.

"I'm fine," Amy said, perhaps too quickly. "Only a little tired after all that traveling." She applied a drop of scent from a crystal bottle to the inside of her wrist; the mingled scents of rose and jasmine perfumed the air. "You look very well yourself," she remarked, sliding her gaze in Aurelia's direction. "And not the least bit weary."

"I napped for nearly an hour, and a bath took care of the rest. Amy," Aurelia hesitated for a moment, "have you heard anything regarding Lord Trevenan's other—visitors?"

"The Durwards, you mean?" Amy pulled a face. "Lady Talbot stopped by to tell me—warn me, rather—that they will be staying at Pentreath as well."

"Good heavens, really?" Aurelia asked, appalled.

Amy nodded, then desisted at a reproving "zut!" from Mariette as she pinned her mistress's last curl into place. "Unfortunately, yes. But according to Lady Talbot, this is a family matter that's best addressed by having her remain here." She sighed. "James made the decision himself. Lady Talbot assures me that the Durwards will not be permitted to make trouble during their stay. She's even had them put in chambers as far from ours as possible. Still, having them under the same roof is bound to be disagreeable. A pity this estate doesn't have a dower house!"

"I will bring your gloves and shawl now, mademoiselle," Mariette announced and whisked away to the other end of the room where the chest of drawers stood.

"Amy," Aurelia lowered her voice, "what do you know of Lady Durward's accusation?"

"Oh, it's nonsense, of course," Amy said at once. "Trevenan's cousin died last January in a fall. There was an inquest, but the coroner said it was an accident—and that he was, well, somewhat intoxicated at the time. I don't recall ever meeting him last year," she added with a slight frown. "He'd have been Viscount Alston then. Aunt Caroline told me that he was the hearty sportsman-type, mainly interested in hunting and shooting—and in no hurry to wed.

"In any case, I know James had nothing to do with his death. He was miles away at the time, and he's got tons of witnesses to prove it. And Papa already knows about this too. James told him when he first asked to court me. I should think all of us have more sense than to believe that spiteful harpy. She's probably hoping for something—money, most likely."

To buy her silence? Aurelia wondered. An uncomfortable thought, indeed.

"James must have the patience of a saint to deal with her as he has," her sister went on. "Not to mention allowing her to stay here after the way she behaved. *I* should have shown her the door at once, and enlisted the staff to send her on her way if she refused to go!"

"Perhaps he hopes to contain her in some way," Aurelia speculated. "I should think it would be far worse to have Lady Durward running all over Cornwall with her accusations, or worse, spreading her slanders in London."

"True," Amy acknowledged. "Not that anyone with a grain of sense would credit what she says. But she could still make life hideously unpleasant for James in the meantime."

And for me. The words hung unspoken on the air.

"I am sure he'll find some way to deal with her," Aurelia said soothingly. "Or Lady Talbot will; she certainly seems formidable enough."

Mariette returned to drape a silk shawl over her mistress's shoulders and fasten the pearl buttons on her evening gloves. Amy thanked her somewhat absently, then rose with a militant sparkle in her blue eyes. "Well, I just hope that harridan won't be joining us at dinner!"

Fortunately, there was no sign of Lady Durward or her husband when they entered the drawing room. According to Lady Talbot, her nephew's other guests had elected to take their meals in their rooms. Aurelia strongly suspected their hostess had influenced that decision, but she could only be thankful the Durwards had absented themselves, for everyone's sake.

She glanced at Trevenan, who was presently standing by

the mantelpiece gazing into the fire; the imprint of Lady Durward's hand could no longer be seen on his cheek, but his dark eyes held an abstracted, even troubled look. What a miserable homecoming this must be for him, she thought with a rush of sympathy. She did not doubt his innocence any more than Amy did. What reason could Lady Durward have to accuse him, and why did she seem to hate him so?

Even as she watched, Lord Trevenan straightened up and came to greet them. True to his breeding, he made no reference to that ugly business in the courtyard, but offered his arm to Mrs. Newbold to begin the formal promenade into dinner. Lady Talbot partnered Mr. Newbold, leaving Andrew to escort his sisters.

The dining room was somewhat cool but not unbearably so. Aurelia's shawl afforded her enough protection from stray draughts, and a fire burned cheerily in the grate. Lord Trevenan and Lady Talbot presided over opposite ends of the table, draped in pale damask and set with gleaming Crown Derby china and silverware so highly polished one could see one's face in it.

Dinner was excellent—a touch plainer than what Aurelia had seen on London tables, but the food was handsomely presented, savory, and plentiful. The fish was especially good, not surprising as Pentreath was so close to the sea. Oyster soup was followed by soles browned in butter, then spring lamb with mint sauce and new potatoes, and two chickens spit-roasted to a rich golden-brown. A sweet course of fresh fruit—strawberries and cherries—and a blackberry tart with cream ended the meal. Aurelia ate with genuine relish and was glad to see that her family also appeared to be enjoying the food; the long journey seemed to have given all of them an appetite.

Conversation was light, even desultory, ranging over a variety of topics that might have been purposely chosen not to give offense. After what had happened earlier, Trevenan and Lady Talbot were no doubt intent on maintaining a relaxed, convivial atmosphere. Not having witnessed that exchange with the Durwards, Aurelia's parents were perfectly at ease; Andrew too seemed inclined to accept the situation at face value. Aurelia wished she could do the same instead of feeling like there was a cache of dynamite with a slowly burning fuse stashed away upstairs. She glanced at Amy, but her twin's face was an alabaster mask: calm and unreadable.

After dinner, the women left the men to their port, proceeding to the drawing room where Lady Talbot offered a choice of tea or coffee. Aurelia accepted a cup of coffee, then gazed about the room, admiring its understated elegance. The house's Tudor charm was evident here: The exposed roof-beams were varnished to a dark gloss, while the walls were painted a contrasting shade of warm white, setting off several oil paintings and a marvelous tapestry woven in deep greens, warm reds, and rich saffrons. Aurelia resolved to have a closer look later.

The rest of the furnishings appeared to have been chosen with equal care—from the chairs and sofa upholstered in muted blue-and-green brocade to the tables, bookcases, and curio cabinets all gleaming with polish. A grand piano stood in the far corner, and the room itself was lightly redolent of citrus potpourri and beeswax. Aurelia took an appreciative breath, feeling oddly at ease. Pentreath might not be as splendid as some of the great estates she and her family had visited, but it seemed far more comfortable, even welcoming: a home and not a showplace.

Lady Talbot's voice recalled her to the present. "Pentreath has not really had a proper mistress since my mother died," the viscountess was saying. "I acted as one for only a few years before my own marriage. And Augusta—my brother Joshua's wife—preferred the Shires, where her family came from, or London." She smiled at Amy. "I am pleased to know that will change, when you and James are married."

"I think Pentreath a very handsome estate, Lady Talbot," Amy declared. "And I look forward to discovering more about Cornwall, as Trevenan has such a deep attachment to it."

"Oh, James is Cornish to the bone, never happier than when he is here! His father was just the same—and his uncle," she added, with the air of one trying to give the latter his due. "I too love my birthplace dearly, and try to spend some time here every summer."

Aurelia couldn't help wondering where the Durwards fit into all this, or the late earl, for that matter. The picture that was emerging of this family was not entirely comforting. Trevenan had mentioned that his uncle was not an easy man to live with, but he had loved his estate. His wife clearly hadn't shared that affection. In what other ways might they have been ill-suited? And how might the children of an unhappy marriage have turned out, and how might they have treated another child whom they possibly saw as an interloper? She thought of Lady Durward's venom toward Trevenan and suppressed a shiver. If Gerald had treated his cousin with the same open hostility and contempt, it was little wonder that James spoke so seldom of him.

"Lady Talbot," Amy began, "that painting over the fireplace—is that one of Thomas Sheridan's works?"

Aurelia glanced toward the painting, which showed a light-house poised like a shining white column against a seascape of vivid blues and greens. Sparsely detailed but striking.

"Why, yes," her hostess confirmed. "You have a good eye, my dear."

Amy shook her head. "I saw this painting, or one very like it, in Mr. Sheridan's studio."

"I don't doubt it's the same one," Lady Talbot replied. "James purchased it and had it sent down last week, with specific instructions on where it was to be hung. It replaced a rather stodgy classical painting of Hades abducting Persephone, as I recall. This is far more pleasing."

"Mr. Sheridan is a very talented artist," Amy declared, with an enthusiasm that surprised her twin. "I've commissioned him to paint my portrait as a wedding gift for James."

"An excellent idea. I understand that Mr. Sheridan is to arrive next week. Do you mean to sit for him then?" At Amy's nod, she added, "There are several rooms here that might serve as a studio. At any rate, you'll find plenty of likely settings for your portrait at Pentreath."

The drawing room door opened then, and the men came to join them. As Lady Talbot busied herself over the coffee service, Aurelia slipped away to examine the tapestry, which depicted a brightly clad procession bearing torches, sheaves of wheat, and bushels of fruit—a celebration of the harvest, by the looks of it. She admired the workmanship, then drifted over to the gleaming Broadwood piano, every bit as fine as the Érard in their Grosvenor Square house.

She was standing over the keyboard, idly wondering if the piano was in tune, when she sensed his presence just at her shoulder. "You must have read my mind, Miss Aurelia. I was hoping I might prevail upon you and Amy to honor us with a song."

Aurelia glanced up at him. He'd been the perfect host tonight, showing no sign of the strain that must be taking its toll on him. But perhaps there was a hint of weariness about his fine dark eyes. "I would be happy to oblige, Lord Trevenan." She ran an admiring hand over the top of the piano. "This is a beautiful instrument. Has it been in the family for many years?"

He nodded. "It belonged to my grandmother, originally. Aunt Judith and my cousin Jessica are the only ones in the family who play now, so the piano's been sadly neglected of late. But my aunt tells me it has been recently tuned. I would be delighted to hear it in regular use."

Music—it seemed little enough comfort to offer, but Aurelia was ready to give it all the same. "Of course," she said at once. "Is there anything you particularly wish to hear tonight?"

"I am happy to leave the choice up to you and Amy," he replied. "But there are a number of songbooks in that bookcase over there, if you care to look through them."

She smiled. "Thank you. I'll do just that."

"Then I'll send Amy over to help you look." He began to move away.

"Lord Trevenan?" She kept her voice low, even as the words practically leapt out of her. "I hope—all is well with you," she ventured as he turned back, his expression quizzical.

"Perfectly well, Miss Aurelia. But I thank you for your concern." His smile did not quite reach his eyes. "I'll send your sister to you now."

She could not help watching as he walked away. If only there was something she could do to help him. But he seemed determined to handle this alone—she only hoped he could weather the storm. Stifling a sigh, she turned to the bookcase to begin her search.

Eighteen

Constant you are,
But yet a woman; and for secrecy,
No lady closer...

—William Shakespeare, *1 Henry IV*

MUCH TO AURELIA'S SURPRISE, MARIETTE RESPONDED to her light tap on Amy's door the following morning. Mademoiselle was indisposed, the maid informed her in a low voice, and—given the nature of her particular ailment—likely to remain in bed for the rest of the day.

Aurelia grimaced in sympathy, easily deciphering her meaning. Amy always had a much harder time than she with her monthly courses. She'd be most comfortable in bed, with hot bricks at her back and a pot of some soothing tisane close by. Fortunately, Mariette seemed to have things well under control, and a breakfast tray had already been requested from the kitchen.

Feeling oddly exposed without her twin beside her, Aurelia went down to breakfast alone. She located the breakfast parlor without difficulty: a cheerful little room with butter-yellow walls and windows facing east into the sunrise.

Lady Talbot—currently the sole occupant of the room—looked up from her place at the table and smiled a greeting. "Good morning, Miss—Aurelia, is it not? You must forgive me," she added as Aurelia nodded confirmation, "you and your sister are so very alike."

If it was a lie, it was a kind one at least, Aurelia thought as she smiled back. "Amy finds herself a bit under the weather this morning and will be taking her breakfast in bed."

"Oh, dear!" Lady Talbot sounded genuinely concerned. "I hope it is not serious?"

Aurelia shook her head. "She will be fine, with time and a bit of rest."

"Ah. I am glad to hear it." To Aurelia's relief, Lady Talbot inquired no further as to the nature of Amy's indisposition; perhaps she suspected the cause, in any case. "The breakfast dishes are laid out on the sideboard. Pray help yourself."

"Am I the first one down?" Aurelia inquired, picking up a plate from the table.

"You are the first I've seen of your family today," Lady Talbot informed her. "However, James has already breakfasted and gone out riding. He's always been an early riser."

Aurelia hardly knew whether to ask about the other guests. She supposed it was too much to hope for that the Durwards might have come to their senses and decamped during the night.

As if reading her thoughts, Lady Talbot said, "Helena and her husband have opted to have trays sent to their chambers."

Opted…somehow Aurelia doubted the choice had been left entirely up to the Durwards, but she was relieved not to be confronting that seething hostility first thing in the morning. She couldn't help wondering, though, how long Lady Talbot could persuade her niece to keep away from the rest of the house party. Short of locking her in her room or throwing her in a dungeon—and Pentreath did not seem to be equipped with the latter.

Banishing such unpleasant thoughts, she approached the

heavy mahogany sideboard, where an array of silver chafing dishes—kept warm by the flames of spirit lamps—awaited her attention. One held porridge, blessedly unlike the lumpy mess that was too often produced by their own cook back in New York. Others held eggs, boiled and coddled, sausages, kippers, streaky bacon, and tender ham fried crisp at the edges. There were a few more exotic dishes as well, such as kedgeree and deviled kidneys. Aurelia couldn't help wrinkling her nose a bit at the latter. She had never understood the English passion for kidneys and other such organ meats, although she thought they did breakfast splendidly in every other respect.

"If there is something you would like but do not see on the sideboard, you have but to ask and it will be prepared for you," Lady Talbot suggested.

"Oh, no—this all looks wonderful!" Aurelia assured her hastily. "I can't imagine needing anything more. I should become the size of a featherbed if I ate this well all the time." She helped herself to coddled eggs, ham, and a small portion of kedgeree, then sat down opposite her hostess. Everything tasted as good as it looked, she discovered on the first delicious mouthful.

Lady Talbot passed her the toast rack. "How did you sleep, Miss Aurelia?" she inquired.

"Very well, thank you." Aurelia took a slice of toast and spread it with strawberry preserves, bright as rubies in their cut-glass bowl. "I think I even heard the sea in the distance."

"You can indeed." Lady Talbot smiled reminiscently. "I would hear it myself every night when I was a girl, sleeping in that chamber. The sound is better than a lullaby."

"I was wondering if I might perhaps have a closer look at the sea today," Aurelia said, pouring herself a cup of tea from the silver service on the table. "What would be the most direct route down to the beach? Lord Trevenan mentioned that there was a staircase."

"Yes, the north staircase. The pitch is not too steep, and there is a banister to hold on to, but the climb does take a while if you are unused to it. You might be better off leaving by the main gateway and making your way down to the cove, though it will take somewhat longer."

Aurelia shook her head. "I would prefer to chance the stairs, thank you. I daresay the exercise will do me good."

"I see you have an adventurous streak, my dear." To Aurelia's surprise, Lady Talbot sounded almost pleased, rather than disapproving.

"Oh, Amy's the daring one in our family," Aurelia replied. "I simply have a great fondness for the sea. When we'd go to Newport during the summer, I would often be the first one up and about." Sitting on the veranda in the mornings, breathing in the bracing salty air…and waiting—or rather, hoping—for Charlie to wander by, she remembered suddenly. The summer before her accident, they had contrived to meet several times in just such a fashion.

She had not thought of Charlie since they'd left London; he seemed very far away just now, and she was glad of it.

"I have never been to America myself," Lady Talbot remarked, "but I have heard that Newport is considered quite the hub of Society there in the summer. Much as Torquay has become here. Is Newport a very exclusive place?"

"Indeed—almost excessively so," Aurelia confessed. "Nearly every prominent family goes there, and so do those aspiring to prominence." She thought of their own status: accepted but not wholly welcome among the more established clans, never entirely certain whether their company would be embraced or rebuffed. "I suppose it's not too different from London during the Season: a whirl of activities, and a very strict code of conduct. Drives to the casino and tennis matches in the morning, sea-bathing just before noon, luncheon aboard someone's yacht, afternoon promenades along Bellevue Avenue, then perhaps a formal dinner followed by a dance. And then up the next morning to start it all over again."

"Gracious, how exhausting!" Lady Talbot exclaimed. "Even in my day, I'm not sure I'd have had the stamina to endure such a giddy round."

Needs must, Aurelia thought, remembering the desperate quest for respectability that drove so many who flocked to Newport each summer. Aloud she suggested, "Perhaps the sea air has something to do with it."

"Perhaps, though there's no shortage of sea air in Cornwall and things are considerably quieter here. I don't doubt that Newport is lovely, but it does sound a bit regimented."

Aurelia smiled. "You would be right on both counts, Lady Talbot. There *is* much to admire in Newport, but I shall find it a relief not to have to conform to such a strict schedule."

Lady Talbot smiled back. "Well, I hope you find Cornwall to your liking, my dear. Are you quite set on attempting the stairs today?" At Aurelia's nod, she continued, "You can reach them through a door in the garden wall. I'll have the key brought for you after breakfast."

"Thank you," Aurelia said. "I'm very much looking forward to the excursion."

They conversed lightly through the rest of their meal, undisturbed by the rest of the party. Afterwards, Lady Talbot had a footman fetch the key for her guest, then gave Aurelia instructions on how to reach the garden. "I trust you will be careful," she added, a little tentatively. "No one has yet had an accident on those stairs, but I should not like for you to be the first. You might consider taking a companion—your maid, perhaps? I would accompany you myself if I did not have certain responsibilities to attend to this morning."

Which doubtless included keeping a pair of uninvited guests out of the house party's way, Aurelia thought. She wondered if Lady Talbot had noticed her limp; well, if she had, there were worse ways to express concern. As confidently as possible, she replied, "I wouldn't dream of taking you away from your duties, Lady Talbot. And there's no need to trouble Suzanne or wake up the rest of my family. I won't rush my descent. Never fear—I'm accustomed to taking extra precautions in a new place. And I should be back well before luncheon."

Lady Talbot relaxed, reassured by this display of common sense. "Well, then, enjoy your adventure, my dear. You will be on Trevenan land, so you needn't worry about being disturbed by anyone who does not belong here. I look forward to hearing your impressions of our beach."

Pocketing the key, Aurelia returned to her chamber. The morning light was still pale, but, on glancing out the window, she fancied the sun was emerging with more conviction now. Ten minutes later, garbed appropriately in a plain blue muslin frock, low canvas shoes, and a wide-brimmed straw hat, she left the house, making for the garden before anyone could stop her.

Lady Talbot's directions were exemplary, and she soon found herself wandering through a fragrant oasis of spring and summer blooms. She made a mental note to come back and explore the garden at a later opportunity. But the door in the high stone wall stood before her now, and she could hear the muted rush and roar of the sea below, a sound that made her pulse quicken with excitement. She fitted the key in the lock, opened the door, and stepped onto the first stair.

The stone shelf felt broad and reassuringly solid beneath her feet; looking down, she saw the rest of the stairs were similarly cut: wide, flat, and spaced just enough apart. The banister was stone as well, weathered but sturdy. Grasping it firmly, Aurelia made her way leisurely down the stairs. Even with her leg, she found the descent fairly easy, and she soon reached the bottom, stepping from stone onto soft sand.

The beach stretched before her, a pale expanse that darkened at the water's edge. On impulse, Aurelia slipped off her shoes, felt the sand fine as crumbled sugar beneath her feet. Yielding further, she dared to peel off her stockings, shivered in sensual pleasure at the touch of cool sand against her skin. Mama never let her go barefoot at home, or brave the summer sun without a hat or a parasol. But what Mama did not know wouldn't hurt her, Aurelia reasoned. Shoes in hand, she made her way down the beach, not stopping until the incoming tide lapped over her toes. She let out an involuntary gasp at the chill and took a half-step back, then looked up and out at the surging sea.

In the morning sun, the tumbling waves were silvery-blue, shot through with green. And so clear—like glass, almost. *"As the wave's subtler emerald is pierced through / With the inextricable heaven's deeper blue,"* Aurelia murmured aloud, remembering the description from *Tristram of Lyonesse*. And the foam on the towering breakers shone whiter than a seagull's back and swirled into patterns more intricate than antique lace.

Newport was nothing like this. Not so wild, nor so glorious. Wide-eyed, Aurelia watched as the waves raced to fling themselves with roaring abandon against the stony shore, sending up flurries of beaten froth. She caught her breath; even from a distance, the sight was exhilarating.

No, Newport was lovely, but for all its moneyed splendor, it did not stop the heart as this did. Nor did it stir the blood and set it racing until every cell in one's body seemed to echo the pulsing song of the sea. Inhaling the delicious salty air, Aurelia found herself quoting other words, far older and more revered than Swinburne's: *"Deep calleth unto deep at the noise of thy waterspouts: all thy waves and thy billows are gone over me."*

The wind off the sea whistled in her ears and flapped the wide brim of her hat. On impulse, she loosened the ribbons under her chin, took off the hat, and stood bareheaded in the sun, letting the breeze ruffle her hair, tease it loose from its pins. Her skirt billowed around her, and she stepped forward more boldly into the surf. The cold felt merely invigorating this time, and she stood with the sea swirling about her ankles, gazing toward the horizon, where the deepening blue of the sea met the softer blue of the sky.

She did not hear the hoofbeats at first, and even when the sound reached her ears, she did not immediately identify them as such. They seemed nothing more than part of the sea's rumble. Not until she felt the ground quiver beneath her feet did she look up to see the lone horseman galloping toward her.

Beneath the open sky, horse and rider moved as one, the latter's head gleaming with the same inky gloss as his horse's hide, making his shirt seem whiter by comparison. Watching him approach, Aurelia experienced a jolt of recognition almost physical in its intensity. No London dandy, transplanted from his usual environs of Hyde Park and Rotten Row.

No London dandy—but James Trelawney, Earl of Trevenan, in his rightful place.

*

James had risen early after an uneasy night. In truth, he'd been relieved when dawn broke and he could abandon the charade of trying to sleep. After breakfast, he'd headed out to the stables, not even bothering to change into what the fashionable would consider proper riding dress. Camborne—his coal-black gelding—had been as eager to see his master as James was to see him. Forsaking the usual bridle paths on the estate, they had instead cantered out the main gateway and down toward the sea, to race unimpeded and undisturbed along the shore.

For a time, the wild exhilaration of the ride—the sensation of Camborne's galloping stride beneath him, the rush of the wind around him—had driven all other thoughts from his mind. But now, slowing his horse to a walk, he found memories of the previous day's ugliness resurfacing. Helena's face, contorted with fury, her strident accusations…and that anonymous letter with its sly insinuations that might prove harder to refute than direct charges would have been.

A coward's weapon, but damnably effective when sent to the right person. And Helena with her festering resentment against the world in general and—it seemed—him in particular had proven to be just that. "Gerald will have justice!" she had insisted, and perhaps she'd even meant it, though James found it difficult to believe she was motivated by any deep affection for Gerald himself. Brother and sister had not been close, even as children; at best they'd tolerated each other. More often than not, they had wrangled as bitterly as their parents. Even at twelve, James had been struck by the lack of affection in his uncle's family.

Nonetheless, Gerald had been part of Helena's daily life until he left for Eton. Was it guilt, perhaps, or regret over their lack of closeness that made her so hot in his posthumous defense? And so eager to assign the blame for his death to James, whom they had both despised and regarded as an interloper? And what did Helena hope to accomplish by branding him as complicit in her brother's death? His execution, or perhaps imprisonment? Or, if proof of his supposed involvement failed to materialize, simply to render his existence a living hell? She and Gerald had already attempted as much when he'd first come to live at Pentreath.

Enough, James told himself. Dwelling on past misery was conducive to nothing but bitterness and self-pity. He should be thinking of how to solve this problem, finding out who was behind that letter—and discovering just how and why Gerald had died. He had not mourned his cousin overmuch—his death had come as a shock, not a grief—but if Gerald's demise was due to foul play rather than mischance, then James owed him at least the time and effort involved in uncovering the truth.

Gerald's death, and his activities in the months preceding it—could there be some connection between them? James thought again, uneasily, of Gerald's involvement with Mercer Shipping, of the exorbitant price he'd paid to buy out two minor shareholders. Uncle Joshua would have had an apoplexy had he known how much his son was spending on this venture.

James felt sure his uncle *hadn't* known—especially since he'd died soon after that fateful game of cards—and he doubted Helena had either. Should he tell her now, share with her the knowledge of Gerald's possibly shady business dealings? If she could be converted from an enemy to an ally...he considered the idea, then dismissed it. At present, her mind seemed fixed upon the idea of his guilt. He would have to find allies elsewhere.

At least Aunt Judith had no doubts of his innocence. While she had cared for Gerald, and Helena too, at times, she had always treated James with what felt like a special warmth— perhaps because his father had been her favorite brother. When he'd first come to Pentreath bereft and grieving, Aunt Judith had been the one to comfort him. It helped to know that, despite the bad blood between him and Gerald, she had never believed him capable of harming his cousin.

So who *did* believe it enough to write that letter? Who could be holding enough of a grudge against him to reopen the wounds of Gerald's death and falsely implicate James, when there was plenty of evidence exonerating him? And to drag Harry and some other fellow into it as well? And was it purely an act of malice, or was there something more sinister afoot?

Troubling thoughts, indeed. And ones he would prefer to keep from Amy and the other Newbolds, although he'd have to tell them something, given Helena's presence at Pentreath. His mother's family, on the other hand, might have some idea of who could be spreading this slander. And whether it was a personal grudge, or one that would have been leveled against any man holding the title of Earl of Trevenan.

He'd ride over to Harry's house after luncheon, James resolved, and show him that letter. But for now, it was high time he headed back to Pentreath. He had a houseful of guests to entertain, chief among them his future bride.

Turning Camborne around, he urged him first into a trot, then—when it became clear that the horse had got his second wind—into a gallop. As they raced along the strand, he felt the lingering traces of fatigue and ill-humor miraculously lift and dissipate, as though blown away on the wind from the sea, and in their place a familiar exultation.

Home. Whatever tangle awaited him, whatever accusations Helena threw at him, he was home—and nothing could dim that pleasure. *In my own country…*

He could have laughed aloud from the joy of it.

A woman was standing on the shore, gazing out to sea. The wind billowed her pale blue skirts, and her hat, trailing blue ribbons, dangled from her hand. She was barefoot too—or near enough, carrying her shoes in her other hand.

Barefoot, carefree—her demeanor at odds with her position. The gilded American heiress, removed from the ballroom and salon, exploring instead the natural world. And becoming a part of it, in a way her acquaintances could not have predicted.

Even before she turned, on hearing his approach, he knew who it was.

Not Amy—Aurelia. He wondered, as he reined in his horse, why he felt no surprise.

She gazed up at him, the water still lapping at her feet. "Lord Trevenan. Good morning."

The sunlight gilded her hair to almost blinding brightness, picking out the darker veins of amber and honey among the flowing gold. Her fair skin had taken on a faint golden tinge as well, and her blue eyes rivaled the sea for richness of color. He thought of the pale, shrinking near-recluse he had surprised in his aunt's conservatory and wanted to laugh. Or, more inexplicably, to weep—and both impulses shook him to the core.

He managed to suppress them and returned her greeting instead. "Miss Aurelia. You're abroad early this morning."

She smiled tentatively. "Forgive me. I couldn't resist the opportunity to explore."

"No need to ask forgiveness." James dismounted, joining her on the sand; he ignored Camborne, who stamped and snorted behind him, frustrated in his wish to gallop further. "I know how irresistible this beach can be. I am just surprised to see you here without your sister."

Aurelia bit her lip, looking hesitant. "Amy is still abed. She finds herself a little indisposed this morning."

Concern roused in him at once. "Nothing serious, I trust? Should I send for the doctor?"

Her color deepened. "Oh, no, that won't be necessary. My sister's complaint is not life-threatening, though it is certainly uncomfortable—and inconvenient."

Enlightenment dawned. "Ah. I hope she makes a quick recovery." He would have some flowers sent up to his fiancée's chamber when he got back to Pentreath.

"Oh, yes. I do think she will be herself within a few days." Aurelia sounded relieved that he required no further explanation. "In any case, I'm the only member of my family awake just now. I suppose the others must be sleeping in."

"Little wonder if they are. It's a long journey from London to Cornwall, even by train." James paused. "Someone knows where you've gone, I trust?"

"Lady Talbot does. She even gave me the key to the garden door."

"You took the north stairs?" he asked in involuntary surprise.

"Well, I certainly didn't *fly* down!" she retorted, looking unexpectedly amused. "These stairs aren't forbidden to guests, are they? After what you told us yesterday—"

"No, of course not," James hastened to assure her.

"You're welcome to use them. I hope you did not find the climb too strenuous?"

Aurelia shook her head. "I took my time descending and held onto the banister all the way. But I'd have climbed twice as far for such a view!" Her gaze returned to the sea. "Is it always like this, so turbulent and splendid?"

He smiled, feeling his mood lighten at her enthusiasm. "More often than not, at least where we are. The sea tends to be gentler on the south coast, and some prefer it so."

Aurelia glanced back over her shoulder. "Do you?"

"Oh, I'm a north coast man, all the way down to my bones. I'd likely find the south coast far too tame, though it has many other features to commend it. Perhaps we might make an excursion down there for the day, once Amy is up and about."

"I'm sure she'd enjoy that. For my part, I mean to entice her down *here*. I've never seen such a sea!"

"Not even at Newport?" he asked lightly, enjoying her obvious pleasure in the sight.

"Not even there," she replied. "And while the sea and sun at Newport are lovely, Bailey's Beach is so stony. I wouldn't dare go barefoot there, the way I've done here."

"Or hatless? Talking of which, you might want to cover yourself again," James advised. "The air is very light here, and the sun stronger than it seems. Your skin is quite fair. I should not like you to suffer a bad sunburn on your first day in Cornwall."

She sighed but donned her hat once again, twisting the ribbons one-handed into a loose knot under her chin. "Very well. I should never hear the end of it from Mama if I came back redder than a boiled lobster. Or worse, with a crop of freckles! And I suppose I should dry off as well, though I'm not nearly ready to go back to the house. It is far too beautiful out here."

"Stay out a bit longer, then," James invited. "I find myself in a similar humor just now, so, if you've no objections to my company—"

"Oh, none," she assured him, returning his smile. "This is your beach, after all." She waded out of the sea, heading for one of the flat rocks a short distance up the sand. Seating herself, she put her shoes down on the sand and stretched out her feet to dry in the sun.

Very shapely feet, James couldn't help but observe, and—to judge from their outline beneath her damp muslin skirt—attached to even more shapely legs. Reminding himself that he had no business admiring such things, he glanced toward the water again. Behind him, a bored Camborne lowered his head to nose at a pile of drying seaweed.

Aurelia said, almost dreamily, "We'd go bathing in the sea at Newport. Nothing too adventurous—just bobbing up and down like corks in the shallows. I imagine it's different here."

"In some ways—less crowded and no bathing huts, of course." James made his own way up the beach and sat down on another rock not far from hers. "My father taught me to swim in the sea here when I was a boy. I wouldn't advise a newcomer to venture out too far—these tides are too strong for someone unaccustomed to them—but you'd be safe enough in the shallows."

"You must have loved growing up here."

James smiled. "I did, indeed. There's always so much to explore when you live by the sea—worlds within worlds. Someday I'll show you some of the caves down near St. Perran. Huge echoing ones, carved out by the tide. Harry and I used to play there as boys. I even kept a few keepsakes in one of them. I thought of it as my treasure trove back then."

"Amy and I had a place like that too, only it was in the hollow of a tree," Aurelia mused. "But weren't you afraid of losing your treasures in the sea?"

"I tried to put them someplace above the waterline. The

tide would have had to rise far higher to reach my hiding place." He paused. "Some of my old playthings may even still be there, unless someone's found and made off with them."

"Would it bother you if they had?"

After a moment's thought, James shook his head. "Not after all this time. Besides, I went back before I left for university and retrieved anything I thought I might grieve to lose. Hiding my things in the cave was mainly my way of keeping them—out of certain hands."

"Your other cousin—Gerald?"

James glanced at her, momentarily startled; given their looks, it was easy to forget how perceptive she and Amy both were. "Very astute of you," he said at last. "Yes, it was Gerald I had in mind. Not that he ever spent much time round the caves or on the beach, for that matter. He used to claim that just looking at the sea gave him *mal de mer,* much to my uncle's disgust. But that didn't stop him from trying to find out our special places, by one means or another. I suspect he resented anyone having secrets that didn't include him." Spoiling something for his "commoner" cousin would have appealed to Gerald as well, James reflected.

"He must have been a difficult person to deal with," Aurelia said after a moment.

James smiled without humor. "He was. But then the same could be said of just about everyone on my father's side of the family—Aunt Judith excepted, of course."

Aurelia fretted her lower lip. "Trevenan, this situation with Lady Durward—"

"It's nothing with which you or your family need to concern yourselves," James said quickly. "I assure you, Helena's accusations are groundless, and I am fully prepared to address any further unpleasantness on that score."

"I don't doubt that, but I should think this matter *does* concern Amy—at least to some extent," Aurelia contended. "My sister is to be your bride and live here with you. Imagine how hard it will be for her if this cloud over your head is not dispersed well before your wedding."

"A valid point," James admitted.

"Amy's already told me that your cousin died in a fall, and you were shown to be miles away at the time," she went on. "So why has Lady Durward accused you of something you obviously didn't do? Does she dislike you that much?"

"It's—a bit more complicated than that." James paused, then continued reluctantly, "The truth is, the exact circumstances of Gerald's death are somewhat unclear. And I suppose the nature of our relationship might have led to speculation in certain quarters."

Her gaze was sympathetic. "I gather you were not on the best of terms."

"No." James exhaled, then turned to stare at the churning surf again. "Gerald and I were never close. Like my uncle, he despised me on account of my mother's family, whom he considered his social inferiors. For my part, I thought him a bully and a braggart. Age did not improve him, and I daresay his opinion of me was likewise unflattering. Fortunately, we moved in different circles, so it wasn't too difficult to avoid each other, most of the time.

"We last met in July, after my uncle died. I came to the funeral, but beyond that..." He shrugged. "Gerald had become Trevenan, and I had other concerns to occupy myself, like running the mine and setting up my own establishment. My father had built up a small property for us on Tresilian land. I inherited it when I came of age."

"So did your cousin come back here to take up his new responsibilities?"

"And miss all those hunting and shooting parties? Not likely. Our solicitor told me Gerald waited until the last possible minute to return to Pentreath." James paused, frowning. "And that is what I find most troubling. Gerald had no love for Cornwall, and yet it was here that he met his death. His body was found at the foot of a cliff, on New Year's Day."

"Which you had nothing to do with, of course," she said with certainty.

He smiled faintly. "Thank you for the 'of course.' No, I was in Cornwall at the time, but attending a party at the Tresilians'. A houseful of people saw me there, and I spent the night. I did not learn of Gerald's death until the following afternoon. It is thought that he lost his footing in the dark while intoxicated. I found that easy enough to believe—Gerald often overindulged in drink, and he did not know Cornwall that well by day, let alone night. The inquest returned a verdict of death by misadventure, which appeared to be accepted by everyone present."

"By everyone?" she echoed. "So, then, why has Lady Durward accused you now?"

He sighed. "Because, a few days ago, Helena received an anonymous letter claiming that, while I did not 'soil my hands' with Gerald's blood, I might have had something to do with how he met his Maker all the same."

Aurelia's eyes widened as she absorbed the significance of his words. "You mean," she began, after a moment, "you're being accused of hiring someone to do away with your cousin?"

James nodded grimly. "Which is a damn sight harder to disprove than my direct involvement. And to make matters worse, two other men—one of them my cousin Harry—have been implicated as well."

"How utterly hateful!" she exclaimed. "Do you know who could have written this letter? Or what he can possibly hope to gain by it?"

He shook his head. "None at all, so far. I went riding in hopes of clearing my head, but as of this moment, I am void of inspiration."

"Some friend of your cousin's, perhaps, trying to make trouble for you?" she suggested.

"I was not aware that Gerald had friends—at least, not in Cornwall. To the best of my knowledge, his intimates lived in London or in hunting country, like Rutland or Leicestershire. Most were the sporting type—hard-drinking, hard-riding…" James paused. "As it happens, I spoke to a few of them before I left London. They don't appear overly grieved by Gerald's death, or inclined to regard it as suspicious, in any way. Nor was I, until recently."

Aurelia bit her lip again. "This seems such an impertinent thing to ask," she said slowly, "but have *you* an enemy, Trevenan?"

"Everyone has enemies. But I had not thought to find one here." Another black mark against his nameless accuser, for trying to destroy his contentment in the one place where he'd always felt secure. "Not unless I count Gerald himself, and we are beyond enmity now." Death had a way of putting paid to old grudges, he reflected somberly.

"Lady Durward seems all too willing to take up where he left off," Aurelia observed.

"I can handle Helena," James said firmly. "And the rest of this business as well."

"What do you mean to do?"

"Try to trace the rumor back to its source, for a start. Harry might be able to help. I'll call on him this afternoon." He paused, studying her face: the contemplative look in her blue eyes, the faint frown between her brows. No fool, Aurelia Newbold; her governess had thought her clever enough to attend college, after all.

"Miss Aurelia," he began, "I know how close you and Amy are, but I would prefer that you not mention this to her—at least, for the moment. Bad enough that I've burdened you with the knowledge." And just how, he wondered, had she managed to get all this out of him when he hadn't intended to tell her a thing? He'd never discussed his past in so much detail with her sister; nor had Amy ever insisted that he do so, or probed beyond what he was comfortable with.

But that was unfair. Aurelia hadn't exactly probed, and yet he'd found himself revealing things he'd only ever spoken of to his intimates—to Harry or, occasionally, to Thomas. A subtle difference in the twins, perhaps, that one should elicit confidences more readily than her sister.

"We are to be family, Lord Trevenan," Aurelia said now, and James had the oddest sense that she knew what he'd just been thinking. "Perhaps you needed to tell someone what was weighing on your mind. But you needn't worry about it going any further than this beach." A faint smile hovered around her mouth. "I've kept a great many confidences over the years."

"Your sister's?" he asked, trying to lighten the mood.

"And my brother's. And my own, of course." Something half-wry, half-wistful flickered across her face and was gone, transient as a butterfly in flight.

"Thank you. I appreciate your discretion." He stood up, stretching his legs. "I should get back to the house. It's a poor host who abandons his guests on their first day in Cornwall."

"I should be getting back as well," Aurelia said, sighing as she reached for her shoes. "Preferably before my mother sees me and goes into conniptions over my little adventure."

James raised his brows. "Your mother frowns on your adventures?"

"Not at all." Her lips quirked. "She simply prefers me to undertake them fully shod, impeccably dressed, sheltered by a parasol, and accompanied by at least one maid."

He laughed. "And here you've managed to circumvent all those conditions! My congratulations."

"I'm fully shod again now. And, well, dressed anyhow," she amended, looking down at her skirts—still slightly damp—with a faint frown.

James whistled to Camborne, still investigating the seaweed a short distance away; the gelding whickered and trotted up to him, eager to be off again.

"He's a very handsome horse," Aurelia observed, getting to her feet.

"Thank you." James stroked the gelding's nose. "This is Camborne. He's strong enough to carry us both back to Pentreath, if you're willing."

An abrupt silence greeted his proposal. Surprised, he looked around and saw that Aurelia had paled visibly.

"I'm not—exactly dressed for riding," she said at last.

James could have kicked himself for his own obliviousness. She was remembering the accident, of course. "Forgive me," he said at once. "I'd thought only to spare you the climb."

"That's all right." She attempted a smile. "I think I'm flattered—that you actually forgot about what happened to me, for a moment."

"You've proved so intrepid in other ways. It's easy to forget that you might harbor some apprehensions about getting back on a horse. Have you ridden at all since the accident?"

She colored, which became her far more than the anxious pallor she'd been sporting. "Yes, actually. A donkey, on an excursion at Bad Ems. He was slow but surefooted—and surprisingly obedient, given how obstinate donkeys are said to be."

"And all was well? You managed to stay in the saddle?"

Aurelia nodded. "It helped to know that I was quite close to the ground and hadn't far to fall if the worst occurred. But a donkey is not the same as a horse, Trevenan."

"True, but the basic principle remains unchanged." James patted Camborne's glossy black neck, his gaze still on Aurelia. "Do you miss riding?" he asked gently.

"I miss it—and I'm deathly afraid of it at the same time," she confessed. "Oh, not of horses, nor even of getting in the saddle. But I *am* afraid of falling—of injuring both myself and the horse." She paused, took a breath before resuming. "Bramble—the horse I was riding when I fell—broke his leg too and had to be shot." Her lips crimped in something that was not quite a smile. "I believe I cried more over that than my own injuries, at the time."

"I am sorry. That's a painful burden to carry."

She shrugged. "A just one. I was foolish, reckless, and we both paid for it." Almost unconsciously, she fingered the scar on her cheek. "But I was the only one who deserved it."

"I wouldn't say either of you *deserved* it," he countered. "Accidents happen even to the most cautious riders. You needn't do anything here that you do not wish to do," he added, "but if you were to ride back with me, I should ensure that we arrive safely."

Again she hesitated. "I don't know if I could—"

"We will not fall." James infused the words with all the certainty he could muster. "Camborne's worked out the fidgets in his legs, so I can promise that he'll behave himself."

She glanced at the horse, her expression turning wistful. "I admit, I've wondered what it might be like to ride again. I don't wish to brag, but Amy and I were both accounted good horsewomen among our set."

James smiled. "I don't doubt that. Back at Pentreath, I've got several horses in my stable that might prove suitable, should you wish to attempt riding again. One mare, in particular, would be ideal for you. She's very calm and gentle."

He thought he could discern the workings of her mind: one more hurdle, one more step on the path back to herself. Then she looked straight at him, and he saw the new resolve in her eyes, around the firm set of her mouth. "Thank you, my lord. I will indeed consider it."

"Excellent." James kept his tone brisk. "Have you proper riding clothes?"

"I could probably find something suitable in my wardrobe. Or I could borrow a riding habit from Amy, since we're the same size. But for now…" She took a step toward Camborne, looked at James again. "It's about time that I tried, isn't it?"

He felt his smile broadening. "Let me give you a leg up. It will be easier for you to ride in front of me, dressed as you are."

Aurelia nodded and stepped closer to Camborne, now standing as still as a horse sculpted in marble. Just before James moved to help her mount, he thought he heard her say something under her breath; it sounded like "Death to the little mouse."

James nearly asked her to explain, but her face—taut with concentration—stopped him. Instead, he held out his interlaced hands and, as she set her foot in them, lifted her to the saddle. She scrambled aboard awkwardly, but settled in more quickly than he'd expected, adjusting her seat and draping her skirts over the pommel. Her back was as straight as a lance, her profile serene beneath her hat, though he suspected her heart was beating at twice its normal rate.

Resisting the urge to cheer, he climbed into the saddle behind her and took up the reins. "Home, Camborne," he ordered, and urged the gelding into a trot.

Nineteen

Blood may be thicker than water, but it is also a great deal nastier.

—E.Œ. Somerville and Martin Ross,
Some Experiences of an Irish R.M.

THE HORSE MOVED SMOOTHLY BENEATH HER, ITS GAIT almost silken on the sand. Aurelia balanced on the front of the saddle and willed herself not to fidget, or worse, panic.

"We will not fall," Trevenan had said, and she had chosen to believe him. They wouldn't be jumping any fences, after all, and they weren't going faster than a slow trot at the moment.

You got yourself into this, my girl—and in more ways than one.

She could feel Trevenan's warmth at her back, and his arms surrounded her as he guided the horse along the path; his hands were light and sure upon the reins. And she could not have said which she found more unnerving—being back on a horse, or being so close to Trevenan physically, something she had taken pains to avoid since their waltz at Amy's betrothal ball.

Amy. Betrothal. She repeated the words to herself with a grim determination, then seized upon the first handy topic of conversation. "So, you call your horse Camborne?" she asked brightly. "After the town of Camborne?"

"His full name is Camborne Hill, actually," Trevenan replied. "From a song about the first steam engine, which made a run up and down Camborne Hill nearly a century ago. But that's a bit of a mouthful for a horse."

Aurelia laughed. "It's more memorable than calling him Soot or Blackie. You've been to Camborne Hill, I trust?"

"Several times," he assured her. "It's just to the south of us. I've traveled widely through Cornwall—and much of the West Country as well."

"That would also include Devon and Dorset, wouldn't it?" she asked.

"Yes, along with Somerset, Bristol, and parts of Gloucestershire and Wiltshire too."

"We've only seen London, and some of the Home Counties," Aurelia said wistfully.

"Well, you'll find some beautiful and varied country there—hills, moorlands, and valleys, as well as the seashore," Trevenan said, as he turned Camborne onto a rough path flanked by low but surprisingly rich grass and shrubs and bushes she couldn't begin to identify. "And some remarkable buildings—Salisbury Cathedral, Bath Abbey, and Stonehenge, of course."

Aurelia shifted in the saddle, trying to adjust to the more rugged surface beneath them and its effect on Camborne's stride. "Pray, tell me more." With so much to be done before Amy's wedding, this might be as close as she'd ever get to seeing these places, she reflected.

He obliged, telling her of castle ruins and picturesque country cottages as they rode along. The grass grew taller and thicker as they headed away from the beach, the bushes yielding to trees, and soon enough, the main gateway of Pentreath came into view.

Trevenan rode through the gates, then took the path leading around the back toward the stables. A good-sized structure, Aurelia observed, which must house a large number of horses, and there was probably a paddock or two beyond. Spying them, a groom came forward at once to take Camborne's reins. Trevenan dismounted with fluid ease, then turned to help Aurelia.

Feeling self-conscious again, she straightened her skirts before letting herself descend into his waiting hands. His grip around her waist was light but firm; she could feel the warmth of his body through her thin muslin dress as he lifted her down, then set her on her feet.

"Thank you," she said a little breathlessly. "I did enjoy that ride, more than I expected."

He smiled. "I hoped you might. Enough to ride again, I trust. Perhaps on that mare I told you about?"

"That's a definite possibility," she conceded, managing to smile back. "But I must go in now. I need to change my clothes, and then I want to look in on Amy."

"Of course." Trevenan stepped aside to let her pass. "That way will take you back to the house the fastest." He nodded toward one of the paths leading away from the stables. "By the by, I mean to have some flowers sent up to Amy, to cheer her recovery."

"She'd like that, especially if you send roses. I'll see you at luncheon," Aurelia added, and hastened toward the path he'd shown her.

Fortunately, no one observed her reentrance into the house. Back in her chamber, she let Suzanne put her appearance to rights: changing her creased muslin frock for a pretty, lace-trimmed shirtwaist and a skirt of lightweight green wool, just right for Cornwall's mild climate.

A quick glance in the mirror showed neither sunburn nor freckles, though she was perhaps slightly ruddier than she'd been when she'd set out on her excursion. Suzanne still seemed astonished that her mistress had allowed herself to become so disheveled; Aurelia heard her murmur "*C'est incroyable!*" as she bore off the muslin dress to be laundered.

Aurelia slipped the key Lady Talbot had given her into the pocket of her skirt; she'd return it when they met at luncheon, but for now, she would check on Amy. She went down the passage and tapped on her sister's door. "Amy, are you awake?" she called softly.

A wan voice bade her enter, and she slipped inside. Amy, looking pale and listless, lay propped up on pillows in bed, thumbing halfheartedly through a novel.

"I am sorry you are not well, dearest," Aurelia said sympathetically, taking a chair beside the bed—a sturdy four-poster like her own, but hung with rose-pink silk.

"It will pass," Amy said with a sigh. "But it could hardly have come at a less convenient moment!" She laid her novel aside and glanced at Aurelia more closely. "You, on the other hand, look very well indeed—positively glowing, in fact. Any particular reason?"

Aurelia flushed, feeling unexpectedly guilty, and gave her sister a brief account of her solitary excursion down to the beach. Like Trevenan, Amy expressed surprise and concern on learning that she'd taken the stairs, and Aurelia hastened to reassure her of their safety.

"As you can see, I'm fine. The stairs are in excellent condition, and I took every precaution. Believe me, it was worth the climb," she added, smiling at the memory of those first exhilarating moments alone on the sand, with the sea surging before her. "You must see the beach, Amy. It's so beautiful—all wild and unspoiled. Newport doesn't hold a candle to it."

Amy's brows rose. "High praise, indeed." She settled back against the pillows once more. "I still think you should have waited for me," she grumbled. "But then you never could resist the sea. I hope Mama didn't catch you out."

"No, fortunately. Lord Trevenan brought me back before anyone discovered I was gone."

"Trevenan?" Amy echoed. "He was there too?"

Aurelia felt herself flush again. "He was out riding on the beach this morning," she replied, trying for a casual tone. "Lady Talbot told me he was an early riser. He seemed as surprised as you that I'd taken the stairs, so he offered me a ride, to spare me the climb back up."

Her sister's eyes widened. "A ride? You mean, you got on a horse again?"

Aurelia nodded. "I thought—well, I thought it was time I *tried* it, at least."

Amy laid a hand over hers. "Was it very difficult for you?"

"At first, yes," Aurelia admitted. "When I got in the saddle, I felt as if I were miles off the ground. But the horse behaved beautifully. I managed to stay on, and we arrived safely." She took a breath. "Trevenan has suggested that I might try riding again."

"Has he?" Amy regarded her intently. "How do you feel about it, Relia?"

"Nervous," Aurelia confessed. "A little frightened, but—a little excited too. I think I *would* like to take it up again, at that."

"Oh, I'm glad!" her sister exclaimed, smiling. "I know how much you used to love riding. And I've so missed riding *with* you, especially mornings on the Row."

"Well, I suspect it may be a while before I can attempt the Row," Aurelia said ruefully. "But perhaps a few turns about the paddock here would be more my speed, at least for now. Trevenan recommended one of his gentler horses for my use."

"I'm sure it won't be long before you're riding as well as you ever have," Amy said staunchly. "And I can lend you a habit and riding boots too. Isn't it lucky that we're of a size?"

"Nothing too fine," Aurelia insisted. "I'm not planning to fall off, but I'd hate to ruin your best riding kit if I do."

They both looked up at a knock on the door. Mariette, who'd been tidying her mistress's linen drawer, immediately went to answer it. Seconds later, she stepped back into the room, carrying a bouquet of brightly hued flowers.

"From his lordship, mademoiselle," she announced, carrying them over to Amy, who perked up noticeably at the sight. "With his best wishes for your quick recovery."

"How gallant of him! And how lovely they are!" Eyes aglow, she sniffed at a half-open pink rose. "Such a scent. You can tell these come straight from a garden, not a shop."

"He remembered your fondness for roses," Aurelia said with determined cheer. "And look, aren't those lupines?" She indicated the tall blue and violet flowers, which towered over the other blooms like the spires of a church.

"Yes, and hollyhocks too." Amy indulged in one last sniff before handing the bouquet to Mariette to put in water. "So thoughtful. I wonder how he knew I was under the weather."

"I told him," Aurelia confessed. "That is, he asked why you weren't with me on the beach, and I mentioned you were indisposed. He was prepared to send for a doctor, if necessary."

"Good heavens!" Amy murmured, but Aurelia thought she looked rather touched. "Well, I trust you assured him that my condition was not so grave as that."

Aurelia nodded. "I assured him you'd be up and about within a day or two."

"Monday," Amy declared emphatically. "No later than that, certainly. If I'm to be mistress here, I can't spend the next week lolling in bed. I want to see the rest of the estate."

"Well, what I've seen of it looks splendid," Aurelia told her. "Trevenan could probably give you a tour, or—if he's otherwise occupied—Lady Talbot."

"That reminds me." Amy leaned forward again. "Is everything all right with James and his other—guests?" She pulled a slight face at the last word.

"We've been spared the Durwards so far," Aurelia replied. "I think Lady Talbot has persuaded them to keep to their rooms, at least for now."

"Oh, good. Though I'm sure the respite won't last—more's the pity."

"Trevenan thinks the same. But surely he and Lady Talbot can keep them in line."

"I hope so, but I just know Lady Durward will try to say something once she's out and about. You know she won't stand for being confined to her room indefinitely. And she's just the sort to put in an appearance at the worst possible moment—from pure spite." Amy lay back with a sigh. "She makes those Fifth Avenue harridans look like the epitome of tact and restraint. I hope James has some plan to counteract her slanders. Has he said anything about it?"

Aurelia hesitated. Trevenan had asked her not to mention the anonymous letter to Amy, and while she would not willingly betray his confidence, neither could she withhold the entire truth from her twin. Amy had the right to know at least part of what was going on. "I think," she ventured at last, "he hopes that his cousins—the Tresilians—might shed some light on how this vicious rumor might have started. He intends to call on them this afternoon."

"If only I could accompany him!" Amy lamented. "He should have someone from our family present, to show our support if nothing else." She lapsed into brooding silence for a few moments, then suddenly brightened. "Relia, why don't you offer to go with him?"

"Me?" Aurelia said, startled.

"Why not? You and James have become such friends. Surely, there would be nothing improper about your accompanying him in my stead." Her eyes sparkled at her own ingenuity. "You could act as my envoy, so to speak! Yes, I like that idea enormously."

"Well, Trevenan might not," Aurelia pointed out, with some asperity. "Under the circumstances, he might prefer to see the Tresilians alone."

"Nonsense. It's only right that the rest of the world should see that we are completely behind him on this. And besides," she added coaxingly, "if you were to go, you could tell me more about these Tresilians who are so important to him. I'd appreciate that *so* much, Relia—knowing what James's favorite cousins are like."

Aurelia sighed, recognizing that she had already capitulated. Her sister was right, after all—Trevenan deserved the comfort of knowing that his future in-laws fully supported him. "Very well, dearest. I shall ask him. Although he might still refuse my offer."

"He won't," Amy predicted. "Not if he has the sense I've credited him with."

❧

"Harry's family lives just outside of St. Perran," Trevenan told Aurelia as he handed her into the gig after luncheon. "About twenty to thirty minutes' drive from here, in good weather."

"Well, we have that at least," she said, settling carefully into the seat. The beauty of the afternoon had fulfilled all the promise of the morning, the sun beaming down from an almost cloudless blue sky. In deference to her mother's wishes, Aurelia had donned a wide-brimmed straw hat trimmed with violets to match her visiting costume of twilled lavender silk.

"We do indeed." Trevenan climbed into the gig himself and took the reins, urging the carriage horse—a tall, placid bay—into an easy trot.

Aurelia relaxed against the squabs as they headed down the drive and out through the gates. While slightly surprised by her offer to accompany him, Trevenan had accepted it without demur after she explained Amy's reasoning. Somewhat unexpectedly, everyone else had approved the idea as well. Aurelia suspected that Lady Talbot saw the advantage of publicly revealing that her nephew remained on the best of terms with his future bride's family.

Trevenan drove as well as he rode, as well as he danced, Aurelia observed—his hands light on the reins that guided the horse down the track. Graceful and competent, without being the least bit showy. One could say the same of the man himself, and here, in Cornwall, he appeared to have shed many of the constraints that had dictated his conduct in town. Despite the cloud over his head, he seemed freer here: more relaxed, more expansive, and, she thought, remembering how he had looked this morning on the beach, infinitely more virile.

She looked away, wondering if she would ever lose this heightened awareness of him, this consciousness of his every breath and motion. Casting about for a safe conversational topic, she said at last, "Amy loved the flowers you sent up. I'd only a glimpse of your garden this morning. Is it as fine as this all year round?"

"Flowers seem to flourish most here during spring and early summer. Although the gardeners at Pentreath work to keep the gardens looking their best, whatever the season."

"Mama likes to garden back home. Unfortunately, Amy and I never got the knack of it."

"My mother was an avid gardener too," Trevenan remarked, smiling reminiscently. "Our garden at Chenoweth—our family home—was her pride and joy. She'd plant roses, daffodils, lupines, and lavender. Especially lavender; she'd make creams and lotions of it, and little sachets of dried lavender, to give to friends."

"I love lavender," Aurelia confessed. "It's my favorite scent."

"I know."

Trevenan's voice was soft, almost caressing, and she felt herself flush, remembering just how he might have come by that knowledge of her. Putting the memory aside, she said brightly, "So, tell me more about the Tresilians. I gather you and Sir Harry are close in age?"

"He's just a year older. But we were inseparable as boys, and close even now. Harry's been head of his family since he was twenty-one. His father, Hugh, was my mother's eldest brother. My own father claimed that meeting the Tresilians—and eventually marrying one—saved him from becoming an irresponsible rogue, like too many younger sons."

"That's quite a compliment," Aurelia mused. "But why did your other uncle—the late earl—object to them so? Supposedly, they were a good influence on your father, and Sir Harry does have a title, of sorts."

"Ah, but a baronet is considerably less exalted than an earl, and then there's the matter of the Tresilians' involvement in trade."

"The mine," Aurelia said, understanding at once.

"Just so. Apparently, it wasn't enough that my mother's family owned a tin mine, but they had to take an active hand in its management and operation." Trevenan's tone was dry. "Clearly, that placed them beyond the pale for many aristocrats."

"But, how foolish!" Aurelia exclaimed. "How can a business prosper unless the owner takes a direct hand in how it's run?" She shook her head. "That's one thing I'll never understand about the English—this prejudice against a gentleman doing honest work for honest money."

He smiled. "An American perspective that has much to recommend it. Fortunately, the Tresilians are just as pragmatic on that score—and thoroughly unapologetic about it. They're impervious to snubs. I suspect that's one reason Uncle Joshua found them so objectionable, though Aunt Judith thinks there might have been another reason for his antipathy."

"Which was?"

"My mother, Carenza." His tone warmed and softened over the name. "She was bright, pretty, vivacious—and she and my father fell headlong in love the first time they met. They married despite my uncle's disapproval, and were very happy together. I suspect Uncle Joshua resented that his brother had the freedom to wed where he chose, and the temerity to make a success of it."

"How sad that he couldn't be happy *for* them instead," Aurelia remarked.

"I'm afraid my uncle's character wasn't capable of that sort of generosity. Instead, he cut off most of his contact with my father, and would not receive my mother at Pentreath. And yet…" Trevenan paused, then continued in a quieter tone, "When my parents drowned in Italy on their second honeymoon, he arranged to have their ashes brought back to Cornwall and interred here. I owe him something for that—and for taking me in, difficult though our relationship was."

"Was he your sole guardian?"

"My parents named both him and Harry's father as my guardians," he said after a moment. "Uncle Hugh was willing to take me in, but he'd five children at home and barely enough room for them, so it was decided that, as a Trelawney, I should live at Pentreath."

Where his aristocratic uncle continually belittled his mother's family, and his cousins bullied him, Aurelia thought. And where affection of any kind appeared to have been thin on the ground. A bleak situation for a boy bereft of loving parents. Aloud she said, "Pentreath is such a handsome house. I am sorry that it wasn't a happier one, when you were growing up there."

He exhaled. "I managed. And there were moments, even then. My father spent his boyhood at Pentreath. I felt…close to him there. And to my uncle's credit, I was not forbidden to see the Tresilians, though I suspect Aunt Judith had a hand in that."

"Your aunt seems wonderfully adept at managing even the most difficult people."

"She is, indeed. Talking of which, have you encountered the Durwards at all today?"

She shook her head. "Your aunt said at breakfast that they were keeping to their rooms. And they didn't come down to luncheon either."

"So I noticed, though I doubt we'll be spared much longer." Trevenan sighed. "I daresay they'll venture out this evening, or possibly tomorrow, if we're lucky."

"I don't understand why Lady Durward dislikes you so. Is it merely that she resents seeing you in her brother's place?"

"That may be part of it," he replied. "But the truth of the matter is, I've never fully understood Helena. We got on no better than Gerald and I, though he was my chief tormentor."

"Were she and her brother close?"

"I wouldn't have said so, myself. They seemed united in their dislike of me, I suppose, but to the best of my recollection, they quarreled just as frequently among themselves."

"You can quarrel fiercely with your brothers and sisters, but still fight against anything or anyone that threatens them," she pointed out. "That happened often enough with Amy and me."

"You and Amy? But you have always seemed to me the very dearest of friends."

"We are. But that doesn't mean we've never quarreled or competed against each other. Less so now, of course, than when we were children," she added reflectively. "Possibly because we've grown up to be quite different people, who might not want the very same things—"

She broke off, struck by the irony of her own words. However much she and Amy had matured, however close they were now, the fact remained that they both wanted one thing very badly indeed: the man who happened to be sitting beside her right now.

And he wanted only one of them, Aurelia reminded herself. He wanted Amy; he was betrothed to her. This odd intimacy that she'd sensed growing between them was nothing more than a fluke—the result of propinquity. If Amy had been on the beach this morning, surely Trevenan would have unburdened himself to *her*, his future wife, rather than his soon-to-be sister-in-law. Or would he? He'd asked her not to discuss this business with Amy, after all.

Trevenan's voice broke into her thoughts. "Well, whatever rivalry you and Amy might have engaged in back in the day, comparing the two of you to Gerald and Helena is quite a stretch. Still," he added, "they do say blood is thicker than water. Helena claims to want justice for Gerald. And as his cousin and successor, I suppose I'm bound to find it for him—if I can."

By now, they had reached the outskirts of St. Perran. The Tresilians lived at the bottom of a valley, Trevenan told her. Not far from the beach, though they did not have the sea at their doorstep, as he now did. As they neared their destination, a lone rider came ambling up the lane. Sighting the gig, he reined in his horse—a fine-looking chestnut—and raised a hand in greeting.

"Trevenan! Good afternoon. I hadn't heard you were back."

The earl halted the gig in turn. "Nankivell," he said, after a brief pause that made Aurelia wonder how well he knew this man. "Good afternoon to you. Yes, I just got in yesterday."

"From London, I understand? Splendid city. I wonder you could bring yourself to leave it. I always regret doing so, myself."

"On the contrary, I am always glad to return home." Trevenan's tone was pleasant but slightly distant.

"And what a charming companion you've brought with you," the other man went on, edging his horse forward. "Might I beg the pleasure of an introduction?"

"Miss Newbold, this is Sir Lucas Nankivell, Baronet, of St. Perran," Trevenan said in that same neutral tone. "Sir Lucas, Miss Aurelia Newbold—one of my guests, from London."

Sir Lucas sketched a graceful bow from his saddle. "Enchanted to make your acquaintance, Miss Newbold."

Aurelia inclined her head and murmured a bland pleasantry in response. Despite Sir Lucas's courtesy and polished manners, she felt acutely self-conscious as his gaze swept over her. As if every stitch of her clothing—indeed, every hair on her head—was being calculated and assessed. *Item—two lips, indifferent red, one visiting costume by Worth, one scarred cheek*…She was suddenly glad that, sitting in the gig, her limp was not visible to this stranger's eye.

It was tempting to take refuge in shyness, to play the little mouse again. *But a cat could look at a king, after all*, she reminded herself, and gazed back just as frankly. Sir Lucas was perhaps a few years older than Trevenan, and while she did not think him as handsome, he was a fine figure of a man, blessed with an athletic form and attractive, regular features. Slate-blue eyes under straight brows, slightly curling brown hair, fashionably cut. His clothes were fashionable too. He wore just the sort of riding apparel a London gentleman might favor for a morning in Hyde Park: dapper, but subtly out of place here in Cornwall. Indeed, there was something just a bit—citified about Sir Lucas, right down to his speech, which bore no trace of a Cornish accent. Indeed, if she hadn't known better, she'd have thought him a Londoner.

"You are on your way to call on Sir Harry, at Roswarne?" Sir Lucas inquired.

"We are," Trevenan confirmed with a brief nod.

"Well, then, don't let me keep you. Pray, give my regards to Sir Harry—and to Miss Tresilian as well." Sir Lucas's eyes and voice changed subtly at those last words, becoming warmer, almost intimate.

A telling sign, Aurelia thought, as was the sudden speculative narrowing of Trevenan's eyes. "I'll tell them" was all he said, as he took up the reins again. "Good day, Nankivell."

"Good day." Sir Lucas touched his hat brim again, then kneed his horse forward.

"A friend?" Aurelia asked in a low voice as they started down the road again.

He shook his head. "More of an acquaintance. Nankivell's one of Harry's neighbors. I don't know the man that well myself."

"I don't mean to criticize, but he strikes me as a bit of a dandy."

"Not too surprising. I gather he has a fondness for London life." Trevenan shrugged. "Well, not every land-owner is content to spend all his time here. Cornwall's still regarded as thoroughly provincial; some prefer to swim in a bigger pond."

"Who'd choose a pond when they could have the sea instead?" Aurelia wondered.

That drew a smile from him. "Just so. But I've accepted that as a matter of individual taste, however misguided."

"He mentioned a Miss Tresilian? One of Sir Harry's sisters?"

"Sophie, the youngest daughter," he confirmed. "And good Lord, I do believe she's ready to come out next spring! It seems only yesterday she was playing with her dolls."

"Oh, young girls tend to grow up very quickly," Aurelia informed him. "How many sisters are there in the family? You mentioned five children in all."

"Two sisters. There's Harry, then Cecily—who's now married—then John—he's Andrew's age—then Sophie, and finally Peter, who's away at school. Harry became guardian to them all after my uncle died, but only Sophie and Peter are still minors."

"Do they all still live in Cornwall?"

"For the most part, although Cecily's husband lives on the south coast. John finished university last summer. He's thinking about reading law, eventually, but for now, he's home helping with the mine. And speaking of which," he added, "here, just before us, is Roswarne."

Cued as much by the lift in his voice as his words, Aurelia glanced ahead and saw the Tresilian home. Roswarne had none of Pentreath's splendor, but it was a handsome resi-dence: part brick, part timber, with the clean, simple lines of Georgian architecture.

"This was a farmhouse, originally," Trevenan told her as

they headed up the drive. "Built toward the middle of the last century. Of course, it's been augmented over the years."

"It looks comfortable. Not as grand as Pentreath, but it has a style of its own."

He smiled. "It does indeed. My mother grew up here, and in some ways, this felt more like a second home to me than Pentreath."

As they neared the front door, a dark-haired man in shirt-sleeves came around the side of the house and stopped in his tracks when he saw them. "Good Lord. James?"

"Harry!" Trevenan exclaimed, breaking into a brilliant smile. "Glad to find you at home!" He brought the gig to a stop and vaulted out as the man strode forward to greet him.

"Delighted to see *you* back where you belong." Sir Harry clasped Trevenan's hand at once. "I'd heard you got in yesterday. I was just thinking of calling on you."

Trevenan laughed, an unexpectedly carefree sound. "I've saved you the trouble, then." He turned to hand Aurelia down from the gig, then proceeded with the introductions. "Miss Aurelia, my cousin Sir Harry Tresilian. Harry, Miss Aurelia Newbold—my intended's sister."

Aurelia studied the man before her. Sir Harry was not especially tall, but he was well-built, broad-shouldered, and compact. His dark hair showed glints of mahogany, and his eyes were the clear grey-green of seawater on a fine day. She could see the resemblance between him and Trevenan, the strong planes of the face as well as the dark coloring. And something more intangible—a flash of spirit and a sense of strength, enduring as the Cornish cliffs.

Now he smiled, revealing a flash of white teeth in an attractively sun-browned face, as he bowed over Aurelia's hand. "Delighted to meet you, Miss Newbold. Welcome to Roswarne."

Aurelia returned his smile. "Thank you, Sir Harry. I am

pleased to meet you as well. Trevenan has told me much of you and your family. All of it good," she added quickly.

"Relieved to hear it. James has nothing but good to say of your family as well." He gestured to a groom who ran up to take charge of the gig. "Come in, and take tea with us."

He led the way inside. The entrance hall of Roswarne was pleasantly bright, with whitewashed walls rather than the dark wood paneling that Aurelia often found oppressive. Music, rippling liquid chords, wafted out to them from a room down the passage. Music so beautiful that Aurelia stopped at once to listen further.

"Sophie!" Sir Harry called. "Put down the fiddle and come out and greet our guests."

The music stopped at once, and seconds later, a girl in a primrose yellow dress appeared in the doorway of the sitting room.

"James!" she exclaimed in obvious delight, before hurrying to embrace him.

"Hullo, infant." Trevenan returned her embrace and kissed her cheek with visible affection.

"Not such an infant now. I'm eighteen at Midsummer!" the girl retorted. "And we're having a party that night, to which you're invited, of course, and—oh!" She broke off as she caught sight of Aurelia. "You've brought a guest!"

"He has," Sir Harry confirmed. "Miss Newbold, my sister, Sophie Tresilian. Sophie, this is Miss Aurelia Newbold. She and her family are guests of James, at Pentreath."

Sophie Tresilian smiled, showing white, even teeth and a flashing set of dimples on either side of a generous mouth. Like her brother, she had rich dark hair, touched with mahogany, but her eyes were a true, vivid green. She mightn't be a classic beauty by London standards, but she radiated such charm and vitality that Aurelia thought she would take very well if she ever had a Season. "I am delighted to meet you at last, Miss Newbold. When are you and James to wed?"

"James is engaged to my sister, Amelia," Aurelia explained hastily. "She finds herself indisposed today, but she's asked me to send her regards, and hopes to meet you quite soon."

Sophie colored prettily. "Forgive the misunderstanding. But you are welcome, all the same, Miss Newbold. Will you stay to take tea with us?"

"I've already invited them," Sir Harry told his sister. "Is anyone else about?"

She shook her head. "Mama has gone to take some scones and cakes to Cousin Eliza. She won't be back for some hours yet. I stayed behind to practice my violin."

"You play beautifully," Aurelia told her. "I noticed when we first came in."

Sophie smiled. "Thank you. Music has always been important to my family—to most Cornish, I do believe. Do you or your sister play any instruments yourselves?"

"I play the piano, and we both sing."

The girl brightened. "Excellent! Perhaps we might play together sometime, or even have a concert? What do you think, James?" she appealed to Trevenan.

"First things first, Sophie," Sir Harry interrupted. "Is John out as well?"

She flashed him a dimpled smile. "He's off visiting Grace Tregarth, as usual."

"I see." They exchanged a significant look. "In that case, we won't see him until dinner."

"And perhaps not even then, if the Tregarths invite him to dine," Sophie replied.

A budding romance, Aurelia thought, charmed. How normal all this seemed, and how different from the formality of yesterday! She glanced at Trevenan, noticing how much more relaxed he appeared in the presence of his Tresilian kin. This was his true homecoming, she realized, among the people who knew and loved him best.

He was shaking his head now, smiling ruefully. "I can

scarce believe what I'm hearing. I'm away for less than a month, and John finds himself a girl?"

"All the more reason for you to stay and have tea with us, then," Sophie declared. "You can catch up on all the local news." She turned to Aurelia. "And today was baking day, so we have scones, splits, and ginger biscuits freshly made. And clotted cream as well."

"Clotted cream?" Aurelia echoed.

"Have you never had it, Miss Newbold? True Cornish clotted cream is fit for the gods."

"My sister exaggerates, but only a little," Sir Harry said, grinning. He clapped Trevenan on the shoulder. "Come, let us all go into the parlor, and I'll have tea brought."

Twenty

For slander lives upon succession
Forever housed where it gets possession.

—William Shakespeare, *The Comedy of Errors*

SITTING IN THE PARLOR, WATCHING SOPHIE SHOW Aurelia how to eat scones the Cornish way by layering butter, strawberry jam, and finally clotted cream on top, James found it easy to forget a less pleasant purpose had brought him here today. He forced himself not to touch the letter, which he'd tucked into the inside breast pocket of his coat before setting out. Time enough for that, when he and Harry found a moment alone. But for now, he let himself bask in it all: Harry's stalwart presence, Sophie's ebullient gaiety, and the comfort of familiar walls around him. This was what he'd missed the whole time he'd been in London; he drank it in like a tonic now, reluctant to mar this warm family interlude.

Soon enough, everyone declared they'd eaten and drunk their fill, Aurelia agreeing that clotted cream was indeed fit for the gods. Once the dishes were cleared away, Sophie invited her to take a walk in the Tresilians' garden. "I'm not impartial, of course, but I think it's the loveliest in St. Perran."

"I'd be delighted to see it," Aurelia assured her.

"James?" Sophie turned next to him, but he shook his head.

"Thank you, cousin, but I have a few things to discuss with Harry."

Harry glanced at him quizzically but made no demur. "I suppose we do at that," was all he said. "Enjoy your walk, ladies."

They went out, the fair and dark heads together, Sophie talking animatedly to her guest. They liked each other, James realized: the American heiress and the Cornish miss, fresh out of the schoolroom. Sophie and Amy would surely become fast friends too, once they met. It boded well for the future that the Newbolds and Tresilians should take so quickly to each other.

"Sophie's grown even prettier than she was at New Year's," he observed. "You'll have to beat the swains off with a cudgel, Harry."

"So I've discovered." Harry pulled a face. "As it happens, Sophie's had a few offers since then, already."

"Good Lord, she's not even eighteen yet!"

"So I told the fellows in question," Harry replied. "And at least one of them has stated his intention of waiting me out."

James strongly suspected he knew who that might be. "Nankivell?"

Harry looked startled. "How did you know?"

"An educated guess. I met him on the way. He sends his regards to you and Sophie."

His cousin frowned, irritated. "Damn his impudence!"

James raised his brows. "I thought he was a friend of yours?"

"He is, in a manner of speaking. But that doesn't mean I'm about to hand over my youngest sister to him, just like that. He's more than ten years older than she, for pity's sake!" Harry's frown deepened. "And there are other reasons I don't favor the match, but I shan't go into them at present. Of course, Mother thinks it's quite a feather in Sophie's cap to have attached a baronet, and one of such ancient lineage, to boot."

"How does Sophie feel about it herself?" James asked.

"Oh, she was flattered," Harry admitted. "What young girl wouldn't be, come to that? But she's not yet eighteen. Time enough for her to settle on a husband when she's had a bit more experience of the world. We're planning to send her to London next spring, for the Season. Perhaps your wife might help her get her sea legs there, introduce her to the right people."

Your wife. The words had an odd formality, coming from his cousin's lips. But Harry was right. By next spring, he would be a married man. "I'm sure Amy would be delighted to lend a hand," he said at last. "She has had quite a triumphant few Seasons herself."

"If she's as delightful as her sister, I can understand why. Sophie certainly seems to have taken to Miss Aurelia; she's got a way with her."

"They both do," James said quickly. "Amy took London by storm when she came over from New York. I thought I hadn't a chance with her, to tell the truth. You'll come and dine with us this week, I hope?"

"I'd be delighted to. I know Mother's very interested in meeting your future bride. However," Harry's gaze sharpened, "I do not think you drove over here today simply to invite us to dinner or to discuss Miss Newbold's charms."

He forgot sometimes how well Harry knew him. "No, more's the pity. There *is* something I must discuss with you—and I fear it is not of a pleasant nature." He drew the letter from his pocket and handed it to his cousin. "My cousin Helena received this a few days ago, at her country estate. She has since descended on Pentreath, demanding retribution."

Harry read over the letter in frowning silence. "What a poisonous screed," he remarked at last, lifting his gaze from the page. "And damned difficult to defend oneself against. It stops just short of open accusation, but one cannot mistake the meaning."

"Well, Helena has swallowed it, hook and line. She came roaring down from Wiltshire, Durward in tow, to strike me across the face and accuse me of complicity in Gerald's death."

Harry grimaced. "Sounds typical of her. She seems to begrudge you the very air you breathe. I don't suppose you were able to send her off with a flea in her ear?"

James sighed. "Unfortunately, no. But I reminded her that I'd been seen elsewhere when Gerald apparently fell from the cliff. *And* I agreed that the circumstances of his death were suspicious enough to warrant further investigation. She's staying at Pentreath for now."

"I don't imagine your fiancée likes that above half."

"No, but she understands the necessity of it. Better to have Helena under our roof where we can contain her than spreading mischief abroad." James paused. "You've been here all this time, Harry. Has this rumor been circulating through the county, as this letter claims?"

Harry did not reply at once, and James felt his apprehension growing.

"There's always talk, isn't there, at the beginning?" Harry said at last, with obvious reluctance. "I won't deny I heard some murmurs when Gerald first turned up dead, but, to my knowledge, the inquest put paid to those. James, if I'd been aware of their resurgence, don't you think I would have told you? And implicating me in the whole business is certainly unexpected."

"I know. And you can't have met Gerald as an adult more than two or three times."

"Enough to dislike him as much as I did when we were boys," Harry admitted. "But how our mysterious letter writer builds a case against me from nothing stronger than that amazes me." He frowned at the letter again. "And bringing Robin into it is even more confusing."

"Robin?" James echoed, confused. "Is he the R. P. mentioned in the letter?"

"I can't think of who else it could be. Robin Pendarvis—you met him here, on New Year's. He's old Pendarvis's grandnephew, his only surviving heir."

"You mean Simon Pendarvis? Gerald's godfather?"

"The very same."

James rubbed a hand over his face. "This tale becomes more tangled at every turn."

He had not known Simon Pendarvis, personally. But the old man had been a crony of his Uncle Joshua. They'd been two of a kind: devoted to Cornwall and not overly tolerant of those who did not share that devotion. No doubt both men had hoped that Joshua's son would feel that same allegiance to his home county, though that had never come to pass. James could not recall Gerald having had much to do with his godfather after he'd gone off to university.

"Old Pendarvis died in early April, just after you left for London," Harry resumed. "Nothing mysterious about it. He'd been ailing for some time, and I suspect he missed your uncle, since they were always thick as thieves."

"So that means Robin Pendarvis has come into his inheritance."

Harry shrugged. "For what it's worth."

"It used to be worth a great deal." Pendarvis Hall, James remembered, was one of the oldest and largest houses in the county. The family might not have had a title, but they'd had an ancient name—and until the last ten years or so, the money to do justice to such an exalted pedigree. "So young Robin is now master of Pendarvis Hall," he mused. "That's still a distinction to conjure with, and it might have made him an object of some envy."

"Like you. But Pendarvis Hall without the fortune to support it isn't that grand a legacy."

James thought of Pentreath. "Did old Simon live beyond his means?"

"In this day and age, doesn't almost every landed gentleman?" Harry sighed. "I hadn't heard that he'd run up enormous debts, like Gerald, but it's a plain fact that money goes less further than it did, unless you've made your fortune on the 'Change."

Or contracted to marry an heiress. The words hung unspoken on the air. Feeling suddenly uncomfortable, James asked, "Does Robin Pendarvis mean to set up his household here, or let the place?"

"Neither, actually. He plans to live in Cornwall, but he has no intention of running the same sort of establishment his great-uncle did." Harry paused. "What he does mean to do with his inheritance will likely ruffle any number of feathers in the county."

James raised his brows. "Is he thinking of breaking the entail and selling outright?"

"No, he means to convert Pendarvis Hall into something else entirely. Something that will help the estate pay its way—a hotel."

"A hotel?" James echoed, startled. "Like the ones they've built in Newquay?"

"Well, perhaps not quite as large as those," Harry amended. "But a respectable size nonetheless, and fine enough to appeal to a—certain class of people."

Moneyed people, James translated without difficulty. "A project of that scope will take a lot of capital," he said slowly. "Unless he has unlimited funds to finance this scheme—"

"He'll need investors," Harry finished. "Well, he's got at least one, James. I mean to put up some of the capital."

"You?" James stared at his cousin.

Harry nodded. "Apparently Robin's been thinking of this for a while. It's not an idle fantasy on his part, James; he's studied architecture abroad for some years, and he feels it can be done without bankrupting either of us. I heard him out when he approached me on this, and," he shrugged, "I'd heard worse schemes, James, put forth by less practical men. He's even offered to make me a partner in the hotel, once it's up and running."

Pendarvis Hall—one of the oldest estates in the county—a resort? Could *he* have taken such a step with Pentreath? James wondered. He doubted it; but then his history with the place ran so deep. Robin Pendarvis had not grown up in his great-uncle's house; strong emotional ties to it might be lacking. Aloud, he asked, "Just how well-fixed is he, now that he's inherited?"

"Well enough, though not perhaps as much as if he'd inherited ten years ago. His legacy will cover some of the costs of renovation and construction. And he owns some shares in a railway company that bring in a tidy bit of interest. But we hope to raise a loan as well."

We—James did not miss the significance there. "It sounds as if you've already decided."

"Perhaps I have," Harry conceded. "But it's only good sense to look to the future—for ourselves *and* Cornwall. I wrote you that two more mines in the district had closed."

James nodded acknowledgment. "But Wheal Felicity is still producing, is it not?"

"It's doing well enough, for now. But times are changing here. It's harder to make a living in the same ways. Some of our men have already emigrated to Australia. St. Perran could use the money that would come from such a place, and its people could use the work. And, forgive my frankness, James, I think Trevenan could too—if you'd consider coming in with us."

"Become a partner in a resort hotel? I can't think about that yet, I'm afraid."

Harry held up a hand. "Understood. But I hope you will give the matter some thought, when you have time to reflect."

James nodded again, absently. Some other thought was stirring. If young Pendarvis was old Simon's heir, but

Gerald had been his godson… "Has Robin Pendarvis ever met Gerald?"

"I don't know. He might have." Harry shrugged. "Since I never counted your obnoxious cousin among my chief concerns, I can't say the subject has ever arisen between us."

James let that go; he'd be the last to deny that Gerald *was* obnoxious, especially to those he considered his social inferiors. "I was wondering whether he could shed some light on this matter of the letter. Or perhaps even on Gerald's last days."

"I'm afraid Rob's gone to London, on business. He left the day before you arrived."

James stifled the oath that rose to his lips. "Do you know when he's likely to return?"

"He hopes to be gone no longer than a week. I know where he'll be staying, though. Do you want me to write him about this?"

James hesitated, chose his next words with care. "A subject this sensitive is best handled face to face. And I'd prefer that Helena's accusations travel no further than Cornwall."

"I see your point. And you're right—no sense in letting this ugly rumor spread."

"No." James exhaled. "You could write and tell him that I am eager to speak with him on a matter of some importance when he returns. But no further details than that, if you please."

Harry regarded him thoughtfully. "I see. Very well, I shall do so. And I promise as well to keep my eyes open, and my ears to the ground, for rumor-mongers here."

"Thank you." James paused as feminine voices and laughter reached his ears. "Sounds like the girls are back from their walk."

"I won't mention this to Mother or Sophie," Harry said in a low voice. "But I should like to take John into my confidence, on the off chance that he might have heard something."

James nodded his consent, relieved that he and Harry were in accord on this at least. For the first time in his life, he felt an element of constraint between himself and his cousin, born of the growing doubts and suspicions he had yet to voice. Praying that it was only temporary, he summoned a smile as Aurelia and Sophie reentered the parlor.

"Welcome back," Harry greeted them easily, even jovially. "Did you enjoy the garden?"

✺

Aurelia had found it easy to admire the garden. The roses were especially fine, grown from cuttings planted by a Tresilian ancestress many years before. "And every spring and summer, they put on the most glorious show," Sophie had said proudly.

"Roses are my sister's favorite flower," Aurelia said. "And I like them too, of course."

Sophie had been eager to hear more about her cousin's fiancée, so Aurelia had obliged. Not too surprisingly, the girl was fascinated by the revelation that Aurelia and Amy were twins. "It must be lovely being a twin," she said a bit wistfully, "like having a best friend who's always there. I've often wished for one myself, secretly."

"But you have a sister, don't you?"

"Yes, but Cecily's six years older and already married with a family. We're very fond of each other, but it's not quite the same. I'm looking forward to meeting your sister, especially if she's as nice as you."

"I'm sure you'll like Amy," Aurelia said confidently. "She's the more outgoing of the two of us, and she's very eager to meet you as well."

They'd lingered a little longer in the garden, then headed back inside, still chatting lightly of flowers and families.

The moment they set foot in the parlor, Aurelia could sense that something had shifted. Something that even Sir

Harry's hearty greeting could not disguise. She glanced at Trevenan, whose face gave nothing away. "Yes, Sir Harry, it was lovely," she said, giving their host her brightest, least revealing smile. "I particularly admired the roses."

He smiled back, though she thought his expression was slightly abstracted. "Thank you, Miss Aurelia. Some of the bushes were planted as far back as my great-grandmother's time."

"So Sophie has told me."

"You must come see our gardens at Pentreath, Sophie," Trevenan told his cousin. "Next week, perhaps, when you dine with us?"

Her eyes lit up. "We're to dine at Pentreath? How splendid! Which evening?"

"I was thinking Wednesday or Thursday." Trevenan's eyes sought out Aurelia's as he spoke; she gave him a small nod of encouragement. Amy should certainly be recovered by then. "Have you a preference, Harry?"

"Thursday might be best. I've business in Truro on Wednesday."

Trevenan nodded. "Thursday it is, then. At seven o' clock."

With the arrangements settled, they took a cordial leave of the Tresilians soon after that. Aurelia waited until their gig had turned back onto the main road before venturing a remark.

"Sophie's a delightful girl," she said, eyeing Trevenan's profile; even now, he looked remote and distant. "And I like Sir Harry too. I can see why you enjoy spending time with them."

His expression warmed slightly. "I am glad to hear you liked one another. They took to you as well, which does not surprise me in the least."

The compliment pleased her, but a more pressing concern weighed on her mind. And on his, she suspected. "Did you have a chance to talk to your cousin, about the letter?"

"I did." A faint furrow appeared between his brows. "I'm

afraid Harry is as much in the dark as I about who could have sent it. But he thinks he knows the identity of the other person alluded to in the letter. A friend and neighbor of his— Robin Pendarvis. And there is a connection, of sorts. Simon Pendarvis—of Pendarvis Hall—was Robin's great-uncle and Gerald's godfather."

Aurelia frowned, considering. "So, is it possible that Robin Pendarvis knew Gerald?"

"It's possible, yes. But I don't know if they met that frequently. Robin and his family never lived at Pendarvis Hall, though Robin is the heir. Simon died in April—of natural causes," Trevenan added hastily. "He was well along in years."

"Can you speak to the younger Mr. Pendarvis?"

"At the moment, no. He's in London, on business, and will be away at least a week."

Aurelia grimaced. "Of all the wretched luck!"

"Wretched timing, anyway. But I can speak to him on his return. Harry's eager for me to talk to him in any event."

"Why is that?"

"A business venture." Trevenan paused. "Pendarvis Hall is a large estate, comparable to Pentreath in size and age. And in much the same condition, I suspect."

Aurelia interpreted this without difficulty. "So it must cost a lot to maintain." A fortune, perhaps. She wondered uncomfortably if Robin Pendarvis had gone heiress-hunting in London.

"Just so. According to Harry, Robin has a rather ambitious scheme to make the estate profitable once more—by converting it to a resort hotel."

"Good heavens! That *is* ambitious." And doubly surprising coming from an English gentleman, most of whom set so much store by ancestral lands and properties. An American entrepreneur might be far more likely to hatch such a plan. "Can he afford to do such a thing?"

"Not on his own. He's seeking out investors, and he's offered to make Harry a partner."

"Gracious!" Aurelia sank back against the seat, trying to make sense of it all. "So, the third man in that anonymous letter is a friend and potential business associate of your cousin. Who also happens to be heir to a country estate and who aspires to become a hotelier, though he lacks the funds to finance the project by himself."

"That is correct." Trevenan's face had gone unreadable once again.

"Is there much support for his scheme here?"

"I'm not sure who else knows about it yet." Trevenan stared at the road before them. "Harry thinks I should consider investing as well. He believes it will be a profitable enterprise, and provide some much-needed employment in the area, now that several mines have closed."

Put in those terms, the hotel scheme did not sound too unreasonable, Aurelia mused. Still, the cost involved might give anyone pause. "Do you agree with him?"

"I don't *disagree*. But I'm not about to get involved until I know more about this venture, and the man proposing it." Trevenan drove in silence for several minutes, his dark eyes abstracted. "I'd give a great deal to know just how well Robin Pendarvis knew Gerald," he said at last. "And whether Gerald stood to inherit anything from his godfather's will."

Aurelia caught her breath as his meaning sank in. Surely he wasn't suggesting—but there was a sinister sense to what he was implying. On the surface, such a concern might seem immaterial now, as Gerald had predeceased his godfather. But if there had been a bequest—something beyond a token gift or amount—to whom would it have gone, afterward? Reverted to Pendarvis's heir, a man eager to sink whatever money he had into this grand hotelier's scheme?

How much might he have resented having to share his inheritance with Gerald, especially if it threatened his plans for the estate? Aurelia suppressed a shiver. Terrible though it was to contemplate, people had killed for less…

"I have said nothing of this to Harry," Trevenan went on. "It seems a foul thing to suspect a man my cousin considers a friend. But God help me, I cannot stop wondering."

Aurelia studied his somber face. "It's not surprising that you should wonder. Robin Pendarvis is a stranger to you. But—do you trust Sir Harry's judgment?"

"Most of the time." He sighed. "But no one's judgment is infallible."

"Of course not," Aurelia said at once. "But perhaps you should wait to form an opinion until you meet Mr. Pendarvis yourself?"

"Indeed. I had resolved to do so. There's been enough rushing to judgment already."

He was thinking of Lady Durward, of course, and her intemperate accusations.

"Might I prevail upon you not to mention this matter to Amy?" Trevenan's gaze was intent on hers. "Not yet, at any rate. I feel I have already imposed enough upon your discretion as it is, by confiding as much in you as I have."

Aurelia stifled a sigh, along with a retort that there was little point in withholding the rest. "Very well. But I think you should tell her what you're facing, and sooner rather than later. Amy is to be your *wife*, your partner in all things. Not some child to be shielded from every unpleasantness. I know *I* should hate it, if my future husband took that approach with me."

He eyed her searchingly. "Should you really? Even if it was from the best of motives?"

"Even then. I had enough of being treated like a weakling after my accident." And to make matters worse, she'd bought into that herself for a time, but that was behind her now. She would not trade a moment of self-knowledge, however painfully acquired, for being wrapped in cotton wool again. "Confide in my sister, Trevenan. She is stronger than you think."

He looked at her a moment longer, then smiled. "So are you."

❧

All seemed tranquil when they returned to Pentreath. Aurelia immediately went up to see her sister and tell her of the visit to Roswarne. Amy seemed pleased to hear that the Tresilians were such a likable family, but relieved that they would not be dining at Pentreath until Thursday, by which time she would be fully recovered.

Not until later, when Aurelia came down to dinner that evening, did trouble rear its head.

Lady Talbot presided over the drawing room as she had the night before. Unfortunately, there had been two more additions to the company: Lady Durward and her undistinguished husband were now present. The earl stood by the hearth not far from Aurelia's father and brother, while the haughty countess sat on the sofa some distance away from Mrs. Newbold, who appeared thoroughly intimidated.

Aurelia glanced instinctively toward Trevenan, who stood nearby with his aunt.

"I fear I could not convince her to remain upstairs tonight, James," Lady Talbot murmured apologetically to her nephew. "But she is under orders to be on her best behavior, or she will not like the consequences."

He nodded, looking composed if somewhat grim. Aurelia could only sympathize with the impossible situation he was in, compelled to play host to a relation who despised him, lest her spite damage his reputation and that of his cousin. "Am I to take her in to dinner, then?"

"Certainly not," his aunt said firmly. "You shall escort Mrs. Newbold as you did last night. Durward can partner Helena here—and *I* have the seating well in hand."

Thank heavens for that, Aurelia thought. She did not doubt Lady Talbot's ability to ride herd on her niece throughout dinner. As for herself, it appeared that she had a parent to rescue.

Mrs. Newbold greeted her approach with undisguised relief. "Aurelia, my dear." She cast a dubious glance at the countess, but carried gamely on with the introductions. "This is Lady Durward. Countess, this is my daughter, Aurelia."

"Lady Durward." Aurelia inclined her head toward Trevenan's cousin.

The countess wore grey tonight—perhaps to show that she was still in mourning for her father and brother?—and her gown was fashionably cut, showing off a handsome, deep-bosomed figure. Even seated, she appeared quite tall. Aurelia, who did not consider herself a tiny female by any means, felt slightly intimidated nonetheless by Lady Durward's extra inches.

But she had not only her own part to uphold, but Amy's *in absentia*. So she straightened her spine and prepared to act the queen for both their sakes, if necessary. It helped to know that she looked her best as well in a gown of apricot silk, trimmed with blond lace, which complemented the new rosiness in her cheeks from this morning's excursion.

"Miss Newbold." Lady Durward's chilly blue gaze swept over Aurelia and—predictably—lingered upon her scar. "I gather it is your sister who is betrothed to Trevenan?"

"She is," Aurelia acknowledged levelly.

"Such a pity she was too—unwell to join us tonight." Her tone insinuated that to be unwell amounted to the gravest liability a future countess could face.

"Indeed it is," Aurelia said, deliberately accepting the remark at face value. "But she's seldom out of sorts for long, and she brings such vivacity to every occasion."

Lady Durward's brows arched. "Indeed? I should hope she understands that not every occasion calls for—vivacity."

Odious woman. "Oh, Amy has an infallible sense of what every occasion requires."

"How extraordinary. I should have expected an American to find herself somewhat out of her depth in English society."

And I should have expected an Englishwoman to have better manners, Aurelia thought. "My sister is forever defying expectations. She's been the toast of London for two Seasons now."

Lady Durward's nostrils flared as though scenting blood. "And what of you, Miss Newbold? Have you enjoyed such a distinction yourself?" Her tone implied the impossibility of such an occurrence.

What a nasty piece of work she was, Aurelia mused. A bully, much like her late brother. Well, one stood up to bullies—preferably before they got the upper hand and thought they could ride roughshod over everyone in their path. She gave a light laugh. "You must not encourage me to be immodest, Lady Durward."

"Immodest?" Lady Durward's lips curved in a feline half-smile. "You surprise me. Given your—condition, I'd have thought you would have found moving in Society difficult."

There could be no question of what she was alluding to. Feeling her mother stiffen indignantly beside her, Aurelia stepped at once into the breach.

"Oh, not particularly. Most of the people I've met are far too well-bred to comment on one's personal appearance. And in any case," she gave the countess her most dazzling smile, "an ugly scar is far easier to live with than an ugly character. Do you not agree, Lady Durward?"

Her mother gave a faint muffled sound that might have been shock or even suppressed laughter. Lady Durward flushed—unbecomingly, as she was high-complexioned already. Aurelia continued to smile at her adversary, even as she braced herself for the next onslaught.

"Dinner is served," Pelham announced from the doorway, coming to everyone's rescue.

The tension dispersed like air escaping from a pricked balloon. Lady Durward turned ostentatiously away from Aurelia as her husband approached; her attempt at the cut direct would have been more successful had she not failed to get in the last word.

Assuming her most demure expression, Aurelia turned away as well—to find that Trevenan and Lady Talbot had drawn nearer and were now eyeing her appraisingly. Just how much had they seen of that last exchange? Fortunately, neither appeared annoyed or offended; Lady Talbot looked almost diverted. And Trevenan...Aurelia thought she saw a faint glint of amusement in his eyes as well. She ventured a tiny smile in his direction—*no more little mouse*—and saw the glint intensify.

Then he was moving past her to offer his arm to her mother, while Andrew, not far behind, came forward to escort her.

Composed and decorous to their last member, the company went in to dinner.

Twenty-One

What if we still ride on, we two
With life for ever old yet new,
Changed not in kind but in degree,
The instant made eternity…

—Robert Browning, "The Last Ride Together"

"THIS IS TAMAR. SHE'S VERY GENTLE," TREVENAN SAID as they paused before the horse's stall. "An ideal mount for a lady, and an unashamed sweet tooth," he added, producing two lumps of sugar from his coat pocket and passing one to Aurelia.

The mare whickered and bowed her head, lipping up the sugar from their outstretched palms. "She's lovely," Aurelia said softly. "A milk-white mare, straight out of a fairy tale."

"We'd call her a grey, here."

Aurelia shook her head at this prosaic statement and stroked Tamar's velvety nose. The mare rolled a liquid dark eye at her, and she smiled. "So, this is the horse you had in mind?"

"The very one," Trevenan confirmed. "My cousin Jessica rides Tamar on her visits here, and she's never come to grief. And I can see the two of you have already taken to each other."

"I think," Aurelia took a breath to calm the butterflies in

her stomach, and continued gamely, "I think Tamar and I will get along famously."

"You need not fear, Miss Aurelia." The gentleness in his voice brought the warmth rushing to her cheeks. "We can start out very slowly, just a turn or two about the paddock."

"Thank you. That sounds just about my speed, for now. Shall you be riding Camborne?"

"He'd never forgive me otherwise." Trevenan beckoned to a groom who came forward to tend to their chosen mounts.

"I am sorry Amy did not feel up to joining us today," he remarked as they walked out to wait in the stable yard.

"I think she slept poorly. The storm last night kept her awake." Aurelia glanced up at the sky: fair for now, but laced with scudding clouds that might augur more rain in the not-too-distant future. Amy, who'd come down to breakfast this morning, had cast a darkling look at those clouds from the breakfast parlor window and roundly declared her deep distrust of them.

"I'm afraid Cornish weather can be unpredictable, even in summer," Trevenan said ruefully. "But these inclement spells don't last forever. Today has dawned fairer than yesterday."

"Indeed it has," she agreed. Which was doubly fortunate, as they could now venture out of doors instead of being confined to the house with the unpleasant Lady Durward. Although Lady Talbot had so far managed to keep her niece from committing any outright discourtesy, the countess radiated hostility toward whoever was unfortunate enough to come into her orbit. It must be exhausting to be so ill-tempered all the time. "I actually thought the storm quite moderate, as summer squalls go."

"It did not distress you, then, as it did your sister?"

"Not unduly, though I wouldn't have liked being out in it," she confessed. "But we've had worse thunderstorms than that in New York, especially in summer. And snowstorms in winter. Does it snow here, in Cornwall?"

"Sometimes, but seldom heavily. Winters tend to be less harsh in the West Country."

The grooms emerged from the stables then, leading the now-saddled Tamar and Camborne. Aware of Trevenan's watchful eye upon her, Aurelia stepped onto the mounting block, told herself firmly that the horse was *not* a thousand miles off the ground, and placed her foot in the stirrup.

Up—and over. Mouth dry, palms damp within her gloves, she settled in the saddle, easing her right leg around the pommel, grateful anew for the soft leather breeches beneath the skirt of Amy's borrowed habit. And even more grateful for Tamar's utter stillness.

"Are you sure you're comfortable in the sidesaddle?" Trevenan, now mounted himself, edged his horse closer to her. "You could practice riding astride, first, if you feel safer that way. I know it's not considered ladylike, but I promise not to tell anyone."

Aurelia mustered a smile. "Thank you. I'll certainly bear that in mind. But I think I can manage for now." She gave Tamar's snowy neck a tentative pat, and the mare heaved what sounded like a patient sigh. "Which way is the paddock?"

She surprised him more and more each day.

Astride a fidgeting Camborne, James watched from outside the fence as Aurelia urged Tamar first to a walk, then to a trot about the circumference of the paddock. No outward sign of nerves or panic. Severely elegant in a plain dark habit, she rode with her back straight as a lance, her seat irreproachable. He could readily believe she'd been an excellent horsewoman.

And would be again, he had no doubt. "Ready for something a bit more challenging?" he asked, as she completed her third circuit.

She tilted her head, regarded him with speculative eyes. "That depends on what you mean by 'more challenging.'"

"A leisurely walk along the estate's bridle path," he proposed.

"I don't suppose that would be too taxing. And if worse comes to worst," she glanced down at herself, "at least I won't be spoiling Amy's best habit."

"Your optimism astounds me," he said dryly. "Pray have a little more faith in your ability to keep your seat and mine to choose a suitable route for us both."

She smiled at him. "Very well. I put myself in your hands, Lord Trevenan."

"I shall hold you to that."

Leaving the paddock behind, they ambled along the bridle path, admiring the lush green lawns and talking easily of this and that. As they rode, James pointed out the various gardens and the orangery, its white walls and mullioned windows gleaming even in the pale sunlight. "My great-grandfather's doing, apparently—he'd a taste for citrus fruit, whether in or out of season. And we have a second glasshouse for other fruits."

"Like the strawberries we've been served at dinner?"

"The very same. And there will be peaches and melons later in the summer."

She gave an appreciative murmur. "I do love English strawberries. They seem to have so much more flavor than American ones."

"You should try wild strawberries in the field," he told her. "But they taste best there. They lose something when you bring them home."

"We'd go berrying sometimes, in the country," she reminisced. "Blueberries, mostly—my Aunt Esther, Father's sister, lives in Maine with her family. We'd come to visit, pick until our pails were full, and there'd be pies that very night." She sighed. "You simply haven't lived until you've tasted fresh-baked blueberry pie."

James smiled. "Then I hope to have the opportunity one day."

They rode for some minutes in companionable silence, then spotting the entrance to one of Pentreath's finest gardens, James reined in Camborne. "Over there is the South Garden, my great-grandmother's work," he reported, pointing it out to Aurelia. "She had a way with plants; almost anything would grow for her. She was especially fond of rhododendrons and camellias, though there's also a magnolia tree planted there—a gift from an admirer."

"Lovely." Aurelia's tone was absent, almost automatic; glancing at her, James saw that her blue eyes had clouded slightly and she was worrying her lower lip.

"My dear, are you in pain?" The endearment slipped out before he was aware of it. "We can turn back now, if your leg is troubling you."

"Oh, no, it's not that! I was just wondering—" She paused, frowning, then made a gesture that seemed to encompass the whole of their surroundings. "All this. The estate, the grounds—who would inherit them, after you?"

James raised his brows, surprised by this turn of thought. "You mean, if I did not have any heirs of my body?"

Aurelia nodded. "If you and Amy should be childless— heaven forbid, of course," she hastened to add. "I know how important sons are considered here, when there's property and a title involved. But just supposing that you didn't have one, who'd be next in line?"

"Not Helena's son, if that's what you were thinking."

"It was," she admitted. "I couldn't help thinking of that letter, and how quick she's been to believe the worst of you. And—forgive me for sounding like the writer of some stage melodrama—I wondered if she might be accusing you in hopes of somehow gaining what you possess. If not for herself, then for her child."

"An interesting theory," James conceded. "Fortunately,

I suspect the odds are against her having me hanged or transported for Gerald's death. But I suppose—if I died without issue—Helena could petition the courts to designate her son my heir by letters patent. But that's only assuming that no further branch of the Trelawneys could be found, in Cornwall or anywhere else. In any case, it seems a far-fetched way to gain control of an estate she never cared tuppence for."

"It may not be the estate so much as the title," Aurelia pointed out. "Most mothers are ambitious for their children, after all. And there's the matter of your fortune too."

He shook his head. "I have hardly any fortune worth the name. My Uncle Joshua left barely enough to keep the estate running, and Gerald left only debts."

"What about your own holdings, in the mines and other businesses? Or," she colored slightly, "Amy's dowry?"

"Reverts to your sister if I die and there are no children of our union. Your father and I agreed on that. She'll have whatever I settle on her too. Helena certainly would not be entitled to any Newbold money. Now," he added firmly, "perhaps we might change the subject? I would prefer not to waste a lovely morning discussing my disagreeable cousin. And as I've told you before, this is not something with which *you* need to concern yourself overmuch."

Vexation sparkled in her eyes. "Trevenan, you cannot take me into your confidence one day, and expect me to forget what you told me the next! Especially not something that affects your future *and* Amy's. I've kept my promise and not said a word to her, but that doesn't mean I've stopped thinking about all this. Or concerning myself—*very* much—with the outcome!"

"Good God!" James stared at her, caught between aston-ishment, annoyance—and something else he could not yet name. "You're nothing if not persistent, Miss Aurelia."

"When it comes to my family's well-being, I'm prepared to

be a great deal more than persistent," she informed him loftily. "Like tenacious, or obstinate—possibly even obnoxious."

The word that came to his mind, startlingly, was "formidable." Bemused, he rubbed a hand over his chin. "I don't suppose you'd be willing to go on discussing flowers and fruit?"

A smile hovered about her lips. "Delightful as they are, you'd suppose correctly. I find Lady Durward every bit as disagreeable as you do, but she's raised problems that cannot be ignored or dismissed."

"True enough. Very well, then. What further thoughts have you had on this matter?"

"Well, presumably that someone *would* benefit materially from your disgrace, if the worst came to pass," she replied. "And if it's not Lady Durward and her son, and if the title and estate are inherited only through the male line, who'd come into them if you were—out of the way? Another Trelawney cousin?"

"I have no idea," James admitted. "I was the son of a younger son myself, and thoroughly astonished when I inherited. Given Gerald's age and general hardiness, I never expected such a thing. But I believe there are one or two extant cadet branches of the Trelawneys, who might conceivably come into the earldom—everyone else being gone. Your guess of a cousin is likely enough. I suppose I shall have to look into it further." And such an investigation would at least keep him occupied until Robin Pendarvis returned from London, he reflected.

She nodded. "I really do think you should, Trevenan. If nothing else, perhaps you can narrow down the possibilities of who might wish you ill."

A rumble of thunder drew their attention upward to the sky. The light had dimmed significantly, and the wispy clouds had thickened into a fleecy mass the color of eiderdown. As they gazed, James felt a cold drop on his brow, followed by several more in rapid succession.

"Rain!" Aurelia exclaimed unnecessarily, wiping moisture from her cheek. "Oh, dear. Amy was right after all!"

James pulled the brim of his hat lower. "Come, the folly's just ahead of us on the path. We can wait out the rain there, though I don't think it will last overlong."

Aurelia tweaked the veil of her hat over her face. "Lead the way!"

Together they urged their horses into a trot.

⁂

The rain had increased to a genuine downpour by the time they reached the folly, nestled among a grove of ash trees. Aurelia gazed in bemusement at the Doric columns and pediment. "It looks like a Grecian temple."

"It's meant to." Trevenan swung down from his horse. "Follies come in all manner of shapes and styles. Personally, I find the temple easier to tolerate in these surroundings than a Chinese pagoda," he added, coming over to help her dismount.

Aurelia slid down from the saddle into his arms, trying not to react to the sensation of his hands clasping her waist; at least her leg had held up under the exercise. "Like the one at Kew?"

"Yes. And I understand there's one in Scotland that looks like a pineapple."

"A pineapple?" she echoed on an incredulous laugh.

His grin flashed briefly in the gloom. "On my honor. I'll show you a print of it someday."

Leaving the horses sheltering beneath the trees, they ducked inside the folly. Overhead, the rain beat a light, insistent tattoo on the roof.

"Is this real marble?" Aurelia asked, gazing around her.

Trevenan nodded. "My ancestor who commissioned this folly would have nothing less. The pillars and roof are marble, imported at great expense from Carrara."

"It's beautiful. I only wish it were watertight as well," she added, dodging a drip.

Trevenan glanced up, grimaced as a drop of water struck his face. "Ah. My apologies."

"It's not your fault. Here." She reached up to blot the water with a handkerchief.

He caught her hand; Aurelia felt the warmth and firmness of his clasp even through the riding gloves they both wore. For a moment, the air seemed to pulse between them, heavy with electricity, then, "Best keep it for yourself," he advised gently, releasing her hand. "You may need it, if there are any more leaks in the roof."

The next few minutes were spent in a fruitless search for a drier place to stand. Jumping back from a particularly copious drip, Aurelia wished it were permissible for a lady to swear. Trevenan sidestepped another leak and regarded the roof with disfavor.

"The placement of these is downright diabolical," he observed.

Aurelia gazed around the folly, saw at last a patch of floor that looked relatively untouched. "Here—this part doesn't seem to be too bad."

The patch was just large enough to accommodate them both if they stood side by side. Outside, the rain pelted down with renewed fervor, its soft patter intensifying to a muted roar.

Crack! Aurelia caught her breath as a flash of lightning turned the world a blinding white. Once her vision had cleared, she glanced toward the horses, still placidly cropping the grass beneath the trees, and shivered.

"Are you cold?" Trevenan asked, instantly solicitous. "Here, take my coat." He tugged off and pocketed his gloves, then began to wrestle with the buttons.

"That's not necessary," she protested, even as he shrugged out of the garment.

"I'm used to Cornish weather; you're not," he pointed out, draping the coat over her shoulders. It settled around her like an embrace, warm from his body and smelling faintly of citrus, clove, and clean male. His scent. Every cell in her body seemed to tingle in response.

She looked up at him, all too conscious of his nearness. Between the wings of his shirt collar, his throat rose in a strong, lightly bronzed column to join the sharp lines of jaw and chin. His hands still grasped the coat's lapels as he drew it close about her, and the expression in his dark eyes was solicitous, almost tender. Even the firm mouth looked softer and more relaxed.

Kiss me. The words blazed across her mind like fire, but no hotter or brighter than the yearning that consumed her, overpowering all else—sense, restraint, even loyalty. *Kiss me. Make me yours—the way it should have been, the way it was supposed to be.*

As she gazed at him, his expression grew abstracted, almost dreamy. Slowly, he lifted a hand as though he would touch her face. Mesmerized, she gazed at his fingers, wondering how they would feel against her skin. And his mouth…how would *that* feel, pressed to hers?

The thunder rumbled again, loud and ominous, like the voice of divine disapproval, and they both jerked back as if singed, Trevenan's hand falling to his side. Shamed, Aurelia dropped her gaze to the floor of the folly. Dear God, what had she been *thinking*? Her sister's fiancé…

A moment's madness, brought on by the storm and their close proximity. *Nothing happened*, she reminded herself—and deliberately did not examine whether she felt glad or sorry.

"Thank you," she said in a small voice. "For the coat, I mean."

"You're welcome." His own voice sounded oddly husky. He swung away from her then and strode back to his former place.

Aurelia eyed him with concern. He stood with his body turned partly away from her, shoulders slightly hunched, arms folded over his middle, as though fighting off a spasm of pain. "Are you all right?" she asked after a moment.

"Fine." He cleared his throat, still not looking at her. "Nature's putting on quite a show," he added. "But it should pass soon."

Aurelia nodded, turning her attention to the sky. She heard the thunder growl again but more faintly this time, and no lightning bolts followed, so she let herself relax. "'I too have heart, then. I was not afraid,'" she murmured, remembering Iseult's reaction to the storm at sea.

"*Tristram of Lyonesse*?" Trevenan's voice sounded normal again.

She glanced at him in surprise, saw that he had turned his head and was almost smiling. "I never told you—the poem is one of my favorites as well," he confessed. "I can only admire a poet who writes so beautifully of Cornwall and the sea. And parts of it remind me of my parents, and how they were together."

And that romance had ended in tragedy too, with a capsized boat in Italy, she thought.

"*But peace they have that none may gain who live,*" Trevenan quoted softly, his dark eyes gone distant and unfathomable. "*And rest about them that no love can give, / And over them, while death and life shall be, / The light and sound and darkness of the sea.*"

"That's a lovely tribute to them," Aurelia said, a trifle unsteadily.

"Not the worst of epitaphs. Although I can't fault the one Aunt Judith and Uncle Hugh chose. 'They were lovely and pleasant in their lives, and in their death, they were not divided.'"

Aurelia swallowed, tears prickling at the corners of her eyes. No, *they* had not been divided, but her heart ached for the child they'd left behind and the man who still felt their loss. "That too is apposite." She looked away quickly, and

saw with relief that the rain had lessened, now falling in a
fine silver curtain.

"Perhaps we should head back to the house," she ventured,
with a covert glance at her companion of the storm. At least
the constraint between them had eased.

"Yes. Perhaps we should," he said after a moment.

Handing him back his coat, she secured her veil again
and headed toward the steps of the folly. "Amy must be
wondering where we are."

"No doubt she is," he agreed, following her. "So, let us
go and put her mind at ease."

Amy just managed not to flinch when she heard the faint
rumble in the air. Abandoning the novel she'd been thumbing
through listlessly, she went to the library window and gazed
out at the darkening sky. Trevenan and Aurelia were mad to
have gone out riding on a day like this, she thought with a
shudder. Of course, it was wonderful that Relia wanted to
ride again, but it could come on to rain at any minute—the
sort of rain that *sensible* people stayed inside to avoid.

Sighing, she drifted away from the window. Despite the
lighted lamps and the fire in the grate, she found the library
oddly...well, not cold, perhaps, but austere. Even remote—as
if it held outsiders at arm's length, waiting for them to prove
their worthiness to be here.

Which was nonsense, Amy chided herself. Pure fancy and
she was not a particularly fanciful person. It was only natural
that she should feel some constraint in a new place, even if it
was to be her home one day soon. And Pentreath was such
a handsome estate; surely she'd find a way to be comfortable
here. She'd *make* herself comfortable here.

She glanced down at her ring, the pretty trio of diamonds
she'd worn ever since her engagement to James was
announced. This was what she'd wanted, after all: a title, a

stately home, and a peer for a husband. And James was young, handsome, intelligent, and kind. She should be thanking her lucky stars that she was engaged to him and not that boorish lout, Glyndon! She was grateful, truly she was. It was no hardship to spend time in his company, though she couldn't help wishing that their tastes in pursuits were more similar. If only he enjoyed Society more—or if only she enjoyed it less, she admitted honestly.

But then, marriages were often compromises, Amy reminded herself. Over the years, spouses learned to make allowances for each other's differences, or found a happy medium with which they could both live. She and James had gone into this arrangement with their eyes open—liking what they saw, but not carried away by passion on either side. Which was just as well. Having witnessed Relia's devastation when Charlie jilted her, Amy had no desire for a love match. But surely she and James could forge an affectionate and satisfying union, made stronger by whatever children they had in the future.

Another, louder rumble made her jump, and she glanced out the window again to see rain sheeting down with noisy abandon. James had mentioned storms were frequent here, though more common in the autumn and winter months. Her stomach sank at the prospect. Perhaps she could persuade James to spend part of the Little Season in London?

The sky lit up with a brilliant flash of lightning, throwing every object in the room into sharp relief. Amy bit back a startled squeak, then gathered up her skirts and hurried from the library, unable to bear it there a moment longer.

In her headlong rush, she did not see the figure in the hallway until it loomed up out of the shadows and caught her by the shoulders. A scream broke from her just as the figure spoke.

"Miss Newbold! It is I!"

The familiar voice cut through her panic, just as it had

once before. "M-Mr. Sheridan?" she faltered, her eyes starting to adjust to the gloom.

He nodded, brushed back rain-wet brown hair; his eyes looked startlingly green in the dim light of the entrance hall. "A trifle waterlogged, but I am he."

"Wh-when did you get in?" Her voice sounded faint even to her own ears.

"My train arrived this morning," he replied. "I wasn't sure just when I would be traveling, so I neglected to wire ahead. But James knew to expect me either today or tomorrow."

"Oh." Amy felt herself begin to relax. "I'm afraid James isn't here at the moment. And I'm not sure where Lady Talbot is. Shall I send someone to fetch her?"

He shook his head. "No need to trouble yourself, Miss Newbold. Pelham's already had the footmen take my luggage up, and he said my chamber should be ready shortly."

"Well, why don't you come into the drawing room and let me ring for hot tea and perhaps some sandwiches?" she proposed. "You must be chilled, traveling in such a downpour."

Sheridan smiled, a startlingly sweet smile devoid of his usual cool irony. "That would be most welcome. Thank you."

Feeling oddly cheered, she led him into the drawing room and pointed out his painting over the fireplace. With a modesty that surprised her, he expressed both astonishment and pleasure at his work being so prominently displayed in a friend's home.

"Well, why wouldn't it be?" Amy asked as she poured tea for them both. "Lady Talbot said it's much nicer than the classical painting that used to hang there."

Sheridan accepted his cup, taking a wedge of lemon but no milk or sugar. "Sentiment, mainly. People become attached to something that's always been there, even if it's unattractive. Or downright hideous, in some cases."

Amy smiled. "Well, fortunately for lovers of art, James isn't ruled by sentiment."

"True. So, what is James up to at the moment? Seeing to some estate matter?"

Amy stirred sugar into her own tea. "Actually, he and Aurelia have both gone riding."

"In this weather?" Sheridan shook his head. "These Cornish. I knew James considers rain of little account here, but I hadn't realized your sister was cut from a similar cloth. Well, never fear. I doubt they'll stay out long if the rain continues."

The prosaic words calmed her. "I told them the weather might change. I didn't trust it myself; that's why I stayed behind."

"Very sensible of you, given the circumstances."

"I do hope they aren't too badly drenched. Aurelia's been so looking forward to riding again. After her accident, I wasn't sure she'd ever bring herself to get on a horse again." Amy sipped her tea. "But James apparently talked her into trying it."

Sheridan's brows rose as he helped himself to a sandwich. "Did he now?"

"Oh, yes. He even said he has the perfect mount for her, and I trust him completely with my sister's safety. They've become good friends, which is a tremendous relief to me," she added, smiling. "I used to worry about what would happen if either of us met a fellow who couldn't understand our bond."

"I'm glad to hear that Miss Aurelia is in such fine fettle these days."

"Oh, she's so much more like her old self. And she seems to have really taken to Cornwall." *More than I have*, Amy admitted ruefully to herself.

"And what of you, Miss Newbold? Are you finding Cornwall to your liking?"

"Well, I haven't seen that much of it so far," she demurred. "A trifling ailment kept me to my room until this morning. But what I *have* seen of it is certainly very—striking."

Sheridan's green eyes studied her with disconcerting perception. "That it is—a wild, beautiful place," he said after a moment. "But there are a number of people who find it a touch…remote, even isolated."

"It does feel a bit like the ends of the earth," she admitted, relieved by his lack of criticism. "Especially when compared to London. But James loves it so here, and Aurelia swears it's vastly superior to Newport, so I am sure—in time—I'll grow fond of it too."

The front door opened then, and laughing voices reached them from the hall. "They're back," Amy noted with relief.

Moments later, her betrothed and her sister entered the drawing room: windblown, their clothes beaded with rain, but their faces brightened by recent exercise.

"James, Relia!" Amy greeted them brightly. "Look who's just arrived."

"Thomas!" James strode forward to clasp his friend's hand. "Glad to see you, old fellow. But why didn't you let me know you were coming today? I'd have sent a carriage to meet you."

"Wasn't entirely sure of my schedule," Sheridan replied, rising to return the earl's greeting. "But things cleared up unexpectedly, so I decided to travel down today, after all. I had no trouble hiring a carriage, which is just as well, considering how many canvases I've brought with me." He turned to Aurelia, bowed over her hand. "Delighted to meet you again, Miss Aurelia—and looking as lovely as ever."

"And you are as flattering as ever, Mr. Sheridan," she returned. "But I am glad to see you here as well."

"I have not abandoned the hope that you will sit for me one day," he told her.

"I may indeed do so, " she conceded. "And perhaps sooner rather than later, though I shall give you plenty of notice beforehand, since I know you have other commissions."

"There are any number of rooms you can use as a studio

here, Thomas," James informed him. "And I'm glad Amy was here to welcome you. You make a splendid hostess, my dear."

"It was no trouble," Amy assured him, warmed by his praise. "Did the two of you enjoy your ride? I hope you did not get too wet and chilled."

Aurelia shook her head. "We were fine, Amy. And our ride was pleasant, despite the rain. We waited out the worst of it in the folly, which you absolutely must see," she added on a gurgle of laughter. "It looks just like a Grecian temple."

James pulled a rueful face. "A Grecian temple with a leaky roof!"

"Leaks can be fixed," Amy pointed out. "I'd love to see it, once the weather's improved. How did you get on with your horse?" she asked her sister.

Aurelia smiled. "Oh, she was lovely—gentle as a kitten, surefooted as a goat. We even got up to a canter today on the way back, though I decided I wasn't ready to gallop yet. Thank you for lending me your habit. Now, I'd best go up and change so I can return it to you."

"Oh, keep it for now," Amy insisted. "It'll save you the trouble of borrowing it again."

"Well, if you're sure you won't need it, dearest," Aurelia began.

"Positive," Amy declared. "I brought more than one habit with me, as you well know. Now, go up and change before you do get a chill!"

"Bossy!" her sister said with affection, then turned to the men. "Trevenan, Mr. Sheridan, if you'll excuse me?" Picking up the habit's damp skirts, she hurried from the room.

"I'd best go up myself," Sheridan said. "Barlow must have my things unpacked by now."

"I'll have a footman show you to your room," James said, going over to the bellpull. Once his guest had gone up, James turned back to Amy. "My dear, if you'll allow me a few minutes to change, I'll give you that tour of the house I promised you."

She smiled, pleased that he'd remembered. "Thank you, James. I should like that."

"I do not mean to neglect you, Amy," he said, almost abruptly.

"Neglect me? It was my own choice to stay behind today. And I must say," she added mischievously, "that I think I had the right idea, given the state of your Grecian temple."

His mouth crooked in an odd sort of smile. "Perhaps you did at that," was all he said as he headed for the door.

Twenty-Two

Slander,
Whose edge is sharper than the sword, whose tongue
Outvenoms all the worms of Nile…

—William Shakespeare, *Cymbeline*

SOMETHING WAS WRONG. JAMES COULD TELL THE moment Harry entered the drawing room with his family on Thursday evening.

He could also see that, whatever was troubling Harry, the rest of the Tresilians had not been apprised of it. There was only pleased expectation on the faces of Aunt Isobel, Sophie, and John as he came forward to welcome them to Pentreath.

"Aunt Isobel, Sophie." James kissed them both on the cheek. "Ladies, you look lovely tonight. John," he clasped his younger cousin's hand, "good to see you. Harry," he took his older cousin's elbow in an easy, affectionate clasp, "if I might have a word with you before dinner?"

Harry's expression eased fractionally as they moved off together, leaving the others to Lady Talbot. "Thank you," he said in a low voice. "I hoped to get you alone for a few minutes."

"I could see by your face that something was wrong."

James spoke in an undertone as well. "Come, we can talk in the library."

They left the drawing room and headed down the passage toward the rear of the house. No one in the library, James observed with relief as he closed the door behind them.

"Now, what's happened?" he asked his cousin.

"This." Harry took an envelope out of his breast pocket and handed it to James. "Another one of those damned letters—sent this time to our banker in Truro."

"What?" James yanked out the single page at once and scanned the contents. The hand was the same, as were the vile accusations, but the tone was sharper. Less insinuating, more accusatory, though it still stopped just short of libel. More damningly, it did not hesitate to name names this time: "Harry Tresilian" and "Robin Pendarvis" were spelled out in full.

James looked up from the letter. "When did Curnow get this?"

"About two days ago. I went to see him yesterday about raising a loan for the hotel venture. He produced the letter and asked me if there was any truth in it. I denied it, of course."

"Does he believe you?" James did not want to think about how bad things would get if their family banker thought them guilty of murder.

Harry did not reply at once, and James's apprehension deepened. "He *says* he does, at least as far as you and I are concerned. He is less certain of Robin, unfortunately—not surprising since Robin's a stranger to him. And he finds the rumor itself deeply disturbing."

"He's not alone in that," James retorted. "So, did he agree to the loan?"

"No—at least, not yet. He wishes to be satisfied as to Robin's character before he'll advance us so much as a penny." Harry exhaled. "James, I know you wish to keep this ugly affair quiet, but as Robin's friend and future business partner, I feel I must inform him of this assault upon his character."

Remembering his own doubts of Robin Pendarvis's character, James hesitated—a fraction too long, as it happened.

Harry stared at him as if he'd become a stranger. "My God, you agree with Curnow." His gaze sharpened. "More than that, you think Robin had something to do with Gerald's death!"

"I didn't say that," James began, uncomfortably aware of how feeble that sounded.

"You didn't bloody have to! I can read your face as well as you can read mine!" Harry paused, his eyes darkening. "We're cousins, James. Blood kin. And beyond that, we've lived in each other's pockets since boyhood. After all this time, does *my* judgment count for so little?"

James swallowed, feeling a chasm starting to open between them. "Harry, I value your judgment as I do that of no other man living. But no one is infallible, not even you. In normal circumstances, I would gladly give any friend of yours the benefit of the doubt—"

"Magnanimous of you," his cousin interposed with heavy irony.

"But these aren't normal circumstances," James continued as though Harry had not spoken. "There's too much at stake, for *all of us*." He emphasized the last words, paused to let them sink in, and saw with relief that their significance was not lost on his cousin.

"Let's not fall out over this," he added in a more moderate tone. "I have the feeling that whoever wrote these letters would like nothing better than to see us at each other's throats."

Harry opened his mouth, closed it almost at once, then sighed. "You're right, damn it all. If we let these rumors divide us, we've already lost."

"Exactly. Whereas if we combine our forces and hold

up our heads, we stand a good chance of coming through this unscathed. And whoever wrote this filth," James struck the letter with his free hand, "will rue the day he put pen to paper."

"Have you any idea who the culprit might be?" Harry asked.

"No, but someone has put an idea in my head that may be worth pursuing." James paused. "I intend to pay a visit to my heir tomorrow."

"Your heir?" Harry echoed, astonished.

"My third cousin, as it happens. Horatio Trelawney, an antiquarian. Married, with three adult children, and living on the coast a few miles north of us."

Harry shook his head, bemused. "I never thought to wonder who came after you."

"Nor did I, which gives you some idea of how unprepared I was for all this." James sighed, rubbed a suddenly stiff neck. "I've spent the last two days looking him up. Wired my solicitor in London about the succession, then went hunting through the family Bible. God, there must be entries in it that go back over a century! Spoke to Aunt Judith too; she's invaluable about such things, but even she didn't know that Horatio was so close to the earldom. There were two other Trelawneys before him," he explained. "But they're now deceased. One was killed in the South African war, the other died more recently and left only daughters. My solicitor wired me this morning with confirmation of their deaths and Horatio's position as heir presumptive."

"Enough to make your head spin, trying to keep it all straight," Harry muttered. "Have you ever met Horatio Trelawney?"

"According to Aunt Judith, Horatio and his family—some of them, anyway—came to my uncle's funeral, and to Gerald's. I haven't much recollection of meeting them. I was still too stunned to find myself an earl." Both funerals had been amply attended, James remembered, though he suspected that had as much to do with curiosity as with the exalted rank of the deceased. Gerald's funeral, barely six months after his father's, had drawn a particularly large crowd, doubtless owing to his youth and vigor at the time of his death.

"In any case," James resumed, "it has come to my attention that Horatio and his family would benefit considerably if I were out of the way."

Harry eyed him narrowly. "You think your heir might be behind these letters?"

"I think we have nothing to lose by investigating this possibility," James qualified. "I'm setting out tomorrow morning. Would you care to accompany me?"

"Gladly." Harry's mouth tightened. "If nothing else, you might need a witness to whatever you see or hear."

"Good thinking." James just managed to conceal his relief. The potential rift between him and Harry had been bridged. "In truth, I'd be glad of reinforcements."

Harry gave a brief nod. "And Robin?" His tone still held a hint of challenge. "Have I your permission to write to him?"

"You may tell him there's an important matter requiring his attention here," James said, after a moment. "But no more than that, if you please."

"Very well," Harry conceded, with visible reluctance. "I shan't go into further details."

"Thank you. Shall we rejoin the others now?"

Something wasn't right. Aurelia could tell the moment Trevenan and Sir Harry reentered the drawing room. Both looked decidedly grim and tight-lipped even as they made an effort to conceal whatever was troubling them.

Aurelia glanced at Sophie and Amy, sitting beside her on the sofa, but the two were still deep in conversation and had not yet noticed the men's return. Lady Tresilian and Aurelia's mother were similarly engaged. Lady Durward, seated haughtily on an armchair a little distance apart, did notice, and her pale eyes narrowed in distaste. Uneasily, Aurelia wondered just how disagreeable the countess was going to be tonight, even with Lady Talbot to keep her in check.

Once Trevenan and Sir Harry's appearance was observed, the formal procession in to dinner began. Aurelia found herself seated between her escort, John Tresilian, and Sir Harry, seated as guest of honor on Lady Talbot's right. Unfortunately, the Durwards were placed almost directly opposite—a necessary evil, Aurelia supposed, since Lady Talbot needed to keep a watchful eye on her niece. For her part, she wished she was not obliged to see the woman's sour face at such close quarters, but at least she knew there was nothing Lady Durward could say that would cow her. Besides, she was only obliged to converse with the people on either side of her; John Tresilian, who was about Andrew's age, seemed as pleasant a fellow as his older brother.

Dinner, always good, was excellent tonight. Trevenan's cook had made a special effort. Lobster bisque and smoked oysters wrapped in bacon gave way to delicately poached salmon with asparagus, then a green goose and a saddle of lamb. Savoring her own meal, Aurelia could not help but notice that Lady Durward consumed each mouthful as though she expected it to poison her, though she drained her wine glass several times. But her husband ate heartily enough.

"Do you find Cornwall to your liking, Miss Aurelia?" Sir Harry inquired.

Relieved, she turned her attention to him. "Oh, yes. I find more to enjoy here each day."

He smiled. "I am pleased to hear you say that. For my part, no place on earth compares. Have you decided what you like best so far?"

"The sea," she replied without hesitation. "I especially love taking the stairs down to the beach. Have you ever done so?"

He shook his head. "I fear not. This is the first time I have been inside Pentreath."

"A pity it's not the last," Lady Durward observed, just audibly enough for her closest neighbors to hear.

Aurelia blinked, scarcely able to believe what she'd just heard. Sir Harry's green eyes cooled, but to his credit, he ignored Lady Durward's obvious provocation, turning again to Aurelia. "Roswarne is further from the sea than Pentreath, but we have a fine beach of our own, should you wish to visit us."

"Best to stay at home rather than intrude where you're not wanted." Lady Durward again, slightly louder this time.

Sir Harry's mouth tightened. "I could not agree with you more, madam," he returned, his own voice edged beneath its surface courtesy. Aurelia could hardly blame him for such a response, even though it seemed as reckless as brandishing a red flag in front of a bull.

The countess's nostrils flared. "In my father's time, you and your family wouldn't have been allowed past the gates of Pentreath, *Sir* Harry," she hissed venomously.

"I daresay. But James is master of Pentreath now, and may invite whom he pleases."

"A jumped-up country squire! And a suspected murderer to boot? What have you to say to that—*H.T.*?" Lady Durward all but flung the last words at him, her voice rising over the other conversations in the room.

A shocked hush descended over the table. Aurelia glanced wildly toward Trevenan at the other end, saw his face darken as he set down his glass. But it was Lady Talbot, breaking off her conversation with Aurelia's father on her left, who spoke first.

"Helena!" she snapped. "Apologize at once! I will not have a guest insulted at our table!"

Both combatants ignored her, the countess's last ugly accusation hovering on the charged air between them. Sir Harry laid down his fork and locked eyes with his adversary. "Let me be frank with you, Lady Durward," he said evenly.

"I have made no secret of my dislike for your brother in life. But considering him an arrogant bully who should have been taught a lesson long ago is not the same as wishing him dead at the bottom of a cliff. Or assisting him there."

It happened too quickly for anyone to stop her. Only Sir Harry perhaps saw what Lady Durward intended, for he moved just one fraction to the side, so that the contents of her wine glass soaked the shoulder of his dinner coat rather than catching him full in the face.

"Helena!" Lady Talbot stood up at once, her dark eyes blazing with cold anger. "Clearly, you are unwell. I shall escort you to your chamber so that you may recover in peace."

"No need to take you away from your dinner, ma'am." Lord Durward surprised everyone by speaking up. "*I* shall escort my wife."

Lady Durward glared daggers at her husband, but to Aurelia's astonishment, the mild-mannered earl did not quail. Instead, he pushed back his chair and stood up, pointedly offering his arm to his wife. Finally, the countess rose with ill grace and accepted his proffered arm.

Aurelia could have sworn the whole dining room held its breath until the Durwards had left. She pitied the earl; no doubt his wife would give him an earful once they were upstairs.

Trevenan spoke at last. "Harry, my deepest apologies. My apologies to all of you," he added, with a glance around the table.

Face impassive, Sir Harry nodded at his cousin and mopped at his coat with a napkin. "You are not to blame, James."

"Certainly not," Lady Talbot declared. "Only Helena is responsible for her lamentable lack of self-control. But let us not permit her to spoil the evening," she added with a determined smile. "Mr. Newbold, I believe you were telling me about the horse races at Saratoga. Have you ever attended Ascot or the Derby at Epsom Downs?"

Aurelia's father quickly followed her lead, and the

lapsed conversations resumed, not pausing even when Lord Durward returned to the dining room to finish his dinner.

So, the ugliness was papered over for now, Aurelia thought. But to judge from the lingering strain she saw on Trevenan and Sir Harry's faces, it was far from forgotten.

❧

The rest of the evening passed in a blur. There was music in the drawing room, Aurelia remembered—Sophie had brought her violin—and everyone did their best to pretend the ugly incident at dinner hadn't happened. The Tresilians left not long after, Sir Harry claiming an early rise, but Aurelia didn't miss the quick glance he exchanged with James on his way out. Something was afoot, and, while it was none of her affair, she couldn't help but wonder.

Upstairs, she dismissed Suzanne as soon as her hair was plaited for the night. Too restless and unsettled to retire yet, she decided to go in search of a book. Something peaceful and soothing, or else so gripping that she wouldn't mind losing sleep over it. Pulling on her dressing gown, she did up all the fastenings, secured the sash about her waist, and ventured downstairs.

Nearing the doorway of the library, she glimpsed the glow of a lighted lamp within. Someone else was also wakeful tonight, she thought as she peered into the room.

Trevenan sat at his desk. He'd loosened his waistcoat and dispensed with his jacket altogether, and the linen of his shirt gleamed with a ghostly whiteness in the lamplight. Beneath a shock of disordered dark hair—had he been running his fingers through it?—his expression was abstracted, almost brooding; slightly to Aurelia's alarm, he cradled a glass of brandy in one hand.

Hesitantly, she called to him from the threshold. "Trevenan?"

He looked up. "Miss Aurelia. Shouldn't you be abed by now?"

"I couldn't sleep," she explained, coming further into the room and trying not to feel self-conscious about being in her nightclothes. At least she was decently covered, and, in his current state of dishevelment, Trevenan was in no position to cast stones. "I wondered if a book might calm me. Why are you sitting here in the dark?"

He glanced at his lone lamp, then toward the fireplace where the evening's blaze had subsided to glowing embers. "I find it helps me to think."

"Does *that* help you to think as well?" Aurelia gestured toward the glass in his hand.

"Sometimes." His mouth formed a faint, sardonic smile. "Or better still, it helps me not to think at all."

"That I can believe," she retorted, a note of censure creeping into her voice.

He raised his brows, swirled about the contents of his glass with an almost provocative air; she'd never seen him in such a mood. "You have something against spirits, then?"

Aurelia met his gaze squarely. "No, merely the misuse of them. Consider Lady Durward's behavior tonight. Surely you noticed how much wine she drank at dinner?"

He exhaled, setting down his glass. "Point taken. But one brandy, after a long, trying evening, is not going to turn me into a toper or a raging boor," he added with some irritation.

"No, of course not," she said at once, trying to sound placatory. "And it *has* been a long, trying evening. But Lady Durward's been dealt with; she can't do any more damage tonight."

Something—some shadow—flickered in his eyes, and she frowned. "But there's something else wrong, isn't there? Not just your odious cousin making a scene." She took a step toward the desk and caught sight of several papers lying off to one side; enlightenment dawned horribly. "Another letter?"

From the way his brows lanced together, she suspected that he was cursing himself for not putting the pages away before she came in. "It would appear so." His voice was curt;

after a moment, he added, more normally, "The second was delivered two days ago to our banker, Samuel Curnow, in Truro. It contains the same accusations as the first, *and* names Harry and Robin Pendarvis as possible suspects, instead of simply hinting at their involvement."

Aurelia fretted her lower lip as she absorbed the implications. "Was Sir Harry able to convince your banker that the letter was libelous?"

Trevenan sighed. "Curnow is willing to give Harry the benefit of the doubt. Robin Pendarvis, however, remains an unknown quantity."

"And you?" she asked. "I trust Mr. Curnow sees no reason to doubt your innocence."

"No, fortunately. He has discounted the slanders against myself and Harry." He glanced down at the letters again, pulled them toward him with obvious reluctance. "All's well and good—until the next one arrives. And there *will* be a next one."

"Yes, very likely," Aurelia conceded with a sigh of her own.

He smiled wryly. "I see you don't dismiss the possibility."

She shrugged. "What good would that do? Ignoring an unpleasant reality doesn't make it go away. I could wish the writer of this poison would tire of his nasty scheme or meet with an unfortunate accident himself, but that won't stop the letters from coming."

"No." He looked down at the letters, his expression darkening. "I go over these again and again, trying to find some clue, some trick of phrasing that might help me discover who could possibly hate us this much." He reached for his glass, took another lengthy swallow.

"Why not put it away for now and come back to it with fresh eyes tomorrow?" Aurelia suggested. "You won't accomplish anything but a headache sitting here brooding and drinking brandy in the dark."

He slanted an unreadable glance at her over his glass. "Sensible Aurelia."

It sounded almost like a gibe. Flushing, she said a bit stiffly, "I try to be."

"And bossy Aurelia too. I hadn't expected that of you. Your sister, perhaps, but not you."

"Perhaps I have hidden depths," she retorted, matching him stare for stare. "You didn't think Amy always called the tune, did you? You'd be sadly mistaken in that case."

Trevenan sighed, shutting both letters away in their drawer. "I suspect I've been mistaken about a great many things lately."

"Including not taking Amy into your confidence?"

His brows drew together, a dark slash of annoyance. "This again?"

There was a hint of temper in his voice as well as his eyes, but Aurelia wasn't about to let it intimidate her. "Yes, this again. I can't understand why you haven't told her the whole of what you're facing."

"Perhaps because one Newbold sister plaguing me about this is more than enough!"

The words stung like a slap; she could almost feel the color leaving her face. Her own fault for prying, she supposed. Summoning what dignity she could, she drew herself up to her full height and strove for enough cool composure to mask the hurt. "I see." To her relief, her voice emerged without a quaver. "My apologies, Lord Trevenan, for intruding upon your private affairs. I wish you good night."

She turned to go, trying to carry herself with the poise expected of an American princess.

"Aurelia!" Trevenan surged to his feet and closed the distance between them in a few short strides. "Forgive me," he said with what appeared to be genuine contrition. "That *was* boorish. I spoke in haste—or perhaps it was the brandy speaking." He reached for her hand, then paused, with his own hand hovering between them.

Aurelia eyed his hand warily, as if it might bite. "Maybe

you and the brandy should say good night as well, before you both say something else that you'll regret in the morning."

She spoke tartly, keeping her defenses well up, but she could already feel herself starting to soften. Only a saint could remain tranquil and unaffected by all that he was facing, and Trevenan was no saint—just a good man beset by problems not of his making. Little wonder, then, that he was impatient and short-tempered now. And she *had* been awfully persistent about him telling Amy, she acknowledged with a pang of guilt.

"I already regret what I've said," Trevenan assured her. "And no doubt you're right about the brandy. I'll stop at once."

Aurelia swallowed. "I do not mean to—to plague you. About Amy or the brandy. It's just that you don't seem the sort, to seek comfort in a bottle."

"I'm not, usually. Call it a momentary lapse, born of circumstance. And as for plaguing me…" He shook his head, offered her a tentative smile. "I have far more cause to thank you than to criticize you. So thank you I will—your loyalty and discretion are deeply appreciated."

"They are no trouble to give, in your case." Aurelia hesitated, then resumed with greater urgency, "Trevenan… James." His name felt strangely right on her tongue; she rushed on rather than let herself think *how* right. "You are not alone. You have family and friends—and a fiancée, who all care for you. Let them in, give them a chance to help you with this."

After a moment, he nodded. "I *will* tell Amy. You are right; this concerns her too."

"Good." Aurelia smiled at him. "You won't regret it. Amy's the most loyal person I know. She never stops fighting for the people she cares for."

He looked at her without speaking, his dark eyes intent on her face. Looked so long, in fact, that Aurelia began to feel self-conscious again. Lowering her gaze, she glimpsed the triangle of bare skin exposed by his open shirt collar, and below that, the outlines of a lean, hard torso, just visible beneath smooth linen. Heat flooded through her at the sight, and she inwardly cursed herself for being so susceptible to his physical presence. Still. Always. Just as she'd been a few days ago, in the folly.

Pushing the thought away, she made herself look up again, only to find him still gazing at her. Self-consciousness quickly yielded to concern. "Trevenan—are you all right?"

He started, visibly coming back to himself. "I'm fine." He paused to clear his throat. "Perhaps—more affected by the brandy than I thought."

"Do you need someone to help you upstairs?" she asked at once.

His brows quirked up. "Good Lord, no." He sounded almost amused now. "I'm not in that bad a case. But I'll say good night now and leave you to your search for bedtime reading. I'd avoid the Gothic romances, if I were you," he added. "They'll give you nightmares."

Aurelia smiled at that, as he'd no doubt expected her to, but she couldn't help eying him with solicitude. "Good night, Trevenan. Pleasant dreams."

He nodded. "And to you as well, my dear."

He strode from the library, leaving Aurelia to stare after him in bemusement. Shaking her head, she turned to face the room again. He'd left his coat behind, thrown over the back of a chair. Idly, she fingered the heavy black broadcloth. It held none of his warmth, not after all this time, but she found herself wondering if it retained any of his scent the way his riding coat had, in the folly. The memory brought a scalding rush of blood to her cheeks, and she snatched her hand back from the coat as if it had been woven of nettles rather than wool.

A book, Aurelia reminded herself. She had come downstairs for a book. With grim determination, she began her search, even as she suspected that sleep might be a lost cause tonight, whatever title she chose.

❧

James stood at his chamber window, staring out at the night sky. Black on black, a nearly moonless night—and all too appropriate to his mood. He'd locked the letters away downstairs, but their poisonous accusations still gnawed at him.

Spite and malice, from a coward's pen. Did this faceless stranger, this invisible enemy who employed such vicious slanders, have any idea just how much James *hadn't* wanted the earldom? God, if he could undo whatever had happened to Gerald that night…

The back of his neck prickled, as if in warning; he turned at once from the window and caught his breath.

His love stood on the threshold, smiling, gazing at him with the tender sympathy he cherished in her. Unbound, her hair spilled over her shoulders like a flood of molten gold, gleaming against the chaste white of her nightgown.

"You shouldn't be here," he told her, but she only glided forward, soft-footed as a shadow, to slip her arms about his neck.

"My dear," James began, then all reason fled as she leaned into him, the soft curves of her body warm and yielding against his own. The scent of her filled his nostrils, made all his senses swim, and sent heat coiling through his lower belly. With a groan, he surrendered to the longing that consumed him, wrapping his arms about her and lifting her off her feet.

Together they sank onto the bed, which received their combined weight without even a creak of springs. She lay beneath him, eyes shining, lips parted for his kiss. The thin muslin of her nightgown fell away beneath his touch like a discarded skin. Marveling, James skimmed his fingers over the plush softness of her lips, the warm satin of her skin, even the line of her scar. Her scar…

He jerked awake, breathless, perspiring—and alone. His

bedclothes were a tangle about his body. He fought his way free of them and stumbled toward the window. Opening the casement as far as it would go, he leaned on the sill and let the night air cool his heated face, while he breathed deeply, in and out. His heart pounded in his chest, a hammer raining blows on an anvil, and his loins still ached with arousal.

A dream, nothing more. But a dream so vivid, so *real*, he could scarce believe it hadn't happened—not even when he looked back at the empty bed.

The bed…fresh linens had been put on it just today, he remembered. Linens fragrant with orris—and lavender, the scent *she* loved so much. The scent of lavender, weaving through his dreams like a silken ribbon, or a strain of music impossible to forget. And scents could be powerfully evocative things. Perhaps if the linens had smelled of roses and jasmine, he would have dreamed of Amy instead.

He grimaced, recognizing that the argument carried more hope than conviction. It hadn't been Amy beside him that day in the folly, when his body had first betrayed him—though at least he'd managed to conceal it. It hadn't been Amy he'd wanted to kiss as though his next breath depended on it. High time he stopped pretending, if only to himself. He stared at the bed a moment longer, still seeing *her* there in his mind's eye, and then looked away. *Shun the demon brandy,* he thought with black humor, remembering her earlier remonstrations to him in the library. Except that he suspected the brandy had had little to do with what had just occurred.

Leaving the window, he dropped onto a chair and leaned his forehead against his braced hands. Two women he cared for, one to whom he had actively pledged his word. But it was the other who haunted his dreams, however determined he was to keep her at arm's length during his waking hours. How the devil was he supposed to do that now?

He sat up long into the night, pondering that question, and did not return to bed until he was too weary to dream.

Twenty-Three

What is a kiss? Why this, as some approve:
The sure, sweet cement, glue, and lime of love.

—Robert Herrick, "A Kiss"

"Dublin?" James echoed, incredulous.

Mrs. Permewan, the Trelawneys' middle-aged house-keeper, nodded vigorously. "Three weeks and more, my lord, and they're not returning for some time yet. Miss Susan and her husband are expecting their first next month. Mistress wanted to be there for her lying-in."

James could sense Harry's barely concealed disappointment. To come so close to answers, only to find them out of reach across the Irish Sea. "Did the rest of the family go too?"

"Why, no. Mr. Frank—that's their oldest—secured a living in Veryan three months ago," Mrs. Permewan said proudly. "Mr. Oliver's chosen to stay with him while the master and mistress are away. Well, no doubt it's dull for him with everyone gone. Likes company, he does."

James felt his hopes revive. "Ah, perhaps I might call upon Cousin Frank, then," he suggested with his most affable smile. "Given our change in circumstances, I should like to improve the connection between our families."

Mrs. Permewan was only too glad to furnish him with Frank Trelawney's direction. James thanked her and subsequently took his leave.

"What do you think then, James?" Harry inquired, once they were mounted and riding back toward Pentreath. "A wasted journey?"

"Not necessarily." James urged Camborne into a trot, Harry doing the same with his own horse. "If Horatio's been in Ireland for that long, he probably didn't write those letters. Unless he wrote them ahead of time and gave them to someone else to post, but that seems unlikely."

"It does," Harry agreed with some reluctance. "Although it might be advisable to call upon his sons and take *their* measure."

"I intend to, but not today. It's too long a journey on horseback. We'll go by carriage."

"Good idea. I'm as eager to get to the bottom of this as you are, James." He paused, frowning slightly. "They don't appear to be destitute, or living in straitened circumstances."

James thought back to the house they'd just left: mellow, Georgian, comfortable rather than luxurious, but there had been no noticeable lack of comfort. "No," he agreed. "Their home was well-kept, and they can clearly afford servants."

"And to travel to Ireland for a good two months or so," Harry observed. "As for your cousin Frank, I know that parish he's been assigned to. Not the richest in the county, but not the poorest by any means. I'd say he was doing fairly well for himself."

"So would I." James rode in silence for a while, thinking. On the surface of it, Horatio Trelawney and his family sounded perfectly amiable, not to mention content with their lives. Not the sort of people who'd write poisonous anonymous letters or, more luridly, conspire to murder one earl and slander another. But then, how could one profess to know another person's true character before meeting him face to face?

Harry said abruptly, "I wired Robin Pendarvis this morning. Just wanted you to know."

"Thank you," James said after a moment. "I appreciate your telling me."

"I kept out the specific details, as you requested. But I told him an urgent matter required his attention here."

"Good. I'm looking forward to speaking with him," James replied as diplomatically as he could. "Perhaps we can clear some things up to our satisfaction."

"Any chance we can keep Gerald's sister from getting wind of this? She's already figured out I'm one of the men named in that damned letter. If she finds out about Robin—"

"She won't. I'll make sure of that." James permitted himself a grim smile. "By the way, you'll be relieved to hear that Helena's kept to her chamber all day. Suffering from the effects of last night's indulgences, according to my aunt. I doubt she'll emerge before evening, if then."

Harry gave a short laugh. "Thank God for small mercies!"

"Just so." All the same, James wondered uneasily how much longer he and his aunt could contain Helena's malice. And more disturbingly, when the next letter would turn up—and where.

❧

"Here, have a pasty." Reaching into the hamper, Sophie pulled out a crusty golden pie shaped like a half-moon and held it out to Aurelia. "Our cook made them fresh this morning."

Aurelia took the pie, still warm to the touch, and bit into it, tasting flaky crust and savory filling: beef, potato, a hint of onion. "Delicious," she managed, when she could speak again.

Sophie smiled, handing another pasty to Amy. "Our cook makes the best pasties in the county, or so my family likes to claim."

"Well, they're perfect for a picnic on the beach," Amy declared.

"Here's something else that's perfect too." Sophie held up a large jug. "Our homemade cider, pressed and bottled last autumn." She took out cups and poured a moderate amount for each of them. "Not too much at once. It can make you quite tiddly if you're not careful."

Heeding the warning, Aurelia sipped cautiously at her cider—crisp, redolent of apples, and tangy with fermentation. She limited herself to one cup, sufficient to wash down the pasty, and feasted her eyes on the tumbling sea before them.

A perfect day for a picnic. The morning had dawned fair and clear, and by the time they had descended the stairs to the beach, the sun was almost at its peak, the sea a brilliant blue-green. A delighted Sophie had declared the prospect the equal to what she saw near St. Perran, while Amy had conceded that this beach might well be superior to Newport's. They'd chosen a spot for their picnic just above the water's edge, settling down on a blanket and talking of many pleasant things, including Sophie's upcoming birthday celebration, as they unpacked the hamper.

Slightly to their surprise, they discovered they were not alone on the beach. Mr. Sheridan had come down before them, settling with his sketchbook on a large rock some distance away. Hearing their voices, he'd looked up and waved, before immersing himself in his work again.

Amy polished off her lunch, glanced in Sheridan's direction. "Have we any more pasties? I was thinking we could offer one to the mad artist. Even genius requires sustenance."

Aurelia shot her sister a warning look, but despite the mocking words, Amy's tone had sounded almost affectionate.

"Oh, we have plenty—and an extra cup for the cider," Sophie replied, rummaging through the hamper again. She unstopped the jug again, poured cider into the cup, and wrapped a pasty in a napkin. "He can have this with our compliments."

"I'll take it over to him," Amy volunteered, getting to her

feet. "I have something I need to discuss with Mr. Sheridan in any case."

"Mr. Sheridan is very attractive," Sophie observed to Aurelia, as they watched Amy make her way toward the artist.

"He is. And talented too."

"Do you—admire him, by any chance?"

"Yes, very much," Aurelia said absently, then, as the significance of Sophie's question sank in, she amended, "that is, I admire his work. And he's one of Trevenan's closest friends."

"I couldn't help wondering. He hardly took his eyes off you or your sister last night."

"That's probably because he wants us to sit for him. Do *you* admire him, Sophie?" That could be problematic, Aurelia reflected. While she liked Mr. Sheridan and found Sophie a delight, the girl was far younger and more innocent than the sophisticated artist.

"Oh, no—at least, not in that way!" Sophie assured her. "The truth is," she colored slightly, "there's someone else I have a fancy for."

"You have a beau?"

Sophie's color deepened. "Perhaps not a beau, exactly. Nothing has been officially decided, but I care for—this gentleman, and I believe he cares for me as well."

"Does your family know about this?" Aurelia asked.

The girl fretted her lower lip, nodded. "Mother is not opposed, though she thinks we should not rush into anything. Harry, though—Harry is less pleased about it. He thinks we are too far apart in age and experience, and that I should consider the attentions of younger suitors."

Aurelia's thoughts went at once to Sir Lucas Nankivell, inquiring after Sophie with that telltale warmth in his eyes and voice. "So this gentleman is quite a bit older than you?"

"Not that much older!" Sophie asserted. "Besides, that's one of the things that attracts me to him—he's a *man*, not a boy." Her chin lifted stubbornly. "In fact, he makes so many of my younger suitors look callow and, well, *boring*."

Aurelia thought back to her first meeting with James. Had not that been one of the things that she had found appealing about him? That he'd seemed older and more mature than the London beaux swarming about Amy. Even then, he'd had a direction and a focus—adult responsibilities that had come to him from his mother's family and, to some extent, even his father's. And, she remembered with an aching sweetness, the chivalry to reach out to a scarred, crippled girl and make her feel, for a few precious minutes, that she was beautiful.

"He's seen and done things I've never dreamed of," Sophie went on. "And he belongs to a wider world I can't wait to be part of!"

Her conviction startled Aurelia. Was Sir Lucas Nankivell really such a paragon? She thought back to the man she'd seen in the lane, with his perfect clothes and almost overly refined speech. And that measuring gaze that had seemed to calculate every penny of her toilette...

Well, perhaps she was not being wholly fair because he hadn't made a favorable first impression on her. No doubt Sophie saw another side to him. "You speak of a wider world," she began tentatively. "Are you sure that your feelings might not change, once you've experienced a bit more of life yourself?"

"That's possible. But I doubt it." Sophie smiled ruefully. "There's a saying in my family: 'Swans and Tresilians mate for life.' We tend to choose early, and not change our minds."

Aurelia studied her thoughtfully. Sophie seemed far older at seventeen than she and Amy ever had—older, and more sure of herself. "Does that always work out for the best?"

Sophie dimpled, suddenly looking her age again. "I would like to say yes, of course, but naturally I can make no such claim. There have been unsuccessful marriages in my family—some quite spectacularly bad—and yet…I do think the good ones have outweighed the bad."

"Does the gentleman share your sentiments, to the same extent?"

"He wants me to comply with my family's plans and have a London Season," Sophie confessed. "To see more of the world, attend parties and dances, and meet other men. And if my feelings do not alter, he says he will be here, waiting." Her lips formed a slightly tremulous smile. "He says I am worth waiting for."

"That's—very generous." More generous than Aurelia would have thought Sir Lucas could be. And his reluctance to take advantage of such a lovely young girl showed him in a far better light. Aurelia privately resolved to be more charitable should she encounter him again.

"Yes, but I already know how it will be." Sophie's young face showed a wealth of determination. "I'll have my Season and enjoy it, for I've never spent much time in London before. But when it's over, I'll return to Cornwall—and to him. To our life together. I mean to stand firm about this, and I know he will too."

Aurelia smiled, pleased for her and just a little envious. How comforting to know exactly what you wanted, and that only time stood between you and the achievement of it! "Then, my dear, I wish you both the very best."

Sophie returned her smile. "Thank you. But what of you, Aurelia? Have you any special admirer yourself?"

Aurelia thought uncomfortably of Charlie's unanswered letter, tucked between the pages of one of her travel books. "There is someone," she admitted at last. "Someone I once knew, who wishes to renew our—acquaintance. But I haven't yet decided if *I* wish that as well."

Sophie nodded her understanding and wisely inquired no further. Unbidden, Trevenan's face rose in Aurelia's memory, as she'd seen it last night in the library: strained, weary, the dark eyes slightly overbright—from brandy or emotion, she could not tell. But for just a moment, he'd stood as close to her as when they waltzed and looked at her with something like hunger…

Which was absurd, she told herself. If Trevenan hungered for anyone, it must be Amy. Whatever she'd seen or thought she'd seen in his eyes was no more than the reflection of what he felt for her sister, his intended bride. The sooner he opened his heart to Amy, the sooner they could begin to face these troubles together, as a couple should.

Trying *not* to think of Trevenan and her sister, Aurelia got to her feet. "The sun's so much warmer now. And we've finished our lunch. Let's go wading in the sea."

On closer inspection, Sheridan was wielding neither pencils nor pastels but a fine watercolor brush. Mindful of his efforts, Amy did not call attention to herself until he lifted the brush away from the page and paused to study his efforts.

"Mr. Sheridan?" she ventured at last. "We've brought you some lunch."

He looked up, his gaze distracted and seemingly miles away. Then, as he recognized her, his eyes came back into focus and he smiled. "Thank you, Miss Newbold. I appreciate your offering. I'd quite lost track of the time." Laying his sketchbook aside on the rock, he accepted the pasty and cider she held out to him.

Amy angled her head to study the sketch. Sheridan was as skilled with watercolor as he was with oils, capturing the sea's shifting hues in alternating strokes of blue and green. For a moment, she experienced the old pang—half-wistful, half-envious—over her own lack of talent.

He followed the direction of her gaze. "I thought I'd make a watercolor sketch or two of my subject before committing it to canvas. That's how I start out, usually."

"It's very impressive so far." Amy peered more closely at the sketch. "Is that—yellow ochre, under the blue and green?"

"It is. I applied a thin wash of it to the paper before adding Prussian blue and viridian. I find cool shades need an under-lying warmth to support them." Sheridan glanced at her. "Not everyone notices that. You have a good eye, Miss Newbold."

Amy shrugged, trying not to feel too pleased by the compliment. "Thank you, but I doubt it's that extraordinary. And in my case, a good eye has never translated into a painting good enough to hang in the Royal Academy—or anywhere else for that matter," she added ruefully.

"I'm sorry." His voice was surprisingly gentle. "I know how frustrating—and painful—it is to feel you cannot create as you wish."

Amy sighed. "Well, no one gets *everything* they want in life. And I'm fortunate in many other ways, so I've reconciled myself to the fact that I'll never be an Angelica Kauffman or even a Mary Cassatt." Though not before she'd shed some private tears over the loss of that girlhood dream, and consigned her portfolio of insipid watercolors and lifeless sketches to the fire.

"Perhaps you simply haven't found the right medium," Sheridan suggested. "But a keen aesthetic sense is not to be disdained, and I'd venture to say you use it more than you know."

Amy blinked. "I do?"

He smiled. "You are one of the few women I know who always looks exactly right: your clothes, your hair, even the angle of your hats. And before you accuse me of excessive flattery, an artist notices such things."

Amy flushed, caught between surprise and pleasure at his words. "I could just have a clever maid," she pointed out. "Mariette is French, after all."

"An asset, no doubt. But I suspect that *you* have the final say in whatever you wear."

"I do," she admitted. "And I can be very stubborn about it, as you've no doubt guessed."

"Can you indeed?" There was a spark of mischief in his green eyes.

Amy suppressed a smile. "Well, if you've forgotten, I'll be sure to remind you once you begin my portrait. Which reminds *me*—when should I come to sit for you?"

"Whenever you're ready, Miss Newbold."

"Tomorrow, perhaps?" she suggested. "Depending on the weather, we can decide whether it should be indoors or out."

"Very well. I've set up a studio in what James calls the old schoolroom: eastern exposure, good light, especially in the early part of the day. We can meet there to start—after breakfast, if that's not too soon for you."

"It's not. But you surprise me, Mr. Sheridan. I never imagined that you rose so early."

His eyes glinted. "Because of my dissipated life in London? I assure you, I am a different creature here. Country life has its own rhythm, quite distinct from that of the town, and I do not pine for one when visiting the other. Besides," his expression grew somber, even intense, "any artist worth his salt knows that the work comes first, town or country, day or night."

"Forgive me," Amy said, contrite. "I did not mean to be impertinent."

"Not at all," he returned politely. "Now, have you decided what you wish to wear?"

"I have a Liberty silk gown, almost medieval in style. High-waisted, flowing. Pentreath has this Tudor charm. I wonder if the gown might complement it."

"A pleasing conceit." Sheridan scanned her intently, as if he was already picturing her so attired. "And a softer, more natural look becomes a bride." He gave a decisive nod. "I said your aesthetic sense was impeccable. Wear the Liberty tomorrow, for your sitting."

Amy swallowed, feeling self-conscious again. "Very well—tomorrow morning, then. Enjoy your lunch, Mr. Sheridan."

She left him biting into his pasty and headed back toward her companions.

❧

Halfway down the stairs, James paused, gazing at the figures frolicking on his beach.

Aurelia and Sophie were already at the water's edge, their laughter floating back toward the onlookers. Amy walked a little more slowly, picking her way down the beach with almost finicky care. *Like a cat*, James thought with an involuntary smile.

His gaze went to Aurelia, standing barefoot in the sea, the way she had that first morning. No seductive phantom, as she had appeared in last night's dream, but a laughing, carefree, slightly disheveled young woman. The only similarity was that both of them glowed more brightly than the sun itself, at least to his eyes.

How strange that it should be the quiet twin who had embraced Cornwall and all its wildness, and the bolder twin who regarded it with a wary eye. In London, Aurelia had been somewhat overshadowed by her more sociable, vivacious sister. Here, in Cornwall, she seemed to be coming into her own.

She looked like she belonged here. The realization struck him with the force of a wave knocking him off his feet.

"James, do you mean to go down or not?" Harry asked testily from behind him.

James roused at once. "Sorry, old fellow," he apologized, resuming his descent.

Sophie looked around just as they set foot on the sand, and waved to them, smiling. So did the twins. Quickening their pace, James and Harry joined the ladies at the water's edge.

Harry slipped an arm about his sister. "Hullo, snip. Didn't know I'd find you here."

"John's gone off fishing with Andrew Newbold," Sophie

explained. "I came too, with a picnic lunch, and we ladies decided to have it on the beach. Now where have *you* two been?" she asked. "You were downright mysterious about it when you left this morning, Harry."

Harry glanced at James, then shrugged and said in an offhand tone, "No mystery involved, actually. We just called on a distant relation of James's who lives up the coast."

"But as he was from home, nothing of import occurred," James added. He did not look at Aurelia, but he sensed by her sudden stillness that she had grasped the significance of his news. He turned instead to Amy and offered his arm. "My dear, will you walk apart with me? I've some things to discuss with you."

∽

So he meant to tell Amy at last, Aurelia thought as her twin accepted Trevenan's arm and the two of them started down the beach together. And it was *right* that he should, she told herself fiercely. Ridiculous to mind, to feel even the slightest bit excluded, now that Trevenan was doing what she had so often urged him to do: confiding in his future wife.

Turning away, she found Sir Harry watching her with disconcertingly shrewd green eyes. Uneasily, she wondered if something in her face or demeanor had betrayed her.

To her relief, all he said was, "You're right about the marvelous view here, Miss Aurelia. Now you must come to St. Perran and see *our* beach as well."

Aurelia managed a smile. "Thank you, Sir Harry. I'd be happy to. Especially those caves you mentioned at dinner."

"They're worth seeing, I promise you. A few are almost as large as Merlin's Cave at Tintagel, and just as atmospheric, in my opinion. And then," he added, "there are some that have more *recent* historical associations."

"More recent?" Aurelia echoed, mystified by the wry quirk of his lips at the last words.

"He means the free trade," Sophie explained. "Centuries ago, smugglers would hide their contraband in the caves, at least until it could be moved to a safer place, like an attic or cellar. Some caves even had connecting tunnels and passageways dug so smugglers could transport the goods unseen, without being spotted by the revenue officers."

"Yes, I read about that in one of my books," Aurelia recalled. "And how most of the gentry sympathized with the smugglers, so they'd turn a blind eye—or actively help them out."

"Yes, well…" Harry cleared his throat. "Times were hard back then, I understand."

Sophie stifled a giggle, and Aurelia stared at him. "Sir Harry, *your* family?"

"Guilty," he confessed with a rueful grin. "Many Tresilians had a finger in that pie. My great-grandfather even had a smugglers' cache built under the floor of our music room at Roswarne. I'd say most of the families on the north coast were involved in the trade, one way or another. Including the Trelawneys, as James could tell you."

"A blot on the family escutcheon," Sophie intoned in a sepulchral voice.

Aurelia laughed. "I wouldn't feel too guilty about it. We have our share of dubious ancestors as well, including some notable robber barons. And then," she added with a wry smile of her own, "there are those who think of American girls like Amy and me as pirates."

"If so, you and your sister are in good company," Harry countered genially. "We Tresilians have a buccaneer or two in our past as well, though not nearly so attractive."

"A true buccaneer?" Aurelia inquired, smiling. "Do tell me more."

He obliged, which soon led to a lively discussion among the three of them about whose forebears were the most scandalous. A welcome distraction, Aurelia thought as she regaled her companions with the history of a particularly disreputable great-uncle. Even if it couldn't entirely make her forget Amy and Trevenan, walking some distance away, or stop wondering just what they were speaking of at this very moment.

They made their way along the sand, heading south. Thomas was there, James noticed, packing up his painting kit. He nodded to his friend as they passed, then looked again at Amy. She was still shod; unlike her sister and Sophie, she hadn't removed her shoes and stockings. Irresistibly, he thought of Aurelia standing barefoot in the sea, then forced the thought away.

"What was it you wished to tell me, James?" Amy's eyes gazed into his with so much trust that he disliked himself even more for making the comparison.

"Mainly how sorry I am. I haven't spent nearly as much time with you as I should."

"Oh, pray don't apologize for that!" she insisted. "I know how preoccupied you've been, and I certainly don't expect you to dance attendance on me every waking moment."

"I know, and believe me, I appreciate your forbearance. But I don't wish you to feel excluded from my confidence. I feel I've wronged you, by keeping you so much in the dark."

Amy's brow furrowed. "In the dark about what, James?"

Tell her, Aurelia had insisted repeatedly. So, at long last, he did, choosing his words with care but relaying all the essential details, however unpleasant. Amy listened attentively, her face growing increasingly perturbed throughout his recital.

"How dreadful for you!" she exclaimed, after he had finished. "Are you any closer to finding out who's writing those awful letters?"

"Sadly, no," James admitted. "I'd hoped to get some answers when I visited my heir, but as he's out of the country entirely…" He shook his head.

She touched his hand. "Well, you know you have my full support, always."

"Thank you." James took her hand, deriving some comfort from the way her fingers twined companionably with his. "Have you any insights to offer, my dear? I wouldn't mind hearing a fresh perspective, just in case there's something I've overlooked entirely."

Amy hesitated, then shook her head. "I'm afraid not. Cornwall is still so unfamiliar to me. I haven't met anyone yet except the Tresilians, and this seems to be such a—volatile situation. I don't want to make things worse for you, by interfering in what I don't understand."

"Of course not," he said at once. "I understand your restraint."

"Try not to worry," she said, giving his hand a consoling squeeze. "I'm sure you'll get to the bottom of this soon. And the evidence is on your side anyway, isn't it? Witnesses saw you at a party that night, and the inquest cleared you of any involvement in your cousin's death. So I shouldn't think these vicious slanders will stick."

"I hope not." James fought back an obscure sense of disappointment.

Amy had said all that was proper, all that was encouraging. She trusted him to handle the situation, without interference from her—a proper, ladylike stance that still showed her loyalty and faith in him. What more could he expect from her?

An image of Aurelia rose in his mind's eye. Aurelia, her face intent, her brow creased in thought: *Who is your heir, Trevenan? Who benefits from your misfortune?*

You cannot take me into your confidence one day, and expect me to forget it the next.

Unfair to compare them like this. They were different people, Amy and Aurelia—he'd understood that from the first. Better to count his blessings, chief among them a sweet, supportive fiancée who believed wholeheartedly in his innocence. "Thank you for your understanding," he said more warmly, gazing down into her lovely face.

She smiled up at him. "Anything I can do to help."

On impulse, James skimmed his fingers along the curve of her cheek, like warm satin to the touch. "I can think of something that might help enormously. If you'll permit me, that is."

Her eyes flared in sudden understanding, and a blush stole up her face, but she did not draw back. "Of course," she said, and stood perfectly still as he lowered his mouth to hers.

He'd last kissed her the night they became betrothed, but, remembering her unpleasant encounter with Glyndon, he'd kept his salute gentle and undemanding. This time, he drew her to him, close enough to feel the soft contours of her body, to let her feel the harder contours of his. Her upturned lips were sweetness itself, and the scent of roses wafted from her creamy skin.

Roses, not lavender. He forced the thought away and deepened the kiss, letting his tongue just graze the tip of hers in a more intimate caress. Amy made a small, startled sound, but did not pull away. Her body stiffened slightly, however, and James released her at once.

"You—you've never kissed me like that before," Amy said, a little breathlessly.

James felt like a beast to have unsettled her. "Forgive me. I did not mean to startle you."

"No, no, it wasn't that. I did not mind. It was just… different." She touched her lips, looked up at him with dazed eyes. "It may take some getting used to."

"You may have as long as you need," he promised.

"Thank you." She essayed a tiny smile. "I think I might quite get to like it, in time."

Relieved, James smiled back at her. "Good. I shall make every effort to see that you do." He offered his arm again. "Shall we rejoin the others now?"

❧

They returned to the house soon after that, and the Tresilians took their leave, John triumphant over having landed a fine lake trout. Amy and Aurelia went upstairs to bathe and change, while James headed for the library to attend to any newly arrived correspondence.

He had just sat down at his desk when Pelham entered, bearing a silver tray on which a single card rested.

"A gentleman called while you were away, my lord," the butler informed him. "He left his card and said he would return tomorrow, before noon."

James picked up the card from the tray and froze when he saw the name printed there, even as a part of him wondered why he felt no real surprise.

Captain Philip Mercer. Mercer Shipping.

Tomorrow, before noon. Yes, this was one appointment he would be sure to keep.

Twenty-Four

The purest treasure mortal times afford
Is spotless reputation.

—William Shakespeare, *King Richard II*

AMY PEERED AROUND THE DOORWAY AT THE LONE figure moving about the old schoolroom. However early she'd risen, clearly Mr. Sheridan had been up even earlier. Morning light from the windows shone upon his loose-fitting white shirt and illuminated the comb marks in his overlong brown hair. Despite his casual appearance, his movements were quick and decisive as he rearranged the various furnishings, then repositioned his easel.

Somewhat hesitantly, she cleared her throat, and he turned around at once. "Ah, Miss Newbold. Good morning. Please, come in."

Amy picked up her trailing skirts and stepped into the room. "Good morning, Mr. Sheridan," she began. "I'm wearing my Liberty gown."

"So I see." Approaching, he studied her from head to toe, his eyes narrowing in thought.

Amy let her skirts fall and held her arms out from her sides so he could see the effect: the heavy overgown of sapphire-blue silk with its brocade collar and long full sleeves, half-open over a high-waisted frock in palest azure. Like a tea gown, aesthetic dress did not require a wealth of petticoats to be worn beneath, and the more daring ladies insisted that corsets weren't needed either, though Amy did not feel quite daring enough to leave hers off. Not yet, at least.

Sheridan circled her, seeming to take in every stitch with those penetrating green eyes of his. Amy caught the scents of sandalwood and linseed oil as he passed close to her, and her body flushed with unexpected heat beneath its flowing silk draperies.

Good heavens, what was the matter with her? She couldn't be sickening for something; she'd felt fine when she awoke this morning. Was it James's kiss, she wondered, that made her so conscious of Mr. Sheridan today? Of how it felt to have a large, warm masculine body so close to hers? That must be it. If James were here, she'd doubtless be having the very same reaction: a sort of pleasant, all-over tingle. Strange how she'd never been so affected during her infatuation with Glyndon. But then, the viscount had never attempted more than a few chaste kisses—not until that horrid encounter in the conservatory! She suppressed a shudder, forcing her thoughts back to the present.

Sheridan had paused in his assessment; much to her surprise, he leaned closer to her and inhaled slowly. "Your scent," he said, after a moment. "Roses—and jasmine?"

She nodded, disconcerted. "A perfumer in London blended it especially for me."

"Lovely. Like a summer garden." His eyes had gone dreamy, even a little unfocused, as if he were savoring a pleasant memory. Then, abruptly, they sharpened into awareness again, and she had the sense of a curtain descending to hide whatever else lay behind those eyes. "A pity that one cannot paint scents, is it not? As to your gown," he added, tilting his head to one side, "that shade of blue is both apposite and becoming. I see you've dressed your hair simply too."

Amy self-consciously touched the filigreed silver combs that held her chignon in place. "I didn't think an elaborate style would suit the gown, or the more natural look you recommended."

"No, you're quite right, and I commend your aesthetic sense again. Simple is best for what I have in mind. However, if I may?" He reached out, teased a few strands free, just at the brow, so gently that Amy scarcely felt the pull. "The human touch," he explained, smiling. "That tiny imperfection that makes us flesh and blood, not marble."

Flesh and blood. Amy had never been more aware of that fact than at this moment. She wondered if she ought to feel offended—just a little—by the liberties he'd taken with her person. And yet she couldn't quite manage it. Relia hadn't resisted either, she remembered, when Sheridan had taken her by the chin and studied her face so closely. Relia, who'd used to hate having anyone outside the family looking at her scar. She would *not* show less self-possession about this than her twin.

Sheridan took a step back and motioned her forward. "Shall we get started, then?"

Amy's mouth was dry, her pulse unusually rapid, but somehow she managed a reply. "Yes, let's not waste all this daylight." Glancing about the room, she noticed the well-padded chaise longue in one corner. "Should I recline, like Cleopatra, on that fainting couch?"

Sheridan smiled. "You *can* recline, if you wish. It's a popular position among my models, much preferred to standing."

"I should think so." Amy headed over to the chaise longue and sank down upon it, finding it quite comfortable—and a good place on which to regain one's composure as well.

"Stretch out on it sideways," Sheridan said, frowning as he surveyed her. "Yes, like that. And then rest your arm—so—on the arm of the chaise. And then your face…" He came up to the chaise, stooped to slip a finger under her chin. "If you will turn it toward me, at just this angle."

His touch was light, almost clinical, though there was nothing clinical in the response Amy found herself having to it. All the sensation in her body seemed concentrated in that small spot beneath her chin, where the tip of his finger still rested.

How many other women had he touched like this, or regarded with such total concentration? Unnerving to be the sole focus of those intense green eyes that seemed to bore into her very soul. Despite her silk draperies, she felt oddly exposed, even a bit…naked.

Flushing at the thought, she moistened her lips. "Should I—should I smile?"

His own lips curved slightly. "Only if you wish to. A forced smile looks dreadful in a portrait, not to mention that a model can find it as hard to maintain an expression as a posture." He got up from the chaise, strode to a chair, which he positioned a few feet away, and picked up his sketchbook and pencil. "We'll start with a few drawings in this position."

Amy cleared her throat. "Do you need me to be completely silent, or may I talk?"

"Talking is fine, as long as I'm not drawing your mouth at the time." Sheridan sounded almost absentminded as he folded back a page in his sketchbook and set to work.

Strangely enough, Amy found herself disinclined to talk now. Instead, she watched the progress of Sheridan's pencil across the page: a few quick, bold strokes—the outline, she guessed—and then slower, more deliberate ones. But she found it more intriguing to watch the artist himself: the absorption on his face, the faint crease between his brows, the way the green of his eyes seemed to deepen in hue as he grew increasingly immersed in his work. He didn't even seem to notice when a lock of leaf-brown hair, glinting bronze and auburn in the strengthening sunlight, strayed over his forehead. Amy's fingers wanted to reach out and push it back, but that would have meant her not only breaking her pose, but leaving the chaise altogether, which she suspected Sheridan would not appreciate.

As if he could read her thoughts, he looked up at just that moment, his eyes narrowing like a hunter's sighting his prey. "Hold still," he ordered, laying his sketchbook aside.

Too surprised to take umbrage at his peremptory tone, Amy obeyed, watching mesmerized as Sheridan left his chair and approached the chaise. Dropping to one knee, he grasped a voluminous swath of her skirts, began to tweak and drape it in seemingly casual folds over the edge of the chaise. The result *was* a bit more artistic-looking, Amy decided, craning her neck to study the effect. Sheridan appeared satisfied as well; his expression lightened and he looked up at her with the beginnings of a smile.

"Pardon me, Miss Newbold, I didn't mean to sound so brusque. I thought it needed a better line," he explained, gesturing toward her gown.

"That's quite all right," Amy assured him, a little breathlessly; his proximity still made her feel unsettled. "I suppose most artists get caught up when it comes to the details."

"Invariably. '*Her mantle laps / Over my lady's wrist too much*,'" Sheridan quoted.

"Or '*Paint / Must never hope to reproduce the faint / Half-flush that dies along her throat*,'" Amy added with a triumphant smile of her own.

His brows rose. "You recognize the poem, Miss Newbold?"

"Of course. Oh, Relia's the one who loves poetry, but I'm partial to your Mr. Browning. He writes about such interesting *people*. The duke is dreadful, but he's fascinating too. I think Miss Witherspoon was a little dismayed when I chose to recite 'My Last Duchess' for one of our lessons rather than something by Tennyson or Wordsworth," she added.

Sheridan grinned like a mischievous schoolboy. "I don't doubt she was!"

"And I've wanted to visit Italy ever since. Have you been there, Mr. Sheridan?"

"Several times," he replied. "Ferrara has some magnificent churches and palazzos."

Amy nodded. "That's what I've heard. And I should like to go to Florence too."

"Perhaps you shall," he said, after a moment. "On your wedding trip."

Her wedding trip. "Yes, of course," Amy said, feeling suddenly foolish. "Only won't James feel uncomfortable in Italy, because his parents died there?"

"He might at first," Sheridan conceded. "But I suspect that his first wish would be to please you, especially if you have your heart set on a honeymoon in Italy." He got to his feet, brisk and business-like once more. "Shall we continue, then?"

Their brief moment of rapport was gone, leaving Amy oddly bereft; she mustered a smile, trying to regain her equilibrium. "Certainly—this light won't last forever." Resuming her pose, she watched as Sheridan returned to his seat and picked up his sketchbook again.

"Captain Mercer is here to see you, my lord," Pelham announced.

James glanced at the clock on the library mantelpiece: just past eleven. "Show him in," he told the butler, and rose to his feet.

Seconds later, Mercer strode into the room. "Good morning, Lord Trevenan. I am pleased to find you at home today."

James inclined his head. "I had some business away from the estate yesterday, Captain Mercer. What is it that you wished to discuss?" He gestured toward the chair opposite his desk.

Mercer seated himself, as did James. "As it happens, I've been occupied in Bristol and then Falmouth for much of this past week. But it occurred to me that we may have some business yet to conduct."

"Do we?" James kept his tone and expression bland, though he knew well enough what Mercer hoped to attain by this interview.

"I read the announcement of your betrothal in the London papers. My congratulations."

"Thank you," James said neutrally, still watching the captain.

"But you see, that impels me to ask whether you are—open to further negotiations."

James leaned back in his chair. "Regarding Mercer Shipping?"

"Indeed," Mercer acknowledged. "I am familiar with Adam Newbold's reputation as a successful businessman; I would assume he has made generous provision for his daughter, on her upcoming marriage to you. Surely with your bride's dowry, you will not need those shares."

"I am betrothed, Mercer, but not yet wed," James reminded him. "My solicitor continues to advise me against selling off my assets for the time being. And as he has guided me unerringly through my change in circumstances, I see no reason to disregard his advice."

Mercer's mouth tightened, and James saw again that inimical flash in his eyes that had unnerved him at their first meeting. "I see. Is there a chance you might consider parting with those shares after your wedding?"

"Perhaps—should the terms be favorable," James replied, refusing to commit himself. "In the meantime, I wonder if we might come to an understanding on a somewhat related matter."

The captain's eyes narrowed. "Which is?"

"My late cousin's activities regarding your company. As it happens, I have made a few inquiries of my own into this affair. And I would hazard a guess that the missing shipment was delivered to your warehouse in Falmouth?"

Mercer's eyes flared briefly in surprise, then his face closed down again. "Your guess—is accurate, Lord Trevenan." His tone was as guarded as his face.

James looked his visitor square in the eye. "Let us speak plainly, Captain Mercer. My cousin is dead, and in no position to defend his actions, though I must confess that those actions do not appear in the best light. If he has unlawfully defrauded you of the profit you would have received from your merchandise, then I am willing to recompense you."

Mercer's gaze sharpened. "Recompense—"

"I have come to share your concerns about your missing cargo, Mercer," James continued. "And I am eager to help you recover either the merchandise, or the cost of it. Perhaps you could provide me with an inventory of what was contained in that shipment. That would seem to be a likely starting point."

"Very well, Lord Trevenan," Mercer said after a moment. "I appreciate your interest in this matter, and I shall send you the inventory at once."

"Excellent." James rose to his feet, signaling the end of the interview. "The sooner we sort out this unpleasant business, the better. Do you not agree?"

Mercer rose as well. "I do, indeed. The shipment contained several valuable goods, including tea and porcelain. Its disappearance has cost my company hundreds, possibly thousands, of pounds in profits."

"I can well imagine. Let me see you out, Captain."

Mercer paused just inside the doorway. "And perhaps once this matter is settled, we might discuss the question of those shares?"

"Perhaps." James motioned his visitor to precede him from the library.

Following Mercer into the entrance hall, James decided he liked the captain no better than he had on their first meeting, though he could not have explained why. Something about the man still made him uneasy—those cool, overly flat eyes and the perfunctory smile that never warmed them. Gerald might have thought he'd got the upper hand on his business associate, but James suspected Mercer could have turned the tables on his cousin in a heartbeat. Why he hadn't was no less a mystery than that missing shipment.

The front door opened as they approached it, and three people entered in a burst of laughter and conversation: Mr. Newbold, Andrew, and Aurelia, all wearing riding dress.

"Good morning, Trevenan!" Mr. Newbold greeted him with a jovial smile.

"Good morning, sir. Did you enjoy your ride?" James inquired.

"I did, indeed. You have an excellent stable. Thank you for allowing us the use of it." Turning his head, Mr. Newbold caught sight of James's visitor, and his affable expression cooled noticeably. "Ah. Captain—Mercer, isn't it?"

Astonished, James glanced at Mercer, whose face had gone similarly rigid. "You know each other?" He did not know why he was surprised; his future father-in-law was in shipping too.

"Mr. Newbold and I have met briefly, in New York," Mercer confirmed, inclining his head toward the older man. "Pray excuse me. I was just taking my leave. Lord Trevenan, I shall send you what you asked, at the first opportunity. Good day."

"Good day," James replied, watching the captain depart.

Once the front door had closed behind Mercer, Mr. Newbold turned, frowning, to James. "You have business with this man?"

"Not exactly," James replied. "Do you, sir?"

"No, and I mean to keep it that way." Mr. Newbold's face set in grim lines. "Trust me on this, Trevenan. You don't want anything to do with Philip Mercer or Mercer Shipping."

"No, I don't believe I do," James assured him. "But Mercer and my late cousin had business dealings of a somewhat suspicious nature, and I'd like to find out just what they were. If there's anything you can tell me about Mercer or his company, I would greatly appreciate it."

Mr. Newbold glanced at his son and daughter, who were looking on with frank curiosity.

"Tell him, Father," Aurelia urged. "You never know what details might come in handy."

"True enough," Mr. Newbold conceded. He turned to James. "What I have to say might not be of any use to you, but I'll tell you what I know."

"Thank you." James studied the Newbolds, his soon-to-be family, for a moment longer and came to a decision. "Why don't we all go into the library and talk about it there?"

"Smuggling?" James stared at Mr. Newbold. "Are you quite sure of that, sir?"

"Reasonably sure," the older man replied. "At least that's what I've heard. Luxury goods, mostly—liquor, tobacco, tea. He's always got plenty on hand, and he always gets top price. And I gather he's approached a few of my colleagues in New York about joining him in the trade."

"But not you."

Mr. Newbold hesitated, then shook his head, much to the relief of Andrew and Aurelia who were watching their father intently. "I own, it's tempting to find ways around paying taxes and tariffs. But a man's reputation is everything in business. Touch pitch, and you defile it."

"Is Mercer's reputation so black in America?"

"Not so black that he's untouchable," Mr. Newbold conceded grudgingly. "But he sails close to the wind, and there are rumors that Mercer Shipping's involved in some dirtier ventures. Stolen antiquities, forged artworks, arms-running, even drugs. No one's caught him red-handed, but the smell lingers, all the same."

"He seems to be more circumspect here," James observed. "Neither my solicitor nor my inquiry agent has turned up rumors of this sort. At least, not so far."

Mr. Newbold grunted. "Makes sense he'd pass himself off as an honest merchant at home. Abroad is another story. How did your cousin get involved with him in the first place?"

As briefly as possible, James summed up what he knew of Gerald's dealings with Mercer Shipping. "Mercer's being very persistent about buying back those shares, but I want to know more about his dealings with my cousin before I make any decisions about that. And then there's that missing shipment to find—if it can be found now, after almost six months."

Andrew spoke for the first time. "Do you think your cousin sold everything off?"

"That has been my theory so far," James replied. "Gerald tended to live beyond his means. He'd have wanted money as quickly as possible. My guess is he'd try to find a buyer for the most valuable goods right away and pocket the profits for himself."

"But what if there wasn't enough time for that?" Aurelia asked. "You said the shipment arrived just before Christmas. Your cousin was dead by New Year's Day. Surely he wouldn't have had the chance to dispose of everything unless he had a buyer right there on the spot."

"Perhaps not," James conceded after a moment's thought. Gerald would also have needed time to sift through the cargo and pick out what was most profitable before Mercer could catch him. Time—and a place, he realized. "So that leaves—hiding it?"

"That would be my guess," Mr. Newbold said, nodding.

"But where?" Aurelia wondered. "I shouldn't think big crates of tea and china would be easy to hide. Your cousin would've had to put them somewhere he could get at, but Captain Mercer couldn't. And someplace where no one else could stumble on them by accident."

"Maybe he buried them in the garden," Andrew suggested with a crooked grin. "Shall we get out the shovels and start digging?"

"He wouldn't have buried them," James said, ignoring the younger man's facetiousness. "Too much chance of damaging the goods. No one's likely to buy broken china or tea that smells of damp earth. Besides, the groundskeepers would have noticed." He got to his feet. "I think it's time I looked into exactly what my cousin was doing just before he died. My thanks to you all."

❧

In all his years at Pentreath, James had never entered Gerald's chamber, nor wished to. He felt like an intruder now—worse, almost a grave robber—as he stood outside the locked door. Locked since the morning of Gerald's funeral and not disturbed since.

It had surprised James, initially, that Gerald hadn't moved into his father's larger rooms, but perhaps he had not been ready to accede to the earldom either. Perhaps remaining in his old chamber had been a comfort, a way to keep the responsibilities of his new position at bay. James felt a reluctant twinge of sympathy at the thought; he kept to *his* old chamber as well.

No putting it off any longer. James turned the key and let himself into the room. Close, musty smell—that was only to be expected. He strode to the window, wrestled it open enough to let in some fresh air, then turned resolutely to his task.

Unlike Gerald's room in the Belgravia house, this contained few of his cousin's belongings. Gerald had arrived at Pentreath just before Christmas, with only enough clothes to see him through a fortnight or so. His valet had testified at the inquest that his lordship meant to leave for the Shires in January, to enjoy the hunting season. But what clothes

Gerald had brought to Cornwall still hung in the wardrobe or remained packed in his trunks. James supposed it would fall to him, eventually, to dispose of them, whether to secondhand shops or missionary barrels. He pushed away the depressing prospect to concentrate on his present business.

It seemed unlikely that Gerald would have stashed the missing shipment in his chamber, but James searched dutifully through the wardrobe, chest of drawers, and dressing room, all to no avail. Finally, he sat down at his cousin's desk and opened the topmost drawer.

An unprepossessing collection of items met his view: pen, paper, and ink, stamps, a box of cigars, and a handful of pennies. He closed the drawer, opened the next.

A stack of maps, loosely folded—now that looked more promising. He spread the first open across the desk. A map of Cornwall: the Cornish coast, to be precise. Not too surprising that Gerald should have such a thing. He'd never known Cornwall that well, after all…

The door burst open behind him, and a strident voice assailed his ears. "What are you doing in Gerald's room?" Helena demanded.

Forcing down his annoyance, James turned in his chair to face her. "Spying now, Helena? I'd have thought that was beneath you."

She drew herself up, affronted, but did not deny the charge, he observed. "I have a right to know when you're pawing through my brother's personal belongings!"

James kept a firm hold on his temper. "Would it placate you to hear that I'm actually trying to discover more about his last days?"

Helena's mouth opened, then closed as his words registered. James resumed before she could get her second wind, "I've spent this morning speaking to a man, the owner of a shipping company, with whom Gerald had done business in the last months of his life."

She stared at him. "What could Gerald have possibly wanted with a shipping company?"

"I gather it was a profitable venture, though perhaps less reputable than it first appeared."

Helena bristled. "Are you implying that my brother was involved in something shady?"

"I am implying nothing of the kind." Stating it outright would be closer to the truth, but James knew better than to fan the flames. "I wish only to discern the full extent of his involvement and to determine whether it might have played a part in his death." Holding her gaze with his own, he continued with steely resolve, "And if you truly desire justice for Gerald, you will not impede my efforts to find answers. Now, unless you have some insights to offer that might illuminate the situation, I suggest you leave me to my task."

Helena flushed, and James braced himself for another explosion. Instead, much to his astonishment, she pressed her lips together, cast him a last fulminating glare, and flung out of the room with nearly as much force as she had entered it.

Would wonders never cease? Perhaps Helena was indeed sincere about what she claimed to want. All the same, it was a relief not to have her breathing down his neck while he searched.

He sorted through the rest of the maps, all of which were of Cornwall. Too much to hope that any would be handily marked with an "X" denoting the stolen shipment's location. But Gerald's reliance on these maps did appear to suggest that the goods hadn't left Cornwall.

Pushing the maps aside, he looked into the drawer again. Pencils of varying lengths and what looked like a black handkerchief, knotted around something else. He picked up the latter, frowned when he felt something hard and heavy concealed in its folds, and untied it at once.

A large iron key dropped with a clank upon the desk.

≈≈≈

Making his weary way along the passage an hour later, James paused as a familiar air, accompanied by a familiar voice, floated out to him from the drawing room: *"I love the white rose so fair as she grows. / It's the rose that reminds me of you."*

Smiling, he peered into the drawing room and saw Aurelia seated at the piano. She glanced up then, caught sight of him, and her hands faltered momentarily on the keys.

"I'm sorry," she began. "I just found this book of old Cornish songs—"

"Please, don't stop," he urged, coming into the room. "That was one of my mother's favorites. She used to sing it with my father."

Aurelia gave him an uncertain smile, but resumed playing and singing. James sat down and let the music and the sweet, sentimental words wash over him. There was comfort for him in that, and in the picture she made at the instrument: poised, graceful, her gilded hair contrasting with the pale lavender of her morning dress. Just so had she looked that morning in Grosvenor Square, when he'd first learned of her musical abilities. It seemed a lifetime ago.

"Well done," he said, when she had finished.

"Thank you. I feel the merest novice next to Sophie; she plays and sings so beautifully."

"No need for comparisons. Piano and violin are like apples and oranges. But Sophie's always been passionate about her music. Harry's thinking of sending her to a conservatory in London, as well as giving her a Season."

"Sounds like the perfect plan for her." Aurelia laced her fingers together, regarded him soberly. "Trevenan, I hope you won't mind my asking if you found anything upstairs?"

"Not a great deal, I'm afraid. Some maps of Cornwall, and a key, which may mean nothing, or everything. I've already spoken at length with the butler, the housekeeper, and my aunt," he added. "The key does not appear to unlock any room or cupboard in the house."

Aurelia frowned. "So, maybe it's to something outside the house. A shed?"

"Or one of the tenants' cottages—there are a few standing empty, I understand. Although," James paused, frowning, "my estate manager tends to inspect them regularly. I should think he'd have found the shipment by now, if Gerald hid it in one of those."

"Might Gerald have paid one of your tenants to hide it for him?" she suggested. "I'm sure they'd know all sorts of convenient hiding places in the area."

"Not a bad theory, but I can't see Gerald taking anyone that deeply into his confidence. Nor would he have wanted to share a penny of whatever profits he got from that shipment."

She pulled a face. "I know it's not proper to speak ill of the dead, but your late cousin sounds just awful."

"An opinion held by many, I'm afraid." And one of the many might well have done for Gerald that night on the cliff, James reflected. "Well, once Mercer sends me that inventory, I'll ride over and check out the cottages myself. It'll help to know exactly what I'm looking for."

A footman entered then, carrying a silver tray laden with letters. "The post, my lord," he announced, presenting the tray to James. "And there's one for you as well, Miss Newbold."

Intrigued, James watched as Aurelia accepted her letter. Who could be writing her here?

She glanced up, flushing slightly. "A friend of mine from France. I wrote to her just before we left London, and gave her your address in Cornwall. I hope you don't mind?"

"Not at all." James's curiosity grew as she slipped the letter into her pocket. But before he could ask any further questions, Lady Talbot entered the drawing room.

"Ah, James, there you are!" she greeted him. "I needed

to ask you whether you'd be willing to set luncheon back an hour or so. Cook's beside herself because the galantine hasn't set properly. I told her not to worry, and just serve the salmon poached with that lemon and herb sauce she does so well. But she says she needs more time."

"That's fine, Aunt Judith," James assured her. "Most of our guests rose rather late this morning. I don't think an hour will make much of a difference." He glanced at Aurelia, who smiled and shook her head.

"Not at all, Lady Talbot." She rose from the piano bench. "I'll tell my family of the change in schedule."

Lady Talbot smiled at the girl as she went out. "Thank you, my dear."

"I should go as well." James picked up his letters. "And see to my latest correspondence."

"James." The unexpected urgency in her voice stopped him halfway to the door.

He turned around, glanced at her inquiringly. "Aunt Judith?"

"We haven't had much chance to speak privately of late, but I couldn't help wondering..." Lady Talbot paused, then asked, with great gentleness, "My dear, are you *happy*? I don't mean about having Helena here," she added, "or about having to deal with those awful letters—who *could* be happy about that?—but about your future. Your marriage, in particular."

James raised his brows, trying to hide his unease at the turn the conversation had taken. "Why wouldn't I be happy? You have no objection to my future bride, I trust?"

"None at all. The Newbolds are delightful people, especially the daughters. It's just..." Again she hesitated, her gaze intent on his face. "Perhaps it's my instincts as a former matchmaking mama speaking, but I have wondered, for some time now, if you were completely certain of your choice. And I think—you know why."

James swallowed, doing his best to meet her eyes. That

was the trouble with close relations: They saw right through you, no matter what you said or did. All at once, the drawing room felt too small, as close and stifling as Gerald's chamber had been. "I gave my word," he said at last, turning back toward the door.

"And keeping your word is an honorable thing. But when the heart is involved…" Lady Talbot sighed. "Dear James, you are too much your father's son to marry for the sake of convenience, or without the sort of love your parents had. I just want you to be sure, really sure, of your choice. Or you may be condemning three people to a lifetime of unhappiness."

From Claudine-Gabrielle Beaumont to Aurelia Leigh Newbold, 9 June 1891

…I do not believe, ma petite, that you are the sort of woman who can be happy without love, or the promise of it at the very least. You say that the first man is lost to you, because he is now your sister's fiancé. But if the second stirs even a trace of affection in you, you might wish to consider seeing him again, if only to determine whether what you feel is love or merely sentiment. If you do not settle the question to your satisfaction, I fear you will always wonder…

Twenty-Five

And holy though he was, and virtuous,
To sinners he was not impiteous,
Nor haughty in his speech, nor too divine,
But in all teaching prudent and benign.

—Geoffrey Chaucer,
The Canterbury Tales: Prologue

"This is the vicarage?" Harry inquired, gazing at the dwelling before them. "A handsome place. Your cousin Frank appears to be doing quite well for himself."

"He does, indeed." *Well enough not to envy a distant, recently ennobled cousin?* James wondered. There was only one way to find out.

They alighted from the carriage and headed up the walk. A pleasant-faced woman opened the door and, on learning their identities, bade them enter. The vicar was currently engaged in writing a sermon, she informed them, but he was always willing to see his relations.

She led them into a cozy parlor, where a man of perhaps thirty sat scribbling at a desk, announced them, and withdrew. Mr. Trelawney rose at once, smiling, and held out his hand. "Cousin James, is it? Welcome. I am glad to meet you again. And you, Sir Harry," he added, with a friendly nod toward his other visitor.

James took the extended hand, studying his host appraisingly. A nondescript man, his cousin Frank—of average height, with brown hair, brown eyes, and pleasant but unremarkable features. His voice was mellifluous, however, and his smile surprisingly sweet. Half against his will, James found himself warming to the man. "I am glad to meet you as well, Cousin Frank. And in somewhat pleasanter circumstances."

"Indeed. My condolences on the deaths of your uncle and cousin; losing them so close together must have come as a shock." Frank gestured toward the sofa in the middle of the room. "Pray sit down. I'll have Mrs. Hughes bring us some tea."

James exchanged a glance with Harry as they seated themselves, knowing their thoughts were running along the same lines. No sign of guilt, discomfort, or even self-consciousness from their host at receiving them; that seemed telling in itself. But this line of investigation could not be ruled out entirely, James thought. Not yet.

Tea and scones arrived in short order, and Frank poured for them all. "So, what brings you to Veryan, cousin? Any particular business?"

"Well, for a start, I wished to explore the connection between our families more fully," James said, with perfect truth. "You are aware that, at present, your father is my heir?"

"I'd heard something of the sort," Frank admitted. "But it seems quite incredible to me. We are third cousins, are we not? Far removed from the succession—or so I thought."

"There were two Trelawneys before your father, but they died without male issue."

"Strange how things turn out. According to my father, a past Earl of Trevenan cut off our branch of the family when my great-grandfather—his younger son—made an imprudent match."

"Were they ever reconciled?" James asked, intrigued.

"Not that I'd ever heard. But my great-grandparents managed well enough, as did their descendants, though there was never much contact between them and the Trevenans."

"Perhaps we might change that now. It seems foolish to be ruled by the past."

Frank smiled. "A good thought, cousin, and a wise one. By the by, I hear that you are engaged. My congratulations. I wish you and the future Lady Trevenan every happiness."

"Thank you." James studied his cousin once more but saw no sign of insincerity. So the man was either as innocent as he seemed, or else a consummate actor. James was almost convinced of the former, but if only there was some way to be certain. Glancing toward Frank's desk, he had a sudden inspiration. "That watercolor, on the wall—is that a Constable?"

Frank followed his gaze. "Why, yes, it is. A gift from my father, on my leaving university. You have a good eye, cousin."

"If I may?" At his cousin's nod, James got up to inspect the painting, positioning himself casually beside the desk. "A fine piece of work. I've always admired Constable's studies of the sky…" Angling his head, he let his gaze fall onto the page Frank had left on his desk—and felt some tension about his chest ease when he glimpsed the spidery scrawl, not at all like the slanting hand that had composed those letters.

"He's a master at capturing light and shadow, isn't he?" Frank remarked.

"Indeed." Turning from the wall, James came to a decision. "Cousin Frank, there is something else I wished to discuss with you, of a less pleasant nature."

The vicar's brows rose. "Oh, dear. I hope it is nothing too serious?"

"I'm afraid it has the potential to become quite serious," James replied. "Recently, Harry and I have become the target of scurrilous rumors surrounding my cousin Gerald's death."

"But there was an inquest! You were cleared of all involvement, as I recall."

"Indeed I was. But within the last few weeks, anonymous letters claiming otherwise have been delivered to several influential people, including our banker." With a glance at Harry, who nodded, James removed the letters from his breast pocket. "I hope you will not be offended, cousin, but I wondered if you might, by any chance, be able to shed some light on this matter."

To his relief, Frank looked thoughtful rather than offended. "I suppose it's only natural to wonder," he murmured, accepting the letters. Opening one, he scanned the page—and James saw his eyes widen and the color drain from his face.

"Cousin Frank," he began, but the vicar shook his head fiercely and strode to the door.

"Mrs. Hughes!" he called into the passage. "Tell Mr. Oliver to come down at once!"

❧

Ten minutes later, Oliver Trelawney—a young man of perhaps twenty-two or twenty-three—shambled into the parlor, yawning and rubbing his eyes. The two brothers could scarce have looked more different: Oliver had the Trelawneys' dark coloring and angular features. But while he was handsomer than Frank, his face held none of his brother's strength or character.

"Good God, Frank," he grumbled around a yawn, "have you any idea what time it is?"

"Long past time for you to be up, brother." The vicar's face was taut, his mouth a hard line. "May I introduce your cousin James, Earl of Trevenan, and Sir Harry Tresilian?"

For a moment, Oliver stared blankly at his brother, then as the names penetrated his brain, paled to the color of whey and swung back toward the door.

Frank caught his brother's arm, thrust the letters under his nose. "Do not even trouble to deny you wrote these! I can tell your hand at a glance!"

"It wasn't me, I swear!" Oliver protested, then as three disbelieving stares riveted themselves on him, "That is, I *wrote* them, but it wasn't my idea!"

The three older men stared at each other, then, "Whose idea was it?" James asked evenly.

Oliver glanced at him for the first time, then dropped his gaze, flushing dully. "He never told me his name," he muttered. "Never set eyes on him before last month, when he approached me one night at the Barleycorn Inn. He offered me one hundred pounds to write some letters over in my own hand. He said it was to right an old injustice in my family and his, and the letters would be sent where they'd do the most good. He never told me who they were meant for."

"What did he look like?" Harry asked, in the same level tone as James.

Oliver avoided looking at him as well. "Tallish chap, brown hair and light eyes, maybe about thirty or so."

James froze, remembering Mercer's pale grey eyes staring at him from across his desk. But before he could ask any more, Frank broke in, his voice at once angry and pained.

"Dear God, Oliver, how could you lend yourself to such a vile scheme? You've got gaming debts again, haven't you? And after everything you told Father—"

"Don't you start, *Vicar*!" Oliver all but spat the word at his brother. "Why shouldn't I make a bit of money off the Trevenans? They've got plenty, and it's not like they've ever done anything for us, not since great-grandfather was cut off—"

"Your part in furthering these slanders shames your honor, and that of *our* family," Frank said, coldly furious. "Whatever happened between great-grandfather and his father has nothing to do with us or our cousin James. Or Sir

Harry Tresilian, whose reputation was also besmirched by these letters you so thoughtlessly penned. Slander and libel—against men who've done you no harm. If they sue you for defamation, it will be no more than you deserve!"

Oliver blanched again, his bravado crumbling. Frank continued, more in sorrow now than anger. "And can you imagine how this will grieve our parents—especially our mother?"

Oliver swallowed, his expression changing from defiant to miserable in the space of a heartbeat. "I didn't think—that is, I never meant..." His voice trailed off wretchedly into silence.

Frank turned back to James and Harry, his face stiff with mortification. "I ask your pardon, gentlemen, for the trouble my brother has caused you. Reparation will be made, I assure you. Shall you wish me and Oliver to call upon the recipients of those letters and make it clear that they are falsehoods?"

"Wait," James said slowly. "I think there might be an even better way to handle this. Oliver," he addressed his younger cousin directly, "the worst might yet be avoided, if you were to tell us everything you know about this man and these letters."

The young man looked up at that. "What do you want to know—Lord Trevenan?"

"The terms of his arrangement with you, for a start. How did you communicate?"

Oliver exhaled gustily, avoiding Frank's gaze. "Well, I said he never gave his name. And we only met the once. He said we shouldn't meet in person again, but he'd send me the letters to copy in my own hand, and then I was to send them to a post office box for Mr. Smith in Truro. And once he had them, he'd send me the money."

James had no doubt *Mr. Smith* was an alias. "How many letters were there, in all?"

"Three. I posted the last one just a few days ago."

"Did you keep any of his original letters? The ones you copied from?"

Oliver shook his head. "He told me to burn them," he muttered, shamefaced.

James stifled an oath. A promising lead gone, and a third letter, somewhere out there, just waiting to set off another explosion.

Harry asked, "Was he a gentleman? The man who enlisted you?"

"He spoke like one. And he dressed like one. But," Oliver paused, frowning slightly, "he didn't sound like he came from around here. He didn't sound—Cornish."

Mercer. The description, while general, did fit, and there was certainly a motive, James knew. "Would you recognize him if you saw him again?"

Oliver hesitated. "I might."

James looked around at all his cousins. "Then this is what I think we should do."

❦

"You believe it to be this Captain Mercer, then?" Harry asked, once they were back in the carriage for the return journey.

"He fits the description—such as it is. More to the point, I have something he wants, and wants badly."

"Those shares in his company."

"He's tried twice to buy them back from me. And he wasn't pleased when I refused. He may believe that if he causes enough trouble for me personally and financially, I'll be more likely to part with them." James exhaled, leaning back against the squabs. "I just don't know why he'd drag you or Robin Pendarvis into it. Unless he knows that I'd never stand for my family being slandered. Or about Robin's hotel scheme, and your involvement in it."

"That may be. Robin's made no secret of his plans for Pendarvis Hall. Talking of which, I've had a reply from him. He's coming back tomorrow and hopes to call on you soon."

"Good. I look forward to his thoughts on this unpleasant business."

"What more proof do you have against Mercer?" Harry asked.

"That's the sum of it, so far. But if we can arrange to have Oliver see and identify him as the man who paid him to write those letters, that should resolve matters tidily."

"So you've proposed. Any ideas on how to set that up?"

"A social gathering, perhaps, that won't arouse Mercer's suspicions. I'll give the matter some further thought." James closed his eyes, suddenly weary to the bone.

"Lucky thing you thought of visiting your heir," Harry observed. "Or we'd still be stumbling about in the dark."

"I can't take all the credit. Aurelia's the one who first asked about the succession."

"Did she now?" Harry sounded impressed. "She's quite a woman."

James opened his eyes. "Yes, she is. You admire her, Harry?" To his disquiet, he heard a faint edge in his voice. Worse, the very thought of Harry admiring Aurelia sent an unpleasant shock through him, a white-hot jolt that felt alarmingly like jealousy.

His cousin did not appear to notice. "Who would not? She's bright, brave, and a lady from top to toe. A pity about the scar, of course—"

"She's lovelier with that scar than scores of women without it!" James broke in heatedly, then stopped, appalled at what he'd just given away.

The silence that descended in the carriage was louder than most explosions. Furious with himself, James stared out the window. He could feel Harry's penetrating gaze on him. Another person who knew him far too well.

"If that's how you feel," his cousin began slowly, "then why—"

James shook his head. A twist of fate, or simple bad

timing…he hardly knew what to call it. He fell back at last on the reason he'd given his aunt. "I gave my word." The statement felt as stark as it sounded. "My pledge. What sort of gentleman would I be to break it?"

Harry did not reply at once, then, "She cares for you," he said abruptly. "And not just as a sister."

James did not need to ask whom he meant. Something inside of him leapt like a flame at his cousin's words, but he throttled it down, not daring to admit the possibility. "Perhaps."

"She does," Harry insisted. "I saw it on her face that day on the beach. Now, would you rather break your word, or her heart?"

"It's—it's not so simple as that." James passed a hand over his face. "Do you think she'd thank me for jilting her sister? For hurting the person she loves most in the world? And," he met Harry's gaze squarely, "I care for Amy too. The last thing I want to do is cause her pain."

Harry sighed. "I think, no matter what you decide, someone will be hurt. Call me selfish or clannish, but I'd rather it wasn't you." He paused, then said slowly, "If, by some chance, your fiancée was to have a change of heart—"

"What?" James interrupted. "Have you seen any proof that she has?"

"Not exactly," Harry admitted. "But, watching her, I've wondered if Miss Amy was truly—comfortable here, in Cornwall. Not that she's ever complained," he added hastily. "But it strikes me that a life in London might be more to her liking."

"I've promised Amy we'll go up to town periodically—at least for the Season," James informed him. "And I have a house in London now."

"So you do. But your heart is here, just as your roots are here, in Cornwall," Harry pointed out. "I'd hope your bride—whoever she might be—would understand that."

His bride. The woman who held his honor, or the

woman who held his heart? He'd dreamed of her again last night, sitting at the piano, the silvery chords rippling from beneath her fingers. In his dreams, he'd pressed his lips to the tender nape of her neck, then stroked and kissed her until their mingled sighs and murmurs of delight formed a song of their own.

James swallowed, longing and reason swirling inside of him like a maelstrom. "I can't—I need time to think…"

"No doubt you do," Harry agreed somberly. "And I don't envy you having to make a choice like this one. Just—try not to leave it too late."

He turned his head to gaze out the carriage window, leaving James to grapple with his thoughts for the remainder of the journey back to Pentreath.

Still in a brown study, he descended from the carriage and entered the house, stopping short when he heard an unfamiliar female voice issuing from the drawing room.

"Visitors, my lord," Pelham informed him. "Acquaintances of Miss Newbold, I believe."

"Thank you, Pelham." James exchanged a glance with Harry as they headed for the salon.

Most of the ladies were assembled there: Lady Talbot, Mrs. Newbold, Amy, and Aurelia, their expressions ranging from polite to apprehensive. And holding court in the middle of the room, chattering artlessly away, was Sally Vandermere. Her brother Charlie stood behind her chair, his gaze fixed on Aurelia, who was looking everywhere but at him.

Watching them both, James felt his heart sink like a stone as Harry's warning echoed almost mockingly in his head.

Don't leave it too late…

❧

"Poor Mama came down with the most awful cold after your ball," Sally Vandermere explained to the room at large. "The doctor recommended a change of air, so Charlie suggested

Newquay. We heard it was all the rage these days. Wasn't that clever of him?"

"How is your mother now, Sally?" Mrs. Newbold inquired, with an air of conscious duty.

"Oh, much better, but I imagine we'll be here until the end of the month, at least," Sally replied blithely. "We're staying at this marvelous hotel—built on the bluff, overlooking the sea. And when I learned we were just a few miles from Pentreath, well, I told Charlie we simply must call on you. I hope you don't mind showing us around your future home, Amy."

Aurelia glanced at her twin, whose already fixed smile stiffened around the edges at these words. Fortunately, Lady Talbot intervened.

"I'm afraid much of Pentreath is still undergoing renovations, Miss Vandermere. But perhaps you would enjoy a tour of the gardens?" She glanced at Trevenan, who gave a brief nod of consent. "Our roses and lupines are especially fine right now."

Sally accepted with delight, and they set out for the gardens, except Sir Harry, who made his excuses and slipped away. Aurelia found herself almost wishing she could do the same.

The Vandermeres' appearance had left her thoroughly bemused. Just this morning she'd tried to answer Charlie's letter, only to consign her efforts to the wastebasket. And now here he was, without her having to pen as much as a single sentence. And looking at her in a way that was unmistakable, that brought back a flood of memories, both bitter and sweet.

What had Claudine said, about making sure of her own feelings? There was still…something there, with Charlie. She was no longer going to deny that, even though she had no idea what that something was. And there might be only one way to find out.

❧

Aunt Judith took the lead on the tour, flanked by Mrs. Newbold and the chatterbox Miss Vandermere. To no one's surprise, Charlie Vandermere ranged himself beside Aurelia, though James noticed he did not have the effrontery to offer his arm.

"Relia," Amy began in instinctive protest, but her twin shook her head.

"It's all right, Amy. You and Trevenan go on ahead," she insisted.

"But," Amy tried again, as James asked, "My dear, are you sure?"

Aurelia colored slightly, but nodded with every appearance of composure. "Quite sure."

So there *was* something going on, though James had no idea what it could be. He offered his arm to Amy, who accepted it reluctantly, with a last glance at her sister, who sent her a faint smile and made a small shooing motion with her hand.

Taking the hint, James escorted his fiancée down the garden path after the others.

Amy fretted her lip, obviously trying to resist the urge to look back as they walked among the flowers, a riot of brilliant color and heady perfume. "Whatever can Stupid Charlie be doing here?" she asked in a fierce whisper. "Imagine him coming all the way down to Cornwall like this! I wish Relia would send him about his business."

What if his business *was* Aurelia? The thought sent a surge of almost primal fury through James; he throttled it down, reminding himself forcibly that he had no rights in this. "I think your sister knows what she's about," he said at last. "So let us trust her to handle this as she sees fit."

Amy opened her mouth, closed it, then sighed. "Very well. I daresay she's capable of dealing with Stupid Charlie on her own. I just wish she didn't have to."

"On that point, we are agreed." James patted her hand and felt suddenly awkward as he remembered Harry's words in the coach. "Amy, are you—happy here, in Cornwall? You need not fear to be honest with me," he added as her eyes widened. "Indeed, I would far rather you told me the truth than tried to spare my feelings on this."

She flushed, fretting her lip again. "I am not *unhappy* here," she said in a small voice. "I don't wish you to think that, ever. Pentreath is a beautiful estate, and Relia has completely converted me about the beach. I think I could become—quite fond of Cornwall, eventually."

"But?" James prodded gently.

Her flush deepened. "I suppose it *does* take some getting used to, living so far out in the country. I'm afraid I am a city girl at heart. But I mean to be a good mistress here, James, truly."

"I know you do." He patted her hand again. "But I also know how you love Society. We will be spending part of the year in London, I promise."

No mistaking the relief on her face. "You won't mind too much?"

"No, no, of course not," he assured her. "Marriage is a partnership, after all—a compromise. Both people should be able to have some of what they want."

She smiled, nodding eagerly. "Yes, that's just how I feel as well! So much more civilized than one person making all the sacrifices."

So civilized, their forthcoming marriage. Why didn't the knowledge make him happier?

"How did your visit to Veryan go?" she asked. "Did you find what you'd hoped to find?"

"In a manner of speaking." James paused, then decided that she might as well know now as later, and gave her a brief account of what he had discovered that morning.

"What an awful man that Captain Mercer is!" Amy

exclaimed afterwards. "I'm so glad neither you nor my father had any dealings with him. And I hope your cousin Oliver is good and sorry for what he did to you and Sir Harry."

"He appears to be. Now all we need to do is find a way for him to identify Mercer."

"I suppose you really can't just invite them all to dinner, can you?"

"That would simplify matters, but, alas, no. We need a somewhat subtler plan."

"Well, at least you have *some* of the answers you were seeking," she pointed out. "I knew you'd get to the bottom of this, eventually."

"I appreciate your confidence in me, Amy." James tried not to think of what Aurelia might have said in her sister's place. Or about what might be happening with Aurelia and Charlie Vandermere elsewhere in the garden.

"You're looking as beautiful as ever," Charlie said as they walked along the path. Much to Aurelia's relief, he'd made no move to touch her. "Cornwall must agree with you."

"It does, very much."

"You received my letter?" he asked, after a moment.

"Yes, I even read it."

"Thank you for not throwing it on the fire."

"I thought about doing that too," Aurelia told him tartly, and saw his lips quirk in a rueful smile that awoke a reminiscent ache in her heart.

"I wouldn't have blamed you if you had. I suspect most women would find my folly—impossible to forgive."

"Difficult, certainly. Impossible…" Aurelia attempted a Claudine-like shrug, even as her pulse quickened. "Who can be sure? We all make mistakes, when we're young and foolish." She paused, seeking the words that would carry her over the next hurdle. "I'd like to think we're capable of learning even from the worst of them—and making the most of a second chance."

Charlie's blue eyes were intent on hers. "What are you saying?"

She took a breath, met his gaze squarely. "I am saying that—if you choose to call on me here, at Pentreath, I am willing to receive you."

His face—still so handsome, once so dear—lit up in just the way she remembered. "You mean it, then? You are giving me a second chance?"

"I am prepared to see—whether any of those feelings we once shared still exist."

"They do," he assured her. "At least, mine do. And I pray yours do as well. You'll see, my dear girl. I will make you care for me again."

He leaned toward her, then checked himself as she drew back. "Forgive me. I don't mean to take liberties so soon. May I call on you tomorrow? Perhaps we might go for a drive."

"That would be pleasant," she acknowledged. "Shall we say, around one o'clock?"

"One o'clock it is, then." Charlie took her gloved hand and lifted it to his lips. "Thank you, Miss Aurelia. I'll make sure you don't regret this."

Aurelia managed a smile, hoping fervently that she wouldn't regret this either.

Twenty-Six

Which of us is happy in this world? Which of us has his desire? or, having it, is satisfied?

—William Makepeace Thackeray, *Vanity Fair*

"You're frowning again," Sheridan observed, laying down his pencil. "This can't be how you wish to appear in your portrait."

Amy hurriedly composed her features into something more serene. "Is this better?"

"Somewhat. But you don't exactly look like a joyful bride-to-be." He studied her with those penetrating green eyes. "Is there something amiss between you and James?"

"Between me and James? No, no, not at all."

"Then what?"

Amy hesitated, then blurted out, "Stupid Charlie Vandermere wants to court my sister again. And even worse, Relia's decided to encourage him!"

"You dislike the gentleman?"

"The understatement of the century, Mr. Sheridan. He broke my sister's heart once by jilting her after her accident. I hate like poison that he's been given another chance to do it again!" Too restless to sit any longer, she rose from the chaise in a rustle of draperies and began to pace. "He took her driving yesterday. And he'll call on her today, mark my words. And bit by bit she'll soften toward him—and then he'll disappoint her, just like he did last time!"

"He might be sincere about wishing to make amends," Sheridan pointed out. "And about winning your sister's heart again. Life has a way of changing us all. Perhaps he has learned the error of his ways and become a better, more dependable man."

"I wish I could believe that. But I trust him about as far as I can throw a grand piano. Honestly, I don't know what Relia's thinking!"

"It's her decision to make."

Amy sighed. "So it is. And that's the only reason I'm not spending every waking moment telling her what a terrible idea this is." Not that she hadn't tried. *"Relia, why?"* she had asked repeatedly, when her sister first told them all of Charlie's renewed courtship and her acceptance of it. But Relia had refused to discuss the matter further, even when they were alone together, and Amy's attempts to press the issue had almost led to an outright quarrel—except that Stupid Charlie wasn't worth quarreling about. They'd agreed to disagree instead, but it still troubled Amy deeply that the person she was closest to seemed to be shutting her out. There must be something more, something Relia wasn't telling her...

"Have you considered that she might still care for him, deep down, in spite of his past behavior? Love forgives all things, they say."

"Oh, *love*." Amy lifted a scornful shoulder. "I'm not sure I believe in it."

Sheridan raised his brows. "A remarkably cynical statement from one so soon to be wed."

"I'm not saying there can't be deep affection and respect in a marriage!" she amended quickly. "I feel both of those for James. But love, romantic love—I just don't think it's for me."

"Why not?"

Amy gazed out the window without seeing anything. "I watched my sister fall in love with Charlie, and I saw how devastated she was by his abandonment." She swallowed, remembering those dark days of worry and anxiety. "Her accident and then the heartbreak on top of that…we feared for her life, Mr. Sheridan! I don't ever want to be that—vulnerable myself. I don't ever want to expose myself to the possibility of that much pain." She turned back to him with a bleak little smile. "So you see, I am a coward at heart."

"That's rather a harsh way of looking at it," he said, half-frowning.

"Harsh?" She shrugged. "I think of it as honest, myself."

"It seems an unkindness, to cut yourself off from love so young."

"Haven't you done the same thing?" she challenged.

He grew very still. "What do you mean?"

Amy inwardly cursed her unruly tongue. They'd been getting on so well during these sittings, and now perhaps she'd jeopardized that by mentioning what must be a very private sorrow; but the die was cast. "Lady Warrender mentioned that you loved her sister Elizabeth—and that she died." *And since then you have had affairs with countless women, and cared not a straw for any of them.*

"I see." Sheridan fell silent for a moment. "It was a lifetime ago."

"But it's left its mark all the same, hasn't it?" she persisted.

He did not reply at once, and the silence stretched between them, like a sheet of ice too thin to skate on. "Elizabeth was—all in all to me, those long years ago," he said at last. "I do not deny I mourned her deeply—and I shall always cherish her memory. But, at the risk of uttering a cliché, life goes on. I am not the boy I was then, but a man grown. My work remains my consolation, though I have known other compensations as well."

A near-perfect speech, Amy thought, delivered with just the right blend of regret and detachment. Completely convincing, if one could overlook the stark pain in his eyes, now darkened to a muddy green—muted now, perhaps, after ten years, but still there, still visible.

Sheridan rose from his easel. "I believe—this concludes our sitting for today."

"I'm sorry!" Instantly remorseful, Amy took a step toward him, her hand stretched out to touch his sleeve. "I didn't mean to pry or offend you in any way—"

"Not at all," he said with perfect courtesy. "But we've been at this nearly two hours. It will be time for luncheon soon enough. You're bound to be hungry," he added, smiling just a little. "I know I am."

"Oh." Relieved by his composure, she asked, "How many more sittings do we need?"

Sheridan glanced back at the easel. "I couldn't say, as yet. But once we decide upon a pose, I can begin to paint. Things should go much faster after that."

"Tomorrow then, at the same time?" Amy asked, trying to sound as calm as he.

His eyes, now their usual clear emerald, met hers, and she felt her pulse quicken. "Tomorrow, Miss Newbold."

❦

"I can't think why you're letting *him* court you again," Andrew grumbled as he and Aurelia turned their horses back toward the stable.

Aurelia shrugged. "Why not? No lady minds being courted by an eligible young man." He'd taken her driving yesterday, just along the coast—a pleasant enough diversion, and Charlie had behaved impeccably throughout. She'd actually enjoyed herself, in a mild sort of way.

"If you were Amy, I'd wonder if you were doing this only because you meant to jilt him later, pay him back in his own coin." Andrew eyed her closely. "You're not, are you?"

"Good heavens!" The thought had never crossed her mind. "No, that would be far too much trouble." She patted Tamar's neck. "Andrew, can't you accept that I have my own reasons for seeing Charlie again, and leave it at that? It's my decision, after all. Mama and Papa have accepted it." Although her mother, at least, had been startled and mystified by her choice.

Andrew snorted. "I'll bet Amy hasn't! Not by a long shot!"

"Probably not, but Amy is holding her tongue for now, and I'd appreciate it if you'd do the same," Aurelia countered. "I mean it, Andrew." She held his gaze until he looked away, scowling, then said in a gentler voice, "You and Charlie were friends for years, after all."

"That was before I knew he'd jilted you," Andrew muttered.

"I'd never have asked you to choose sides."

"I've chosen one anyway—yours."

His brusque admission touched her. "Thank you. But you don't have to worry now. I can take care of myself." She reached across the short distance between them to touch his sleeve. "Shall we canter now? If you can keep up, that is," she added provocatively.

Andrew made the only response an older brother could make to that, and they urged their horses forward, clattering neck and neck into the stable yard five minutes later. Flushed and laughing, they dismounted and made their way back to the house.

No sooner had they entered than Aurelia heard a familiar voice call her name. "Charlie!" she exclaimed, turning toward him. "I hadn't expected to see you so soon."

"I couldn't stay away. Good morning, Andrew," he greeted his former friend uncertainly.

"Vandermere." Andrew, stony-faced, gave him a curt

nod. "It's almost time for luncheon. I'm going up to change," he told his sister, and strode past them both to the stairs.

Charlie watched him go with obvious regret. "I deserved that, I guess." He turned back to Aurelia, touched the wispy veil on her hat. "You've been riding?"

"Yes, I started last week and now I'm out on horseback almost every morning." She smiled. "It feels wonderful to ride again. I even raced Andrew back to the house today."

"Racing?" He stared at her in shock. "After what happened before? How could you take that kind of risk?"

"We were just cantering," Aurelia protested. "I know I'm not ready for a full gallop yet."

Charlie exhaled, reached out to take her shoulders. "Thank God for that! Promise me you won't do anything so dangerous again."

Aurelia resisted the urge to shake off his hold. "I came to no harm, as you can see."

"But you could have! I still remember the day you fell—"

"So do I, vividly. And everything that came after," she added with a touch of acid.

He flushed, and Aurelia felt a pang of self-reproach. Charlie was only being solicitous and kind. If he'd behaved like this four years ago, she'd have felt so safe, even cherished. Why did she find his concern irritating rather than comforting now? She said, more gently, "I do know the difference between being active and being foolish, Charlie. Trust me on this, please."

"I'm sorry," he said. "I know I'm being overprotective, and that I've got no right to tell you what to do." His hold on her shoulders slackened, though he did not release her entirely. "It's just that your safety means everything to me—and so do you."

That did touch her, and she managed to smile. "I do appreciate your concern, Charlie. And I promise to take care when I ride."

He smiled back, his relief palpable. "Thank you, my dear girl—for humoring me."

"Aurelia?" Lady Talbot spoke up from behind them. "Luncheon is in half an hour, my dear. Mr. Vandermere, shall you be joining us?"

Charlie glanced at Aurelia, who nodded. "Yes, thank you. I'd like that very much."

Lady Talbot inclined her head. "I'll see that another place is laid for you."

"I'd better go up and change," Aurelia said, glancing down at her riding habit. "Would you mind waiting in the drawing room?"

His gaze was as warm as a summer day. "Not if it means waiting for you."

～

"A gentleman to see you, my lord," Pelham announced, as soon as James set foot inside the door. "A Mr. Pendarvis. I've put him in the library."

"Thank you, Pelham. I'll speak to him right away." He paused, remembering Helena's still-simmering hostility. "See to it that Mr. Pendarvis and I are not disturbed."

"Very good, my lord."

A man was standing by the window, but he turned at once when James entered the library. "Lord Trevenan." He stepped forward, extending his hand. "I understand from Harry that you wish to speak with me?"

"Indeed." James shook his visitor's hand, taking the opportunity to study him closely. Robin Pendarvis appeared to be his age, a tall, spare young man with dark brown hair and intensely blue eyes in a strong, angular face. "What has my cousin told you, exactly?"

"Merely that an unpleasant situation had arisen here that affected all three of us," Pendarvis replied. "He said you would fill me in on the details."

"And so I shall." James gestured for Pendarvis to be seated, and sat down himself in the chair directly opposite. "To begin with, you, Harry, and I have been the target of malicious letters insinuating that we conspired to have my late cousin killed."

Pendarvis stared at him. "Good God!"

His obvious shock went a fair way toward banishing any lingering doubts James had about his innocence. "Absurd, I know. But it's caused considerable upheaval, nonetheless. Two letters have been received, one by my cousin's sister, another by our banker in Truro."

Pendarvis's mouth tightened. "Do you know who's responsible for these accusations?"

"Only in part." James gave a brief account of what he'd discovered in Veryan. "My cousin Oliver certainly bears some of the blame, but he was not the originator of this scheme. There is someone I suspect, though I lack conclusive proof as yet. A Captain Philip Mercer, who had some business dealings with Gerald in the last months of his life."

"Philip Mercer, of Mercer Shipping?"

James stared at him, wondering if he'd found yet another connection. "You know him?"

"Not personally. But my great-uncle owned a few shares in his company when he died."

"So did Gerald—rather more than a few, which all came to me on his death. Mercer has twice approached me about buying them back. Much to his displeasure, I refused him."

Pendarvis nodded. "I received a letter from Mercer a few weeks ago, asking if I'd be willing to part with my shares. He offered a handsome sum, but I told him I couldn't yet see my way clear to divesting myself of any part of my great-uncle's estate." He shrugged. "I haven't heard back so far. But then, I don't hold many shares. Acquiring yours—or rather, your late cousin's—might have seemed more imperative."

"He may also believe that slandering us both and causing

us financial difficulties might make us more receptive to his offer," James pointed out.

"If I may ask, just how deeply was your cousin involved in Mercer's company?"

"At the time of his death, Gerald had gained control of nearly a third of the business. Worse, he appears to have stolen a shipment of goods from Mercer's warehouse in Falmouth and hidden it somewhere." James grimaced at the memory. "I offered compensation, and Mercer sent over the inventory yesterday. I spent this morning searching the empty cottages on my land to see if Gerald might have hidden the cargo there, but," he shook his head, "nothing."

"That must be difficult, learning that your cousin behaved—less than honorably."

"Like a thief, you mean?" James sighed. "Unfortunately, I've learned several unpleasant things about Gerald since this business began. And I had no good opinion of him to start with."

"I met your cousin," Pendarvis said, almost abruptly. "Only once, but you must have wondered, when my name came up in those letters, if there was any sort of connection."

"I did," James acknowledged, relieved that Pendarvis had raised the subject himself. "When did this meeting take place?"

"Several days before he died. I came to visit my great-uncle at the Hall. Your cousin was there, having a brandy with him in the drawing room."

"He was?" None of this had been mentioned during the inquest, James recalled. "Did you know that Gerald was his godson?"

"Not when I first came in. But your cousin apprised me of it soon enough. Pardon me if I offend you, but I was not overly impressed by him. To be honest, I rather disliked him."

"You would not be the first to do so. What business did Gerald have with your uncle?"

Pendarvis shook his head. "I'm not certain. On the surface,

it appeared to be an ordinary social visit, but something about it—didn't feel right to me."

"Were they discussing anything of note?"

"Not that I could tell. Great-Uncle was rambling on, as he often did, about the glories of Pendarvises past. The mines and fisheries they started, the houses they built, even their involvement long ago in the trade—and your cousin was drinking it in like mother's milk and urging him to go on." Pendarvis paused. "That's what struck me as false, I suppose. As far as I knew, he'd never troubled to visit Great-Uncle Simon before, yet here he was now, hanging on his every word. I couldn't quite believe in it. Not that it mattered," he added wryly. "Neither of them paid the least attention to me. Besides, it seemed ungracious to spoil an old man's pleasure in a visitor, so I went up to bed, and by the next morning, your cousin had gone."

Puzzling indeed, James reflected. Why would Gerald, of all people, be interested in the doings of the Pendarvis family? Especially since his father's attempts to interest him in the Trelawney history and lineage had met with sullen indifference. James could well remember his uncle's fury and Gerald's sulks when the latter had refused to learn any part of the family tree. No, if Gerald had come to visit Simon Pendarvis, it could only have been because he wanted something from him. Money, perhaps? Had he sought to ingratiate himself with an old man he usually ignored in hopes of being named in his will?

Pendarvis said, as if reading his mind, "I considered my great-uncle's will, of course. He died before he could change it to reflect—what happened in January, but he'd left your cousin three thousand pounds, which has since reverted to the estate. Not an inconsiderable sum," he added, looking James straight in the eye. "But I would never have killed for it."

James met his gaze with equal honesty, his last doubts of the man vanishing. "Of course not. Thank you, Mr. Pendarvis."

Pendarvis relaxed just enough for James to realize how tense he'd been before. "Robin," he invited, with the barest of smiles.

James smiled back and offered his own Christian name in return. "James. Now, if you would permit it, I'd like to speak with your staff at the Hall—that is, if they're the same ones who worked for your great-uncle last Christmas. They might remember more about Gerald's visit."

"I haven't turned anyone off since I inherited," Robin assured him. "You may talk to whomever you wish, though I believe the butler and housekeeper may be of the most use here. Is tomorrow afternoon soon enough?"

"That would be fine, thank you." James rose from his chair. "Might I offer you something? Tea, or a glass of sherry?"

"No, thank you." Robin rose as well. "It's time I headed back. There's much work being done at the Hall, and it goes more smoothly when I'm there to oversee it."

"Ah, yes, the hotel scheme. Harry's told me something about it."

"I thought he might. Perhaps you'll let me show you some of the plans tomorrow?"

"Perhaps—if time permits." James followed his visitor out into the passage.

The front door opened as they neared it, and Aurelia came in, smiling and becomingly flushed. She stopped short when she saw them, her eyes widening. "Good afternoon, Trevenan. Mr...." She let the word trail off questioningly.

James introduced them, saw the flash of speculation in Aurelia's eyes on hearing Pendarvis's name.

"Pleased to meet you, Miss Newbold," Robin said, sketching a bow. "But I must be on my way home. I'll see you tomorrow, Trevenan."

"Tomorrow," James confirmed with a nod.

Aurelia turned to James as the door closed behind Robin. "Is everything all right?"

"More or less. I'm satisfied that Pendarvis wasn't involved in Gerald's death. In fact, he's told me some things that might prove useful. Apparently, several days before his death, Gerald visited Simon Pendarvis."

"Why would he have done that?"

"That's what I intend to find out, by talking to Pendarvis's staff. I can only hope that bears more fruit than my search of the cottages," he added, grimacing.

"So the shipment wasn't there?" she asked with sympathy.

"Not so much as a potsherd." Weary, James rubbed a hand over his face. "Bolts of silk and muslin, more than a dozen crates of tea and porcelain—I've practically memorized that inventory. They can't all have vanished into thin air."

"Of course not," Aurelia said bracingly. "Your cousin found a good hiding place, that's all. But with you, Sir Harry, and now Mr. Pendarvis working together, I'm sure it's just a matter of time before you discover it. In the meantime, why don't you go and have something to eat? You missed luncheon, after all."

James managed to smile at her. "Sensible, as always. I'll ring for some sandwiches."

"That's sensible too." She smiled back at him, headed for the stairs.

"Aurelia?' He did not know what made him call to her, but as she glanced back at him, he found himself asking, "Has Mr. Vandermere called today?"

She hesitated, flushing slightly, then replied, "He has. In fact, he joined us for luncheon. I was just seeing him out now. He'll probably call tomorrow too."

His heart seemed to constrict at her words. "Are you sure—this is what you want?"

A bittersweet smile ghosted about her mouth. "Are any of us ever sure of what we want?" she said at last, and hurried up the stairs without waiting for an answer.

Twenty-Seven

Their heads neared, and their hands were drawn in one,
And they saw dark, though still the unsunken sun
Far through fine rain shot fire into the south;
And their four lips became one burning mouth.

—Algernon Charles Swinburne,
Tristram of Lyonesse

"I'D HEARD YOU WERE BACK. I THOUGHT I'D COME BY,
pay my respects."

The words floated out to James as he and Harry rode through the gates of Pendarvis Hall the next day. He frowned to himself; the well-bred voice was familiar, but he could not place it immediately. Then, entering the courtyard, he saw Sir Lucas Nankivell, astride his chestnut hack, talking to Robin, who was standing on the front steps of Pendarvis Hall.

"Very neighborly of you, Nankivell." Beneath the surface courtesy of Robin's voice, there was an undertone that James could not identify.

Perhaps Nankivell heard it too, for his next words sounded slightly less affable. "I hope you've given some serious thought to our last conversation. My offer still stands, you know."

"Thank you, but I prefer to retain my shares for now."

"Is that wise? A scheme as ambitious as this," he gestured toward Pendarvis Hall, "could only benefit from a quick infusion of capital. Especially if you lack investors."

"Oh, I haven't given up hope of finding those." Robin turned his head, caught sight of his visitors. "Trevenan, Harry—welcome to Pendarvis Hall."

Nankivell glanced in their direction as well. "Ah. Good afternoon to you both." He touched his hat. "How is your family, Tresilian—all well, I trust?"

"Very well, thank you," Harry acknowledged, his tone carefully neutral.

"And Miss Sophie?" Nankivell went on. "I saw her out riding just the other day."

"Sophie is fine. She's looking forward to her birthday celebration next week."

"Ah, yes." Nankivell patted his horse's neck. "Eighteen—a woman grown, at last."

No mistaking the significance of his remark. To James's relief, Harry did not rise to the bait. "So she tells me," he said equably. "But she's still quite young, for all that. You'd understand, I'm sure, if you had sisters yourself."

"No doubt I would." Nankivell inclined his head. "Well, if you'll excuse me, gentlemen, I must be on my way. Pendarvis, I hope you will reconsider my offer."

"I promise to give it the attention it deserves, Nankivell." Again James heard that not entirely cordial undertone in Robin's voice, though he could not tell if Nankivell had. The baronet merely nodded again, kneed his horse to a trot, and rode out through the gate.

"What was that about?" James asked, once Nankivell had gone.

"I inherited some railway shares from my maternal grandfather," Robin explained. "Sir Lucas wishes to buy them, but since they provide much of my income, I refused him."

Harry grimaced. "Can't say I'm surprised. Apparently he's been trying to buy up shares in railways and other such ventures for the last six months, at least. With only limited success."

"Is Nankivell in debt, then?" James inquired, surprised. "He looks prosperous enough."

"I daresay he does, at first glance," Harry agreed. "But there have been some whispers going round the county that his mine is exhausted, and that he's taken out a mortgage on his estate. Of course, he might be better off if he spent more time tending to his interests in Cornwall instead of gallivanting off to London for half the year," he added censoriously. "Anyway, Nankivell's finances are among the reasons I don't favor a match between him and Sophie."

James wondered if he was imagining the admonitory note in his cousin's voice, and glanced at Robin, who seemed unaffected. "Indeed. Your sister deserves a man who can provide for her." He beckoned to a groom to take charge of the horses. "Come in, please, both of you."

James studied the house as he followed his host up the steps. Once a modest medieval manor, Pendarvis Hall had been rebuilt during Queen Anne's reign, and now rivaled Pentreath for size—if not elegance, to his partial eye. But no one could deny its grandeur.

Robin caught the direction of his gaze and smiled a little wryly. "Impressive, is it not? But I doubt many can live on that scale now, unless their estates can support themselves."

"And that's why you mean to transform the place into a hotel?" James asked.

"Among other reasons." Robin led them inside. "But even if I could afford to live like Great-Uncle Simon, my parents are long dead, and the Hall is far too large for one man alone."

"You might marry and have a family," James suggested.

Robin's face went still and expressionless. "I am not in a position to consider that just now," he said at last. "But I don't want the Hall to pass out of the family altogether. This way, I can ensure that the house survives in some form, *and* retain all the staff. Talking of which, whom do you wish to speak to first?"

༄

The butler, a tall, austere Cornishman by the name of Praed, remembered showing Gerald into the drawing room where he had left both host and guest to their brandy and returned below stairs. A good half-hour later, Mr. Robin had arrived and been shown in as well. All told, Gerald had stayed nearly two hours; unusual for that time of night. While Praed could not recall what the gentlemen had been discussing, he observed that Mr. Pendarvis had been much affected by the death of the previous Lord Trevenan, and inclined to dwell upon the past.

Which confirmed what Robin had told him, James reflected, but did not explain Gerald's apparent fascination with his godfather's reminiscences. "Did my cousin make any further visits to Mr. Pendarvis?" he inquired, without much hope.

"Not to my knowledge, my lord."

"Thank you, Mr. Praed." James glanced at Robin, who sent the butler back to his duties.

The housekeeper, Mrs. Dowling, came in next. Her account was similar to Praed's, though unlike the butler, she hadn't actually spoken to Gerald. But she'd kept track of how long he'd stayed, just in case he spent the night and an extra chamber needed to be readied.

"Mrs. Dowling, did you notice anything unusual about the house, after my cousin's visit?" James asked. "Anything at all, however minor?"

The housekeeper frowned. "Well," she began, after a lengthy pause, "this may have naught to do with your cousin, my lord, but…sometime after the master died, I noticed the key to the old lodge was missing. I couldn't think where it had gone. We'd the locksmith in to make a new one just before you came to take charge of the Hall, sir," she added to Robin.

"A key?" James stared at her, his mind racing. "Would it happen to be an iron key, plain and slightly rusty, about this long?" He held his thumb and forefinger about four inches apart.

"Why, yes. It was about that size, as I recall."

James exhaled, forced himself to remain calm. "Thank you, Mrs. Dowling." He turned to Robin and Harry. "I found such a key among Gerald's personal effects, just a few days ago."

"Then, gentlemen, I believe we have a lodge to open," Robin said, getting to his feet.

❧

The old lodge was located across the park, no distance at all on horseback. Within minutes, they were dismounting and making their way to the door.

"I haven't set foot inside this place in years," Robin admitted, taking out the key. "It's so far from the main house and dropping to bits, besides. I was actually thinking of razing it and having something else built on this site." He opened the door, stepped gingerly over the threshold. "Mind the cobwebs."

The parlor stood just off the narrow entrance hall, its furniture shrouded in holland covers and several large wooden crates stacked in the middle of the floor. Shipping crates, bearing the stamp of a familiar name...

For one stunned moment, they all stood and stared at the missing shipment, now so miraculously found. Then Harry swore fervently, breaking the spell, and moved to investigate the cargo. Shaking off his paralysis, James proceeded to do the same.

"Great-Uncle must have slipped your cousin the key on

the sly," Robin said, joining the search. "Good God, hiding the shipment here might even have been his idea!"

James paused, frowning. "He'd have condoned Gerald's theft?"

"I doubt your cousin told him the whole story. He probably compared what he'd done to the free trade, hiding luxury goods right under the nose of the law. That would have appealed to Great-Uncle's sense of adventure, and his love of the past." Robin handed James one of the crowbars they'd brought with them. "Shall we open these and see just what's inside?"

They worked in silence, prising off the lids of the crates. James found himself mentally marking off the items in Mercer's inventory. Porcelain vases and bowls in delicate hues and intricate patterns, trinkets of jade and ivory, bolts of brocaded silk and airy muslin...

He straightened up from the last crate. "Everything seems to be here, except the tea. There should be about half a dozen crates of it."

"He might have been able to sell that right away," Robin suggested.

"Perhaps," James conceded. "There's certainly enough demand for it." He glanced around the roomful of cargo. "I suppose we should inform Mercer the shipment's been found."

"Wait." Harry held up a forestalling hand. "I've just thought of a way to kill two birds with one stone." He glanced at James. "I say we move all this to Roswarne now, and contact Mercer—somewhat later. Perhaps on Midsummer Eve, if your Trelawney cousins are willing to join us that night?"

James met Harry's gaze with perfect understanding. "Under the circumstances, I'm sure they'll be glad to accept your invitation."

෫෮

The sea was lively today, its rolling waves crowned with lashings of foam. Aurelia walked along the sand, hoping the sea's tumult would calm her restless thoughts. And the solitude, of which she had far less now that she'd agreed to see Charlie again.

But that wasn't fair. She'd made the decision to let him renew his courtship, and so far, their meetings had been pleasant, though in a somewhat muted way. Nostalgically sweet, like a bouquet of pressed flowers, without the heady fragrance or promise of fresh-picked blooms. But this was old affection, not new, Aurelia reminded herself. And could not former love revive, given the right circumstances? The shadow of his desertion lingered, but it was growing fainter, more a memory of disappointment now than the heart-wrenching betrayal it had been. They were careful in their dealings with each other, as kind and considerate as they knew how to be. Maybe *too* kind and considerate, if such a thing was possible.

Which was infinitely preferable to rancor and bitterness. Except that, with each day that passed, she felt increasingly unsettled and dissatisfied. *How is that for clarity, dear Claudine?*

"Aurelia?" Charlie's voice spoke up from behind, startling her. Between the roaring surf and the soft sand underfoot, she had not heard him approach.

"Lady Talbot tells me you often walk here," he explained, as she turned to face him. "I hope you don't mind my joining you."

She did, actually, but it would be rude—and unkind—to say so. "Not at all."

Charlie gazed out at the water. "Beautiful waves. Reminds me of Newport. Remember that first summer we were courting?"

"I remember." It seemed a lifetime ago, those days when she'd lingered on the veranda, hoping for a glimpse of him.

"I don't think I've ever been as happy, before or since. Have you?"

More recent memories arose in her mind—of a dark-haired

man holding out his hand to her as a waltz played in the distance. Of that same man lifting her to the saddle and swinging up behind her. And just yesterday, watching her with those night-dark eyes and asking her if this—this tentative, painstakingly polite courtship—was what she wanted. "It was a very special time for us, Charlie," she said at last. "But one oughtn't to live in the past."

"Of course not," he said quickly and agreeably—almost too agreeably, Aurelia thought, then chided herself for being overly critical. "Indeed, I should like very much to talk of the future. Shall we walk?"

She took his arm and they began a slow promenade along the water's edge. "So, what are your plans after this summer?" he asked. "Will your family be returning home for the wedding, or does Amy mean to marry here, in England?"

Home. It took a moment for her to remember that was supposed to be New York. "Oh, Amy has her heart set on getting married in New York, probably sometime in September or even October." A grand Society wedding, befitting her status and fortune. Aurelia would have preferred a smaller, more intimate ceremony, but she reminded herself forcibly that she wasn't the bride. "And then she and Trevenan will most likely winter abroad, for their honeymoon," she continued, ignoring the wistful pang that always accompanied that thought.

"And will you be traveling as well, or do you mean to stay at home this winter?"

"Oh, the latter, I suspect. I did rather miss Christmas in New York last year—sleigh rides, caroling, even skating parties." She managed a smile. "I may even chance a few turns about the ice this winter, now that my leg is so much stronger."

Alarm flickered in Charlie's eyes at this professed ambition, but to his credit, he refrained from expressing the reservations that had irked her before. "Well, you've always had spirit," he said manfully. "And what about spring? Will you be returning to England then?"

Where Amy would be settling in as Trevenan's wife? Not a chance of that, Aurelia thought. Aloud she said, "Oh, I haven't decided yet. I was actually thinking about college. You know Miss Witherspoon always hoped at least one of us would go. What about you, Charlie? Are you missing New York, and your job at the bank?"

"A little," he admitted. "I'm enjoying my holiday, but a part of me is looking forward to taking up my work again. Of course, I'm very much the junior partner there, but Father's bringing me along in the expectation that I'll succeed him in the fullness of time."

That came as no surprise to Aurelia. Mr. Vandermere had always had very definite ideas regarding his only son's future. "I am sure you'll fulfill all his hopes for you."

"Maybe. I've always tried to please him. But that doesn't mean I can't have—or cherish some hopes of my own." He paused, clearly working up to something. "And that's why I've come today. Not just to discuss the future, but *our* future in particular."

"*Our* future?" Aurelia echoed, startled, her hand dropping from the crook of his arm; she was still getting used to their having a present.

"It's time, don't you think?" To her amazement, he lowered himself to one knee and reached for her hand. "Aurelia Newbold, will you do me the honor of becoming my wife?"

Shock crashed over her like a wave, followed at once by panic. "Charlie, it's only been four days since we started seeing each other again!"

"But we've known each other far longer, haven't we? Some people might say a proposal was overdue. But whether it's been four days, four months, or four years," his mouth quirked in that rueful smile she'd once loved, "my affections haven't changed. Every day we've spent together has just convinced me that we shouldn't have parted in the first place."

Aurelia bit her lip, gazing at her first love. "I wish I could be as certain."

Charlie flushed. "I know you have a lot to forgive."

"That's not it—at least, not entirely. Does your family know what you intend?" Aurelia couldn't imagine his parents being any more pleased by this than they'd been four years ago.

His gaze was steady on hers, a man's gaze now. "They know I mean to propose to the finest lady I know, and that I won't be talked out of it. A fellow has the right to choose his own wife—if she'll have him." His voice softened. "So will you, dearest girl?"

"Charlie…" Aurelia paused, fumbling for the right words. "I'm sorry," she managed at last. "I didn't expect—I need more time!"

Contrition spread across his face. "I'm the one who should apologize," he said, getting to his feet. "I shouldn't have rushed you. It's just—well, I wanted to put our past behind us, once and for all. And to show you I'm serious about making a fresh start with you."

"I understand." And she did. Some small part of her even warmed at his sincere desire to make amends, but a far larger part insisted that she wasn't ready for this. "But given how—complicated our history has been, I think it's all the more important that we not rush into anything now. Would you give me some time—a week at least—to think over what you've said?"

"Take all the time you need." He took her hand, hesitated a moment, then raised it to his lips. "I'll be on my way now, but may I call on you again, perhaps in a day or two?"

"Of course." She summoned a smile. "Until then, dear Charlie."

"Until then." He released her hand and strode toward the stairs.

Aurelia did not watch his ascent. Turning back toward the sea, she closed her eyes, her thoughts and emotions in chaos once more.

"He went down on one knee," a familiar voice observed sardonically. "How gallant of him. I didn't know they still did that in America."

Aurelia opened her eyes to find Trevenan, astride Camborne, staring down at her, his expression unreadable. "You saw?"

His lips thinned. "A bit hard to miss, a grown man kneeling on the sand." He swung down from his horse, stood face to face with her. "Am I to wish you happy, then?"

She glanced away. "I haven't given him an answer yet."

"But you're considering it?" His voice sounded oddly taut.

Aurelia shrugged, trying for nonchalance. "A lady should always take the time to consider a proposal of marriage from a gentleman."

"Even one who's disappointed her?" he challenged. "You've forgiven him so quickly?"

"Quickly? It's been four years, Trevenan. Charlie and I are different people now."

"You could still do better than Vandermere." His brows drew together. "And you've just started seeing each other again. What the deuce is he about, asking you this soon?"

"He says he wants to put the past behind us, and start afresh." Aurelia picked up her skirts, walked a few steps away from him. "I'd say that was a worthy goal, wouldn't you?"

Trevenan followed her. "If he's being wholly honest about it.'

Indignant, she turned to face him. "You doubt his motives?"

"I'd question the motives of any man who'd behaved as he had!" Trevenan paused, then resumed more gently, "You don't have to accept him, Aurelia. I understand he was your first love, but there are other fish in the sea."

Unexpectedly, Aurelia felt her temper fraying. "If you

only knew how sick I am of that phrase!" she exclaimed. "I must have heard it a thousand times after my accident!"

"That doesn't make it any less true," he countered. "You of all people shouldn't have to settle for less than you deserve or want."

"What I want," she began with some heat, then quickly changed course, "is for everyone to stop treating me like a fool or a simpleton just because I'm seeing Charlie again! Why shouldn't I let him court me? Why shouldn't I explore my feelings and see where they lead?" She stopped, breathless and suddenly furious: at Trevenan, at herself, at everything that had brought them here. "And why shouldn't I marry him, and have a life of my own?"

He stared at her, his dark eyes unfathomable. "You could meet a better, worthier man."

She laughed, a strained, harsh sound. "I've already met one—he's marrying my sister!"

The words blazed forth, hanging in the air as though etched in fire, impossible to recall or deny. They stared at each other, scarcely breathing—then, in an instant, Trevenan closed the distance between them in one stride and pulled her to him, arms banding around her like iron.

Their mouths met in a fierce mutual claiming, and the world went white around them—white as lightning, white as the heart of a flame. Closing her eyes, Aurelia let herself fall, deep into a void where all that existed was his touch, his taste, and the hot, urgent press of his lips against hers. *This*, she thought hazily. Yes, *this*. And knew by his response, the guttural moan low in his throat, that it was the same for him. *Love, that is first and last of all things made…*

They parted to a hand's span, still dazed and breathless. Looking up, Aurelia saw her own desire and longing mirrored in his eyes. Exultation flared, only to extinguish itself a moment later, turning into something that felt almost like fury. Pushing him away, she stepped back and blurted out, with the wild illogic born of pain, the question that had haunted her since her return.

"Damn you, James! Why couldn't you *wait* for me?"

～

Why couldn't you wait for me?

Her words, all the more poignant for their lack of reason, struck him like a blow to the heart: a scathing indictment of every choice he'd made since becoming Trevenan. And she stood there, her eyes blazing at him: furious as he'd never seen her, and so beautiful his soul ached. No use pretending anymore, even if he'd wanted to. They'd deceived themselves long enough.

"I'm sorry." The words rasped out, dry as Sahara sand. "Forgive me. You were so *fragile*, then. I heard you'd gone away, and I thought—and then your sister..." He shook his head, defeated. "God help me, Aurelia, I should have known my own heart!"

The anger faded as quickly as it had come upon her. "Then God help us both," she whispered, her eyes brimming.

He took a step toward her; she shook her head, retreated. "Don't, please."

"Aurelia—"

"I can't do this to Amy!" she broke in wildly. "I can't betray my sister! She can't ever know about us. I'll go away, right after the wedding—"

"You could run to the ends of the earth, and my heart would still follow you."

She shook her head again, whether in acknowledgment or denial of his words he could not tell. "Amy doesn't deserve this, not from us."

James swallowed. "I know. And I gave her my word. I do care for her, Aurelia. I even thought I could love her."

"You *can*! You will. She's so easy to love, James, so beautiful and bright. And she cares for you. I can see it in her eyes." She straightened, her eyes still brilliant with unshed tears. "Women have honor too, my lord. I could never be happy if I spoiled *her* happiness."

A lifetime of unhappiness…his aunt's words echoed in his mind. "I know," he managed at last. "I'd expect nothing less from you, when it comes to loyalty and love."

Her lips formed a tremulous smile. "Thank you, for understanding."

James cleared his throat. "Just promise me—one thing. That you won't marry," *Vandermere*, "any man who doesn't love you with all his heart and soul. Who won't do his utmost to make you happy. Because you deserve happiness, every bit as much as Amy."

The tears spilled over then, but she brushed them away impatiently, nodded. "I promise." Her voice was little more than a whisper. "I should go up now."

He nodded as well, feeling as if his heart was lodged in his throat, and watched as she made her way to the stairs and began to climb, every step taking her further away from him. His match, his mate, the love of his life…lost to him through his own well-intentioned folly.

Only after she'd disappeared from sight did he get back on Camborne and make his own way back to Pentreath.

He did not follow her. Hurrying through the gardens, Aurelia told herself fiercely that she was glad, because if he had…she did not think she could have denied him whatever he asked.

She'd thrown every obstacle she could think of between them—honor, reason, her love for Amy, her unresolved feelings for Charlie. And they'd all gone up like tinder with one kiss. One kiss that made a mockery of all her attempts to keep her love for him at bay. And now, to know that he wanted her just as badly…

Again she relived that moment on the beach, the consuming fire of that kiss. Body and soul aflame, desire coursing through her veins, awakening sensations in all the secret places that a lady wasn't supposed to know about, let alone think about.

But Aurelia had known about them ever since those heady days of first love with Charlie. Lying in bed at night, she'd conjure his dear face, imagining his lips on hers, his hands caressing and exploring every inch of her body. And think with a delicious shiver of what they'd do once they were married—dreams and fantasies too intimate to share with anyone, even Amy.

Charlie…what answer could she possibly give him, when the face she now saw in those secret fantasies was no longer his? And had not been his, for a very long time?

Pausing beneath a tree, Aurelia closed her eyes and fought for composure. The kind of composure she'd needed after her accident, when all she'd wanted was to scream aloud, in pain and frustration. How ironic that, after her long struggle to recover, she should find herself in the same agony of mind, if not body.

But she was stronger now. What had happened just now must not happen again—she and James had agreed on that. For everyone's sake, they must go on as before, live the lives they had determined to live, even if it was on separate continents. *Parting is such sweet sorrow…* There was nothing sweet about this sorrow, but perhaps, in time, it would become less bitter. She could hope for that, at least.

Opening her eyes, she saw that she'd nearly reached the house. She took another moment to collect herself, then almost ran the rest of the way, praying that no one would notice or comment on her entrance.

She made it safely upstairs and was heading down the passage toward her chamber when her luck ran out.

"Relia?"

The last voice she wanted to hear just now, the last person she felt up to dealing with. Guilt, remorse, and something darker that she didn't dare to name rose up in a cresting wave that threatened to drown her where she stood. She forced it down, then turned to face her twin.

"Amy, dearest." She hoped her smile didn't look as forced as it felt.

If it did, Amy did not appear to notice, fortunately. "I feel as if I haven't seen you all day," she said, almost plaintively. "Whatever have you been doing?"

Kissing your fiancé. And being kissed by him. The wave reared up again, was forced back again. "Walking on the beach," Aurelia replied, trying for a light tone. "You know how I love it down there." She changed the subject quickly. "You look lovely in that gown. Are the sittings going well?"

Amy's expression brightened. "Oh, yes! Mr. Sheridan and I have nearly decided on a final pose. I feel certain this portrait will be everything it should be—and more."

So confident, always. What must it be like, to be so sure of oneself all the time, Aurelia wondered. To know exactly what one wanted, and to be completely certain of getting it? She looked at Amy—beautiful, composed, unsuspecting Amy—and, for the first time in her life, felt a spark of resentment that was close to hatred. Words trembled on her tongue, words that could smash that composure, that utter certainty, to smithereens...

Horrified at herself, Aurelia stamped out that rebel spark. Dear heaven, what was she thinking? *My twin, my heart*—the person she loved most in the world. Except, perhaps, for one other now. But James would not want her to do this, either—to devastate someone who'd done nothing to deserve it. "*I do care for her,*" he had said. "*I even thought I could love her.*" How he'd despise her if he knew how close she'd come to hurting Amy! Almost as much as she'd despise herself.

Swallowing back her too-ready confession, she replied,

"I'm sure Trevenan will be delighted with it." After his name, his title felt strange, even foreign, in her mouth.

Much to her surprise, Amy colored at her remark. "Yes, of course. James. Naturally, I hope he'll be pleased."

Aurelia looked at her twin more closely. Was there something almost—guilty in Amy's response? As if, perhaps, her future husband was *not* foremost in her thoughts? Curiosity roused, sharp and avid, and a whole slew of questions with it: *Do you love him? Do you want him, burn for him—as I do? Do you dream of being his* wife, *not just his countess? Would you even have looked at him if he'd been plain Mr. Trelawney, and not the Earl of Trevenan?*

Disloyal thoughts—she should be ashamed of having them, especially when she knew, better than anyone else, how much love Amy had to give. And love could grow in a marriage, Aurelia reminded herself, even if it wasn't present at the very beginning. Her parents were proof of that. Stifling curiosity and jealousy alike, she asked gently, "And you, dearest? Are *you* happy—about marrying James, I mean? The wedding's just a few months away."

"Of course I'm happy," Amy said quickly. A shade too quickly? "It'll be lovely to have everything settled at last," she went on, "and James is such a good man, isn't he? So straightforward and honorable. You always know just where you stand with him."

Standing on the beach, locked in his arms, his mouth pressed so hungrily to hers…

"Yes, he's—he's nothing if not honorable." Relief and disappointment were waging a fierce tug-of-war inside of her; she could not have said which one was stronger.

Amy's gaze sharpened at the strain in her voice. "Relia, are you all right?" She took a step closer, frowning. "Stupid Charlie called, didn't he? If he's done anything to upset you—"

"He hasn't," Aurelia broke in. "I think I've had a little too much sun, that's all." She summoned a suitably wan smile, no hardship under the circumstances. "I'll feel much better after I lie down and rest for a while."

Amy's expression softened at once. "You poor dear! Do you need anything else, a cool drink, perhaps? Let me come with you. I can ring for Suzanne."

Aurelia shook her head. "No, thank you, love. I'd prefer to be on my own just now. I'll see you at dinner," she added, and hurried away before Amy could offer to accompany her again.

Reaching the safety of her chamber, she closed the door and leaned against it—bracing herself for the difficult days, months, *years* ahead. The knowledge that she'd tried to do the right thing seemed cold comfort, but she clung to it with the desperation of a shipwreck survivor clinging to a spar.

It's just as I said. Amy cares for James.

Because if she didn't, I'd fight her for him. So help me God, I would.

Twenty-Eight

In the mouth of two or three witnesses shall every word be established.

—2 Corinthians 13:1

ST. JOHN'S EVE, AND THE LIGHTED WINDOWS OF Roswarne gleamed golden in the dusk, bright as the midsummer bonfires James remembered blazing on the cliff tops when he was a boy. Once his party, consisting of his aunt, the Newbolds, and Thomas, had alighted from the carriages, he led them toward the house, where the Tresilians waited to receive them. He spared a moment to be thankful for Helena's absence. Not that she'd have deigned to attend this ball in any case, but her recent altercation with Harry had made her doubly unwelcome here.

James kissed Sophie, looking quite the young lady in a pale green gown that complemented her eyes. "Many happy returns, cousin. Save me a dance for later?"

"Of course." Sophie smiled back, but he thought she looked just a touch distracted. Before he could ask what was troubling her, she turned to greet the nearest Newbold, "So glad you came, dear Aurelia. How lovely you look in that color—periwinkle blue?"

James did not turn his head, though he'd noticed how well

the shade flattered Aurelia's fair skin and bright hair. They studiously avoided each other's company whenever possible now, the memories—and the regrets—too keen for them both. At unguarded moments, James still recalled the sensation of her body, warm and pliant against his, and the searing intensity of that kiss, so different from the tentative salutes he and Amy had exchanged. How could two women be so similar on the surface and so different underneath?

He glanced guiltily toward his betrothed, radiant in blush pink as she greeted his cousins. For Amy, he'd felt affection and even attraction, but nothing like the hunger her sister roused in him. And yet it was to Amy that he'd pledged his word and his honor. She'd entered into their contract in good faith. He could no more justify betraying her than Aurelia could.

"James." Harry spoke low in his ear. "If I may have a private word?"

Alerted by his cousin's tone, James followed him into the library at the back of the house. To his surprise, Frank and Oliver Trelawney were already there. While their presence here tonight was part of Harry's plan, James could tell at a glance that something had changed.

"What's happened?" he asked at once.

Oliver swallowed. "I received another letter to copy today, for an extra twenty pounds."

"You did?" James stared at him. "Have you brought it with you?"

"We have," Frank replied, taking the letter from his breast pocket and handing it over.

James opened and scanned the letter: the accusations were the same, but the hand was different—and still unfamiliar.

"Is it Mercer's writing?" Harry asked.

"I couldn't say. The inventory I received was written by one of Mercer's clerks. But this is valuable evidence nonetheless. Well done, both of you," James added to the Trelawneys.

"We're happy to make amends, Cousin James." Frank eyed his brother pointedly. "Isn't that right, Oliver?"

The younger man flushed but nodded. James tucked the letter into his own breast pocket. "I'll take charge of this, for now. You understand the rest of the plan?"

"We wait in the ballroom with the other guests until you and Sir Harry bring in Captain Mercer so Oliver can identify him," Frank replied. "Simple but effective. And Sir Harry says he's asked the local magistrate to be present, just in case Mercer proves resistant."

"I thought it best not to leave anything to chance," Harry explained.

"When do you expect Mercer?" James asked.

"At half-past seven or thereabouts." Harry consulted the clock on the mantel. "A quarter-hour from now. Robin will be here soon as well."

"Then, gentlemen, let's get in place," James proposed. "The sooner this is resolved, the better for us all."

"Amen," Frank said fervently, and shepherded Oliver from the library.

❧

At exactly half-past seven, Mercer strode into the library. "Good evening, gentlemen." His gaze went at once to James. "I understand you've found the shipment?"

"We have," James replied. "Gerald hid it in an old lodge house on the Pendarvis estate."

Mercer's brows rose in genuine surprise. "Good God, how did it come to be there?"

"My Great-Uncle Simon was the late earl's godfather," Robin replied, then gave a brief account of how they'd discovered the missing cargo in the lodge.

"Given the condition of the lodge, we thought it best to move the goods elsewhere for safekeeping," James explained. "Harry suggested Roswarne, since it was closest."

Mercer came to a point like a hunting dog. "The shipment's here, then?"

"In the morning room, just down the hall. You can inspect it yourself, of course, but according to the inventory, everything is here. Except for the tea."

Mercer's tone sharpened. "The tea is missing?"

"I'm afraid so." Looking more closely, James saw a flash of rage in the captain's eyes, so intense that he had to force himself not to recoil. "Gerald probably found a buyer right away."

The fury burned for a moment longer, then Mercer's eyes went flat and opaque again. "No doubt," he agreed colorlessly. "Well—I appreciate your efforts in recovering my cargo."

James inclined his head. "I regret we could not recover it all. Do you wish to see it now?"

"Yes, thank you." Mercer turned to Harry. "You said the morning room, Sir Harry?"

"Indeed. Follow me." Harry led the way down the passage to the salon where they'd transported the crates from the shipment a day earlier.

Mercer moved about the room, lifting the crates' lids and asking the occasional question, but James thought there was something almost cursory about his inspection. Uneasily, he remembered the rage in the captain's eyes on hearing that the tea was gone: the justifiable anger of a merchant cheated of the price of his goods—or something far more sinister?

Mercer straightened up from the last crate. "You're right, Trevenan. Everything else appears to be here. Sir Harry, might I arrange to have all this transported to my warehouse?"

"Of course. I'll loan you our baggage wagon, and my servants can start loading it right away. In the meantime, why don't you come and take some refreshment while you wait?" Harry suggested, with easy hospitality. "We're celebrating Midsummer's Eve and my sister's birthday tonight. Half the county must be here, so there's plenty of food and drink."

"Very well," Mercer conceded after a moment. "A glass of wine might not come amiss."

"I can promise that and more." Harry avoided his cousin's gaze, but James knew their minds were running along the same track. Not long now…

The ballroom at Roswarne wasn't especially large or grand, Amy reflected as she gazed about it, but the arrangements of massed roses and lilies gave it a festive air, and so did the floral garlands draped over the window bays. On the whole, this party was less formal and more openly celebratory than most balls she had attended in London. A buffet table laden with hot and cold delicacies had been set up against one wall, and some guests had eagerly descended upon the food. Laughter and conversations hummed from every corner of the room, while several couples—including Relia with John Tresilian—pranced across the dance floor to a lively polka.

Amy found her toe tapping in time to the music and wished she could join the dancers. But the women outnumbered the men here, so she would simply have to wait her turn. James wasn't in the room, at present, but she understood that he and Sir Harry were trying to resolve the matter of those nasty anonymous letters tonight. She hoped fervently that they succeeded, and tried not to look too wistful as the polka ended and the musicians struck up a waltz.

"Miss Newbold." She glanced up to find Sheridan, striking in his black and white evening kit, standing beside her. "May I have this dance?"

Amy stared at him for a moment, then rallied. "You may, Mr. Sheridan, and thank you."

She took his arm and let him lead her onto the floor. Had they ever danced together before? On reflection, she did not think they had. After all, he'd seemed to disapprove of her, and she'd convinced herself that she disliked *him*—neither of which had turned out to be true. At least, Amy knew she did not dislike Mr. Sheridan; for all his sophistication, he was capable of kindness and, as she now knew, deep feeling. Much to her relief, their recent conversation about Elizabeth had not caused a rift between them. He'd been as courteous as ever in their subsequent sittings, if perhaps a little more guarded. But then, it couldn't be easy for him to talk about the first love he'd lost so tragically. Mindful of that, she hadn't raised the subject again.

They stepped into the dance, entering the flow of waltzing couples as smoothly as one stream joins another. Dancing with Mr. Sheridan was subtly different from dancing with James. The artist was a fraction taller and lankier, his movements sharper, even angular somehow, though no less polished. His scent was different too, sandalwood rather than citrus and clove. But James's scent made her feel safe and secure, while Mr. Sheridan's...

She looked up suddenly—and lost herself in his eyes. Not warm, dark eyes like her fiancé's, but vivid, piercing green eyes. Artist's eyes that found beauty and meaning in the world around them, which his artist's hands strove to capture. One of those hands was resting at the small of her back now. She felt its warmth even through layers of silk and kid, and an answering warmth seemed to spread through her entire body as she registered his touch. Through her body and all the way up to her face, which must be redder than a beetroot right now!

Flustered, she summoned a smile and said brightly, "You waltz so well, Mr. Sheridan."

He lifted his brows. "That surprises you?"

"Maybe a little," she confessed. "I'm so used to thinking of you as the eternal observer."

He gave her the unguarded smile that had so astonished her the first time she saw it, and swept her into a graceful turn. "Even an observer may wish to join the dance of life, sometimes."

Life, Amy thought bemusedly, as she followed his lead. That was what she felt dancing with Mr. Sheridan. Not safe or secure, exactly, but *alive*. More alive and exhilarated than she'd ever felt while dancing with a man. Even James, she realized, with a pang of guilt.

She should be thinking of *him* right now: her kind, honorable betrothed, so unfairly beset by those awful slanders. Not of Thomas Sheridan, cynic and sophisticate, who probably had this unsettling effect on every woman who came into his orbit.

Amy glanced up at the artist from under her lashes. Not as handsome as James, but far too attractive for his own good—and hers, she acknowledged with an inner grimace. Hadn't she once resolved not to fall victim to his charms? He certainly seemed indifferent to her own, except as a subject for painting. Best to keep to her resolve then—and regard him as nothing more than a talented artist and close friend of her future husband.

But as the music slowed, fading into soft minor chords, Amy found herself wishing perversely that their dance could have lasted longer…

❧

"Amy and Mr. Sheridan seem to be enjoying their waltz," Sophie remarked, nodding toward the couples revolving on the dance floor.

Still fanning herself vigorously after the polka, Aurelia followed her gaze. "So they do." Her sister and the artist seemed to have formed a genuine rapport of late. She wondered if James had noticed, or if he'd been too preoccupied with the missing shipment—so unexpectedly recovered—and the anonymous letters. Amy had mentioned that he and Sir Harry were trying to resolve that business tonight, which must account for their absence from the festivities.

At the moment, their absence was easy to overlook; the

ballroom was packed with the Tresilians' friends, relations, and neighbors, with more guests arriving each minute.

Aurelia glanced at Sophie, who was plying her fan half-heartedly, her pretty face shadowed with anxiety. Indeed, she'd seemed distracted since the party began. "Are you all right, my dear? You don't seem to be enjoying your birthday celebration very much."

"Oh, no, I'm quite well," the girl assured her hurriedly. "And it's a lovely party. It's just—" She broke off, biting her lip, clearly undecided about whether to continue.

"Just what?" Aurelia prompted in her gentlest voice. "You *can* tell me, you know."

Sophie hesitated, then, after a quick glance around, confided in a low voice, "I haven't mentioned this to anyone else, but—I received something upsetting in the post today."

"The post?" Aurelia echoed, a nasty suspicion starting to form in her mind.

Sophie's next words confirmed it. "An anonymous letter, containing the most beastly accusations against Harry, James, and," she paused, flushing, "Mr. Pendarvis."

Aurelia's hand tightened around her fan. "What sort of accusations?"

"The letter—implied that they had something to do with the late Lord Trevenan's death. It's not true, of course," she added hastily. "I didn't believe it for a second. But the fact that such a rumor exists at all…" She shook her head, looking unhappier than ever.

Aurelia breathed out, a slow exhale. "Do you still have the letter?"

"Yes, though I thought about burning it right away."

"Under the circumstances, it's just as well that you didn't," Aurelia told her. "Sophie, dear, you need to show this letter to Sir Harry at once. Trust me on this."

Sophie's eyes widened, and she rose immediately. "It's in my room. Will you come with me?"

"Of course," Aurelia replied, standing up as well.

Together, they slipped discreetly from the ballroom.

◦◦◦

James strode down the passage toward the ballroom. Harry lingered some distance behind, chatting easily with Mercer and Robin, playing the genial squire to the hilt. Buying him time, James knew, to locate Oliver and arrange for him to identify the captain.

He'd scarcely set foot in the ballroom when an agitated Oliver materialized beside him.

"Cousin, he's here!" the young man hissed, grasping his sleeve. "The man who paid me to write the letters—I've seen him."

"But," James began, bewildered, glancing back toward the doorway, where Harry and Mercer had yet to make an appearance.

"He's over there," Oliver insisted, "standing by that window!"

James followed the line of his cousin's gaze and froze, caught between shock and recognition. *Tallish, brown hair, light eyes…* "Are you sure?"

At Oliver's frantic nod, he came to a swift decision. "You and Frank—go to the library and wait for us there. I need to speak to Harry."

Oliver hurried off; within seconds, James saw the brothers depart the ballroom together. Moments later, Harry, accompanied by Mercer and Robin, entered. Still acting the amiable host, he escorted Mercer to the refreshment table, inviting him to partake of whatever he pleased.

Keeping one eye on the man Oliver had identified, James headed for the refreshment table, drew Harry a little aside, and discreetly informed him of what had just occurred.

Harry's eyes widened, then narrowed, his face hardening. "I see," he said, and there was a world of meaning in that curt phrase. "Well, let's get to it then, shall we?"

He strolled over to the man standing by the window and clapped a hand on his shoulder. "Ah, Nankivell! Just the man I wanted to see. May I have a word with you, in the library?"

⁓

Much to James's relief, Nankivell accepted Harry's invitation without apparent suspicion. Perhaps he thought that Harry had had a change of heart about his courting Sophie. But his rather complacent expression vanished once he entered the library and saw the men waiting there. Not only the Trelawneys, but Major Arthur Henshawe, one of the local magistrates. He looked even less pleased at the sight of James and Robin entering behind him.

"Good God, Tresilian!" he exclaimed. "I assumed you meant a *private* word."

"Did you?' Harry inquired, his tone deceptively pleasant. "Pardon the oversight. James, would you close the door?"

James obeyed, then looked at Oliver. "This is the man, cousin?"

"It is," Oliver confirmed, pointing at Nankivell. "This is the man who approached me last month and paid me to write letters defaming you, Sir Harry, and Mr. Pendarvis."

"What nonsense is this?" Nankivell demanded furiously. "I've never seen this *puppy* in my life! And I certainly know nothing about any anonymous letters!"

A charged silence fell, then Major Henshawe, a stocky, greying fellow whose mild expression concealed a sharp mind, inquired, "Who said they were anonymous, Sir Lucas?"

Nankivell opened his mouth, then closed it with a snap, realizing that he'd betrayed himself. And at that moment, the door opened and a breathless Sophie burst into the room.

"Harry!" she exclaimed. "I must speak to you at once!"

"Not now, Sophie," he began, but Aurelia, entering on Sophie's heels, interrupted him.

"Please, Sir Harry—it's very important," she insisted.

Harry glanced at his sister. "Very well, then. What is it?"

"I received an anonymous letter today," she said, producing it from her reticule. "Saying the most awful things about you and James! I didn't know what to do, but Aurelia told me to bring it to you right away!"

James stared at Aurelia, as did everyone else. She colored but stood her ground with the queenly certainty he so loved in her. "I thought you'd know what to do with it, Sir Harry."

"Thank you, Miss Aurelia. I do indeed." He handed the letter to Oliver. "Familiar?"

Oliver glanced it over, nodded. "This is the last one I copied."

Nankivell snatched the letter from him, scanned it as well, and gave a scornful laugh. "Wrong again, *gentlemen*. This isn't *my* handwriting!"

"We never said it was," James replied equably. "But *this* is, I believe." He took the fourth and final letter from his breast pocket. "Oliver received it just this afternoon. As you see, it's in the original hand. Quite different from his." He passed it over to Henshawe for inspection.

Nankivell paled slightly, but his mouth was tight. "You can't prove it's mine."

"On the contrary, I think we can," Harry retorted, walking over to the writing desk in the window alcove. "My mother keeps her most recent correspondence here, including all the responses to our invitation for tonight's party. Yours is certainly among them—and I don't doubt it contains enough of your handwriting to show a match with that letter."

Emotions stormed across Nankivell's face in rapid succession: shock at having his guilt exposed, fury at those who'd unmasked him, and even now, a stubborn unwillingness to admit defeat or wrongdoing. He clamped his mouth shut, but his very silence spoke volumes.

"In God's name, Nankivell, *why*?" Harry said at last.

Robin spoke for the first time. "I suspect *I* can answer

that. It comes down to money, for the most part. He's hungry for my railway shares—and certain other things beyond his reach."

"Like my sister," Harry added grimly. "I suppose this is also his revenge against me, for rejecting his suit."

Nankivell reddened and looked away.

Sophie stared at her former suitor. "I would never have believed it of you, Sir Lucas! Slandering my brother, my cousin, and—Mr. Pendarvis?" A telltale flush crept into her cheeks at the last name, though she avoided looking at Robin. "Insinuating that they murdered Lord Trevenan? How could you write me something so *vile?*"

"I meant to protect you, Miss Sophie!" Nankivell protested, breaking his silence.

"Protect me?" she echoed, incredulous.

"From *him.*" Nankivell gestured toward Robin, and James saw the enmity flash sharp and cold between both men. "This upstart, this Johnny-come-lately…" A sneer edged into the baronet's voice. "Just what do you know about this fellow, Miss Sophie? I could tell you things."

Sophie ranged herself beside Robin, her head held high. "I know that *he's* a gentleman, Sir Lucas. That's all I need to know."

That silenced him, much to everyone's surprise. Flushing again, Nankivell glanced away from his rival and the girl he'd tried to win, who would never be his now.

"Are you now admitting to authorship of these letters, Sir Lucas?" Henshawe inquired.

"Damn you." Nankivell's voice was barely audible. "Damn all of you. Yes."

Unruffled by the baronet's imprecations, Henshawe resumed, "Then we must discuss whether any of you three gentlemen wish to bring a defamation suit against Sir Lucas. Or whether you would prefer him to make restitution by other means."

"Pardon me, Major Henshawe, but I would rather not take part in this discussion," Robin said, his face and voice expressionless; James noticed that he did not look at Sophie. "I will go along with whatever Trevenan and Sir Harry decide."

Henshawe inclined his head. "Very well, Mr. Pendarvis, if you're sure—"

"I am." Robin turned to his host. "I'll be on my way home now. Good night, Harry."

Harry accepted his hand, his expression grave. "That might be best. Good night, Rob."

"Mr. Pendarvis!" Sophie protested, stretching out a hand as if to touch his sleeve. But he stepped back out of reach, with a slight shake of his head.

"Good night, Miss Sophie." His voice held a mixture of tenderness, regret…and finality. "And to all of you," he added, then strode from the library without a backward glance.

"Let him go, Sophie," Harry urged his sister, who was gazing after Robin with such naked longing that James could not help but ache for her.

"I can't!" she choked out, her eyes brimming, and hurried from the room.

After a moment, Aurelia followed, the sympathy plain on her own face. Nankivell stared at the floor, his expression bleak, even haggard now. Self-serving and calculating though he was, he may have genuinely cared for Sophie, James thought. Even the Trelawneys looked shaken.

Henshawe alone was unaffected. "Shall we continue, gentlemen?"

❧

Emerging from the library some time later, James headed back toward the ballroom. The sprightly strains of music he could hear in the distance seemed to come from another world entirely, one in which bruised hearts and vicious slanders played no part.

He caught sight of her lingering in the passage, the gaslight casting a soft glow on her golden hair and periwinkle-blue skirts. She turned her head at his approach, and their eyes met in a silent understanding James knew he would share with no one else.

She spoke first, her blue eyes anxious. "Is everything all right now?"

"Well enough," he assured her. "None of us want the bother of a defamation suit, but Nankivell will be making restitution. He's to inform Helena and Curnow in writing that the accusations against us were malicious and unfounded. Harry proposed a financial settlement as well. Nankivell's none too pleased, but he'll pay, rather than let his misconduct become public."

"There's something I don't understand, James. If Sir Lucas's true targets were Sir Harry and Mr. Pendarvis, why did he drag you into this?"

"Because an ugly rumor attached to an earl is far more sensational than one attached to a baronet or a mere mister." He gave her a wry smile. "I was a convenient scapegoat, my dear."

Aurelia grimaced in disgust. "So all that trouble and distress he caused you, personally, was just so he could discredit Mr. Pendarvis and punish Sir Harry?"

"In a nutshell, yes. But don't forget Robin's railway shares. If those rumors prevented him from obtaining a loan, he'd probably have had to sell them to finance his hotel scheme. And Nankivell would have been right there to snap them up."

She shook her head. "All that damage for such a petty aim! Well, at least Sir Lucas is getting his just deserts, financially. What happened with Captain Mercer?"

James sighed. "He's packed up his cargo and departed without incident. Whatever else he's done, he wasn't responsible for those letters, or for what happened tonight. How is Sophie?"

"She's with her mother now. Mr. Pendarvis is gone." By the twist of her lips, he surmised that things had not gone well there. "He told her to forget him, and find someone worthier. Someone without any shadows in his past—whatever that means. Men!" she added scathingly.

James knew better than to try to defend his sex at that moment. "Poor Sophie. I'm afraid she's had anything but a happy birthday tonight."

"It's miserable, being crossed in love."

The vehemence in her voice struck him like a blow to the heart. "Aurelia—"

"Sophie's asked me to stay the night," she went on, avoiding his gaze. "I think I will. She's so unhappy now—she might be glad to have a friend near. I'll let Mother know." She glanced at him then, and smiled with the wistful sweetness that was uniquely hers. "And *you* should find Amy and dance with her. It would be a shame to let that music go to waste."

James listened for a moment. "It's a waltz." He doubted he would ever hear one without thinking of her.

Her smile trembled, then firmed again. "All the better. Good night, James." She turned away and glided past him, disappearing into the ballroom like a wisp of blue smoke.

Let her go, James told himself. And despite his resolve, heard deep within his heart an echo of Sophie's cry.

I can't.

Twenty-Nine

One face looks out from all his canvases,
One selfsame figure sits or walks or leans...

— Christina Rossetti, "In an Artist's Studio"

"MR. SHERIDAN?" AMY CALLED SOFTLY AT THE schoolroom door the following morning.

Receiving no response, she opened the door and peered into the room: empty. So she was here before him, for once. Well, they had returned somewhat late from the dance at Roswarne last night—and without Relia, who'd stayed behind to comfort a distraught Sophie. Amy didn't know the whole story there, but James had mentioned that the matter of the anonymous letters had been resolved, if not altogether happily. Something to be thankful for, she mused.

Picking up her trailing skirts, she entered the schoolroom. All was in place for her next sitting: a carved wooden chair, very like a throne, had been positioned with its back to the mullioned window, whose myriad panes glowed faintly in the pale morning sun. Sheridan's easel and stool stood ready as well, just waiting for the artist to appear—as she was.

They'd decided on a pose two days ago, and Sheridan had brought in some props to make the portrait more dramatic.

A small but colorful tapestry would hang on the wall beyond her right shoulder, and to the left of her chair, he'd set a low table, on which a crystal bowl of newly opened roses—pink and white—would stand. And in her right hand, Amy would hold a fan of peacock feathers, just so, their iridescent hues complementing the rich blue of her draperies.

Amy drifted over to Sheridan's worktable, where he'd set his palette and paints. His sketchbooks were there too. He was almost always drawing something, even when he wasn't in the studio. Idly, she drew one of the sketchbooks toward her, opened it at random, and caught her breath in shocked recognition at what she saw. Scarcely able to believe her own eyes, she continued to leaf through the sketchbook, her astonishment mounting with each successive page.

Images of the same young woman—walking, riding, dancing, or simply sitting and gazing out to sea. Dozens of drawings, taking up more than half the pages in the sketchbook...

"Miss Newbold!" Sheridan's voice thundered behind her, making her jump. "What the devil are you doing?"

Amy turned around at once. The artist loomed over her, his face as furious as his voice, his green eyes burning. "M-Mr. Sheridan," she began, flushing like a guilty school-girl. "Forgive me, I was just—"

He cut off her apology with icy precision. "I would prefer that you not invade my privacy, Miss Newbold."

"You left this out, for anyone to see!" she defended herself.

"I did not expect—" He checked himself, held out his hand for the sketchbook.

Amy held on to it stubbornly. "These drawings...they're all of *me*."

He flushed but did not deny it. His silver tongue seemed to have deserted him, for once.

"Thomas." She spoke his given name for the first time, tasting the syllables, the curious rightness of them on her tongue. "How long have you been drawing these? Drawing me?"

Sheridan cleared his throat, looked away, apparently striving for his customary nonchalance. "For a while. I'm always looking for compelling new faces to paint. I believe I told your sister as much."

"So you did. I was there when you tried to get her to sit for you. Except that it's not Relia you've been sketching all this time—and I'd like to know why."

He shrugged a shoulder, still not looking at her. "One must stay in practice, after all."

Amy swallowed, forced words past the constriction in her throat. "P-poppycock!"

His gaze swung back to her. "I beg your pardon?"

"I said, *poppycock!*" Voice stronger now, she challenged him, "Look me in the eye, Thomas Sheridan, and tell me the *real* reason you've been drawing me."

"Miss Newbold—"

"Tell me!" she insisted, locking her eyes with his.

He went still, so still she could see the pulse beating in his throat. Suave, sophisticated Thomas Sheridan, never at a loss for words, stood there like a block, staring back at her with eyes gone the dark, dense green of malachite or forest shadows. Silence hung between them, heavy and strangely electric. And something stirred in Amy—striving to break free, reaching out blindly for what it had never known before.

She launched herself at him, the sketchbook falling to the floor. His arms came up, though whether to receive her or ward her off, she could not say. But her arms were twining about his neck, drawing his head down. He gave a stifled groan, and then his mouth, hot as a fever, took hers.

He kissed her hungrily, even fiercely. Not in the chaste, careful way that James kissed her, on the rare occasions he acted upon their betrothed status. Nor yet in the greedy, almost punishing way Glyndon had kissed her during that awful meeting in the conservatory. Underneath all that hunger was a tenderness and care she had never thought to find.

And she was kissing him back just as eagerly, drowning in sensations. Not just the taste of that beautiful, ironic mouth, but the lean warmth of his body against hers, the scent of sandalwood clinging to his skin. Even his hair…she thrust her hands through its glossy, autumn-brown length, marveled at how fine and soft it felt. Such a contrast on a man who reminded her time and again of a rapier: sharp, elegant, and potentially lethal.

But that sharpness hid a heart as tender as a new leaf, a heart that had been shattered into pieces once before…

He grasped her shoulders and put her from him with a firmness belied by his shaking hands. Amy heard herself utter a low moan of protest that would have mortified her a day ago.

Sheridan took a step back, shook his head as though trying to clear it. "This cannot happen." His usually clear voice sounded husky, as if he hadn't used it for years. "It was my fault that it even went this far. I should've destroyed those sketches, hidden them away…"

It took several tries to make her own voice work. "Why didn't you?" she whispered.

Sheridan swallowed but did not reply. She could see the warring emotions in his eyes, the faint sheen of perspiration on his brow. How could she ever have thought him cold and detached? "I will not do this. I will not dishonor us both. I will not betray James."

"Thomas…"

He shook his head again, backed further away. "Good-bye, Miss Newbold."

Wrenching his gaze from her, he strode to the door and was gone before she could say another word, his footsteps dying away down the passage.

Amy's legs trembled beneath her, and she sank down upon the floor, her lips swollen and tender from his kisses, and the world as she'd known it knocked clean off its axis.

❧

"The accusations were baseless?" Helena stared at Nankivell's letter of confession as if it had been written in Greek.

"Entirely." *Terribly sorry to disappoint you*, James thought, but he resisted the urge to say it aloud; sarcasm would accomplish nothing. "The originator of those anonymous letters had his own motives for slandering us, none of which included avenging Gerald's death."

Helena frowned over the pages, but the wind seemed to have gone out of her sails, for the time being. "It appears I was—mistaken, about you and the others." The words came out slightly strangled, but James suspected that was as much of an apology as he could expect from her.

He inclined his head in acknowledgment, and Lady Talbot said briskly, "I am glad that ugly matter has been resolved. And now we can all concentrate on other, more pleasant things."

"Indeed, ma'am." The unobtrusive Lord Durward surprised them all by speaking up from his corner of the library. "I think it is time for Lady Durward and myself to take our leave. We have imposed upon your hospitality long enough."

"Durward," Helena began imperatively, but her husband stared her down.

"Our son awaits us in Wiltshire, my lady. We must return to him."

The unaccustomed firmness in his tone stifled whatever protest she'd been about to make. In as quiet a voice as he'd ever heard from her, she asked, "Trevenan?"

James did his best to conceal his surprise. "Cousin?"

"Have you made any progress in your investigation of my brother's death?"

"I can tell you nothing new, I'm afraid. My most recent theory was partly disproved by what happened last night."

To his surprise, the admission did not provoke an angry outburst or accusations of incompetence. "Shall you continue to pursue it?" she asked, still in that subdued tone.

"I intend to, though I am not wholly sure which course to follow at this moment," James replied with complete candor. "Nor can I promise that my efforts will bear fruit. It's possible we may never know the whole truth of how and why Gerald died. But if I should learn anything new, I would not hesitate to inform you of my findings at the earliest opportunity."

"I'd appreciate that." Helena moistened her lips, looking oddly tentative, even vulnerable.

Almost human, James thought. "I understand what is due to family."

Perhaps a week ago, she would have jeered at the very notion that they were family. Now, she gave a jerky nod and rose from her chair. "I should go up and start packing. Durward," her gaze sought her husband, "perhaps we might leave tomorrow morning?"

"An excellent idea," he replied. "Trevenan, Lady Talbot, if you'll excuse us?"

"I must say," Lady Talbot remarked, once the Durwards had left the room, "I never expected to see Helena behave so—reasonably. She was downright conciliatory!"

"Indeed," James agreed absently, still bemused by the first civilized conversation he could remember having with Helena in years, if not longer.

Lady Talbot studied her nephew. "Just what theory *did* you have, before last night?"

He gave her a brief account of Gerald's involvement in Mercer Shipping and Mercer's repeated attempts to buy back his shares. "As it turned out, he wasn't responsible for those letters. But I imagine he'll offer again at some point. I may even accept this time, rather than have to deal with him further. And after Gerald, I expect Mercer's just as eager to be rid of me."

"I'm not surprised to hear their partnership was a disaster," his aunt observed, with a sigh. "Gerald always had to get the upper hand, even if that meant poking and prying into things that were none of his affair. Mind you, Captain Mercer sounds rather shady himself, so I doubt you'd regret severing ties with him." She turned to go. "I should see to luncheon. Do you know if Aurelia will be back from Roswarne by then?"

James shook his head. "She may still be helping Sophie. Personally, I wouldn't expect her before dinner, at the earliest."

"Luncheon for nine, I suppose. I'll see you then, my dear."

Alone, James leaned back in his chair, frowning to himself. The matter of the letters resolved, his feud with Helena settled…he should feel relieved, calm. But thoughts of Gerald, and all the questions that remained unanswered, circled like a flock of restless birds overhead.

His aunt's words lingered in his mind, teasing his memory.

Always had to get the upper hand.

Poking and prying into things that were none of his affair.

Prying into things…

James sat bolt upright, his mind racing. Then he sprang from his chair and strode from the library, making for the stairs and his cousin's room.

"Nearly there!" Sophie called back over her shoulder with a forced brightness that made Aurelia's heart ache in sympathy for her.

Sir Lucas Nankivell had a lot to answer for, she thought darkly. The only good thing was that Sophie hadn't been in love with him, after all. But while Mr. Pendarvis might be a far worthier man than the baronet, his pride and secrecy were creating problems of their own.

Sophie had arisen that morning, still pale and heavy-eyed from tears the previous night, but determined to act as though nothing was wrong. As though the man she had cared for *hadn't* walked away, leaving her heart in pieces on the ground. As though she wasn't secretly waiting for a knock on the door or the arrival of a letter that would somehow put everything right. Aurelia recognized the signs all too well; hadn't she done the same after Charlie left her? It had taken years to get over her own first love; she hoped Sophie's romance would end more happily.

After watching the hope continually flare and fade in her friend's eyes with each passing hour, Aurelia had proposed this expedition to the caves at St. Perran as a distraction. Sophie had seized upon the notion at once, and within half an hour, they'd donned riding gear—Aurelia borrowing a habit from Lady Tresilian—and set out for the shore on a pair of dependable hacks.

The sea came in sight, a changeable blue-grey in the afternoon sun, and they urged their horses into a trot, reining in only after they'd reached their destination and heard the soft crunch of sand beneath their horses' hooves. Sophie dismounted with the fluid ease of a born horsewoman. Aurelia alighted more slowly, but with a confidence she'd thought never to regain. She caught Sophie's eye, and the girl smiled without constraint for the first time that day.

"The caves are down that way," she announced. "And fortunately for us, the tide is out. Where shall we start?"

"Wasn't there a cave Sir Harry and James used to play in, when they were boys?"

Sophie shrugged. "They were in and out of all of them, but I *think* I know which one you mean. Follow me."

Leaving the horses to recover their wind, they made their way along the sand toward the great rocks, hollowed out by the sea. Sophie paused before a cave with an opening that reminded Aurelia of a mouthful of jagged teeth. "This may be it. I don't know these caves quite as well as Harry and James," she added apologetically, and ducked inside.

Aurelia followed, stepping into the cave's cool depths. The sand, pale gold in the sun, gleamed bone-white in the shadows, and the brackish but not unpleasant smells of sea-washed stone and beached kelp enveloped them. Peering into the gloom, she wondered how many centuries it had taken for the relentless tide to carve out such a deep recess in solid rock.

Sophie lit one of the thick candles they'd brought and shone its beam over the ridges and grooves of the cave's walls. "Look, there's the hole where James used to hide things!"

Charmed, Aurelia came closer and saw a small hollow worn into the stone, just about at eye level. "He did say *above* the water line," she murmured, smiling as she envisioned a boy reaching up to tuck his treasures out of sight. Nothing there now but a battered tin cup, black with tarnish. Still, she was glad that his nasty cousin had apparently never found his hiding place.

"It's not the deepest one here," Sophie said, illuminating the back of the cave with her candle. "There's another a bit farther down—Echo Cavern, it's called. We used to go in and make all kinds of noises at the echo—clap, sing, shout silly words. Harry thinks it used to be a true smugglers' cave, one that connected with the tunnels they used to hide contraband."

"A smuggler's cave? Then we absolutely must go there next," Aurelia declared. No doubt any contraband stored there had been retrieved long ago by the free traders or the excisemen—or less romantically, rotted away in the damp and darkness. But it was the adventure that counted.

Sophie actually laughed, a sound of genuine amusement, then led the way out of the first cave and down to the famous Echo Cavern.

A much larger cave, Aurelia observed, perhaps because the rock protruded much further onto the beach. And deeper too. She lit her own candle before entering in her friend's wake.

Sophie lifted her hand to her mouth. "Hullooo!" she called into the cave.

Ullooo—ullooo—ullooo, the echo resounded back at them.

"Impressive," Aurelia said, keeping her own voice low. "But maybe a little eerie."

"Before I was old enough to know better, Harry and John told me it was a ghost living in the cavern, who made that noise. Aren't brothers horrid?" Sophie lifted her candle and pointed down the rough stone passage. "See how much further back this goes? You'd think it would get narrower, but it opens up into a much wider space. Harry thinks the smugglers used charges to blast a bigger opening."

"Those tunnels you mentioned?" Aurelia asked, raising her own candle.

"Exactly. I haven't been down this far in years," Sophie continued as they ventured further along the passage. "I do hope nothing's collapsed after all this time."

Luck seemed to be holding, however, and the passage did indeed open up into a larger, wider space—almost a chamber, Aurelia thought, gazing about in astonishment.

A large mass at the far end of the chamber caught her eye. Frowning, she stepped forward, shone her candle over it. "Sophie, are you sure no one's been using these tunnels?"

The girl's candle joined her own at once. "Good heavens, what *is* that?"

"It looks like a tarpaulin—with something underneath."

Exchanging a glance, they crept toward the mysterious mass.

"It *is* a tarpaulin," Sophie said, gingerly taking up a fold of dirty canvas. Aurelia did likewise, and they pulled back the tarpaulin, dropped it on the sand—and stared in shock at their discovery. Six wooden crates, stamped with the words "Mercer Shipping."

Sophie caught her breath. "Aurelia, is that—?"

"The rest of the missing cargo," Aurelia finished for her. "Yes, I believe it is." She stepped back from the crates, made herself speak calmly. "Sophie, would you ride back to Roswarne and fetch Sir Harry? Tell him what we've found, and tell him to bring a wagon."

&

Some fifteen minutes later, Aurelia looked up from her vigil over the crates as the sound of horse's hooves outside the cave reached her ears.

So soon? Even if Sophie had reached Roswarne by now, Sir Harry would have needed time to ready a wagon. Frowning, she reached for one of the candles. "Who's there?" she called, and tried not to shiver as the echo tossed her question back to her: *Who's there—there—there?*

"Aurelia?" Unbelievably, it sounded like James's voice. *Relia—Relia—Relia*, the echo mocked.

"I'm in here, James! I've found the cargo," she added, wishing it were possible to silence an echo.

She heard him break into a run, his footsteps preternaturally loud in the passage. Within seconds, he emerged into the chamber, his gaze lighting at once upon the crates.

"Good God." It sounded almost reverent.

He was carrying a lantern, she noticed, and a crowbar. "You knew?"

"I had a suspicion." He walked over to the crates, set down the lantern. "Something Aunt Judith said, about Gerald prying into things that weren't his business. I remembered how he was always trying to find out my secret hiding places. And then I wondered if he'd managed to discover the biggest secret hiding place of all. Once I took another look at those maps in his room, I was almost sure of it. They were all of roughly the same area of the coast, and Echo Cavern appears on every one." He picked up the crowbar and set to work on the nearest crate. "I've got to hand it to Gerald—I'd never have imagined he'd go to such trouble to hide these."

She picked up the lantern and held it for him. "How did he learn about this place?"

"My guess is Simon Pendarvis told him. His family was up to its ears in the free trade. They may even have built these tunnels." James eyed her speculatively over the lid of the crate. "Now, how did *you* end up in the thick of this, and why am I not more surprised?"

"It was pure coincidence," she pointed out with dignity. "Sophie and I just happened to be exploring these caves today. I sent her to fetch Sir Harry, as she can ride much faster, while I kept watch on the cargo."

"Good thinking," he approved, resuming his labors.

"And this is the tea? Do you suppose it's still good after six months in a cave?"

"We'll find out soon enough." The lid came loose at last, and he lifted it away.

Together they peered into the crate, filled almost to the brim with what looked like black wood shavings. *Tea leaves*, Aurelia thought, stifling an absurd pang of disappointment. Well, what had she been expecting? Jewels, state secrets, or stolen antiquities like the Elgin Marbles? "At least there's still some aroma left," she remarked.

"Mm." James thrust his hand deep into the tea leaves, felt around…and then frowned, lifting out what looked like a ball of dried leaves, tied with twine. "There's something wrapped up in this," he said, taking out a pocketknife and cutting the twine.

The leaves fell away to reveal a small brownish cake, about the size of a silver dollar. James took a cautious sniff, then held out the cake to Aurelia, who did the same: the pungent, sickly-sweet odor caught at her throat, but was oddly familiar. Memories of her accident drifted into her mind: splints, bandages, the cloying smell of laudanum…

She looked up, startled. "Opium!" Congress had levied a heavy import tax on opium and morphine just last year, she remembered.

James gave a grim nod. "Raw opium, smuggled in among the tea leaves. I'll wager the crates are full of these little balls."

"Clever of you to figure it out," a new voice observed. "Now step away from my cargo."

They turned sharply to find that Captain Mercer had entered the chamber behind them. In his hand was a revolver, aimed at James's heart.

Thirty

GUN DRAWN AND AT THE READY, MERCER ADVANCED into the chamber, his gaze intent on the crates. "I knew these had to be here, somewhere, when they weren't found with everything else."

"And now we know why they weren't." James matched the captain's coolness. "Gerald learned your secret, didn't he? That's why he stole the shipment."

Mercer's lips thinned, and his eyes—the coldest grey eyes Aurelia had ever seen—went even colder. "Some fool dropped one of the crates while unloading—it broke open right in front of him. Once your cousin knew about my operation, he wanted in on it."

"Along with a bigger cut of the profits."

Mercer's face hardened. "Half the business. *My* business."

"Gerald always was greedy," James observed, his tone

almost conversational. "I suppose he stole the cargo when you refused his terms?"

The captain gave a curt nod. "He also said that unless I gave him what he wanted, he'd turn me in to the law." His hand tightened around the revolver. "I wasn't going to allow that."

"Which is why you killed him," James stated flatly.

Aurelia bit back a gasp, not sure whether she was reacting to the accusation or James's almost matter-of-fact tone.

Mercer ignored her. "He had an accident. Which he brought on himself, I might add."

James's eyes narrowed, though he still sounded eerily calm. "So, you were there, then—that night on the cliffs."

"His idea of a meeting place," Mercer confirmed, his face darkening at the memory. "He stood there, boasting of his own cleverness, convinced he had me right where he wanted. He said I'd never find my cargo without his help. That it could be right under my nose, and I'd never know it. Obnoxious little toad." He shrugged. "I hit him, of course. He went right over—too bad for him he was standing so close to the edge."

Aurelia glanced at James, saw his mouth tighten at this casual admission. Mercer might not have murdered Gerald, but he'd been directly responsible for his death all the same. "Too bad for you as well," he said. "Gerald died without telling you where he'd hidden the cargo."

"That's not a problem now." Mercer's gaze rested on the crates. "I'd wondered this morning if Gerald had thought to use these caves. When I saw you turn up with your crowbar, I was almost sure of it. You and Miss Newbold have done an admirable job of finding my cargo. Pity it's the last thing you'll ever do."

Aurelia saw the gun swing toward her like a deadly little eye, and wondered why she wasn't more terrified. They'd sealed their fate the moment they discovered Mercer's secret.

They weren't leaving Echo Cavern alive if he had anything to say about it. But Sir Harry was on his way, she remembered. *If they could just stall long enough…*

James stepped in front of her. "Let her go, Mercer. She has nothing to do with this."

"She knows what's in those crates." The captain's voice was implacable. "But if you have some chivalrous wish to die before her—" Again he aimed the gun at James's heart.

"Wait!" Aurelia burst out. "It doesn't have to be like this, Captain," she said, attempting a winning smile. "You don't have to shoot anyone. Trevenan's not like his cousin—he won't say anything, will you, my lord? I'm sure it's no one's business what you carry aboard your own ships," she prattled on, even as her ears strained for the sound of hooves.

James was staring at her in wonder and—she hoped—understanding, but Mercer regarded her with amused contempt. "An unusual opinion, coming from Adam Newbold's daughter."

Aurelia shrugged. "Oh, I never pay any mind to Papa's *business!*" She made it sound like a disease. "But since you've mentioned him, I know he'd pay a great deal to have his daughter and his future son-in-law back safe and sound. Why, he'd probably pay *much* more than whatever you could get from all that!" she added, with an airy gesture toward the crates.

The mention of money actually got Mercer's attention; at least, she thought she saw a faint flicker of interest in those cold eyes. "Would he indeed?"

She nodded, and felt her scalp prickle as a faint jingle from outside the cave reached her ears. Sir Harry, coming with his wagon? "Of course he would!"

"Aurelia, hold your tongue!" James snapped in a louder, angrier voice than was necessary. Had he heard it too? "Mercer's not going to let us go!"

Following his lead, Aurelia raised her own voice, letting

the echo carry their warning to whoever might be in earshot. "He might, once he sees what valuable hostages we'd make!"

Footsteps sounded at the mouth of the cave, and Mercer spun around, aiming his gun toward the tunnel entrance. James sprang forward, tackling the captain head-on. They fell to the ground in a tangle of thrashing limbs, grunting and swearing as they fought for the gun.

Glancing around frantically, Aurelia saw the crowbar, lying forgotten by the open crate. Even as she caught it up, she heard the crack of the revolver, followed by a sharp exclamation of pain. Turning, she saw to her horror that Mercer had clambered to his feet and was leveling his gun at James, still prone on the ground, his right hand clamped around his bleeding left arm.

She swung the crowbar with all her strength at Mercer's head, felt it connect with a sickening crunch. He collapsed in an ungainly sprawl, the gun dropping from his hand. Shaking with reaction, the blood pounding in her ears, she stared down at his motionless form.

"Aurelia, the gun!"

His voice, slicing through the fog and paralysis. Dropping the crowbar, she scooped up the gun and turned to see him struggling upright, his face drawn with pain, but blessedly alive.

"James." It emerged as a breath, rather than a word. But his dark eyes kindled into fire as he heard it. Without a word, he stretched out his uninjured arm, and she flew into it, felt it close around her as his mouth sought hers again and again. Wrapping her own arms around him, she kissed him back no less fiercely. Words spilled out between kisses, a breathless jumble of assurances and endearments. "Safe. Love. Thank God…"

"James! Aurelia!" Sir Harry erupted into the chamber. "I heard a gunshot—" He stopped short at the sight of them embracing, with Mercer unconscious at their feet.

"Good work, cousin," he remarked prosaically as they turned to him with identical dazed expressions. He prodded

Mercer with his foot, drawing a faint groan in response. "I've brought some rope. Shall we start by tying this bastard up?"

❧

"See that these are sent to Lady Talbot and Lady Durward at Pentreath, right away." James handed over the sealed letters.

"Very good, Lord Trevenan." Accepting the letters, the footman bowed and withdrew.

Alone in his guest chamber, James sighed and pushed back his chair from the desk. Hours had passed since that tense encounter in the cave, hours since Mercer—barely conscious and still groaning weakly—and his cargo had been turned over to the proper authorities. He, Harry, and Aurelia had all given statements about what had happened in the cave and then been sent on their way without further questioning.

James flexed his aching arm, now cleaned and dressed. According to the doctor Harry had summoned on their return to Roswarne, the bullet had apparently passed through the upper arm without striking anything vital, so the wound would heal soon enough with rest and proper care. The doctor had left tincture of willow bark and a mild opiate to relieve any fever or pain, but James had not yet availed himself of either.

He rose and went to the window, gazing out at the darkening sky. Once again, he relived those moments in the cave—the blazing pain in his arm as he struggled to rise and fight again, Mercer looming over him with that damned revolver, and a golden-haired avenging angel swinging the crowbar that brought their enemy down.

His Aurelia, bright, brave, and beautiful: the woman who'd saved his life, which would never again belong to him alone. Aurelia, who held his heart so completely that he no longer had even a piece of it to give to any other woman—not even the sister who so closely resembled her. And somehow, he had to convince her of that.

If he could even get to her, that was. On their return, Sophie and Aunt Isobel had borne her off to another chamber, and he hadn't seen her since. Was she asleep now, exhausted by their ordeal, or lying awake, fretting over what had happened? She'd struck down Mercer to save them both, but anyone unaccustomed to violence would have been shaken at having to resort to it. And James did not want her to suffer even a moment's guilt or grief over that cold-blooded bastard. His own blood turned to ice when he remembered how Mercer had turned his gun on her. Thank God Harry had arrived in time.

Filled with a new resolve, he turned from the window. If Aunt Isobel wouldn't let him see Aurelia, she could at least tell him how she fared. He strode toward the door, and stopped short when he heard the tentative knock.

"Enter," he said after a moment.

The door opened, and Aurelia herself stood there, holding a tray and smiling at him, a little uncertainly. She wore a robe and a nightgown—borrowed from Aunt Isobel by the look of it—and her golden hair lay across her shoulder in a single plait, like his dreams, almost, but so much better. "Your aunt thought you should have something to eat, after all this time."

For a moment, he stood where he was, drinking in the sight of her. Then he took her gently by the arm and drew her inside, closing the door behind them.

❧

Safe—and whole. Aurelia felt the hard knot of fear in her stomach loosen, then dissolve at the sight of him standing in the doorway. Despite the doctor's assurances that he'd sustained only a minor wound, she hadn't been able to banish her fears until she saw him again.

"Your arm," she began in instinctive protest as he took the tray from her now.

"Will heal quickly, I'm told." He set the tray on the dresser, turned back to her.

"I'd have come sooner, but Sophie and Lady Tresilian wanted to know everything," she rushed on, feeling absurdly shy with him. "And then the doctor came to tend your wound, and your aunt thought I should wash and change and—"

She fell silent as he took her by the shoulders and drew her to him. This time, his kiss was not the desperate, almost feverish response to barely averted danger, but rather, the slow, deliberate caress of a man determined to do something properly. She closed her eyes, her lips parting beneath his like a flower. He deepened the kiss, his tongue brushing lightly against hers, an intimate touch that made her shiver, even as warmth flooded through her entire body. She leaned into him, wanting more, striving to give all she could. Her hands slid along the strong planes of his face—the face she'd seen in her dreams, waking or sleeping, for the last year—and buried themselves in his hair; the dark waves felt as thick and soft as she'd imagined they would.

"James," she murmured against his lips. "Dear God…"

He made a sound low in his throat that might have been laughter. "Now, that's something I don't hear every day." He pulled away just a little, gazing at her with steady dark eyes. "Listen, dear heart—I'm not marrying your sister. It would be the worst thing I could do, for all of us."

Aurelia swallowed. "I know." From the moment she'd swung that crowbar in the cave, she had known—less in her head than in her blood and bones—that she wasn't fighting for Amy, but for him and herself and the future they were meant to have together. And that life was too short and too precious to waste it denying the truth of one's own heart.

"I thought it would be dishonorable to break our engagement," he went on. "Now I see it would be far more dishonorable—and unjust—to proceed with the marriage when I love someone else. When I love *you*."

Her eyes flooded, even as her lips trembled into a smile. "I love you, James." She freed a hand to dash away the tears. "I can say that now, with all my heart and no divided loyalties."

He searched her face. "Truly? I know how close you and Amy are."

"She's half my soul. But I would have lost her anyway if she'd married you. I would have stayed away—I couldn't have borne it…"

He kissed her again, brushing away more tears with gentle fingers. Sighing, she leaned her head on his shoulder. "I just pray that she can forgive us both. That she'll understand."

"We'll make her understand," he promised. "My word on it."

She believed in his word. And even more than that, she believed in what they could accomplish, together. Raising her head, she kissed him, shyly at first, then with growing confidence as he responded, his mouth working a subtle magic on hers that made her senses sing. Desire coursed through her, a tidal wave of longing sweeping away all else before it.

She felt an almost physical sense of loss when he drew back and touched her hair, bound in a loose plait for the night. "You should go back to your chamber now." His eyes looked dazed, and his voice, like his hand, was not quite steady when he spoke. "I can't answer for the consequences, if you stay."

"There would be consequences?" Aurelia paused as a sudden daring stirred to life inside of her. "Then I definitely want to stay!"

His brows arched over widening eyes. "Aurelia, you don't know—"

"Yes, I do. In theory, anyway. Mama told me a few years ago." She fought down a giggle at his expression; it wasn't often she could shock the man she loved. "And I mean it,

James! I want to be with you tonight—and every other night for the rest of our lives." She twined her arms around his neck, pressed closer to him. "We could have *died* today. And I can face anything, anything at all, tomorrow, if we have tonight! Don't send me away."

"Oh, God." It emerged as a near-groan, and he kissed her once more, so fiercely that her head swam and even her name seemed a distant memory. Then, unbelievably, he pulled away.

"Look, dear heart," he began, over her soft protestation, "I want you just as badly, in just the same way. But we *have* to do this right." He touched her plait again with aching tenderness. "I want no shadows between us, no regrets, and no reproaches. Nothing to taint what we have."

Longing, frustration, and a strange sense of pride in him all tangled inside of her at his words. "James—"

"One more day, Aurelia, to sever what must be severed. And then, I promise, we need never be apart again." He cupped her cheek, traced the seam of her lips with his thumb. "It will be all the sweeter for the waiting—I promise that too."

He was right, she knew, though that made the delay no easier to bear. Poised precariously between tears and laughter, she leaned against him, savoring his warmth and nearness while she could. "Honorable to the last," she managed to choke out. "Is it any wonder that I love you?"

"No more than I love you." He kissed her again, more gently this time. "Because you understand honor too. Now, go— before I change my mind and take you right here and now."

He wanted her, as deeply and urgently as she wanted him. Aurelia knew enough about men's bodies to sense that much. With persistence she could have overborne him, made him do as he threatened; instead, she detached herself reluctantly and stepped back, sighing. "*All night safe sleeping in her maidenhood.* No wonder Iseult of Brittany turned sour."

He smiled, skimming a finger down her cheek—the scarred one. "'*As the dawn loves the sunlight I love thee*,'" he quoted. "Sweet dreams, my love."

Slightly mollified, she headed for the door. "Sweet dreams, my lord."

"Aurelia?"

She paused with her hand on the knob. "Yes, James?"

"For what it's worth, I expect to sleep very badly tonight."

She gave him a look of pure mischief before whisking out of the room. "Good!"

Thirty-One

I'll have no husband if you be not he.

— William Shakespeare, *As You Like It*

"Mr. Pendarvis is here to see you, Sir Harry," the Tresilians' butler announced, entering the breakfast room the following morning. "And Lord Trevenan, your carriage has arrived."

Sir Harry and James exchanged a glance, as did Aurelia and Sophie. "Thank you, Parsons. You may show Mr. Pendarvis in here."

"And you may tell the coachman that Miss Newbold and I will be departing shortly," James added. Aurelia felt his fingers brush hers under the table and hid a smile in her teacup.

"Very good, Sir Harry, my lord." Parsons bowed and withdrew.

"Good morning, Rob," Sir Harry greeted his friend as he strode into the room looking more than a little agitated, Aurelia observed with interest.

Mr. Pendarvis nodded almost absently. "Forgive the intrusion, Harry, but I've just heard that there was some trouble here yesterday, and someone was injured?" His gaze went at once to Sophie, who colored at this evidence of concern for her, but gave a small shake of her head.

"That would be me," James replied. "But not seriously—a graze on the arm, nothing more. And I'm glad to say, the trouble's been resolved."

Mr. Pendarvis relaxed. "I'm relieved to hear it, Trevenan. Might I know the details?"

"I'm about to return to Pentreath, but Harry can fill you in." James pushed back his chair and turned to Aurelia. "Are you ready to go, my dear?"

Aurelia nodded and rose, smiling around the table. "Thank you all for your hospitality."

"You're very welcome." Sophie smiled back, even as her gaze kept drifting toward their latest visitor. "Would you care for some tea, Mr. Pendarvis? Or a bite of breakfast, perhaps?"

He hesitated, not looking at his host, but Sir Harry said, "Yes, take a plate and join us, Rob. I'll tell you what happened, once I've seen James and Miss Aurelia on their way."

The last thing Aurelia saw as she left the breakfast room was Sophie pouring tea for Mr. Pendarvis and looking more hopeful than she had for the last two days. So perhaps things would end well there, she mused, whatever shadows Mr. Pendarvis claimed were in his past.

Outside, the Pentreath coachmen presented James with a sealed note from his aunt, which he slipped into his pocket for the present. Bidding farewell to Sir Harry, he and Aurelia climbed into the carriage and settled back in comfort against the cushioned seat.

Alone together. Aurelia found herself smiling, despite knowing what awaited them both at Pentreath. Breaking the news to Amy and even Charlie…she couldn't help but quail at the thought. But neither could she regret that she and James would finally be together, and that soon they could bring their love out into the open.

He touched her cheek, a feather-light caress that made her tingle. "Tired, dear heart?"

"A little," she admitted. "But mostly preoccupied."

He said gently, "I'll do my best to spare Amy's feelings, when I tell her."

"I know you will." She laid her hand over his. "I fear I have a heart to bruise as well."

"Vandermere." To his credit, he spoke the name without even the slightest grimace.

She nodded. "To tell the truth, I'm dreading it. I believe he was sincere about wanting another chance with me. And I thought—I owed it to him to try, for old times' sake. But I'm not the girl I was then. We've both changed too much to go back to the way things were."

"Would you have married him, if we hadn't both come to our senses?"

"Not after you kissed me. That clarified things considerably." Lacing her fingers with his, she decided that a change of subject was in order. "What does Lady Talbot say in her note?"

He took out the note, opened it, and scanned the contents. "Mainly that she's relieved we came to no serious harm. And that Helena and Durward have departed for Wiltshire, though Helena wishes to convey her thanks for uncovering the truth about Gerald's death."

"Under the circumstances, I'd say that was the least she could do," Aurelia observed tartly. "But it's a start, I suppose. Anything else?"

James looked up from the page, frowning. "Thomas has also left, for London."

"Heavens, that *is* unexpected!" Surely Mr. Sheridan hadn't finished Amy's portrait already; she wondered uneasily if hostilities had broken out again. "When did this happen?"

"Late yesterday afternoon. I hope nothing's wrong there."

❧

Amy gazed about the schoolroom, now as desolate as a field after the traveling circus had departed. The wooden chair still stood where it had yesterday, and the props that were to have been used—the tapestry, the feathered fan, the crystal bowl—sat discarded on the low table. Gone were the easel, the canvases, the paints, the palette…and the artist.

Gone. Between one hour and the next, it seemed, and with a stealth she could never have imagined, Sheridan had departed. And without a further word spoken between them.

This, after a revelation and a kiss that had sent her reeling. And now had her rethinking everything, especially the careful plans she'd made for the future.

Amy shivered, hugging herself against an inner chill. What she was contemplating now must be madness, sheer folly even. To change her mind, let her castles in the air go, on the strength of what she had seen in another man's eyes…the practical, calculating Amy of one year ago—even three months ago—would never have considered such a thing.

But that girl hadn't kissed Thomas Sheridan, or felt the ardent quiver of his body against hers, and her own body's response to that—a response she'd had to no other man. Easy to explain away, of course: Sheridan was so much more experienced than she, and doubtless adept at rousing these feelings in women. But how, then, to explain her apparent effect on *him*? The hunger in those green eyes when he kissed her, the haunted look in them when he broke away?

Other memories crowded into her mind: Sheridan rescuing her from Glyndon and then thrashing him soundly, making him apologize in writing, listening without judgment to her doubts about life in Cornwall, laying aside his role of observer to waltz with her last night…

He cares—and it frightens him. Because of what he lost before, in Elizabeth. It frightened her too, and so did the hollow ache inside of her whenever she thought about not seeing him again. Or worse, seeing him when she was irrevocably tied to someone else.

"I will not dishonor us both. I will not betray James."

Dear James, who deserved far better and for whom she hadn't spared a thought since kissing Thomas. She'd given her word, along with her family's money, to be his countess and the mistress of Pentreath. How could she even think of betraying him? But—wouldn't marrying him when she suspected she cared more deeply for Thomas Sheridan be a worse betrayal?

No easy answer, but at the very least, she owed James honesty. So once he returned from Roswarne, she'd tell him of her doubts, and together they would decide what should be done.

Resolved, she left the schoolroom, closing the door behind her. As she descended the stairs, she heard the front door open, followed by the sound of two familiar voices. James and Relia—they were back! She quickened her pace, reached the first floor landing…and stopped dead when she caught sight of them in the entrance hall below.

They stood close together, not touching, not even speaking now, but in their stillness and silence Amy read a world of meaning. The resulting flash of insight was as blinding as the proverbial lightning bolt: her betrothed and her twin were in love.

Shock, then relief, crashed over her in waves, bringing with them a sense of release so powerful she could have burst into song—or hysterical laughter. What a mess they'd all managed to make of what ought to be the simplest thing in the world!

Simple—and she would do her best to set it right. How could Relia have kept such a secret from her for all this time? And how she must have suffered, believing James lost to her! And how Amy loved her for her selfless restraint!

But it would be better, far better, as it was.

She gave a light cough to gain their attention, and had to stifle a laugh when she saw how quickly they moved apart, their faces wearing almost identical expressions of guilt.

"Relia, James." She smiled at them both. "I think—you have something to tell me?"

⁓

Neither James nor Amy could ever have imagined that the dissolution of their engagement would be so painless. And yet, given the liking and regard on both sides, perhaps it wasn't so peculiar, James reasoned, reluctantly accepting the ring Amy insisted on returning.

"You are one of the finest women of my acquaintance," he told her. "And you deserve a husband who can give you his whole heart on your marriage."

"Thank you, James." Amy regarded him with unrestrained affection. "I am fond of you too. Indeed, I esteem you above almost every man I know. But I think, upon reflection, that we may not suit as well as we first thought. And not merely because you and Relia love each other to distraction." She paused, her expression growing pensive. "Even as your wife, I doubt I could ever be completely at home in Cornwall, while you are at home here as you are nowhere else. I'm not selfish enough to demand that you live in London, where you'd be miserable beyond a doubt. Fortunately, my sister seems to love Cornwall as much as she loves you."

"Fortunate, indeed," James agreed, pocketing the ring. "Although I think, in different circumstances, you and I would not have done so poorly together."

"Probably not." She smiled at him. "But I suspect you and Relia will do a great deal better than that."

He returned her smile. "On that we're agreed. May I—call you sister?"

"Indeed, you may. Dear brother." Her smile turned wicked. "Better you any day than Stupid Charlie!"

"Mr. Vandermere—Charlie," Aurelia paused, looking into the face of her first love, then made herself continue, "I cannot in good conscience allow you to persist in your court-ship of me, nor offer you false hope. So much has changed in the last few days. Enough to make me understand that—we cannot go back to the way things were between us."

Contrary to all expectation, it was painful to give pain to him, to see the hope in his face die away. He nodded once, twice, swallowing visibly. "I see. There's someone else, isn't there?"

"Yes," Aurelia confirmed. "I care for Lord Trevenan. And he cares for me as well."

"But Amy—"

"She and Trevenan have ended their betrothal, amicably and with no ill will. As it turns out, Amy was having doubts as well." Again she experienced that giddy sense of relief that she *hadn't* ruined things for her twin.

"The Earl of Trevenan prefers you to Amy." Charlie sounded almost dazed to hear it.

Aurelia raised her brows. "Is that so incomprehensible?"

Charlie flushed. "Of course not! *I* did! It's just…" He floundered to a stop.

Taking pity on him, she explained, "It isn't merely that Trevenan prefers me. It's knowing that, when he looks at me, he doesn't see someone broken and in need of mending."

"You think that's how I see you?" He sounded startled.

"Isn't it?" she countered gently. "The truth now, Charlie."

For a moment, she thought he'd continue to deny it. But from the bleakness in his eyes, she perceived that her accident was as sharply etched on his memory as on hers.

"I still remember—how you looked, that day…" He swal-lowed again. "So fragile. And I came to break your heart. I should have had more faith in my own."

"I am sure the pressure and the expectations on you were

enormous. Your parents wouldn't have wanted you to wed an invalid. And I—well, I convinced myself it was the right thing to do, to offer to set you free." That she had hoped he'd refuse to go had been her mistake, or rather, her naïvete. What had she told James? She'd made it easy for Charlie to leave her, and so he'd gone. But not, she realized now, without regrets or doubts...or shame.

He shook his head. "You don't have to make excuses for me, Aurelia. I spoiled everything that was between us, through my own selfishness and cowardice."

"And so you tried to make up for it, by courting me again."

"I'd hoped there was a way back, for both of us."

"I think, for a time, I hoped the same. But we aren't the same people we were then." She managed a smile. "We can't go back, my dear, so we must go on—separately."

He gave a jerky nod. "I have never met your equal. I never will."

Aurelia's eyes stung. "Hush! I think, in time, you will meet someone who is right for you now. Clinging to the old dream wouldn't be fair to either of us. But I can remember that dream fondly now, without bitterness or regret."

"Truly?" His eyes were suspiciously moist, but she saw the shadow of hope in them yet.

"The girl I was can forgive the boy you were, long ago," she told him. "And the woman I am now wishes you only the best. You tried to make amends, Charlie, belatedly but sincerely. I will always—esteem you for that."

"Might I," Charlie cleared his throat, "might I kiss you— one last time?"

Aurelia nodded, not trusting herself to speak. Her first love cupped her face and pressed his lips to hers. Tentative and sweet, like the children they had been—because Charlie hadn't been so very much older than she, nor so much more worldly. If matters had been different, they might have married and lived to a contented old age together. But things being as they were…this kiss was a shadow, compared to what she had found with James.

She lifted a hand to his cheek. "Be happy, dear Charlie. You do deserve to be."

"So do you," he said, his voice oddly choked. "You deserve every blessing life has to offer. I hope Trevenan agrees."

Aurelia smiled. "He does, I assure you." Then, knowing how painful it must be for him to hear her talk about James and herself, she asked, "Will you and your family be staying in England for the rest of the summer?"

Charlie shook his head. "I expect we'll be sailing for home soon. Father's already returned to New York, and Mother and Sally are eager for Newport in August."

It seemed another world now, and one she found she did not miss, though she would remember it with a touch of nostalgia from time to time. "I wish you and your family a safe journey."

"Thank you." A brief touch of her hand, and he was gone, striding away through the garden, the sunlight glinting on his fair head. Safely alone, Aurelia let some tears fall for what they had once shared, but other, more pleasurable thoughts soon dispelled them.

Some minutes later, James came to sit beside her on the garden bench. "All is well?"

"I think so. Or it will be—in time." She sighed. "I was truly sorry to cause him pain. Does that sound strange?"

He shook his head. "You cared for him once. And one's first love is always special."

"It is. But," she turned to smile at him, "it doesn't hold a candle to one's last love!"

"I'm relieved to hear it," he replied, and kissed her until the past receded entirely and only the present, bright with promise, remained.

After a time, James stood up and held out his hand. "Come, love. Amy thinks the three of us should go and talk to your parents, and sort it all out between us."

"By all means." Taking his hand, Aurelia let him lead her into their future.

～∞～

"All's well that ends well, wouldn't you say?" Amy remarked that night as the twins sat together in Aurelia's room, having the heart-to-heart talk they should have had long ago.

Aurelia nodded, still astonished at the relative ease with which their situation had been resolved. A tense moment had occurred at the start of the family meeting, when Papa had fixed James with a stern eye and declared, "I'll have you know, Trevenan, that my daughters are not interchangeable." But James had only taken Aurelia's hand and replied with the steadfastness she loved in him, "That is what I have come to realize, sir." Once all the explanations were made, reconciliation and resolution had swiftly followed. Aurelia suspected that Amy's blithe acceptance of the situation and visible lack of regret had also smoothed the way.

"I should have seen what was happening right under my nose," Amy said, a bit ruefully. "More than that, I should have seen how much better suited you and James were."

"Amy," Aurelia began in instinctive protest, but her twin held up a forestalling hand.

"I mean it, Relia. When James was in trouble, I stood aside, telling myself he could handle it. *You* were the one who jumped in feet first, determined to help."

"I told myself I was doing it for you," Aurelia confessed. "I didn't know I was capable of such self-deception."

"Maybe self-deception is a natural complication of being in love. But the best woman won," Amy added in a rallying tone, "or rather, the woman who's best for James won."

"I never saw this as a rivalry, dearest. I tried so hard for it not to turn into one, even when—" Aurelia broke off, not wanting her twin even now to know how difficult it had been.

"Even when you resented my good fortune most?" Amy asked without rancor, smiling.

"Even then. Oh, Amy, are you so sure that you don't mind?"

"Surer than I've been in a long time. To tell the truth, it's almost a relief that you're taking not only James but Cornwall off my hands."

"It's a beautiful place," Aurelia defended her future home.

"So it is, but not for me. My stay here has shown me what a social creature I am! Much too frivolous to live far from London, though I shall enjoy visiting you and James here."

"You'll always be welcome." Aurelia paused, studying her twin's bright face. "Dearest, I only wish you could be as happy! Or at least stop holding love at arm's length the way you do."

"I know, I know. I've never let anyone get close enough for me to love him."

"No, I meant that you've never let anyone get close enough to love *you*," Aurelia corrected. "And you deserve it so much, Amy. To love and be loved in return."

Amy fell silent, her face growing pensive. "Do you know what I've always admired about you, Relia?" she said at last. "You were brave enough to risk your heart, twice. Charlie disappointed you cruelly, but you didn't let that stop you from loving again. From loving James. I would give a great deal—for that sort of courage. As it is, I'll have to rely on plain old American nerve! Good thing Aunt Caroline is still in London."

Aurelia eyed her warily. "Just what do you mean to do?"

"You have your man," Amy declared, kissing her on the cheek. "And now I think it's time, and past time, for me to get mine." She rose from the sofa they'd been sharing and headed for the door. "Good night, dearest."

"Good night," Aurelia echoed.

Alone, she reflected on her twin's last words. Who else could Amy have meant but the recently decamped Mr.

Sheridan? How extraordinary! She hoped Amy knew what she was doing. If Mr. Sheridan broke her twin's heart, he'd have *her* to answer to.

A light tap on the door, followed by a low voice calling her name, drove all else from her thoughts. Smiling, she rose to admit her fiancé. *Hers*—the knowledge was impossibly sweet. She spared a moment to be thankful that her family's rooms were all out of earshot, then feasted her eyes on him as he slipped inside, clad only in a dressing gown, sashed loosely about the waist.

He gazed at her, his eyes kindling like dark fires, and a smile, at once ardent and tender, stole across his face. All the sweeter for the waiting, he'd promised her—and now they need wait no more. At long last they were together, as they'd been when they waltzed in his aunt's conservatory, more than a year ago. Just James and Aurelia, with no shadows between them.

And just as he had that night, he held out his hand and she took it without a word. What more needed to be said?

༄

Aurelia watched from the bed in growing excitement and anticipation as James shrugged out of his dressing gown and draped it over a chair. So handsome—with his broad shoulders, lean torso, and long limbs, the last marred only by the bandage around his left arm. By lamplight, his pale olive skin took on an almost golden cast that made a dramatic contrast to his dark hair and eyes. When he turned around to face her, she flushed as red as fire. Miss Witherspoon's long-ago lessons on anatomy seemed inadequate, to say the least.

Seeing her expression change, he paused. "Aurelia, if you're having second thoughts—"

She shook her head. "It's not that. Your body is so beautiful. Perfect. I—I wish mine were, for you." She pulled the sheet closer around her own naked form, suddenly shy again.

"I have scars you haven't seen yet, just as off-putting as the one on my face."

He came to perch on the side of the bed, his night-dark eyes gone soft as shadows on velvet. "Loveday." The Cornish endearment was music on his tongue. "There is nothing, absolutely nothing, about you that isn't beautiful to me. Beautiful—and desirable."

Joy rose in her, golden and glowing as a sunburst, banishing the last vestiges of self-doubt and inferiority. Smiling, radiant, she let the sheet fall and reached for him instead.

Nothing about her that wasn't beautiful to him.

Like the flood of her hair, all amber-shot gold in the lamplight, now loosed and falling heavily over her shoulders. Crowning glory—he lifted a lock, let the strands slide like silk between his fingers.

Like her face, with its delicate features and speaking eyes. The fine nose, and upturned lips, with that wistful sweetness lurking at their corners. The skin, so petal-soft, even to the curving line of her scar that now seemed to him less a blemish than a grace note to her beauty.

Like her body, with its high, round bosom and trim waist, her fair skin flushing the translucent pink of a pearl when he touched her, lightly but intimately. He touched her as if he had never known another woman so, sliding his hands over contours and curves. And down, to the gentle flare of her hips and beyond.

The scars on her left thigh brought an involuntary murmur of pity from him, but the limb as a whole was still sound and shapely. He kissed his way up its length, felt her shiver beneath the pressure of his mouth and murmur his name, her fingers reaching down to twine in his hair.

At the juncture of her thighs he found the triangle of soft fleece, slightly darker than her hair, and teased it gently with his fingers as he sought her opening. The tender seam parted beneath his fingers and he slipped one inside, probing the moist heat of her core.

Aurelia gave a soft gasp at the intrusion, but relaxed as he began to stroke her, lightly, then more firmly, until she arched against his hand, seeking still more. He coaxed her further along, higher, faster—and felt a surge of fierce triumph when she neared the peak, eyes widening, breath catching... and then climaxed, her body shuddering its release, her face transcendent with discovery. *The bud of her sweet spirit broke... Thrilled, and was cloven, and from the full sheath came / The whole rose of the woman, red as flame.*

"Beautiful," he murmured when she lay quiet in his arms once more. "And all mine."

"Always yours," Aurelia whispered, reaching up to caress his face. "From the moment you first asked me to dance. Didn't you know?" She turned in his embrace. "Make love to me again, James. I know there's more to what we're doing than this."

"This part may hurt you," he warned, stroking her hair back from her face.

No stranger to pain, she smiled and shook her head. "I'll wager I've known worse." Her hand trailed over his chest, then began sliding downward—seeking, exploring...

He stifled a groan when her fingers closed around him, squeezed gently. "Torment," he said, and heard her low laugh against his heart.

He rolled over, pinning her neatly to the bed. She was still laughing, her eyes bright with mischief, her hands ready to wreak further havoc on his person. Another dance, in which they were equal partners: stroking, caressing, and finding out what each enjoyed most. He reveled in her eager exploration of his body, teased her again to the brink of fulfillment, and at last, positioned himself at her body's opening and entered by slow degrees, trying to give her the chance to grow accustomed to the feeling of him inside her.

Despite his efforts, she stiffened, surprise and discomfort playing across her face. He paused at once, suspended within the tight heat of her inner passage. Sensations rippled and pulsed along his length, but he remained still for her sake, doing his best to ignore them. But then, just as he was berating himself for a clumsy oaf, her expression eased and she began to relax, carefully adjusting her position to accommodate his presence.

Penitent, he touched his lips to her brow, her eyelids. "Loveday, shall I—"

"Stay with me, James." One leg lifted, wrapped tentatively about his hip. "Stay with me."

He kissed her again, soothing her with hands and voice, then began to move within her, building up a gradual rhythm that eventually drew her in. They rocked together, a gentle rise and fall like a ship riding at anchor, while sensations welled up between their joined bodies…and crested at last, hurling them both into the torrent.

Gasping and shaking, they clung together as the storm broke around them. Then, limbs heavy with lassitude, they slept in each other's arms—for the first of what would be many nights in their long life together.

Thirty-Two

He gazed and gazed and gazed and gazed,
Amazed, amazed, amazed, amazed.

—Robert Browning, "Rhyme for a Child Viewing
a Naked Venus in a Painting of the Judgment of Paris"

TWO DAYS LATER, AMY PRESENTED HERSELF AT HALF
Moon Street, much to the surprise of Sheridan's housekeeper,
and was shown into the studio to await the artist's return, as
he'd reportedly stepped out to buy some new brushes.

Alone, Amy breathed in the familiar, almost comforting
scents of turpentine and linseed oil. Elizabeth Martin's
portrait seemed to smile at her from the wall, wishing her the
best of luck in winning the heart of their extraordinary man.

"Your sister told me you'd have wanted him to be happy,"
Amy murmured to the portrait. "I don't know if you'd have
approved of me, but I mean to do my best to make him so."

Happier than the likes of Lady Crowley could, at least, she
added to herself.

Turning from the portrait, she reviewed her plan of
action. Honor and friendship mattered deeply to Sheridan;
she understood that now. As long as he believed her bound
to James, he would make no move to claim her. Even now

that she'd freed herself, he might still hesitate. Just as well that she was a brash, pert, forward American set on having what she wanted. A veritable pirate, after all; she would board his ship and demand his complete surrender. The image made her smile, and quelled the butterflies rioting in her stomach. Emboldened, she set to with a will.

It took less time than she'd expected to get ready. Her Liberty silk gown was so easy to don—and remove, especially when one dispensed with petticoats and corset, as she had today. She pulled the combs out of her chignon as well, letting her hair tumble down her back, then arranged herself upon the sofa, draping a sheet around her in graceful folds. The day was quite warm, fortunately, so she did not feel the least bit chilled.

Her pulse quickened when she heard his step in the passage. She wondered just when she had come to recognize it. Then the door opened, and she turned a smiling face in his direction.

"Amelia!" Sheridan stopped abruptly, swallowed. "Miss Newbold," he resumed in a painfully neutral tone. "Might I ask what brings you here?"

"Cornish Railways," she said brightly. "I arrived in London yesterday."

He flushed, still something of a novelty to see. "That is—not what I meant."

"No?" She feigned surprise. "Well, then I wished to consult you about my portrait."

"Your portrait?" he echoed, dumbfounded. "You still want—"

"I want you to finish your commission, of course. I trust myself to no one else's hands."

He turned away, setting down his brushes. "You might be better served by another artist."

"Oh, I doubt that, very much." When he turned back, she let the sheet drop just a little, exposing one shoulder, and saw his throat work as he swallowed again.

"Your Liberty gown," he husked, after a moment. "Shouldn't you be wearing it?"

"I *was* wearing it when I came. But I've changed my mind about its suitability. Perhaps you can suggest something else?" She lowered the sheet still further, showing more bare skin.

A muscle twitched at the corner of his jaw. "Miss Newbold, you shouldn't be here. The future countess of Trevenan—"

"But I'm not going to be a countess," she informed him blithely.

"Not going to be…" His eyes narrowed. "What happened?"

Much as she enjoyed teasing him, she sensed it was time to speak in earnest. "James loves Relia—and she loves him too, as it turns out. So I've called off the engagement and wished them both happy. The wedding may take place as soon as next month, I'm told."

Sheridan appeared thunderstruck. "James is marrying your sister—and you don't mind?"

"Why should I? I suspect they'll be very happy together. They really are much better suited than he and I," she added. "If I hadn't been so blinkered by my own ambitions, I'd have seen it a lot sooner, but at least I saw it in time."

He frowned. "Are you quite certain? I can't imagine many women being pleased at having their plans for the future overturned, especially not one about to become a countess."

"As it happens, I'm considering a new plan for my future." At his inquiring look, she explained, "Being a countess would have been very grand, but I think it might be grander still to marry—the person you love most." The words felt strange but oddly right on her tongue.

He stilled, absorbing what she had said. "I thought you didn't believe in romantic love."

"Something's—happened to make me rethink my position." Amy paused, feeling an unaccustomed shyness. "I told myself over and over that I didn't want to be that vulnerable. That I didn't want to risk my heart or my peace of mind.

Except," she looked directly into those fathomless green eyes, "it wouldn't be just me taking the risk—would it, Thomas?" Something moved in his eyes—she didn't think it was aversion or indifference—so she continued, "And maybe, *two* people taking a risk for love—is what makes it all worthwhile."

"Amelia," Sheridan began, and stopped. But the way he said her full name, the caress of his tongue against the syllables, gave her the courage she needed for the rest.

"Would you marry me, Thomas? I know I'm a little vain and more than a little frivolous, and probably fonder of Society than I should be. But—I'm even fonder of you. I," she swallowed and tried again, "I believe I love you. Which I've never said to any other man, so you see, you must mean a great deal to me. And I think, perhaps, you care for me as well?"

His eyes warmed. "More than you know—and for longer than you know," he said at last. "You call yourself vain and frivolous. Well, I don't deny your faults, but heaven knows *I'm* no paragon! You are also loyal, generous, and brave. Entirely worthy of being loved."

"Oh," Amy breathed, feeling the strangest melting sensation in the region of her heart.

"What has grown between us," he resumed, almost haltingly, "is not something I expected or sought, any more than you did."

"Because of James? Or—Elizabeth?" She spoke the second name with some trepidation.

"Both, really. James is my closest friend. And Elizabeth had been a part of my life and my dreams since we were children. I never expected any woman to take her place in my heart. Or to make a place for herself there that would become just as essential—as you have."

Her eyes as well as her heart now felt full to overflowing; she stretched out her hand, but Sheridan still hung back. "I'm not a peer of the realm, nor ever likely to be," he warned.

"Oh, that!" Amy waved a dismissive hand, and the sheet slipped down a little more, which Sheridan ignored like a perfect gentleman. "You're a great artist, which, in my opinion, is far more impressive. You're also clever, kind, honorable, and never dull, which is the real reason I proposed to you." She paused, shaking her head in bemusement. "*I* proposed to *you*! I may never live that down, Thomas. Must I ask you to kiss me as well?"

Sheridan's severe mouth curved in that wonderful smile. "No," he replied succinctly, then crossed the room and took her in his arms, sheet and all.

The kiss was all she had hoped for: tender and passionate at once, sweeping all doubts before it. Wrapping her arms around Sheridan's neck, she lost herself in his embrace, the heat of his mouth on hers, the lean hardness of his body against the softer contours of her own.

She did not remember when the sheet slipped to the floor, but the drift of his hands over her bare skin roused her to new heights of sensual pleasure. His hands, with their long, tapering artist's fingers…she bit back a gasp as they skimmed over her breasts, teased her nipples erect and tingling, and cried out when his mouth replaced his fingers, sucking gently at the peak. And still his hands moved, sweeping down to caress the slight rise of her mound and finally the hidden bud within her cleft. A moan broke from her throat as he rolled his thumb over that spot in deepening circles, and the sensations swirled ever higher, spilling over at last in a surging flood that coursed through her body, leaving her limp and breathless in its wake.

When she came back to herself, the sheet once again covered her from neck to knee. But Sheridan lounged beside her on the sofa, a lazy smile on his face and his shirt fully open—had *she* done that?—over his bare chest. His eyes had gone the tender green of new spring leaves.

"All right, sweetheart?" he inquired, stroking her face.

"Mmm," she sighed, snuggling closer to him. "That was lovely. Why ever did you stop?'

His arm tightened around her. "Because, my lady pirate, for all your wiles, you're still an innocent. And because I've no intention of exhausting my repertoire before our wedding night."

She pulled back to look at him. "Our wedding night? So you're accepting my proposal?"

"It would appear so." Sheridan threaded his hands through her hair. "You and your sister," he mused. "What man stands a chance against either of you?"

Amy smiled. "Just as long as you remember that." She reached up to draw his head down to hers. "And now that that's settled, would you kiss me again?"

He obliged, combining his vast experience and newfound ardor in a kiss the likes of which neither had ever known. And, after a while, the sheet slipped quietly to the floor again...

Epilogue

Aura Lea, Aura Lea,
Take my golden ring;
Light and life return with thee,
And swallows with the spring.

—W.W. Fosdick, "Aura Lea"

Six weeks later

CORNWALL HAD SEEN ITS SHARE OF BEAUTIFUL BRIDES, but few could recall one as dazzling as the new Countess of Trevenan. And fewer still noticed the fading scar on the bride's cheek or the slight halt in her step as, escorted by her father, she paced down the aisle of the Cathedral of the Blessed Virgin Mary in Truro. Many noticed her gown, a simple but stunning creation of cream satin and lace—made in Paris, the more knowledgeable guests whispered—that complemented her fair coloring perfectly. But all of them noticed her smile, which outshone the sun on this glorious summer day, and Lord Trevenan's expression of dazed delight as she neared the altar.

A sumptuous wedding breakfast was held at Pentreath, the earl's estate, to which nearly everyone of consequence in the county was invited. Other notable guests included extended relations of the former Miss Newbold, come all the way from America, and an elegant Frenchwoman of middle years who had befriended the bride during a lengthy sojourn abroad.

The bride and groom were to spend the wedding night at Chenoweth, the house the earl had owned as plain Mr. Trelawney, before embarking on a honeymoon tour of the West Country.

"I'm still amazed you don't want to go someplace more extravagant for our wedding trip," James told Aurelia as they enjoyed a private moment in the garden, gazing out over the sea, brilliantly blue in the distance. The muted roar of the waves drifted up to them from the beach.

She smiled. "I've been to Paris and the Riviera, James. And Germany, of course. All lovely places, but unless you have a burning wish to go there yourself, I'd just as soon we stayed in England. You made the West Country sound so wonderful when you described it to me."

"Well, loveday, if you're sure. The Continent's not going anywhere, after all." James took her hand, smiling at the rings shining on her finger: the sapphire she'd admired in Wickes and Taylor, and the simple gold band he'd given her mere hours ago. "Come to that, I'm even more amazed that you didn't opt for a lavish double wedding in New York with Amy."

Aurelia shook her head. "Oh, that wouldn't have suited me at all! I never wanted a grand show. I just wanted to be married to you. This," she gestured toward the house behind them, still filled with laughing, chattering guests, "was more than enough for me. Amy and Mr. Sheridan are more than welcome to my share of the limelight."

James chuckled. "Poor Thomas! Even he might find a big Society wedding in New York a trifle overwhelming."

"He might take it in stride," Aurelia countered. "Think of all the material he'll find there for his paintings. Although it's possible they'll marry sooner, rather than later. Amy told me she's eager to discover the extent of Mr. Sheridan's repertoire—whatever that means."

James suspected he knew exactly what that meant, but he wasn't about to share that insight with his bride. Although, talking of eagerness…he slipped an arm around Aurelia's waist. "Well, there are advantages to an early wedding. Not having to wait, for example."

She colored, and another smile, at once shy and oddly secretive, played about her lips. "I was thinking the exact same thing. And early weddings can help conceal certain—indiscretions."

James stared at his wife, as the import of her words sank in. "Aurelia," he husked at last. "Dear heart, are you sure?"

"Almost sure," she confessed, her eyes glowing like the sapphire in her engagement ring. "Certain signs are there, though I'm feeling perfectly well. I suppose a doctor could confirm it more quickly, but…I may be carrying your heir already. Are you pleased?"

For answer, he drew her into his arms and kissed her until they were both breathless. Then, his arm about her waist, his other hand clasping hers, the Earl of Trevenan guided his wife into a gentle waltz beneath the summer sky, with no other accompaniment than the sound of waves lapping against the shore and two hearts—soon to be three—beating in perfect time.

THE END

Acknowledgments

So much goes into the making of a book that it would probably take years to name and acknowledge everybody who was involved, even peripherally. But special thanks are due to the following people.

To my agent, Stephany Evans, for her encouragement, patience, and willingness to soldier through multiple drafts. And to Becky Vinter, also at Fine Print, for last-minute suggestions that made the manuscript stronger.

To my editor Leah Hultenschmidt for loving *Waltz with a Stranger* from the start but still thinking of ways to make it better, and to Aubrey Poole and the rest of the Sourcebooks team for putting together such a beautiful book.

To Angela, friend and beta reader *extraordinaire*, for pushing me through this one by insisting on knowing what happened next.

To Jules, Suzanna, Jean, and the rest of the After Hours crew for your support and camaraderie over the years. I am a better writer, especially of romance, because of you guys.

To Elizabeth and Lisa, for wanting to say they knew me when. Well, you did—and I hope you'll agree I've improved since then!

To readers past, present, and to come—thank you all.

About the Author

Pamela Sherwood grew up in a family of teachers and taught college-level literature and writing courses for several years before turning to writing full time. She holds a doctorate in English literature, specializing in the Romantic and Victorian periods, eras that continue to fascinate her and provide her with countless opportunities for virtual time travel. She lives in Southern California and is currently at work on her next book. Visit her on the web at http://pamelasherwood.wordpress.com.

How to Tame a Willful Wife

by Christy English

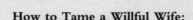

How to Tame a Willful Wife:

1. Forbid her from riding astride
2. Hide her dueling sword
3. Burn all her breeches and buy her silk drawers
4. Frisk her for hidden daggers
5. Don't get distracted while frisking
   her for hidden daggers…

Anthony Carrington, Earl of Ravensbrook, expects a biddable bride. A man of fiery passion tempered by the rigors of war into steely self-control, he demands obedience from his troops and his future wife. Regardless of how fetching she looks in breeches.

Promised to the Earl of Plump Pockets by her impoverished father, Caroline Montague is no simpering miss. She rides a war stallion named Hercules, fights with a blade, and can best most men with both bow and rifle. She finds Anthony autocratic, domineering, and… ridiculously handsome.

It's a duel of wit and wills in this charming retelling of *The Taming of the Shrew*. But the question is…who's taming whom?

For more Christy English, visit:

www.sourcebooks.com

Miss Lavigne's Little White Lie

by Samantha Grace

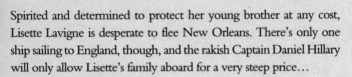

Spirited and determined to protect her young brother at any cost, Lisette Lavigne is desperate to flee New Orleans. There's only one ship sailing to England, though, and the rakish Captain Daniel Hillary will only allow Lisette's family aboard for a very steep price…

Daniel prides himself on running a tight ship, and he knows a lady will be nothing but trouble on a long voyage. Yet he can't help but break his own ironclad rules when Lisette persuades him that being gentlemanly just this once is his wisest course of action…

"Evocative… There is a charm in Grace's prose that will delight readers." —RT Book Reviews

"Grace's fabulously fun debut will dazzle readers with its endearingly outspoken heroine and devilishly rakish hero." —Booklist

"Clever, spicy, and fresh from beginning to end." —Amelia Grey, award-winning author of *A Gentleman Never Tells*

"A delightfully witty romp seasoned with an irresistible dash of intrigue and passion. Samantha Grace is an author to watch!" —Shana Galen, award-winning author of *Lord and Lady Spy*

For more Samantha Grace, visit:

www.sourcebooks.com

New York Times and USA Today bestselling author

Lady Louisa's Christmas Knight

by Grace Burrowes

❦

'Tis the season for scandal...

Years ago Lady Louisa Windham acted rashly on a dare from her brother, and that indiscretion is about to come to light. She knows her reputation will never survive exposure. Just as she's nearly overwhelmed by her dilemma, Sir Joseph Carrington offers himself to her as a solution...

But Sir Joseph has secrets as well, and as he and Louisa become entangled with each other, their deceptions begin to close in on them both...

❦

Praise for RITA-nominated
Lady Sophie's Christmas Wish:

"An extraordinary, precious, unforgettable holiday story."
—*RT Book Reviews* Top Pick of the Month, 4.5 Stars

"Burrowes continues to write outside the usual Regency box with strong characters and humor similar to Amanda Quick's." —*Booklist*

For more Grace Burrowes, visit:

www.sourcebooks.com

The Wicked Wedding of Miss Ellie Vyne

by Jayne Fresina

❧

When a notorious bachelor seduces a scandalous lady, it can only end in a wicked wedding.

By night Ellie Vyne fleeces unsuspecting aristocrats as the dashing Count de Bonneville. By day she avoids her sisters' matchmaking attempts and dreams up inventive insults to hurl at her childhood nemesis, the arrogant, far-too-handsome-for-his-own-good James Hartley.

James finally has a lead on the villainous, thieving count, tracking him to a shady inn. He bursts in on none other than "that Vyne woman"...in a shocking state of dishabille. Convinced she is the count's mistress, James decides it's best to keep his enemies close. Very close. Seducing Ellie will be the perfect bait...

❧

Praise for *The Most Improper Miss Sophie Valentine*:

"Ms. Fresina delivers a scintillating debut! Her sharply drawn characters and witty prose are as addictive as chocolate!" —Mia Marlowe, author of *Touch of a Rogue*

For more Jayne Fresina, visit:

www.sourcebooks.com

Waking Up with a Rake

Connie Mason and Mia Marlowe

**The fate of England's monarchy is in
the hands of three notorious rakes.**

To prevent three royal dukes from marrying their way onto
the throne, heroic, selfless agents for the crown will be
dispatched…to seduce the dukes' intended brides. These
wickedly debauched rakes will rumple sheets and cause a
scandal. But they just might fall into their own trap…

After he's blamed for a botched assignment during the
war, former cavalry officer Rhys Warrick turns his back
on "honor." He spends his nights in brothels doing his
best to live down to the expectations of his disapproving
family. But one last mission could restore the reputation
he's so thoroughly sullied. All he has to do is seduce and
ruin Miss Olivia Symon and his military record will be
cleared. For a man with Rhys' reputation, ravishing the
delectably innocent miss should be easy. But Olivia's
honesty and bold curiosity stir more than Rhys' desire.
Suddenly the heart he thought he left on the battlefield is
about to surrender…

For more Connie Mason and Mia Marlow, visit

www.sourcebooks.com

When You Give a Duke a Diamond

by Shana Galen

---- ⌘ ----

He had a perfectly orderly life...

William, the sixth Duke of Pelham, enjoys his punctual, securely structured life. Orderly and predictable—that's the way he likes it. But he's in the public eye, and the scandal sheets will make up anything to sell papers. When the gossips link him to Juliette, one of the most beautiful and celebrated courtesans in London, chaos doesn't begin to describe what happens next...

Until she came along...

Juliette is nicknamed the Duchess of Dalliance, and has the cream of the nobility at her beck and call. It's seriously disruptive to have the duke who's the biggest catch on the Marriage Mart scaring her other suitors away. Then she discovers William's darkest secret and decides what he needs in his life is the kind of excitement only she can provide...

---- ⌘ ----

For more Shana Galen, visit:

www.sourcebooks.com